To Amanda & Julie

Wishing you Abundant Joy & Success

Love Lonely

Enjoy

Book 1

By William C. Cole

Love Lonely

Limitless Publishing, LLC
Kailua, HI 96734
www.limitlesspublishing.com

Formatting: Limitless Publishing

ISBN-13: 978-1-68058-012-9
ISBN-10: 1-68058-012-4

Dedication

Diane
My wife of 34 years, there is zero chance of me being the person I am today without you by my side.

Lee & Aaron
My two amazing sons who I spend far too little time with, I do care. Unless I am kicking your butt on the golf course.

Deb & Robin
My Sisters who have always so graciously and unconditionally welcomed my family with open arms.

Thank you

Never, ever, let someone tell you, you can't run after your dreams

Chapter 1

David sat on a fence that separated the family's stables from the remainder of the race track. It was his favorite spot to sit and contemplate all that life had tossed his way. Today he'd been dealt some bad cards.

Dressed in faded jeans, denim shirt, and cowboy boots or as he referred to them his ass kicking boots, he looked good. Six foot two, strong legs and a butt developed from his professional hockey career. A true fan could pick a hockey player out of a crowd by his physique. David always thought of himself as a pretty cool guy, a what-you-see-is-what-you-get person for the most part, one the guys wanted to hang with and the ladies wanted to sleep with.

But today it was best for all to stay clear.

"David," she paused, "David," Renée repeated. Her words jolted him from his reverie. The trance had been brought on by the exhaustion of the previous twenty-four hours. "David, detective Slocum needs to go over a few things with you. Are

1

you good to go here?"

"Yeah, I'm fine. Where is he?"

David followed her around the stable. Or what was left of it.

Even though he was dead tired, awake for well over a full day dealing with this horrific situation, he was still aware of Renée's body as she led the way. When she arrived from France, speaking broken English and with few employment opportunities, David took a chance and hired her. It paid off big time as she was quickly becoming one of the most respected horse handlers in the country. She wasn't the head of his team yet, but someday she'd be calling the shots.

As Renée walked in front of him he couldn't help but take a fleeting look at her backside. Actually, he found himself becoming more and more mindful of her. His thoughts, he knew, would remain just that—thoughts. He had no intentions of acting on them, because he loved his wife, Sandy. David had had numerous female companions throughout his life. Single professional athletes had no lack of attention from the opposite sex. Some of the married ones also had their fair share of little social gatherings. But he was totally committed to his marriage. One of his life survival guidelines was, "what goes on in this head, stays in this head."

"David, this is Detective Slocum from the Louisville Police Department. He's handling the investigation of the fire."

"Please to meet you Mr. Watson," the detective said.

"Please, call me David."

"As your assistant mentioned, I am here to investigate the fire. However, I've just been informed that I'm no longer the lead on the case. I've been ordered to gather as much information as possible and turn it over to the FBI. It seems a bit odd, but you get used to odd in this business. I am sorry for your loss. We will do everything we can to assist the Bureau."

David knew it wasn't that unusual to learn of the FBI involvement. His father-in-law probably put a call into the Director of the FBI or maybe even the President. He knew them both. He seemed to know them all. They weren't golfing buddies, but they did see each other when frequenting the same cities. His father-in-law's substantial campaign donations and support came with a "when I call you, you call back receipt."

"Thank you for your help detective. We appreciate your and the fire department's swiftness. You first responders saved the lives of a lot of horses. We lost two, but if it wasn't for their quick actions," he paused. "Well you know what I mean," he choked up.

Growing up on a farm he had endured the ending of the livestock's lives quite often. It never got easier. He had a hard time discussing the two horses that perished in the fire.

"With regards to the FBI, don't take it personally. Jacob McGinnis, my father-in-law has an uncanny way of becoming the one in charge. I'm sure you would have resolved this without outside assistance."

"Thank you for the vote of confidence, David.

I'm sure they will determine the cause in a timely manner. I have a few questions for you but since we expect an FBI agent on site in the near future, I won't take up anymore of your time right now."

"Detective, I won't be far if you need me."

"Thank you, we will keep you abreast of the investigation."

David and Renée made their way back to the other side of the stables. They settled at the spot on the fence he referred to as his office. A lot of decisions were made there. Each of them rested a leg on the first cross pole then leaned their arms on the top. Nothing was said. They stared at the full moon surrounded by glistening stars. They spent a great deal of their time at this exact location alone and together. Here many conversations took place about pretty much everything. Some of those talks maybe should have been reserved for people in personal relationships, not employer-employee dialogue. Tonight there would be little bantering.

He could feel her forearm ever so slightly touching his. This wasn't the first time it happened. It was a warm night with the smoldering of the fire making it feel even hotter. Renée wore a short sleeve top and the arms of his denim shirt were rolled up. It wasn't that their skin actually touched, but rather the hair on their arms rubbed against each other. He liked it. It felt nice. The contact was so gentle he wondered if she noticed. She must feel it. What was she thinking? Although it had been a trying day, he felt comforted by the touch.

"What's on your mind?"

"Really, Renée, you don't want to know."

His reply not only referred to the frustration brought on by the day's events, but his thoughts about the solace he found in her subtle touch.

The more he reflected on the senseless loss of the two animals, the more enraged he became. No matter what caused the fire, he should have been able to foresee and prevent it. That was his job.

"Oui, David I do. I'm not sure what to do here. I need to know my next step, s'ils vous plait," she said, substituting French into her response.

Renée also experienced serenity when they shared these get-togethers. She had grown fond of David. It was an attraction she kept closely guarded, with no plans on revealing, at least for now. But tonight her mind was not on the allure. She was visibly upset by the tragedy and seeking some direction to assist her with navigating her way through the remainder of the evening.

David understood her French excerpts. Spending a couple of years playing in the NHL with the Montreal Canadiens, it went without saying that the fans and press expected to converse in their mother tongue. So he learned enough to stay on the good side of them. After all, ultimately they paid his wage and he never took that for granted.

"We need to get some rest and let the authorities deal with this. They know what they're doing and will get to the bottom of it soon. It's best we don't get in their way," he answered her.

"You've never handed over the reins to anyone nor been worried about getting in someone's way since I've known you."

"This time I think it would be best to let the

proper people investigate without my interference," he said knowing full well that he couldn't keep his nose out of any problem that directly affected his family. Renée knew this, he knew she knew, but nothing more needed to be said.

"Can you leave our numbers with—" his cell started to ring, "—the detective so he can reach us if need be?"

The phone kept ringing.

Renée turned to leave then hesitated, turned back, "David."

"What?"

The cell was still ringing. A sound he could live without the rest of his life and not miss it for one second.

"Your phone. You might want to answer it. It's probably Sandy." She left to track down the police officer.

He looked down at his iPhone screen then up again and she was gone. He pressed talk.

"Wattsy, are you okay?"

It was Sandy his wife of seven years. From time to time she called him by his hockey nickname. It was a title bestowed by teammates, who had most likely been checked into the boards a few too many times.

He was surprised by the call. She was supposed to be in Paris for the remainder of the week on one of her fund-raising excursions. But the call display indicated she was on her aircraft.

"Hey babe," he answered.

"Are you okay?"

"I'm fine."

"Wattsy, I can't believe this happened, I'm on my way home. They told me we lost West Coast Breeze and Overtime."

She started to weep. Not break down I'm dying tears, but more reserved, controlled but still real tears. She was referring to the two thoroughbred horses that perished in the stable fire. These were world class racehorses, worth millions of dollars. Her sorrow was not related to the financial loss but rather her love for the animals. Sandy had an authentic passion for them.

"We did lose them. We'll figure out what caused the fire shortly."

"Is my father there?"

"No, not personally, but you can feel his presence everywhere, no matter which way you look," David answered sounding slightly exasperated.

Sandy picked up on it but let it slide. Her father was rich, very rich and powerful. She knew that he would be directing the event from his office at their ranch. He'd be on his telephone speaking to someone that not too many people had access to. His tone would be low key, relaxed, and soft spoken. The person on the other end of the line would be meticulously zoned into the conversation not wanting to miss a directive that may be coming their way. They would be agreeing and assuring Mr. Jacob McGinnis that all was being taken care of and he shouldn't worry as the proper people were being put in place. The situation would be resolved as expeditiously as humanly possible.

"I thought you were going to stay in Europe until

the end of the week. Babe you didn't have to come home early, I can handle this."

"I know you can. That's why I married you. You kind of remind me of my father," she said jokingly.

But it was true. David would never back down from a challenge. He'd face adversity head on. Life didn't have a lot in its arsenal that could throw him off his game.

Sandy admired this trait knowing it was instilled in him at an early age and reinforced throughout his professional hockey career. The dedication and discipline was similar, although not as intense as the preparation she had subjected herself to over the years.

"As soon as our plane lands, I'm coming to the track."

The plane she was speaking of was her father's private jet. She used it more than he did. Some kids get cars as a gift. Sandy got a luxury aircraft.

"When do you land?"

She told him they expected to touch down within the hour.

"There's nothing you can do here and I was just preparing to head back to the ranch. I'll meet you there. Thanks for coming home. I'm looking forward to seeing you. It's almost been a week now."

"Woo, a week without sex with your hot wife, you poor boy."

"And that would be one of the reasons I love you so much," they hung up. No arguments from either side.

David arrived at the ranch within a couple of

hours of speaking to his wife. Sandy wasn't home yet. He took a quick look for his father-in-law but he was nowhere to be found. This wasn't all that surprising. The ranch was so big he suspected someone could live there for days without being noticed.

He then made his way to their private quarters. Sandy and David lived in a residence attached to the west wing of the estate. It was theirs and their privacy was respected by her father and his staff. The suite measured in at about four thousand square feet. They were adamant about doing all the chores themselves, the cleaning, cooking, and laundry. David insisted on this if they were going to make the ranch their home—although he knew he really didn't have much of a choice about where they lived. It came with an unspoken segment of their wedding vows. He felt a bit like a sellout, but regained some pride knowing he could still clean up after himself. Sandy, who was not raised in this style of living had become accustom to it. David liked to believe she respected it.

A long, hot shower was foremost on his mind. It took lathering a few times to rid himself of the smell of smoke. Once clean, he let the steaming water pound on the back of his neck. It wouldn't have taken much for him to fall asleep right there. He stayed for what seemed to be an hour but it was only fifteen or twenty minutes. David dried off, threw on his pajama bottoms, and made his way to the bedroom. He looked around for Sandy in hopes she had arrived, knowing full well it was still too early.

William C. Cole

After attaching his iPhone to the docking station, he tapped an app and instantly a Toby Keith song began to play. There were hundreds of songs from all genres of music downloaded on it. Tim McGraw, Kenny Chesney, Toby, Blake Shelton, along with a number of up and coming country artists received the majority of airplay. Growing up on a farm in northern Alberta, Canada, you listened to country music. He loved it. The songs told a story. There were a couple of guitars sitting around which he attempted to play every once in a while, whenever time permitted. It was always a country tune.

David folded the sheets back and stretched out on the bed while awaiting the arrival of his wife. She would be home soon. He was excited about having this beautiful woman beside him tonight. He thanked his lucky stars each and every day that he was the person she chose to share her life and bed with. Sandy was very open-minded when it came to their bedroom activities. Although he was aware she had a number of relationships before theirs, he felt privileged to be the one she now comes home to. Her healthy sexual appetite made him wonder if she ever slept with anyone else since they'd been together. After all, she did spend a great deal of time traveling.

Sandy was an only child, born into money. She always lived with her father and continued to do so, albeit in a separate suite. Her mother passed away from cancer when she was young. This was a woman who turned heads when entering a room. She had shoulder length blonde hair, was thin, not skinny, but in great physical shape. David was captivated by her physical fitness. He couldn't get over how she sculpted such a perfect washboard stomach. She jogged, biked, and worked out in the gym as much as her demanding schedule permitted. David often complimented her on the results. He'd say, "Babe, if I was asked to create the perfect female body, hands down you would be the mold."

This young lady oversaw the philanthropy division of her father's business. She excelled at it, dining with the President of the United States and the First Lady. She'd been greeted by the Queen of England. Socializing with movie stars, heads of states and many other influential people was a regular part of the profession. Waiting in line at a grocery store checkout, David would see her on the cover of magazines, standing next to some celebrity or other public figure. It didn't bother him. Actually he was proud of her accomplishments. Sandy would have achieved great success no matter what upbringing she was exposed to. She was all that, yet the most grounded and down to earth person he had ever met. To meet her and not know her background, you would think of her as the girl next door. Tonight that girl was all his.

As he was beginning to drift off, the phone rang. It was Renée.

"Hello Renée, is something wrong?" he answered, not all that surprised by the late night call. It wasn't a common occurrence, but it had happened more than once.

"Are you okay? Everything is wrapping up here. They want to continue at sunrise."

"I can't believe you're still there. Go home, get

yourself some rest. You have to keep focused. We have important races to prepare for. I can't have you falling asleep riding a training session. Now pack it in, go home."

"Soon, you okay?

"Yes I'm fine. Now go or you won't be okay the next time I see you," he replied with a lighthearted threat.

"Okay, I'm going. Is Sandy home?"

"No. Not yet. I'm expecting her soon. Now go."

"Tell her I said hello. Goodnight, David," she signed off.

They hung up. His head once again hit the pillow, this time with a hint of a smile on his face. He did enjoy their interactions.

At that moment the door opened. It was Sandy.

"Wattsy, I'm home. How are you holding up? Did we learn what started the fire?"

"Not yet. But I'm sure we'll have the answers tomorrow."

"I want to have a look around first thing in the morning," she told him.

"There's no need for you to rush over there. They have the scene secured and won't be releasing it back to us until the investigation is complete. Listen, I need to be there early to take care of a couple of things, so why don't you catch up with your father or go for a jog to shake off the jet lag and meet me there early afternoon."

"Are you sure?"

"Yes, by then we will know more."

"Okay then. I'm going to go take a shower," she leaned over and gave him a kiss.

"For what you have gone through today you still look pretty good for an old beat up hockey player."

"Nice," he jokingly replied.

"Maybe we can figure out another way to shake off my jet lag."

"I have no idea what you're talking about."

With that she turned, walked slowly towards the shower in a sexy swagger losing her clothing one piece at a time until there was nothing but her. He knew what she meant, and oh how badly he wanted her.

"Wait a minute, now I know what you mean," he smiled.

He rested his head on the pillow again and within seconds he was out for the count.

***

It took Sandy a good half hour to finish up. Returning to find her husband fast asleep was a disappointment. She had been looking forward to slipping into this bed since leaving for Europe last week. It was understandable knowing how difficult the past hours must have been for him. In all honesty she was actually surprised to find him still up when she arrived. So she wasn't going to wake him, not purposely anyhow. Nevertheless, that didn't ease the fact she was horny. Folding the blankets back, she gave him a kiss on his cheek, then nestled into her side of the king size bed.

A few minutes passed but sleep was not imminent. Becoming more and more aroused with thoughts of what might be forthcoming in the morning, when both were rested, she couldn't wait. She began to ever so lightly pinch her nipples with one hand while stroking her stomach with the other. It wasn't long before she was experiencing wetness. Lying on her back with both legs slightly spread apart, her fingers found their way to the vicinity of need. From above, it would appear both of them were sound asleep except for the delicate movements below the satin sheets where her fingers were becoming wet. As she became more stimulated, she began to move her moist fingers from between her legs to his manhood. She would go back to pleasuring herself and then move them back to him. Sandy repeated her movements a number of times until he soon became hard, bathed in her juices. As she was nearing an orgasm, muffling her moans with a folded pillow over her face, David woke up. No man could continue to sleep while being finessed like this. They didn't make tired enough to compete with it. God he loved this girl. They made love. They slept.

Chapter 2

Monday through Thursday David would meet with Sandy's father Jacob in the latter's office, located on the main floor of the estate. Eight o'clock was the predetermined time. Mr. McGinnis would have preferred seven, but David bartered for an extra few minutes of sleep. In his hockey days, most games were played in the evening. After, they would be shuttled from the dressing room to a waiting bus, to a chartered flight and on to a new city. Mornings were reserved for rest and recuperation. You didn't come out of these games without bruises. Ice bags were such a wonderful thing.

Since his retirement, he worked for his wife's father. David controlled the thoroughbred division of the business. Their stable was known to produce some of the world's finest racehorses. The breeding fees alone amounted to tens of millions of dollars per year. David did a first-class job overseeing the operation. Jacob allowed him to make the majority of the decisions. David appreciated this. These meetings consisted of a quick update on whether or

15

not Mr. McGinnis could be of any assistance. The answer was always thanks, but no thanks, everything seems to be in order.

This morning was not much different from others, except for the fact that when he entered the room, Mr. McGinnis was entertaining a guest.

"This is my son-in-law, David. David this is Special Agent James Scott from the FBI," Jacob stood up from behind his desk to introduce them.

He wasn't all that surprised to be standing next to a FBI agent. His father-in-law was wealthy and connected beyond comprehension, a regular on the Forbes list of the world's most powerful people. David earned an average of four million dollars a year playing hockey. Being frugal with his earnings, he really didn't have to work another day of his life. However, in comparison to his father-in-law's wealth, his was chump change. He wasn't quite sure of all that Sandy's father's businesses encompassed. Jacob had offices in a number of major cities, but spent most of his time at the ranch. It was magical to watch at times. Witnessing him pick up the phone and have a short conversation with the person on the other end, and that was that. The situation resolved. Things were in motion and the outcome was always in favor of Jacob McGinnis. He could place you on a board of directors, or get an invite to whatever event he wished to attend. That was his business, so David didn't spend a great deal of time scrutinizing it. All his energies went into his own responsibilities.

"Pleased to meet you," David replied.

"I spoke with the Director of the FBI yesterday,

and she has sent us Special Agent Scott here," Jacob began, "he was kind enough to fly in this morning. I've been told he is the most experienced arson investigator in the country, if not in the world."

"With all due respect Special Agent Scott, nothing I or the local authorities have seen led us to believe that this is a case of arson," David interjected. "I'm sure there is a simple explanation for the fire."

"Mr. Watson," agent Scott began.

"Please, David is fine."

"David," he continued, "I hope what you say is correct, but since I'm already here, would you mind if I wandered over to the stables to take a look around? Your father-in-law has made it clear that all decisions relating to this are yours."

For the most part anyway, David thought. But he knew it had been predetermined that the FBI agent was going to leave the room to command control of the investigation and was okay with it. He didn't think the fire was set on purpose. Agent Scott's visit would only confirm that.

David grew up in a small town where nobody had cause to lock the doors of their homes. Their keys were left in the ignition of the pickup trucks parked in the driveways. He found it hard to believe that anyone could be that insensitive to endanger these animals on purpose.

"Absolutely," David replied. "I'm heading over there shortly, would you like a ride."

"No, but thank you, I have transportation."

"Well then," David stood, "our head trainer, Serge Thompson, should be there this morning.

He'll be able to assist you with most of what you need. But be warned, he possesses quite the ego. He is the best horseman in the country and knows it. Should he frustrate you to no end, which he often does, ask for Renée, our assistant trainer. She can walk you from one end to the other blindfolded. Maybe that's who you should start with," he said enlightening the agent of the chain of command. "I'll be there in a couple of hours if you need to discuss anything."

They shook hands. David made his way towards the door but before reaching it he turned back to catch both men watching him leave. He looked at the FBI agent with a piercing stare, for what seemed to be an uncomfortable length of time—a facial expression not many had witnessed. Speaking in a searing tone he warned, "If this fire was deliberately set Agent Scott, it would be in everyone's best interest to resolve it quickly. Use all the resources available to you. You will want to find the people responsible for it," he paused, "before I do."

With that he exited the meeting, not bothering to listen to the lecture he was getting about leaving the situation in the hands of the proper authorities and that he should not do anything that would be considered an act of vigilantism.

***

Sandy woke up. David was gone. He had let her sleep. She was disappointed, as she was looking forward to an encore of last night's activities. But it wasn't to be. She put on a track suit in preparation of a morning jog. The plan was to take a quick ten mile run. At that distance she would barely break a sweat. Exercise, particularly running and martial arts had become an obsession of hers early in life. She relished the high, craved the mental cleansing they provided. Blessed with beauty, becoming a world class model would have been a walk in the park. But she preferred the athletic route. Exercise, at the intensity she performed on a daily basis, could only be achieved if one was in immaculate physical condition.

Walking down the stairs she caught a glimpse of two men in the foyer saying their goodbyes. One was her father. The other she hadn't seen before. Yet, she knew he was law enforcement. Her best guess was FBI. She had the ability to size up a person within seconds by their shoes, clothing, hair, their demeanor, being extremely accurate in her assessment of one's capacity. She had to be.

The door closed, her father turned and there she was standing idle halfway down the staircase. When entering the ranch through the twelve foot high doors, the grand rustic staircase supported by hefty wooden pillars, was the center of attraction.

"Daddy, I'm home," she said leaning on the railing.

"Yes you are. Come here and give me a hug," he spread his arms.

She ran down the stairs to embrace him.

"You need to spend more time at home and less time flying all over the world young lady."

"That's a plan. We'll work on it. I do miss you guys so much," she said referring to her father and her husband.

They made their way into his office and he sat on the black leather couch situated along the wall facing his desk with a view of the pasture where the horses grazed. Sometimes he would sit there for extended periods of time, gazing out at the animals roaming the land.

He tapped the cushion, "Come, sit."

She sat beside him. He patted her hand with his.

"When are you going to give my jet a break?"

"Soon, I promise."

"How did the trip work out for you?" He teased with a wink, "Did you catch the bad guy?"

"Don't I always," she replied sporting a cute little smile.

"I've been spreading your wealth to a number of well deserving organizations," referring to their charitable work throughout the world.

"We've done some great work daddy."

At an early age Sandy established an urgency of helping the unfortunate by the giving of her time. It was a natural progression for her to administer this side of her father's estate.

"Seriously," he said, "are you going to be home for a while. I worry about you. And I'm sure David feels the same."

"I will try. You do realize it's not always my choice."

"I know," he sighed. "But that doesn't mean I have to like it."

"Well father you should have thought about that before and registered me in ballet lessons."

"Anyhow enough of that," Sandy changed the

subject. "Do we know how the fire started? Was that the FBI that just left?"

"Yes he was. What gave him away?"

"His hair cut. His spit-shined shoes. A suit of good quality, better than local authorities would wear, but not extravagant. Funny, with all the thought that goes into their training, they neglect to teach the agents to wear their weapons when having a suit tailored. He holstered a gun on his left side, a backup strapped to his lower right ankle," she smiled then asked, "should I continue."

"Lord no. You're boring me to death," he waved her off the subject.

"We would like to think there is a simple explanation as to the origin of the fire. However, should it not be, I did make a call to the Director of the FBI. She has asked Special Agent Scott to have a look at the scene. He is an expert in this field," Jacob explained.

"Was that necessary, I'm sure the local authorities employ people who are quite capable of resolving it."

"Well one can never be too careful. This agent is one of the best in the world. If he clears the fire as accidental, we can put it to rest. But if it was intentional, we need to know."

"Ok, you win," Sandy conceded. "Have you been to see the damage?"

"No, but I'm getting updated frequently. Everything seems to be in good hands. I would just get in the way. David is handling it."

With a slight smirk Sandy moved her head ever so slightly back and forth. Which meant, sure father, we know who is in control. He shrugged his shoulders.

"I'm going for a quick run then meeting David there in a couple of hours, would you like to jump in and keep me company?"

"No, I prefer to stay here. I have a couple of other pressing matters to deal with today."

As she was raising herself off the couch, her cell phone rang. Falling back into the seat, she stared at the phone, then up at her father. He signaled for her to answer. She did. She listened. She nodded. Then spoke to the person on the other end.

"Of course I'll be there. Nothing could keep me from attending. I'll see you in a few days," a pause then, "I will. Take care."

Hearing the conversation he knew what it meant. Once again his daughter would be departing.

"You're leaving us again, aren't you?"

He knew the answer, but didn't like it. He wanted his daughter here, at home. Guilt of engineering the life his daughter lived festered within him, but at the same time he was as proud of her as a father could be.

"That was King Ahmed. Fyad's wedding has been moved up to this weekend. The date was changed a couple of months ago. When he learned I hadn't been informed he wanted to personally apologize. I couldn't possibly miss it. I'll need to leave in a couple of days. David is not going to be pleased. He was planning on me accompanying him to the stake races in California on the weekend, and then we were going try to fit in a couple of days in New York. We had also made arrangements to attend the wedding together later this year. There is absolutely no way he's going to miss the races. Please don't mention this until I have a chance to explain it."

"By the way father, the King extended an invitation to you," she relayed a message received during the conversation. "He said something along the lines of, he would find time to show you what a real race horse looks like."

She was referring to the King's breeding of the finest thoroughbred horses on his side of the globe as Jacob McGinnis had the distinction of so doing in the USA.

"Daddy, maybe David and I could sneak away to New York tomorrow. It's not great timing, but David said himself there is not much we can do until the authorities finish up. If I can convince him, would it be okay if we took the plane." Sandy asked.

Sandy and David would often get away for a day or two to visit New York. They acquired a fondness for the theater. In addition, they would take in an NHL hockey game once in a while. David was still well connected within the hockey community. Just over five thousand men had ever played in the NHL. It is a small brotherhood that you became a part of when you've made it. These guys looked after one another. There was never an issue with securing seats to a game when they were in town.

Both were busy people, so there was an appreciation for these quick trips. In addition, they put aside two weeks each year to get lost somewhere in the world. Normally they wouldn't stray too far from home as Sandy routinely traveled so much. Actually David had his concerns about how much his wife was out of the country. Nothing was said to her. He had the utmost trust in her, and would never think of intruding on her travels. She would always give him a summary of each trip. They kept in touch once a day, no matter where in the world her excursions took her. A quick call, but mostly text, was the chosen form of communication. Sandy tried to sell him on Skyping or FaceTime. He felt there was something a touch weird about how the current generation interacted. A text or call was fine with him. The other stuff he wasn't buying into.

"I should get going," she said once more pushing herself off the couch.

Again they were interrupted by the chime of a phone. She carried two. The one ringing was not the same one she had spoken to the King on. This one had its own distinctive tone. Only a handful of people had access to its number. Most of those expected it to be promptly answered. When it rang, her adrenalin kicked into high gear. Her father knew the meaning of such a call.

She answered, "Hello. Yes I was just speaking with him," she listened, then spoke again, "yes I'll be there. I'll contact you as soon as I arrive." She ended the call. No goodbyes were exchanged.

"I better go."

"Okay," he said giving her a hug. "Let me know what you decide and see if you can find some time for me before you head abroad."

After her run she returned to their suite, blended

a smoothie with fresh fruit and juice. David had been to the grocery store when she was away. She showered, dressed and then walked to the garage to find her glistening, candy apple red, Corvette Stingray named Pumpkin. It was her carriage.

Upon arrival at the stables, the reality of the fire set in. The aftermath was noticeable. She could smell the burn. Clean up was on hold until the FBI finished their investigation. Her thoughts drifted to the loss of the two horses. She made herself a promise to make sure both would have a proper memorial built for them at the ranch.

Sandy and Renée noticed each another simultaneously.

"Renée, it's been a while," Sandy said extending her arms.

They gave each other a hug.

"How are you? Have you had any rest in the past couple of days?"

"Oh, I'm fine," Renée replied. "Sleep, it's so overrated. What about you? You must be exhausted from your flight. I'm a bit jealous that you travel to my homeland so often."

"Well, why don't you hop aboard sometime when I fly to France? Spend a few days with your family. I will go about my business, then pick you up on the way back, and bring you right back here."

"Thanks Sandy, you're so sweet. Someday I may take you up on that. When I was there a while back for my aunt's funeral, I realized how much I miss home. If I can swing a few days off somewhere down the road that would be wonderful."

"Don't worry about booking time off, I have an

in with your boss and my ways of persuasion."

At that David came around the corner of the stable. He walked up to them, put one arm around Sandy and gave her a quick kiss on the cheek.

"So what kind of trouble are you two conniving up?"

"Just girl talk and if I recall from last night, you're definitely not a girl."

"Really, I'm not sure what you are referring to."

"Oh, is that right. Well if I were you I'd dig deep. If your memory doesn't reappear within a few seconds, you won't need it any longer, because, there won't be any more nights worth remembering."

"Oh you mean last night, last night," he said while rubbing the side of his cheek with his fingers as if he was deep in thought.

"That's my boy. You get to live another day."

"Okay, you two. This is becoming too personal for me. I'm going to get back to work and leave you love birds alone to discuss your bedroom activities in private. David is there anything you'd like me to do?"

"Could you please check in with the FBI agent, and see if any progress is being made."

"I will," she began to walk away but paused as she received further instructions from her boss.

"Renée, allow him complete access to anything he wants. The quicker he determines the fire was ignited by a natural cause, the sooner we can clean up, and move on," he paused briefly then continued. "But keep an eye on him. Don't let him get too far out of your sight."

She nodded then went on her way. David stared at Renée a fraction of a second longer than he should have. Sandy took notice.

"She's hot," Sandy proclaimed.

"Sandy!"

"Look at her butt."

"Sandy!"

"She *is* hot."

He didn't reply this time. Taking a long breath, he lowered his head while shaking it back and forth, as if he was saying, I can't believe this. He had gotten accustomed to his wife's blunt comments. So this didn't surprise him. But it didn't ease the shock factor.

"Are you doing her?"

"Sandy!"

She gave him that little schoolgirl smile and shrugged her shoulders.

"Why would you say something like that? Have you looked at yourself in the mirror lately? Why would I want to be with anyone but you?"

She didn't reply, continuing to look at him with that brattish smirk.

"Besides, being married to someone that possesses your sexual appetite, I couldn't muster up enough energy to have an affair."

This time he got a grown up smile. Impressive comeback she thought.

"I need all that time you're away just to recuperate."

"I'm just saying," Sandy said, "she's hot."

"Enough about Renée," trying to change the subject, noting that she was enjoying the razzing a bit too much.

"Okay, but I would sleep with her."

She was relentless.

"You would sleep with Renée?"

"Well I might, that is, if I wasn't married to you."

"You would sleep with a woman?" he repeated.

"Why not, is there something wrong with that?"

He shrugged not knowing exactly how to reply.

"I thought you pro athletes were a free spirited bunch. After all, what about the stories of your partying with those groupies or what did you refer to them as, oh yea, puck bunnies."

"That's different, Sandy. Enough, I have to get back to work."

"Okay, but," she said, always being the one to have the last word, "my college roommate and I would make out every once in awhile when we were bored. It was quite an interesting experience."

"Wow, I learn something new about you every day. Why is it I have the feeling that you will continue to surprise me with these revelations until the day I die?"

"Babe, I've only just begun."

Chapter 3

After a persuasive hour or two David agreed to the quick trip. His mindset wasn't on relaxation. It had been absorbed in the aftermath of the fire, besides, they were about to spend a weekend together in California. Only after the FBI informed him the stable would be closed for a minimum of three days did he agree, not without protest. The horses had been moved to the ranch for the time being, so there was little left he could do. Renée and Serge would be attending to the animals twenty-four seven. Sandy prevailed.

The next morning they left for New York. A couple of day's rest, shopping, shows and so on. They were flying in her father's jet, which she put to use more than he did. It was a Gulfstream 650 with a price tag of eighty-five million dollars. Its fuel range was seven thousand nautical miles. This worked out well for Sandy. She rarely had to fly on a commercial airline during her worldly adventures.

Not much was said during the short flight. Both were exhausted. David tired from spending the previous two days at the track, Sandy jet lagged after spending the last ten days on the other side of the world. Now she was facing a return trip. Not the same destination, but far away from her husband. On one hand she craved the action. On the other, she would find herself day dreaming about cuddling up on the couch next to David, reading a good old fashion book. Some of her best memories were the two of them being together, with no words being spoken. Just feeling the warmth of his body, the sound of his breathing made her feel safe, toasty and peaceful. In a few years, she hoped to reduce her commitments, be more of a partner. Truth be told though, she wondered if that day would ever come. Telling him about her upcoming departure would wait until they had dinner and enjoyed an off-Broadway show.

One of their favorites was a small theater, off the beaten path. It featured two shows in the same building, one upstairs that seated two hundred ninety-nine people and one downstairs, that accommodated two hundred forty-nine. David preferred the one on the lower level. It featured a thrust stage, otherwise known as an open stage. Three of its sides extended into the audience, offering a unique experience that brought a great deal of interaction between the actors and the audience.

After dinner they set out on foot for the theater. It was only a few minutes away. This was New York, walking was quicker than hailing a cab. Nothing on four wheels got you from point A to point B very quickly. They were holding hands, savoring the time together. Life seemed so busy, precious times like this were special.

During the walk Sandy decided she should break the news about her upcoming departure.

"David, I need to go overseas again," she kind of cringed, one eye closed, easing her head away from her husband ever so slightly. Similar to what one would do when they expect the other person to react angrily. David said nothing. No reaction whatsoever.

"David," she said in a slightly higher pitch. Her tone was like someone gently waking someone up, not wanting to startle them, "David, did you hear me?"

"I heard."

Just as he began to answer, two young men appeared from a doorway and stood directly in front of them.

"Give me your wallet," the thinner of the two demanded. They were being mugged.

"Hey man look, we don't want any trouble. We don't carry cash, I probably have fifty bucks tops," David put his hand in his pocket to take out the cash.

"Here," he handed it to them. "Why don't you guys just let us pass here and we can forget this happened."

"That ain't going to happen rich guy," at this point the kid doing all the talking pulled out a knife and pointed it at David.

"I said give me your wallet," he threatened. "Maybe we're going to take a walk to a cash machine then you can show us how poor you are. You rich guys think people like us are stupid."

The kid talking was standing directly in front of David, the closer of the two to Sandy. The other guy was standing to David's right, one foot on the road and the other on the curb, as if he was ready to block anyone coming at them from the street.

From the second the two appeared Sandy's mind kicked into analyzing the situation. Tuning out everything around her not related to the initial threat. Being conscious of what was being said, but focused on their movements, gestures, and demeanor. She was trained to do so. Within a split second, she knew they were drug addicts in need of a fix. Not high at the moment, but in desperate need of cash to score a hit. Crashing addicts are irrational, very dangerous. She determined the threat had to be resolved immediately. Both were very unsteady on their legs—nervous. They would be no match for David who being a farm boy and playing hockey most of his life, was a pretty tough guy. But she also knew David would talk to these guys all night long before he became physical. He still had a lot of faith in mankind. It was a wonderful attribute. Tonight these boys didn't care about mankind or anything else other than getting high.

The guy with the knife was the first person who needed to be neutralized. The other kid was younger, a follower. He would probably run off as fast as he could if the mouth piece was put down. They were crashing addicts supported by weak and shaky legs. Their reaction would be much slower than a sober person. Her impassioned study in martial arts taught her to instantaneously recognize every vulnerable part of an adversary's body. She knew how much damage any blow to this guy would cause. If the kid forced her hand, he would soon be visiting the nearest emergency department.

"Buddy, I'm not going to give you my wallet," David was saying when she found herself tuning back into the conversation.

Nobody took notice that she had slipped out of her shoes. The importance of preparation was instilled in her. At that instant the kid with the knife made a move towards her husband.

Sandy instinctively reacted. She spun right and made a 180 degree crescent spinning hook kick, landing the back of her heal directly into the rear of the kid's knee. He buckled backwards, forcing his upper body and knife to face skyward. Her attack flowed smoothly. All in one fluid motion, she spun back with an open fist and drove the palm of her right hand upward into the bottom of his jaw, simultaneously landing a kick to the other attacker's face. As the knife-wielding kid was dropping to the ground she disarmed him. Within a split second the assailants were both down, both out cold—blood spewing from their faces. She inflicted enough damage to keep them off the streets for a few days. A visit to the hospital would be the smart move, but Sandy knew they were more apt to lie low until their wounds naturally mended. But nobody was dead, which might have been the outcome should this had been a life or death situation. Within seconds of their appearance Sandy knew how quickly the encounter was going to escalate into a dangerous situation. She could name the individual bones she had broken, and length of time they would take to heal. The threat nullified, executed with precision.

David stood in silence as his wife casually dropped the knife into the city drain, then put her shoes back on and readjusted her clothing. He understood she excelled in self-defense, karate and all that stuff. Her father insisted she learn how to defend herself. So martial arts training instead of dance classes was never a choice. She had lightheartedly demonstrated a few moves on him, but this was the first time he'd seen the damage his wife could wreak on a human being. It was a chilling experience.

With that girlish smile and wink she said, "We should be getting ourselves to the show," putting her arm around his, directing him away from the scene.

David was concerned that people would have taken notice of what had just transpired. He visualized police cruisers racing to the scene. Both of them being cuffed and spending the night behind bars. Sandy knew better. This was New York City. No one was calling the cops. No one probably witnessed the ordeal. If they did, they would have thought it was a drug deal gone wrong.

"Well," David said as he was being whisked away from the scene, "you really know how to make a guy feel inferior."

"David, I know you had the situation under control. I was just a bit anxious to get to the theater. I'm aware you're a rough and tough jock. But you Canadians are a bit too polite."

"Somehow, I don't think I'm quite as tough as you. I wish I would have met you earlier in life. I would have taught you how to skate. You'd have made a great defense partner on a few of my hockey teams."

"EH," She blurted out making fun of his Canadian accent.

***

After the evening's entertainment, they settled in back at the hotel lounge for a nightcap. There had been no further mention about the confrontation. Both thoroughly enjoyed the night at the theater and the conversations that took place were in reference to the production. There were other things on their minds, which they wanted to discuss. David was first to initiate a change in topics. "Sandy, I need to get serious for a minute."

She wasn't comfortable with these weighty discussions and replied, "Do we have to David. We're here to have some fun and relaxation."

"Yes. We need to have this talk. I love you more than I thought it was humanly possible to love someone. I'm so lucky to have met you. There is nobody I'd rather be with. That is the reason you need to hear me out."

"Did you do something you shouldn't have?"

"No Sandy, I didn't. I'm serious here. I'm worried about your traveling. I know you do wonderful things with your money, and I appreciate the compassion you apply to that part of your life. I can deal with you not being around all the time. I do completely trust you."

"Then why the urgency?" Looking directly in his blue eyes she added, "I'm not expecting to go at this pace for the rest of my life. But for now, that part of my life is important to me. It is who I am. You've known this since we met."

"I know, it's just," he hesitated, "I understand there's more to your travel than meets the eye. You have always been up front about that. Maybe it's me being paranoid, or jealous. But it does worry me. It can be a dangerous world."

"David, when a company such as ours spreads as much money as we do around the world, it takes on a life of its own. Everyone wants you to attend or speak at their function. So many people want a piece of you. I wouldn't feel comfortable leaving that in someone else's hands. Am I micromanaging, possibly? Being selfish, of course I am. That's who I am. I need to be at the helm of this. At least for the time being," she paused, raised her glass and took a sip of the drink.

David remained silent knowing she hadn't finished. He was a good listener. A trait he practiced after something she explained to him early in their relationship. She was having a stressful day and venting. He had automatically thought she wanted him to come up with a solution or console her. When he started to reply, she stopped him dead in his tracks, her eyes almost burning a hole in him. She told him, 'I don't want you to fix this. I want you to listen. I just want you to listen, that's all, nothing more, nothing less.' He got the picture. From that day forward, if she had to get something off her chest, David was the best listener in the world. He wouldn't say a word. He was cool with that.

Sandy continued, "We do find ourselves in remote places one may not see as the norm for a philanthropist's work. Our network has no prejudice. It touches every part of the world, wherever we can make a difference."

"Listen, I get it and I'm okay with it. What happened tonight brings my concerns back to the forefront. The way you handled yourself startled me. It felt more like a military attack, rather than someone utilizing a defensive martial arts discipline. The look on your face scared me, Sandy."

"It was a serious situation. He was about to stab you. I did what was necessary to defuse the situation, no more. Do we have to discuss this tonight? There are only a few hours left before we leave."

"Okay, I'll drop it for now, but I would like to sit down with you soon and talk about our future. We need to start making plans to start our own family. Life with you is so full of surprises. But I trust you, I love you, so enough said, for now."

"Thank you."

It felt as if she had more to say but nothing was forthcoming.

"Well," he paused, "what?"

She smiled, "Come with me I'll show you."

She grabbed his arm leading him to the stairwell. The door of their suite wasn't even closed and her clothes were decorating the floor. The learning trend continued. She surprised him with moves he hadn't realized a couple could physically achieve. He did luck out when he met this woman.

Breakfast in bed was served up by way of room service. She had to revisit the explanation about her leaving. Before she could bring the topic up David started.

"You know we should be heading home soon. I have quite a bit of prep work to do for the race this weekend. The horse is being flown out to California tomorrow night. I've booked our flights. Maybe we should continue this in the California sun."

Oh boy, she thought to herself. This is going to be a tad more difficult than she hoped.

"Babe, I can't go with you. As I was trying to explain before those kids interrupted us last night, I have to head overseas again."

"You're not coming. You just got back."

"I'm sorry," she apologized. "I have to leave soon."

"Where are you headed?"

She so wished she hadn't put those two kids down last night. It was sure to raise more suspicions with her husband, especially combined with revealing her destination.

"Saudi Arabia," she said sharply, offering no other explanation.

He looked at her a bit startled.

"I know you have access to more money than most third world countries do. But correct me if I'm wrong, from what I understand doesn't Saudi Arabia have more than say, everyone."

"David this isn't a fund-raising jaunt, or a spread

the wealth expedition. I had a call yesterday from King Abdullah. Fyad's is being married this weekend. The wedding date has been moved up. He called personally to confirm my attendance."

"I thought he was getting married in a couple of months."

"That was the original plan. He didn't offer me the reasoning behind the change. You know I need to attend this wedding David. Why don't you join me? You were originally planning on coming. Serge and Renée can deal with the California race. I could even ask my father to go with them and oversee the weekend."

"You know I can't. I'd love nothing more than to be with you, but I need to be at the track. To be honest, because of the fire, I may have to miss the race myself. I do have meetings set up mind you, but they can be rescheduled. There are some breeding contracts which need to be finalized," he explained. "I have way too much on my plate right now babe. Besides, I'm really not that comfortable socializing with Kings and Queens."

"Are you sure? They're actually really nice people. Believe it or not, they can be a lot of fun once the front door is locked."

"Sorry, I can't go. It's okay, you go. Just make sure you don't stay too long."

She got up and headed for the shower. He followed. A half hour later they reappeared, smiling.

Shortly thereafter, they were packed and called for a car to take them to the airport. It was a short flight. Nothing further was said about her trip. They talked about the fire and the upcoming race weekend at Santa Anita Park in Arcadia, California. This was the race track that saw the legendary horse Seabiscuit rise to fame during the great depression with a Canadian Jockey on him. A little tidbit of the sports history that David took pride in. He lived a great deal of his life in the USA, but was still quite proud of the achievements of his fellow Canadians.

It was a gorgeous day. The sun was shining brightly through the jet's windows. As they touched down, David wished they could just take off again in the direction of a secluded Caribbean island. He was longing for a week or two of R&R with his wife. But that was not going to happen anytime soon. He was supposed to be in California for the weekend, but may even have to put that aside because of the fire. And she was off to the Middle East.

The plane taxied to a private hanger. Once the engines were shut down, the door opened and the ladder appeared. David and Sandy made their way down and then walked to the structure.

"I'll get the car," David said as he followed his wife closely.

She turned to him, "David I'm not going back to the ranch. I have to leave now. The guys are filing a flight plan and we take off within the hour."

"Wow. I wasn't expecting that. When you say soon, you mean it."

"When I shortened my last trip, I canceled a speaking engagement. If I leave right away, I can fulfill my prior commitment. It's a choice audience, the corps d'elite. I should make an effort to attend if

I can make it happen. The Save the Children foundation stands to raise serious cash at the event. The more I can accomplish on this trip, the longer we can spend on that extended vacation in the middle of nowhere that you've been day dreaming about."

He looked surprised, "how did you know that's what I was thinking about."

"Another one of my amazing talents," she answered with a seductive smile. "I've been relishing the thought of self-imposed exile with you, on some deserted island."

"Come here," he said reaching out his arms.

He gave her a kiss, while hugging her tighter and longer than normal not wanting to go in separate directions. They knew it was inevitable this was going to be a part of their lives. But savoring the here and now was special. These partings were becoming more frequent. Nevertheless, it didn't get any easier.

Eventually they found a way to say their goodbyes, and went their separate ways. David out the front doors of the hanger to retrieve his vehicle from the parking facility reserved for those who were privileged in ownership of a private jet. He was heading directly to the stables.

Sandy exited the way she entered, by the hanger door facing the tarmac. She walked to and climbed the stairs of the aircraft. Her next few days were going to be a trying exercise—believing in the magnitude of the task at hand justified the frequent separations from the man she loved.

Chapter 4

Around the same time David and Sandy were entangled in the shower, Renée was opening her eyes to a new day. The sun was penetrating through the window, brighter than normal. Most days at this time she would be beginning her routine at the stables, but not this morning. There were two reasons for this. First, it was going to be a late night because she had to prepare one of their finest horses for transportation to the West Coast. He had to be ready to be driven to the airport by seven that evening.

The second reason was lying beside her, still fast asleep. Meeting in the parking lot while leaving the stables late last night, they decided to grab a night cap at The Dead Heat, a bar and grill not far from work. It is a favorite gathering spot for the people who frequent the race track. Owned and operated by two retired jockeys, Sebastian and Leven, both world class riders and highly respected by the inner circle of the racing world. Most thought they had retired much too early. However, Leven had a couple of nagging injuries that he was dealing with on a daily basis. Not severe enough to hamper his riding ability, but annoying enough to remind him that he wasn't getting any younger. Sebastian was a few years younger and had some good years left in him. He easily could have extended his successful career. The two men had become close friends throughout the years of competing against one another. When the opportunity to purchase the establishment came around, a partnership was formed. They saw it as a way to stay in touch with the people in the business far into the future, albeit in a different capacity. It allowed them to experience the camaraderie they had become accustomed to.

Renée and her sleepover weren't regulars. The majority of their time was spent working and sleeping, with the odd timeout for a bite to eat. On occasion they ran into each other, and it typically led to a drink or two. There was a lot of common ground, as Renée was a trainer and her guest was a jockey, actually North America's current leading jockey.

Renée's home was a spacious two-bedroom condominium, located close to the track. If asked, she would describe her décor as comfy. There were lots of pillows, comfortable couches, large lazy boys that you could fall into, each with its own reading lamp hovering over it. She loved to read, and wanted to feel relaxed no matter what piece of furniture she found herself occupying.

Plopped in one of those chairs located at the side of her bed, she sat reading, which was unusual for this time of day. But it had been an enjoyable night, she felt content, a morning without a worry in the world. She would read for a while, until her guest awoke. Then a quick breakfast would be in order before finding their way to work. This was a noncommittal relationship. They had been together only a few times within the past year. The encounters were enjoyed by both, fulfilling each other's sexual appetite, minus any emotional ties. Intense, exhausting, uninhibited, open-minded. Neither took it too seriously. There was a lot of laughter and kidding around during the hours they spent jumping each other's bones. A quiet morning of relaxation and recuperation was the right choice.

"Good morning."

Renée turned with a smile on her face and was greeted by the same.

"Good morning. You were sleeping like a baby."

"I was wasn't I? You have that effect on me," her guest replied. "Why don't you come join me?"

"Seriously," Renée questioned in a jokingly manner, then giving her guest a quick wink with a sexy little smirk on her face.

"We both have to get to work. I'm already going to be late. I have a busy day ahead of me."

With that she leaned onto the bed with one knee and gave Gabriela a kiss on the forehead.

"Time to get that tight little jockey butt up and ready," Renée said.

She did get up and they went into the kitchen area, each sporting only a t-shirt that barely covered their bottoms.

Gabriela was smaller than Renée by a whopping five pounds. She was on a regimented diet. She was required to meet a weight restriction each and every race. Her goal was to maintain a weight of 105 lbs or less. Most races required weighing in at 115 to 126 lbs. The Kentucky Derby, one of the world's most prestige's races, carried a weight restriction of 126 lbs. This included the weight of both the jockey, and his or her equipment of approximately ten pounds. These rigid standards were always on her mind. She refused to adapt the lifestyle of some other jockeys. There were widespread methods of shedding that crucial pound prior to stepping on the race day scale by self-induced vomiting and the use of laxatives.

Both were naturally petite young women. Renée's weight was similar, topping 110 on a bad day. Gabriela was five foot one inch, and Renée five foot two. If someday her decision was to pursue a career as a jockey, she would have to match her friend's weight. For now she was satisfied riding exercising laps each day.

When they made love it looked like two teenage girls hidden underneath the covers. However this visualization was the only similarity. These were two accomplished, self-assured, educated, open-minded women who possessed an unquestionable knowledge in the art of lovemaking. Two women small in stature, significant in attainment.

Renée wouldn't label her sexual preferences. There had been men. Gabriela was only her second female partner. Not much thought was put into the gender of who she slipped under the sheets with. She didn't entertain often, but when she did meet someone who intrigued her, she let her guard down and engaged in fulfilling her needs. It wasn't uncommon to go months without companionship. When she first moved to the USA to pursue her career, she remembers not having sex for two years. This didn't concern her. She had perfected self-gratification and although it wasn't as memorable as some of her encounters, it did provide some intense orgasms. Her mother had quashed the myths about this method of stimulation at an early age. It wouldn't make her go blind. It wasn't something to be embarrassed about. The satisfaction it produced was an acceptable form of pleasure. Having an open relationship with her parents provided the foundation of her extraordinary state of self-confidence.

Renée and Gabriela sat at the breakfast counter nibbling on fruit, drinking smoothies.

"That was an awesome night, Renée. We should find the time to do this more often."

"We'll see," she paused, "but you know that's not what I'm looking for right now. Look on the bright side. This way it feels like it's our first time, every time."

"You have a point," Gabriela smiled. "Where did you learn some of that stuff," referring to her being well versed in the bedroom. "That thing with the ice cubes, how did you come up with that? I almost passed out. I didn't realize an orgasm could be so powerful."

"Well you know what they say about us little French girls," they both laughed.

"Merci pour les Français," Gabriela said, thanking the French.

"C'est mon plaisir," Renée replied.

They ate, dressed and found their way to work. Gabriela traveling in her Cadillac SUV while Renée rode her bicycle. One requirement of her housing search was to find a location that would allow her to bike. Besides the obvious benefits, this form of transportation provided her with alone time. So much of nature's offerings were passed over when traveling in a vehicle. By the time she arrived at the track, she felt like she could take on the world. On those days it didn't seem to be a practical mode of transportation, she rode her BMW HP4 street motorcycle. A thoroughbred race horse was painted on the gas tank.

The track was buzzing with activity when she arrived. Everything was nearly back to normal. The only indication of the destruction was a small crew beginning to reconstruct the building back to its pre-fire form. The authorities released the scene within a day. Today's task was preparing for the return of the horses.

She was met at the stable's office by Serge the head trainer. As usual, he seemed to have everything in order. Putting aside his flamboyant style on race days he was one of, if not the best trainers in the world. Renée couldn't have kept better company. She never judged his over-the-top outfits worn on the race day and she was able to overlook his arrogant mannerisms. He was the best, she knew it. Success breeds success. Surround yourself with the elite. She was doing just that. Listen, learn, question and absorb. You will achieve your quest much sooner.

"A late night, Renée," Serge greeted her. "You're normally a much earlier arriver."

"I apologize. I did have a late evening and should have been here sooner."

She made no excuses. Messing up sometimes in life was a given. Always admitting her errors and being prepared to face whatever consequence they bore, was a quality characteristic. Although coming in a bit late on a day that probably wouldn't end until close to midnight wasn't a big deal. Just tell it like it is.

"Never mind that," he said. "Actually, I think you should indulge in late evenings more often. You need to introduce more personal time into your schedule. Spending as much time here as you do is not healthy," he hesitated. "Then again your presence reduces my workload so perhaps a little more personal time and a little less work."

"Merci," she thanked him in French. "I'll work on that."

Serge pointed at one of the chairs in front of the desk, "Please, sit."

She did and he sat opposite her on another old broken down chair. This wasn't your typical office it was more of a break room for the crew. The floor was stained, walls and furniture beat up. It had a couple of saddles sitting in the corner, no books, an old wooden desk, a coffee pot and a small microwave. Not much else.

"We need to discuss a couple of things young lady," Serge said.

Renée had a sudden rush of guilt but wasn't sure why. Had she done something wrong? To the best of her knowledge her duties were being fulfilled in the highest of standards. Serge gave her instructions on a daily basis, which she followed to the tee. These meetings were far and few between. On occasion she wondered if Serge had misunderstood her frequent interactions with David.

"You look a bit uncomfortable," he continued. "I told you I wasn't concerned with you being late."

"No, I'm good Serge. What's on your mind?"

"I want you to take the lead in California this weekend. I'm going to take care of the race card here," he told her.

Her face did little to hide the shock she was feeling. This wasn't what she was expecting. The lead trainers of a stake race were in the public eye. Quite often they were interviewed on national sport networks. Even after hearing it she couldn't quite grasp what he was saying.

"Serge this is one of our most important and prestigious races of the year. I can't recall you ever missing a card like this."

"Listen up," he paused. "You can handle this. I have complete confidence in your ability to oversee this properly. I'm not sure you actually realize how talented a trainer you have become. However, you may have to brush up on your hobnobbing."

"My what?" she asked.

Renée wasn't familiar with that term. As a matter of fact she was amazed at the endless list of phrases Serge threw at her. Hobnobbing was a new one. Being from England, Serge had a complete repertoire of sayings that seemed peculiar to her. This one was an old English phase from the 1700's, originally meaning to drink together and later taking on a general expressing of chumminess.

"Hobnobbing," Serge repeated himself. "It will be expected of you to socialize in the owner's booth at this race. You need to parade our horse in the winner's circle when we win. We will win. You can't wear jeans."

"Are you sure about this,, Serge," Renée once again questioned what he was proposing. "This is what you live for. It's your arena, your day in the spotlight."

"Renée, you're going and everything will work out fine. Would you like to borrow one of my suits?"

Both burst into laughter. Serge was known for his flamboyant outfits and top hats which he flaunted at these stake races. He played the part of the world's most respected horsemen. The press would be disappointed at his absence. Interviewing Serge was good for their ratings.

After the giggling subsided she replied, "I'm pretty sure I can find something to wear, although it may be more subdued than your attire."

"Good then, it's settled. You will give our entry a short run today and then begin preparations for transport to the airport tonight. Steven will accompany him to Los Angeles. I've booked your flight. You fly out tomorrow at noon. David will take care of the business end of the trip so you can put a hundred percent of your energies into Charlotte's Choice and bring home the winning saddle cloth."

Uneasiness came over her at the mention of

David. She wasn't sure how he would take to the change in plans.

"How does he feel about this? I mean David."

"I don't know. We haven't told him yet. Actually I haven't seen him today. I will inform him when he arrives. I'm sure he will be okay with it. He speaks highly of you and believes in your capabilities. But that said I'm the head honcho of this barn and I have decided you're going. He won't question my decision."

"This brings me to the second item I wish to discuss with you," changing the subject. "As we speak David is at his residence meeting with Mr. Watson and Special Agent Scott. Renée, the fire was deliberately set. It was an act of arson. This is disturbing news. We've been asked to jog our memories. See if we can recall anything that seemed out of the ordinary within the past two months. Give it some thought. Ask around."

"How could that be? As of late last night it was believed to have been ignited by natural causes."

"I don't have any more information at this time. When I last met with the FBI Agent he confirmed the findings. I was not privy to anything further. He was heading to the ranch to brief David and his father in-law. There is nothing more I can tell you."

"When is David expected?"

"I'm not sure. But I would think sometime this afternoon. We will be updated then. But right now, we need to keep our minds focused on winning that race this weekend. You with me?"

"Okay, let's do this," she stood up quickly, confidently leaving the room ready to take a giant leap in her career.

***

Jacob and David listened intently as Special Agent Scott apprised them of his findings.

"So remember when you were a kid and playing with alleys, or as some call them marbles. Imagine spreading half a dozen of those in piles of hay throughout the stable. That's exactly what happened. The difference here is the marbles actually had a tiny, powerful computer chip in them. Once the device is activated electronically by a cell phone or a computer, they heat up to an extremely intense temperature similar to a stove top element on high. They do not explode or burst into flames. However, placed under a light dry material they will ignite it. In this case it was hay. I would think this is the reason the local fire investigator determined there were multiple areas of origin for the fire."

He sat quietly for a moment anticipating questions. None were forthcoming.

"This method of arson is rare and expensive. Coined a Marble Burn, it can be activated from any location in the world. Gentlemen, you have been targeted and we need to look at reasons why someone wishes to inflict this kind of damage on you. We only know of two individuals that produce this sort of system. They are secretive as to whom their clients are. Both live in Europe. The world is a large geographic area to begin a search such as this, so we need to begin narrowing it down by determining motivation. It was not meant for mass destruction. The rare times we have come across it, its purpose was one of distraction, rather than damage."

Without responding to the Special Agent's explanation, Mr. McGinnis picked up the phone and tapped the intercom.

"Yes, Jacob," his executive assistant Brooklyn Albright immediately answered.

"Would you step into my office for a minute?"

Seconds later the office door opened and she entered with her iPad in hand. She appeared so quickly it was as if she was waiting outside the room with her hand on the door knob. Brooklyn was a brilliant woman in her mid-fifties. She was Harvard educated, attractive, fit, a professional married to her career. Jacob had enticed her to move from Washington DC to become his executive assistant a number of years ago. Brooklyn had been the private secretary to the President of the United States for eight years prior to joining Jacob. She was compensated with a very generous high six figure salary and a private residence on the ranch. Intelligent, dedicated and by spending two terms sitting at a desk adjacent to the Oval Office, she was well connected. Brooklyn was the President's Rock of Gibraltar. If you wanted to enter the most elusive office in the world, you had to make your way past her. No one, even the First Lady, entered that room without her authorization. She had approved Jacob's access on more than one occasion. Now here she stood, saying nothing, waiting for instructions from Mr. McGinnis.

"Brooklyn," he began, "Agent Scott has

determined that the fire at our stables was intentionally set. We need to assist him in any and every possible way to ensure a speedy conclusion to this situation. Please provide him with all the material or information he requires."

She said nothing, nodding that she understood. The actual meaning to his instructions was to allow Agent Scott access to most files, not all. Certain files would never to be seen by anyone, other than herself and her boss.

"Special Agent Scott if you would follow Miss Albright she will assist you immediately. All of her other business matters will be put aside until you are satisfied with your examination." He had heard enough, now he expected that the situation to be fixed.

"Miss Albright will fill you in on any threats we may have received, or any disgruntled persons or employees we may be associated with. She possesses far more knowledge of this kind of information than I do. I would appreciate you informing me when you've apprehended the persons responsible for this."

At that the men stood, shook hands and the FBI Agent left the room with Brooklyn.

David spoke for the first time since the meeting commenced. "When they do determine who did this, I'd like five minutes alone with them."

Jacob addressed him, "David this is not hockey game. The FBI will find our culprit and they will be brought to justice. Now, don't you have some business to attend to at the stables? This is a big weekend."

"You're right I do need to get going. Are you coming to California tomorrow?"

"That will not be possible. I will take in the races here. My schedule is full," he said as he spread out his hands referring to the files lying on his desk. "Besides I don't have a plane. Your wife has hijacked it once again. Speaking of planes, Brooklyn has your tickets on her desk. She booked two tickets thinking Sandy was going to accompany you. Maybe you could offer it to Serge. That would make for an interesting flight."

"I'll ask if he is interested."

They both had a little chuckle then David made his exit. Jacob sat back at his desk. The smile disappeared. An eerie facial expression crossed his face. He would allow no more than one week for this investigation to conclude before he picked up the phone to ruffle some feathers. Someone was going to pay dearly for this attack. They had targeted the wrong family.

David arrived at the stables. All seemed well. The construction crew repairing the damage caused by the fire was moving at a nice pace. Everything else was quite normal. Some of the horses had been returned. They were being walked and groomed. There were a number of horses from other stables being put through their paces on the track. It was a gorgeous day. The sun was shining, not a cloud in the sky. Even with the events of the last few days, he felt revitalized once he entered the area where the horses were housed. The smell, the people, the innocence of the animals all made for a peaceful environment. At this instant there was nowhere else in the world he'd rather be.

He walked along the outside of the stalls and said hello to any stable hand he came across. In search of either Serge or Renée he was making his way to the lunch room/office. They had a busy weekend ahead of them, and he wanted to make sure preparations were on schedule.

"David, wait up."

Turning to the direction of the voice, he saw Renée jogging to catch up to him. He stopped and waited for her. Always brightening his day, always in good spirits—at least on the outside no matter what challenges she was facing, was an attribute he admired. She caught up, out of breath, but still smiling. His day just got better.

"Hey Renée, how are things going around here? I've been gone less than two days, but it feels like a lifetime."

"Everything is fine. Serge told me that they suspect that the fire was set on purpose," changing the subject.

"That seems to be the consensus. I'm sure the FBI will figure it out. However young lady, we need to concentrate on our upcoming races."

"All seems to be running smoothly and on time," Renée answered. "Serge has made a few changes to our schedule, but I think it would be best if you discuss it with him."

"What changes?"

"I'm sure he would rather explain it himself. I'm good with whatever you two decide." Then she added in French, "si c'est okay avec toi," meaning if that's okay with you.

56

"C'est très bien," he answered.

"Where is Serge?"

"I'm not sure, I'll call him," reaching for her phone.

Serge picked up immediately. They talked briefly then she slipped the cell into the back pocket of her jeans.

"He'll meet you at the office in five."

"Good, I'll catch up with you later," then turned in the direction of the office.

Renée was hoping that he would be okay with her taking Serge's position in California. Being the head trainer of a favorite in a premiere horse race, would definitely propel her career a notch or two.

David arrived at the office before Serge. He opened the refrigerator, snatched a bottle of water then sat on one of the rickety chairs putting his feet up on the desk. The majority of his time during the ride to work was taken up by talking on his Bluetooth, arranging meetings for the upcoming trip. So this was his first quiet moment since he touched down this morning. His thoughts drifted to the events which had unfolded yesterday. Witnessing his wife destroy those two thugs was disturbing. Knowing she was a master in martial arts was one thing. Standing beside her as she pulverized them was another. The visualization of the episode was short lived as Serge soon appeared in the doorway.

"David, it's nice to see you found your way back," Serge began with an authoritarian emphasis to his voice.

Everyone including himself knew David was the

boss. But he also knew he was the best in the business. He didn't like being instructed on how to do his job, and he wasn't that keen on seeking approval on his decisions.

David very rarely questioned Serge's judgment when it related to the training of the horses. Actually he valued his opinions. After all, he was one of the elite trainers in the world. Serge's ego and his commanding of the spotlight did not bother David in the least. Frankly, he was entertained by it. Yet the trainer was an employee and if push came to shove, David would prevail.

"Well, I'm glad to be home Serge, although it has been less than two days. It's nice to see you too," David replied.

"Two long days," Serge added. "Can you bring me up to date on the fire?"

"The FBI has determined that it was set intentionally. Some sort of computer chip device which heats up to such an intense temperature it ignited the hay. The chips are small much like a marble. It can be activated remotely from anywhere in the world. Someone who had access to the stables placed them in our stalls."

"I find it hard to believe a fellow horseman would take that kind of action," Serge seemed sincerely shaken at this news.

"I doubt that it was anyone from this track. But the FBI feels confident they will resolve it quickly and prosecute the guilty parties."

He then changed the subject, "Are we on schedule for transporting the kid to the West Coast? We need to focus solely on our weekend race. Let the authorities do their job, at least for the time being."

"I agree," Serge replied then hesitated before informing him about who was going to make the trip. "I'm sending Renée to California this weekend, and I will oversee our local races. I think under the circumstances it would best one of us stayed close to home."

"Serge this is a stakes race, one of the most important of the year. Why would you not want to be there? If anyone should stay here it should be me. I can rearrange my meetings." He paused giving it some thought then continued, "do you really think Renée can handle this?"

"She's been ready for some time now. I believe you will find her quite prepared for the task at hand," he was going to explain his decision further but David put his hand up to stop him.

"I'm okay with it Serge. I appreciate your believing in her. I'm not sure I fully understand why you want to miss it. But it's your call. Have you confirmed her travel arrangements?"

"Everything has been taken care of."

David stood, shook his hand and patted him on the shoulder then added, "I'm heading back to the ranch within an hour or so. If you need anything call me." Then both men left the office and went their own ways.

David had all the confidence in the world pertaining to Renée's handling of the weekend. Something about Serge passing up an opportunity that would most definitely present him a day or two in the limelight didn't sit well. These races were heavily covered by the media. Renée could handle the horse just fine, but it was going to be interesting to see how well she deals with the press. David smiled to himself. This was going to make for an intriguing trip. He was looking forward to it.

After leaving the office, he once again made his way through the stalls chatting it up with the stable's employees. Spending time around the horses was a gratifying aspect of his job. He had a true love for these animals, cherishing every moment he could spend with them. He stood having a conversation with one of the groomers while rubbing Charlotte's forelock. Charlotte's Choice was the horse being transported to California that evening by cargo plane in preparation for the upcoming race.

Renée came around the corner but stopped when she saw David, and slowly backed off, leaning her shoulder on the wall. She wasn't hiding, but more observing as she kept herself out of sight, not wanting to interrupt her boss's conversation. There was something to be said about a man that could treat an animal with such tenderness and care. Renée wanted to savor the scene. When she witnessed David's interaction with the thoroughbreds, it heightened her admiration towards the man. Her pausing, in part, could also have been her subconsciously delaying the conversation with him—fearing he might have declined Serge's request for her to take the lead in California.

The interlude was short lived as he took notice of her, motioning for her to join him. She smiled and walked towards them. David said something to

Monica the groomer. She was one of the crew that would fly with the horse tonight. Besides Renée and himself there were three hands that would make the trip. They would chaperon the horse twenty-four seven, never letting him out of their sight. David ended the chat, shook her hand while tapping her on the shoulder, then made his way in the direction of Renée, who was approaching. When they came together he continued walking which forced Renée to make a quick ninety degree turn to keep up with him. They didn't speak until outside the stables.

"Did you speak to Serge," she said expecting to hear bad news about her upcoming travels.

"I did," he replied not adding anything further.

They continued to walk side by side. Knowing she was champing at the bit to find out if he approved the change in schedule, his first thought was he was going to have a little fun with it. Not letting her hang too long, but a few minutes would be enjoyable. Always the jokester he saw no harm in a little teasing. It broke the seriousness of the day.

When he was playing hockey he had been known to participate in a prank or two. During one of his Junior Hockey years, the team had a player that was always the last out of the shower. On most nights he was the last player to get on the bus, which delayed many departures. One night after a late practice David came up with the idea. During practice they solicited the arena attendant's approval and verified that they were the last booking on the ice that particular night. There would be nobody in the facility when they were done. So once practice was over they all changed and showered a little quicker than usual. True to form this one player was last to enter the shower. Once he did, they cleared the dressing room of everything, taking his towel, equipment, clothes and putting them at center ice. The poor guy had to walk out on the cold ice surface butt naked to retrieve his clothing. He was laughing harder than the remainder of the team who were hiding in the lobby peeking through the glass.

David realizes that type of behavior would not be allowed in this day and age. It would be shunned, labeled hazing or harassment. But he believed it was all in good fun. This was a tight-knit group. These guys would go to war for each other. They were a brotherhood. If you messed with one, you messed with them all. During the next road trip following the practice, they allowed that player to be first in line when the bus stopped for food, a position which was normally reserved for the star of the game or the captain. He got to select the movies for the ride. It had all been in good-spirited fun and the player himself was impressed with whoever thought it up. But it was a team and the whole team took credit for the idea. David did not condone bullying. Contrary to some people's belief, he felt in this case no harm had been done. It was part and parcel of belonging to a sports team. The razzing was present in this environment. It always had been and would always be.

"I understand everything is in order for Charlotte's flight."

"We are on schedule and should be leaving within the next two hours for the airport. I would like him to have an hour or so to settle on the aircraft before its departure."

"Good. I have to attend to a couple of things this evening so I'm heading out now. If you need anything call me," he could see she was a confused as to why the subject of her going to California hadn't been brought up.

He was right, it was killing her. She didn't know if he approved of the plan, or had he not and was leaving it to Serge to break the news. Certainly if he agreed with it, he would have touched on the subject by now.

David started to walk towards the parking lot. As he got about ten feet in front of Renée, he turned back. She was walking away. Taking a second to admire her, he recalled Sandy's comments from the other day. She does have a great butt.

"Renée," he called out to her.

She turned towards him, stopping as he approached.

"I was informed by Serge that he has asked you to join me in California this weekend."

Here it comes she thought. Aware how important the race was she would understand David wanting the veteran trainer overseeing it. Although she knew she was quite capable, there would be no hard feelings for what she was about to hear.

"You're going to need to have Serge cancel your flight reservations," not offering any further explanation.

There it is Renée thought. That damn Serge he should have cleared it with David before letting her get her hopes up.

"Ok, I'll go find him and let him know," she said in a lower disappointing voice.

As she turned to walk away he called out her name again. She stopped and thought to herself, what now, your crushing me here, let's just get on with it.

He looked at her sporting a devilish smile, "Can you be ready by ten?"

"For what David?"

"I'll pick you up at ten tomorrow morning."

"David, you're going to California tomorrow," reminding him.

"I know my flight leaves at one and I thought it would be nice to have some company."

"I don't understand. If you and Sandy need a ride to the airport, I'm sure the staff at the ranch can arrange it," adding, "I will have a lot to oversee here David with you and Serge both gone."

"Strange, I thought you were coming to California and Serge was staying here," he pretended to act surprised.

"You just told me to cancel my tickets."

"I did, didn't I," David said. "I want you to cancel your tickets, because I have two first class tickets and there is only one of me. Flights can be so boring. It would be nice to have some company."

"What about Sandy. You told me she was joining you."

"She left for Europe this morning. No telling when she'll be home." He went on, "by the way I think it was an excellent call to have you take the lead at this race. You will do a fantastic job. You're ready for this young lady. It's your turn to shine."

Renée gazed in wonderment at her boss. She couldn't find any words to respond. Being resigned to staying behind her brain wasn't synchronized with her speech. The surprise was noticeable.

"Renée, are you okay? Renée, tu es bien avec ceci?" he repeated it in French thinking words in her native tongue might bring her back to earth.

"Oui, David I'm fine," she responded. "You said ten, yes, I'll be ready."

"Good, I'll see you then."

With that he turned and continued his walk to the parking lot, got into his vehicle and drove away. Renée walked to the race track to have a look at one of their horses which was being put through a training session. She made her way to the end of the path that the horses are paraded to and from the stables. There were four or five horses running. One was slowly walking towards the open gate, returning to the stalls when the jockey stopped and dismounted handing the reins over to a groomer. It was Gabriela.

She approached Renée, who was leaning on the fence, her eyes glued to one of her horses. So zoned in she didn't notice Gabriela until hearing her.

"Renée."

When she realized who it was a smile came across her face.

"How's your day going," Gabriela continued. "I thought I might see you out on the track this afternoon."

"I would have loved to have been riding. But I had way too much to take care of," she replied.

"That's too bad. I know how much you look

forward to it."

"I really do."

Gabriela went on, "Listen I won't be seeing you for a few days. I got a call this morning and caught a ride for this weekend's stake race in California. So tell Serge I intend on occupying the winners circle," she joked.

"Well don't get your hopes up. I'm leaving for the west coast tomorrow afternoon. Serge is sending me as lead trainer for the race. I'm planning on winning."

"Serge is not going. This has to be a first."

"You're surprised. Imagine how I am feeling."

"Well congratulations. It is well earned. You are one of the best, and now it is your time to show them what you're made of. I'm really proud of you." Then she suddenly realized this meant they were going to cross paths sooner than later, "we need to get together for dinner, drinks or—"

Renée cut her off, "I'd love to."

"Okay, great. I'll get in touch with you after settling in," Gabriela said. "This has the makings of an intriguing trip."

Chapter 5

Sandy's pilots filed a flight plan to France. Her flying time was estimated at approximately nine hours. She decided to spend the next day in Paris before making the additional six hour trip to Saudi Arabia. The board of the Save the Children Foundation was overwhelmed when informed she was able to attend after all.

She spent the first part of the Atlantic crossing catching up on sleep. The activities of the past couple of days hadn't allowed for much rest. Next, an hour or so dedicated to the preparation of the address she was scheduled to present. When the word was out that she might be returning to Europe sooner than expected, a couple opportunities to speak at functions were offered. She chose to fulfill her original commitment. Charities whose goal was to enhance the well-being of children would always be her preference.

The remainder of the flight was split between reading and staring out the window of the plane, letting her thoughts drift from David, to the wedding she was attending, then back to David.

Recently a good deal of her time was spent reflecting on her future. Her husband wanted children in their lives. Was it a deal breaker? Would she lose him if her decision was to remain committed to her present lifestyle, or was it possible to continue at this pace and properly raise a child? The answers were not clear, and the search for them was becoming more pressuring each day. She did promise herself one thing. Once this detail was completed she was going to retreat to the ranch for an extended period of time. A heart to heart with her husband was overdue.

When they arrived at Charles de Gaulle airport she was whisked through customs. Anywhere on this side of the world when her name was entered into an official computer, the instructions were to clear her through without the formalities that most travelers were accustomed to. Over the years she had befriended some very powerful allies. Sandy carried a status similar to a Head of State. Her plan was to grab a bite to eat then bed. What lie ahead would require her utmost attention.

***

Waking up early, she put on a jogging outfit then made her way down the stairs to the hotel lobby. She left the room key at the front desk not wanting to carry anything with her during the run. The only item allowed to participate in the journey was an iPhone which contained a wide variety of her favorite music, different playlists for different moods.

Paris was such an inspiring city to run in, so much history. A jog along the banks of the River Seine was as breathtaking as it gets. Passing by the Eiffel Tower, running alongside yesteryear's structures, with their secrets hidden between the walls, was a setting to be relished by true romantics. Such magnificent views whichever direction one faced. It was simply stunning.

The goal was to run a pace of six minute miles. A slower tempo for part of the jog was to be expected while taking in the scenery. After all the years of rigorous training she was as fit as any Olympian athlete. Her resting heart rate was forty beats per minute. The norm for an elite female athlete was nearer to fifty. She could have run faster but this was a nice pace for someone facing a fourteen hour day.

After the run she walked a block or two allowing her heart rate to lower. En route back to the hotel, a stop at a small café she frequented when in Paris was in order. They blended up a peach-mango smoothie with a scoop of protein. Once back at the hotel she retrieved the key from the front desk. Completing her day's workout she climbed the stairs two at a time. A flight of stairs was an excellent form of exercise. She was surprised it wasn't a common practice with most people. It was such a simple way to implement a little fitness into a person's daily routine.

Sandy locked the door then striped her way to the powder room for a well deserved shower. As the wash progressed, she surrendered to self gratification. It was going to be one of her extended showers. The stimulation actually began during her run. Occasionally during an exercise session she would experience what was learned to be an exercise-induced orgasm. She first experienced this sensation during her teen years. Training mostly in a male predominate environment she felt embarrassed at the onset of the episodes. It was important to recognize them when exercising in the public. With time Sandy learned to control the awkwardness.

Sandy educated herself about the sensation. With some research and the quizzing of a trusted sports psychology professor, to her surprise she learned it was natural for a woman to feel sexually aroused during extreme exercise. The explanation given was, studies concluded that women build tension in their legs before an orgasm. When a woman exercises, they release endorphins and dopamines, which are essential for an orgasm, combined with the tension in the lower extremities can cause the stimulation. The orgasms were referred to as coregasm. On a positive note, Sandy felt it was quite a motivator to hit the gym.

Once finished, she leaned on the vanity with both arms, wiped the fogged mirror and spoke to her blurred reflection, "Oh my God, I spend way too much time alone."

Arriving at the charity luncheon on time, she spent an hour or so getting reacquainted with people she hadn't seen for quite some time. Shortly after everyone was seated, she was introduced as the guest speaker. The event was a thousand-dollar-a-plate dinner. Most in attendance were multimillionaires. Her goal was to open as many cheque books as possible. The Save the Children association was one she spent numerous hours campaigning for. She had links with many well deserving non-profit organizations, but those who assisted or came to the aid of children, no matter where in the world they lived, were close to her heart.

The hostess of the gathering introduced Sandy, "Ladies and Gentlemen would please welcome our special guest this evening, Sandy McGinnis-Watson."

Sandy set her glass of water on the podium. She thanked her hostess and began speaking, "My dear friends, it is an honor to stand in front of you today. The work of the Save the Children organization has become dear to my heart."

She went on for about ten minutes talking about the goals of the charity. A brief outline of their recent achievements was touched on. You didn't want to bore these guests. It was best to have them well fed and happy. Maybe loosened up by way of the spirits being served. They were all aware why they had been invited. A short speech or two would be acceptable, but most wanted to get down to business. For that reason Sandy felt it was time to wrap up her talk.

"We haven't been very careful with taking care of the earth we live on," she continued. "We've polluted our water, created holes in the ozone layer, and paved the fields that once grew the food we eat. It's been profitable to beat it up. People are losing their lives every day in conflicts over geographic and religious disputes. It would astound you to learn how many children are caught in the crossfire." She wanted to paint a bleak picture but on the other hand, didn't want to dampen the mood of her listeners. So it was time to mention the positives then bring the speech to an end.

"It is however, encouraging that governments and citizens worldwide have taken positive steps to reverse this damage. What we need to ensure is that every child in every corner of the world, has access to safe water and a nourishing diet. A pledge to provide an education for every one of them, void of prejudice, and antagonism, is one of our goals. Let us visualize a world in which those who grow to become our leaders retain the innocence they once knew while playing in the local playground. They see no color or race. All equal."

With one last stitch effort to rally the troops, she decided to tell a story about one of David's coaches attempt to motivate his team.

"Some of you know my husband David," abruptly changing the subject. "For those who don't, he was a professional athlete before an injury ended his career. Well, listening to some of the stories he has told," she almost started to whisper as if telling a secret, "would make you think, it might have been a head injury that forced him into an early retirement."

She heard a few chuckles from the crowd, their serious faces soon turning to smiles. It was as if they were looking for a reason not to be thinking of all the dire events in the world which she brought to light.

"Now, being married to an athlete bestows a sense of duty which requires you to listen to accounts of events that took place during their career. Keep in mind, in my case that meant tales of twenty some athletic, wealthy men, traveling, dressing and showering together for ten months out of each year. Most of these anecdotes I believe weren't meant to be discussed in public, although some have been rather interesting," she paused. "If you will indulge me for another minute or two I would like to share one with you today. Then we eat."

"One year David's team began to falter near the end of the season. They still had a chance to make a comeback and be in contention to win the league championship. The coach felt that his players were not playing up to their potential. In David's words, the coach had called them a bunch of spoiled overpaid lazy so and so. Now, I must interject and say that after hearing these tales, I have come to the conclusion that an athletic coach must not only possess a sound knowledge for the game in which he or she is teaching, but equally important, they must be an exceptional motivator."

She then fast forwarded the story. "After the loss of another important game the coach informed all the players that they would have to pack and carry their own equipment to the bus, which was waiting at the rear of the arena. All professional teams employ staff to manage the gear. They had been given the day off. The coach informed the players in harsh terms, that for the remainder of the season there would be no need for equipment handlers. He explained since some players in the room weren't prepared to play like professionals, there was no need to be treated as one," she took a sip of water.

"The players didn't say a word to him. They learned from the early age of five that nothing good would come from disputing what a coach says."

Feeling she might be getting a bit long winded. It was time to get to the point. "So the team packed their gear and loaded it onto the bus. When everyone was accounted for the coach took the front seat which was always reserved for him. The bus was sitting on a slant, but no one said a word. The reason it was tilting to the side was because the coach had the bus company hire a towing service to remove one of the front wheels and hide it out of sight. When they were ready to depart, the coach turned to the bus driver instructing him in his grumpy voice, 'Okay, let's go'. The driver turned to him replying, 'sir we can't move, we're missing a tire'. The coach said, 'I don't care, just go'. The driver repeated, 'I can't drive this thing with nine tires, we need ten.' This went back and forth until a couple of the veteran players came to the aid of the driver. They moved to the front of the bus and told the coach they would go out and have a look, which they did. Stepping back on, they confirmed that for some strange reason there was a wheel missing. Not acknowledging them the coach turned and again said to the driver, 'let's go. Why do need all the tires to move this thing?' Before the driver could respond, the captain of the team spoke to the coach, 'Look I know you're upset at us, but don't take it out on this guy,' referring to the driver. 'We can't drive until we replace the tire," Sandy took a moment so the people in attendance could visualize the situation.

"At this point the coach stood up and turned to address his players. 'Guys I don't see the problem here. The bus still has nine tires. It's only missing one.' A player near the back of the bus spoke up, 'come on coach you know we can't move without all the tires working.' Now it was time for the coach to drive home the point of this whole exercise. 'Is that right? Seems like a strange statement coming from someone on this team. For the last three weeks we have played game after game with six players being on the ice, but only two or three of them actually doing anything. The others were nowhere to be found. Gentlemen, we've been missing players. Apparently you guys believe this damn bus can't go anywhere when it has one of its tires missing. How the hell do you think this hockey team can go anywhere missing players? This is a team sport. Only teams win in this league. A team needs all its wheels. It can't move forward without them. We need every single tire performing at its peak. And let me assure you gentlemen, we will win.' With that he took his seat, nodded to the bus driver and said, 'get that damn wheel fixed.' The players got the message. Motivated by what may have been construed as an act bordering on insanity, they went on to win the league championship."

"At first, I thought the coach's performance was over the top. The more and more I thought about it, his behavior inspired a group of young men who had forgotten their roots. What they sacrificed to achieve those childhood dreams." She brought the story its end.

"So let's Save the Children. They are the future. Let's provide them with the finest education available. Let's feed them so they never have to experience hunger again. Let's teach them to cherish the earth they live on. Let them live a life void of chauvinism. Everyone in this room is part of this team. Let's make sure this bus has all of its wheels. I solicit you to open up those cheque books, and don't be shy with the zeros. It's our time to give back."

At that point she held up an envelope and informed her listeners, "We at the McGinnis Foundation would like to get this started with a donation of one million dollars. Thank you."

They stood and clapped. Sandy took her seat and enjoyed an exquisite meal. After an hour or so of socializing, she began to offer her goodbyes. Save the Children was the winner of the evening. Those in attendance were far more generous than anyone had anticipated. More money was raised that evening than at any other single event the organization had hosted.

Sandy made her way to the airport where her jet was fueled, flight plan filed, and her pilots prepared for takeoff.

Chapter 6

David parked his jeep out in front of Renée's condo. He arrived fifteen minutes early. Being raised on a farm, punctuality became an important trait, taught to him at an early age. The tardiness of some who felt it acceptable to arrive a few minutes later than they were expected, didn't sit well with him. His staff was aware of it. Meetings at the ranch or the stables, started on time. The exception to the rule was Serge. His superior mentality made arriving late okay, if not a necessity in his own mind, reinforcing his importance. David found it quite comical.

Since inviting Renée to join him on the flight, he was experiencing an unanticipated reaction to the travel plans. They shared a close, but professional relationship. Nothing was ever alluded to by either that would lead the other to think otherwise. But at this instant, he was having a flashback of being on a first date. It threw him a little off-kilter although it was a pleasant feeling. The two of them spent numerous hours together with no lack of conversation. Sitting there he found himself wondering what they would talk about for the next five or six hours. When on common ground, the chatter flowed with ease. He hoped the interaction on the trip would come naturally, but the thought of it was a touch unnerving.

Renée was well aware that David would arrive early, so she was packed ready to roll an hour before the scheduled time. She was dressed in tight black lululemon yoga pants, a cadet blue cool racerback tank top covered by a nice grey asana jacket. Not the wardrobe normally worn, but a comfortable choice for a flight.

The weekend was going to elevate her career to a level few trainers achieve in a lifetime. The odds favored her horse winning his race. Being in her twenties and to be given this much responsibility surpassed her wildest dreams. Yet here she was, the top dog, calling the shots for a stakes race with millions of dollars on the line. Nothing was going to throw her off her game this weekend.

She rolled her luggage into the hallway, and then turned taking a moment to scan the room, reassuring herself nothing was being forgotten. Everything was good, all accounted for. Now in the hall with the door almost closed she abruptly stopped, opened it and jarred her suitcase against it to stop it from closing. Renée re-entered and made her way to the bathroom. She stood in front of the mirror, fluffed her hair, and then touched her face with the fingertips of both hands examining her makeup. Picked up a perfume bottle and sprayed a touch on each wrist. Now she was ready. She locked the door and pushed the down button.

David was waiting in the lobby when the elevator doors opened. They both smiled at each other. He was pleasantly surprised with how her attire accentuated her figure. Seldom had he seen her dressed in anything other than denim. There was a short hello from both of them. The doorman held the foyer doors open. David threw her luggage into the back seat of the Jeep.

"You two have a great day," the doorman said.

"Thank you, Daniel, enjoy your weekend," Renée replied.

The doorman smiled and nodded his head at her. David opened and held the passenger door. Not trying to impress anyone. It was second nature to him, taught how to act like a gentleman by his father and grandfather. He'd hold a door open, adjust the chair of a lady as she sat, and walk on the street side of the sidewalk. Corny but appreciated. Sandy often commented, "You Canadians are crazy polite."

With Renée now seated, David caught a scent of her fragrance. It smelled good. He would have to be mindful his thoughts weren't noticeable on the outside. They were embarking on business trip, nothing more. Savor the present situation in silence and keep it professional, he repeated to himself.

The conversation was sparse during the drive to the airport, a little personal, a little business. For the most part they remained silent. The flight would provide ample time to address any subject they wished to discuss.

After clearing security, they arrived at the gate as a boarding announcement was being made. First class, first on.

"Would you like the window or aisle," he asked Renée.

"Either works for me David."

He made a motion with his hand guiding her to the window seat.

"This is comfortable," Renée said referring to the first class seating. "I've never flown first class before. To be honest I always thought it was a bit of overindulgence." She nestled into the luxurious seat, reserved for those who could afford it, "although it's possible I could become accustomed to it," she said with a smile. They both laughed.

All were on board. The plane taxied to the runway and to David's delight immediately took off, no delays. Once the aircraft reached its determined altitude the flight attendants began serving the passengers. For the most part, first class fliers were pampered. The beverages arrived quickly. Dinner wasn't what one might expect from a five star restaurant, but it was good.

"David, could you brief me on what the FBI determined started the fire," Renée asked in a concerning way.

David explained the materials were used to ignite the fire. He went on to say that it was arson and at this point no one was quite sure as to why someone would want to harm the animals.

"This is a big money game we play in. Sandy's father is wealthy beyond belief. You don't get to where he is without making enemies. The FBI knows this technology was developed in Europe. There are only a handful of people who build the igniters. We just have to put our trust in the authorities. I'm sure it will be solved in a timely matter. But young lady, now we have to concentrate on the upcoming race. The show must go on," he ended the conversation about the fire.

"Your right, it's a sad world we live in when two beautiful horses are sacrificed because of someone's vendetta," she added.

They had been in the air for a couple of hours now. For a large portion of it David and Renée had been nonchalantly coming in contact with one another. First their arms touching while resting on the armrest, then their legs would touch ever so slightly. At one point during the flight they took a break from talking to read. Renée curled her legs onto the seat, and rested her head on a pillow, leaning against the window. After a couple of chapters she dozed off. In her sleep her legs unintentionally stretched out and David could feel them wiggled in behind his backside. When she awoke she seemed unconcerned or embarrassed about the position of her feet. She did remove them as she straightened up. They were both at ease with this closeness.

The plane landed and they made their way to a waiting car that drove them directly to the hotel. By traveling with only carry-on luggage, the transfer from the airport to the hotel lobby was quick and effortless. David had reserved two Jr. Suites a couple of rooms apart on the same floor. Once the front desk clerk handed over their swipe cards, they made their way to the elevator. What a treat he thought. If he was with his wife he'd be hiking it up the stairs. She would tease him to no end if he refused to join her climb to the proper floor. It did have its benefits as a source of exercise. But today the elevator was his choice of transport. They reached the floor, walked down the hall to Renée's room.

"How about we have some dinner," David asked.

"Sure, I'd love that."

"Good, I know this little café not too far from here. They serve up a mean Steak Frites," David said a little too enthusiastically.

"C'est merveilleux," she replied in French having difficulty containing her excitement. This was proving to be a delightful trip.

"Ok, say, in an hour? I'll meet you in the lobby."

At that she opened her door and disappeared inside. David found his room, settled in, unpacked, and took a quick shower. Once done, he parked himself on the couch wearing only a white towel. With his legs resting on the coffee table, he retrieved his mobile phone. There were no messages from his wife, so he dialed her number, not really expecting an answer. When in Europe each minute of her day was accounted for. More often than not, she didn't answer. He would send a short text. Sandy would normally get back to him within an hour or two. Rarely did a day go by without contact of some form. It was those odd occasions, when she didn't get in touch with him for a couple of days that concerned him. It was as if she vanished off the grid. He knew her trips included more than met the eye which he attributed to Jacob somehow having a hand in it. She was probably on a mission to smooth over some secretive deal, or obtain an insight to this or that for the benefit her father's business. Trust of an absent partner was essential in the success of this kind of relationship. He hoped to discover more about her travels someday. But for now, he was satisfied with her explanations. Sandy answered on the first ring.

"Wattsy, I thought you'd never call," she joked.

"How's your trip going? By the way where are you?"

"I'm at the Palace. King Ahmed insisted I stay here. Have you arrived in L.A.?"

"We got in a couple of hours ago."

"We who?"

"Renée flew out with me. Serge decided to stay behind to oversee our local entries. He feels she is ready for the big show."

"Why wouldn't she have accompanied Charlotte's Choice? Isn't that what trainers do?"

"I had an extra ticket—yours."

"I'm stuck here, and she gets to be with the one person in the world I wish I were with. It doesn't seem fair. But good for her, pass on my congratulations. She worked hard for this day."

"I will. When are you coming home?"

"The wedding is tomorrow. The King asked if I could stay on for a day. There is some business he would like to discuss with me, and prior to the wedding he will be devoted to entertaining the guests who have been arriving hourly. From what I've seen so far, they include every single Middle East country. Most represented by their leader. It's actually quite an extravagant affair."

"Okay," he took a breath, "Sandy, promise me that when you get home we find time to hang out. We need to find some, our time. I love you so much, kid. I want you here."

"Wattsy, I love you to death, you know that. I want nothing more than for us to be together. It's just been an arduous few months. After this trip I'm going clear my schedule. You have my word on it. I will be all yours, to do what you wish with me," she promised.

"Oh I can think of a few things. But seriously, yes, I would appreciate that. Listen, I know it's early in the morning there so I will let you go. We're going to grab some dinner, then make it an early night. I want to be at the track first thing in the morning."

"We?" she inquired again in a jokingly tone.

"Renée and I," he replied.

"Make sure it's just dinner."

"What's this, do I detect a tad of jealousy from the great Mrs. McGinnis-Watson. As a matter of fact based on our last conversation with regards to Renée, I should be the jealous one."

"If I recall correctly, I just made mention that I would sleep with her if I was still back in college and if I were not faithfully married to a wonderful ex-jock," she playfully answered.

"Great, my wife has the hots for my trainer. That's all I need," he said.

Sandy enjoyed this bantering back and forth with her husband. Her life was trying at the best of times, so it was refreshing to find a few light moments.

"Goodnight, David, you should run along to your

dinner. And David—"

"What?"

"Keep your eyes in their sockets," referring to David's quick peeks at the backside of Renée's jeans. Sandy was trained to observe everything.

"Goodnight Sandy, talk to you soon. Take care. Love you," he signed off.

***

"Love you too," she said as they both ended the call.

It was still early in the morning when Sandy hung up. Too early for roaming around the palace, so she decided to relax in the luxury room the King so graciously provided. She laid back onto the king size bed with a beautiful lace canopy supported by four gold plated pillars.

A number of years ago she spent some time at the Palace. One summer she led a training program with the King's son Fyad. The King, his son, and Sandy became close friends. Over the years they stayed in contact. She closed her eyes, drifting back in time.

At the age of seven Sandy lost her mother to cancer. Old enough to understand that for the remainder of her childhood, there would be no brother, no sister, just her and her father. There would be no mother on the sidelines of her soccer games or other sports or dance competitions. At graduation she would only see a single pair of proud, teary eyes. One set of shoulders to cry on. It made her angry. Her father picked up on this immediately, which was the main reason he enrolled her in a martial arts class. He felt this discipline would provide an outlet for her frustration. Teach her self-defense, along with contributing to her physical and mental well being. She took to it like a duck to water, quickly progressing through the skill levels. By the age of eleven, she attained the highest level taught locally. It was suggested by her instructor that she spend the summer in China training with a Grand Master. Only a select few were extended an invitation to the teachings of such caliber. Throughout her teenage years she spent her vacations studying with the world's best. China one year, Japan another year, the Middle East in addition to other counties. Unbeknownst to her, her future was beginning to take shape. Lying there with her eyes closed she reflected on those years.

It was the summer after graduating from Harvard that she reunited with the King's son. They were the same age. Both had earned the distinction of being considered Grand Masters of Martial Arts, known as two of the best. Although they lived in different worlds culturally, and were separated by a vast distance, their similar upbringings forged an irrefutable bond. They were only children of wealthy parents, who took their art form seriously.

That summer they decided to give back and offer two four week sessions for a free introduction course of martial arts to underprivileged children. The first would be in Saudi Arabia, the remainder in the USA. One evening, after a day of lessons, the King's son informed Sandy that at the end of the month he had accepted an invitation into a secretive combat-orientated exercise, which was scheduled to last one full year. He would both join in the training, and teach advanced martial arts during the exercise. The program was reserved for thirty elite soldiers, inclusive of Special Forces from the USA, along with its allies. It would be the cream of the crop, the best of the best. Each individual invited would train the others in their own specialty.

Fayd was approached and asked to recruit Sandy into the group. He was instructed not to take no for an answer. Her area of expertise in hand-to-hand combat would be superior to all, including Fyad. She was given an outline of the commission. It would be self contained, with one outside contact needed to arrange transportation and such. Only a handful of high-ranking government officials knew of its existence, enough to secure financing for the undertaking. It was going to be an excruciating undertaking, far beyond what any of them experienced in the past. The architect of the project looked for one outcome only. Those who survived would become the most dangerous soldiers in the world, machines. They would be deployed by their respective countries, in the most delicate situations. The estimate was less than half would be capable of seeing it through to the end.

Her mind was made up to join five seconds into briefing. This was her, this was her life. Nothing else mattered. To take her obsession to the next level was the only thing that made sense.

Fayd already predicted her response and had discussed her inclusion in the program with his father, who in return, spoke to her father, prepping him on the dangers they were about to embark on. Sandy's only concern was securing the exceedingly high security clearance required to partake. Fyad assured her that wasn't going to be an issue.

As she lay there, a smile came to her face, recalling her father's reaction when she informed him the next morning that she would be gone for a year. It was as if he had been expecting something like this from her. His wasn't surprised that her passion had progressed to this level. Knowing how determined his daughter was he didn't try to change her mind. He listened, analyzed the pros and cons. He was aware of the risks involved in elite warfare training, and knew once a person entered into that brotherhood, there was little chance of resuming a normal lifestyle. If what Sandy accomplished in her short life could be considered a normal lifestyle in the first place. One promise he made to her at an early age, was that he would support any path she elected to follow. No exceptions. Saying little he listened. Respecting her decision, she received his blessing. The calls had already been placed the day before. The security clearance was fast tracked.

One month later Fayd and Sandy traveled to a secret location in Virginia. They would not be coming home for twelve months. Training began in the USA, relocated to the tropical rain forest in Malaysia, then counter-terrorism exercises in Israel. Many other countries would present their own distinct challenges before the conclusion of the year. The ones accepted into the program were a select number of men from the USA's Navy Seals,

Green Berets, the British SAS and the Shayetet 13 from Israel and Fayd. Sandy, the lone female, was the only non-military personnel invited to partake. Never had a female been afforded an opportunity to train at this level. Sandy recalled the first time she put a Navy Seal flat on his butt during a man to women drill. She smirked. Good memories.

There was a knock at the door. Lying on the bed in a bra and a pair of Calvin Klein undies, she grabbed for a shirt and a pair of track pants.

"I'll be with you in a minute," she acknowledged the visitor in a raised voice.

"Breaker, it's me," she heard a reply.

It was Fayd. She was only referred to as Breaker by those few who spent that year together. A nickname her counterparts coined after they sustained a fracture or two partnering with her in sparing sessions.

Knowing it was Fayd, she only threw on the shirt not attempting to button it up. After all they'd seen each other naked many times during some of their brutal exercises. One such operation saw them paired off together then parachuted into the Malaysia jungle naked. They were expected to survive for two weeks with no supplies. Once on the ground the parachutes were soon modified into makeshift clothing. The only other item in their possession was a watch. It doubled as a GPS device monitored by their instructors. It could be activated as a distress indicator for an emergency. That did not occur once throughout the year. This group of soldiers would go to their grave before asking for assistance.

It had been a long time since they'd been in each other's company. She opened the door. Both took a second to stare into each other's eyes. A warm smile came over their faces. Hearts fluttered faster than they ought to. Only those who endured what they did together would understand the bond between them. Their spouses would never see that side of them. Actually, odds were, they would never see the other nine who completed the year. Even if they did, all the painful, gruesome details would not be spoken about. So it was something shared by only the two of them.

"Breaker, I missed you."

She backed up while he closed the door behind him. They embraced longer than normal.

"Yes, it's been far too long, Fayd," she said. "You look good. Life must be treating you well," complimenting him.

"I may look good, but you, my dear," he hesitated, looking at her from head to toe, spreading his hands apart. "How do you Americans say it, you look awesome."

They gave each other another hug.

"My father said you arrived late last night. I apologize that I was unable to greet you at the airport but I just flew in late myself."

"Not a problem. Your father's people were more than gracious."

"Being here has me reflecting on our past."

"It changed us forever didn't it? Our fathers were correct in that there would be no return to a normal lifestyle."

"Fayd," Sandy said moving on to the present.

"You're getting married. I'm so excited for you."

"Thank you for coming," he replied. "It means a great deal to me that you have taken time out from your busy schedule to be here."

"Nothing, and I mean nothing, was going to keep me from attending my best friend's wedding."

They sat on the bed, talked about his wife to be. He had a lot of questions with regards to how much of their past she discussed with David. Seeking her advice as he felt at a crossroads of wanting to fully commit to the future Princess, but knowing the reality was he could never reveal certain aspects of his past or present commissions.

Sandy assured him it would work out. Yes, certain responsibilities would need to remain unspoken. She'd been able to succeed in her marriage. Fayd would no doubt find a true partnership with the future Princess.

They had come a long way. Look at them now. When they parted ways at the end of that ferocious year, both suspected that neither of them would ever marry. That was just about the time the CIA took an interest in Sandy.

Chapter 7

David and Renée sat across from each other at a small table for two, located at the café's front outside patio. Both ordered their drink of choice—beer. They were enjoying each other's company outside of the customary confines of the workplace. A glowing candle sitting in the center of the table flickered off their faces. It was a warm night with a slight breeze. Most people sitting on the patio were couples. The day, nightfall, that instant, had a romantic aura to it. Not by design, but most certainly present. This was supposed to be an employer having dinner with an employee, nothing more. Yet they both could not help but be taken in by the alluring ambiance the evening was providing.

The main discussion centered on tomorrow's training session in preparation of the race. They were in agreement with the methods Renée would use to ready the horse. What they were not particularly on the same wave length was how the jockey should be instructed to position the horse during the race. Renée had spent an immeasurable amount of time with this thoroughbred, so David would surrender to her plan of action. After all, both he and Serge agreed she was ready. In all fairness she understood the horse better than anyone else. So this weekend's race was Renée's to run as she saw fit.

"David do you think it would upset Sandy if she had knowledge of us having dinner tonight?"

"I don't see why it would concern her," he replied. "Sandy spends most of her time on the other side of the world having dinner with a variety of people. Its work, isn't it?"

There was a growing mutual unspoken sentiment that there was more to this relationship. Neither was clear on whether the line would ever be crossed, but there definitely was another flame burning here other than the one in the middle of the table.

"Absolutely, just work," she was quick to answer, overemphasizing it. Yet it brought a grin to her face.

He noticed the uneasiness of the reply and thought he caught a glimpse of what might have been construed as a wink directed his way.

The food was served. The next hour was spent eating, talking about the business at hand, with a bit of flirtation thrown into the mix by both of them. Then supper was complete, the waiter cleared the table.

"Well," David said, "this has been a pleasant day. You make for good company young lady. I haven't enjoyed myself like this for a long time."

"Careful there cowboy, we should be getting back to the hotel before we redefine the meaning of a working relationship."

She immediately regretted her words. The wine was beginning to speak for her.

"You make a good point. A good night's sleep is in order. We have a big day tomorrow."

With that David caught the waiter's attention to settle up.

Renée felt slightly aroused. Spending so many hours with David at the stables, the attraction was always present. Having him this close during the flight and dinner had elevated a desire for him. Toss in the playful conversation of the past few hours it was no wonder she was a little captivated. She was relieved they decided to head back to the hotel. She didn't want her boss to take notice.

David wasn't exempt from the sensation brought on by the evening. His thoughts were similar. The present setting provided an ambiance nourishing the path that neither was sure they should take. With a little persuasion, a pleasant outing could have easily reverted into a complicated state of affairs.

They made it back to the hotel without incident. The exchange during their walk was without flirtation. Neither of them was prepared to initiate the crossing of the fine line they were walking. And neither was prepared to expose to the other their present level of desire.

The elevator door opened. They walked down the hall. Renée's room came first. Stopping at her door, it was taking all the restraint both of them could mustard up to refrain from throwing the door open and tearing off each other's clothes.

"Hey, it's been a great day Renée," David told her, while intently staring into her eyes.

"Thank you. It has been a refreshing break from our regular routine."

"That it has," he replied, "and we still have the remainder of the weekend in front of us. I'm looking forward to sharing a couple more dinners."

"I'd like that."

"Good, but now we should get some sleep. How about we meet up for breakfast then catch a ride over to the track together."

"Oui, cela semble bon," she responded in French expressing her approval.

"Ok, I will call you in the morning, goodnight."

He wasn't sure if he should shake her hand, give her a quick kiss on the forehead or hug. Any contact at all seemed inappropriate. They awkwardly smiled at each other and he walked down the hall to his room.

Renée entered her room, locked the door then fell on her bed stomach first. She started kicking the bed and punching the pillows with both arms and feet. Mumbling to herself, "You idiot, that's your married boss. You idiot, you idiot, you idiot, God, I made such a fool of myself, you idiot!"

After her little tantrum she striped her clothes off, went to the washroom to splash cold water on her face trying to come back down to earth. A shower would have to wait until morning as she returned to the bed disappearing under the covers.

Replaying the day over and over, it wasn't long before her eyes closed and she was drifting off. Then the phone rang.

She realized it was her cell that was chiming. Her heartbeat instantly did double time. Presuming it was David calling with a change of heart wanting to take the relationship to the next level. Oh my god, what am I going to say to him. Fuzzy from near sleep it took a second to gather her composure. She decided right there and then she wasn't going to resist the temptation any longer. If he wanted to come back to her room or her to his, she would agree.

"Hello," she answered not checking the call display as she was so certain it was him. At the moment there was only one other person on the face of the earth, David.

"Renée," she heard a woman's voice on the other end.

There was a moment of silence. It took an instant for Renée to pull herself together.

"Gabriela?"

"Is this a bad time? Do you have company?"

"No, Gabriela, I'm alone," she answered while straightening up into a sitting position on the bed. Resting her back on the head board and pulling a sheet up over her naked body.

"Are you in town?" Renée questioned her not knowing when she was expected to fly in.

"Actually I flew in this morning and spent the afternoon at the track. I thought I might run into you there but your groomers told me they weren't expecting you until tomorrow."

"Oui, we arrived a few hours ago and thought it was best just to get an early start in the morning," Renée explained.

"We?" she heard Gabriela say.

"David and I," informing the inquisitive mind on

the other end of the line.

"Sandy is back in Europe so David offered me her seat. We felt it was too late to accomplish much at the track, so we opted to go out and have dinner."

"Renée is he there with you now," whispered Gabriela. "You seem preoccupied."

Renée sighed, "No Gabriela, he's not here. We had dinner, a nice conversation and then it was back to our separate little rooms. Just like two respectable co-workers, one of which is happily married, are expected to behave."

"I'm sensing from the tone of your voice that the end result of the evening may not have been what you had envisioned."

"On the contrary, it's exactly what I expected," she said.

"I said envisioned, not expected."

Renée let it slide then changed the subject, "What hotel are you staying at?"

"I'm at the Beverly Hill's Four Season's."

Coincidentally they were lodging at the same place.

"What floor are you on?"

"I'm in room 808. Why, are you thinking of coming over," Gabriela teased.

"No, but if you're in the mood you could take the elevator to the tenth. Knock on suite 10C and then we can continue this discussion in person," inviting Gabriela to her room.

"What are the odds?" Gabriela was pleasantly surprised by the turn of events.

Forty-five minutes later they were entangled in each other well on their way to closing out the day with a rapturous climax.

***

Meanwhile, David had taken a shower. He poured himself a drink, retrieved a Martin Cruz Smith novel from his luggage and planted himself in one of the luxurious chairs. The plan was to read for an hour or so, and then it was down for a good night's sleep. It was a book he had been trying to get to for months.

The challenge was clearing his thoughts of Renée from his head. He had genuinely enjoyed her company. Yes, she was attractive. Yes, the thought of sleeping with her had crossed his mind. He liked being around her. It felt good.

Momentarily he was lost in the novel before his preoccupation won over. Struggling to clear his mind knowing full well he shouldn't feel this way. He had the most beautiful wife, who loved him dearly. She was unrivaled in the bedroom. By far the best partner, lover, and friend anyone could ask for. It would be ludicrous to jeopardize the relationship. That being said it wasn't until today, spending time with Renée that he realized how lonely he actually was. Sandy's frequent absence was unbeknownst to him beginning to take its toll.

He stopped reading and stared at the book for a short time before closing it. Laying it down on the coffee table he got up from his chair. If someone was to quiz him on the first two chapters of his reading he wouldn't be able to answer one single question correctly.

David made the decision to go down the hall and knock on her door. A need for companionship was influencing his choices. Common sense was being outweighed by his yearning. He would tell her that he was too restless to sleep. Ask her if she wanted a nightcap and chat for a while longer. If she was receptive, he would invite her to his room or maybe she would invite him into hers. Either way he was going to get dressed and make his way down the hall.

David knew it was an inappropriate move on his part. He wasn't going to barge in and suggest they have sex. Even if that opportunity presented itself he wasn't convinced he would act on it. Just sitting there, looking into one another's eyes while continuing the conversations of the past hours was sufficient in itself. But he was determined he was going. Throwing on a pair of jeans and t-shirt he snatched his room keycard and made his way to her suite.

The number on the door was Suite 10C. He studied it, making certain he actually was at the correct room. Knocking at the wrong one would surely be an embarrassing situation. But no, he was confident it was the correct one.

He took a couple of deep breaths. This was so wrong in so many ways he was thinking. But yet he found himself raising his arm, clenching his fist in preparation of knocking. Just as he committed to making the movement of tapping he thought he heard a voice or voices from within the room. He pulled his fist away which was about a fraction of an inch from the door or a millisecond from announcing his presence.

There he stood leaning his head towards the door but he could no longer hear any voices. Being in a nervous state he reasoned that maybe there had been no voices after all. His mind was clouded by a fixation. It had to be his imagination trumping reality, so his arm rose once again just as the voices or noises became more audible.

This time he did hear something. It wasn't talk. It was moaning. There were two voices. He was positive this was the suite he had reserved for her. After all they stood right here not more than a couple of hours ago. There was no doubt about it. The sound was of two people in the act of making love.

David quickly returned to his room more confused than when he left, praying no one had noticed him. Could he have made a mistake with the room numbers? They had just spent the better part of the day together. There was never any indication that she was planning on meeting someone after they parted ways. He had no knowledge of Renée even knowing someone in Los Angeles. Something wasn't adding up here. His emotions switched from desire to alarm, to concern for her safety all within minutes.

Should he call her or go back down the hall and make up some lame excuse for knocking on her door. No, he couldn't do either. She was a grown woman who owed him no explanation with regards to her personal life. It was best to clear his mind and put this whole incident to rest.

He washed up, went to bed and turned the lights

off. As he lied there it dawned on him, could Renée have been watching some risqué show on the television? Was that what he had heard? It had to be. It was the only thing that made sense. He convinced himself that was what he had heard. The more he thought about it, the more comfortable he was with the theory. And the more he thought about it the more allured by her he became. He wanted her.

This is getting out of hand. You need to grow up. You're a grown man. This is high school stuff. So get a grip on yourself man. This infatuation of yours is dangerous, was his train of thought before falling asleep.

Chapter 8

Early the next morning Serge sat across the desk from his oncologist.

"Serge, there is no good way to say this. I wish there was," the doctor began to break the bad news.

"Doc, there is no need to sugarcoat it. I've lived a full life with no regrets. I'm prepared for whatever the diagnosis is."

"Okay, fair enough," the doctor continued. "Your cancer cannot be treated. It's terminal. All we can do at this point is to provide you medication to ease the pain."

"You know Doc, I knew. I'm not sure if it's common that a person realizes the end is nearing before being officially told, but I did. How long do I have."

"Three months, maybe six."

The doctor thought to himself, this never gets easier then continued, "It will give you time to get your matters in order. I would be more than happy to meet with your family. I would also like to make an appointment for you and your family with one of our counselors here at the clinic. They will guide you and your love ones through this difficult time. They are very good at what they do."

"Thank you, doctor," Serge replied than asked, "can I travel overseas?"

"When would you consider making such a trip?"

"You see, Doc, I came to America pursuing a dream to become one of the best horsemen in the world. I accomplished what I set out to do. But, in doing so, I've had to sacrifice my personal life. I never married, nor had children. What I do have is a brother and a sister among a number of other relatives I rarely see. I sometimes think I led a selfish life. But I had a dream," he stopped for a minute.

Both men sat quietly for the moment. The doctor was prepared to sit with Serge all day if that was what his patient needed. He had broken devastating news such as this far too many times. Everyone reacted differently. The one common factor was the doctor would be there until the end, providing them with every ounce of support he had at his disposal.

"I have some business to attend to this weekend then I would like to leave. I would say Monday, Tuesday at the latest," he informed the doctor.

"I will make arrangements for your medicine today. How long will you stay?" the doctor asked.

"I'm not coming back."

The doctor deciphered what Serge was saying then gave him his blessing followed by some instruction. "Serge, I hear what you're saying. I respect your decision. I am going to prescribe you twelve months worth of medication which I would like you to pick up here tomorrow. I would like you to inform my medical assistant of the address you will be residing. Arrangements will be made with one of my colleagues in that country to oversee your needs. You will be in good hands."

"Thank you, doctor," Serge stood up, shook the oncologist's hand.

"I wish I could have done more."

"You did everything you could," he thanked him again then turned and walked towards the door.

"Serge," the doctor spoke, "you weren't selfish. Attaining one's dreams is not a selfish act. I am certain those loved ones you speak of are extremely proud of your achievements. Far too few conquer their visions."

"Thank you, you're a kind man."

Serge left the office and made his way to the parking lot. He found his truck, opened the door, jumped in and began to cry. He had been aware of his failing health and that the end was near for some time now. But there was bewilderment about hearing the words from your specialist.

He pushed a button and spoke into his Bluetooth, "dial."

A robotic female voice asked, "Please say the name or number."

"The boss."

The call was answered on the second ring, "Mr. McGinnis' office, how may I help you."

"Brooklyn, its Serge. I'll be at the ranch in an hour. Would you be kind enough to pen me in with Jacob?"

"Serge, he has a tight schedule today. Can we do this tomorrow?"

"No, tomorrow will be too late. Truth be told, it's already too late. I will be there in an hour, please work your magic," he made it clear there was no other option. Then he pressed the end call on the steering wheel column.

David woke up early. The goal was to be in the hotel's fitness center by six. A three quarter hour workout then he would call Renée and they should be ordering breakfast by seven thirty. Then off to the track.

He dressed in his exercise clothing, grabbed his iPhone, keycard, opened and closed the door. With a clearer head, a quick glance at Renée's room on his way to the staircase reaffirmed that it was most definitely her room. Just as he was exiting the hallway to take the stairs down to the gym, he heard the sounds of a door closing. Instinctively he turned and took a look down the hall. He couldn't believe his eyes. Was he hallucinating? The door was Renée's suite or the one next to it. He couldn't be a hundred percent sure as the person who came out was already in the hall. It wasn't Renée who was making her way down the corridor to the elevator. But it was a familiar face. David recognized her. It was Gabriela D'Angelo. He knew her. She was an A-List jockey. His stable had been perusing her to ride for them for some time now without any success.

He quickly stepped into the staircase landing not wanting to be noticed. Keeping out of her line of vision he watched her light up the wall button to summon an elevator. What was she doing here on the West Coast? There were only two stake races and he had an entry in one of them. At her caliber, it would take that level of card to lure her to L.A. He made it a point to know his opposition and he didn't like to compete against her. She was the best, winning more than not. Her name didn't appear as the jockey on any of the horses. She must be a last minute replacement. And what the hell was she doing in Renée's room.

***

Gabriela thought she caught a glimpse of a man entering the staircase at the far end of the hall. She hadn't seen his face, just the back of him and only for a split second. There were no recognizable features. Yet, she had this unsettling gut feeling. Riding the elevator alone, her thought was, I hope to god that wasn't David. But something inside her was saying it was. In her line of business you rely on instincts. When mounted on an eleven hundred pound horse running more than forty miles per hour surrounded by ten others, it was a necessity. She never fought them. You had to feel your horse, make split second decisions. Did he want to run, did he want to chase the horse in front of him. Were the other horses going to pass her or block her in? She had to feel the whole race and react. What she was feeling now was that the man in the hallway was Renée's boss, David.

***

When Jacob was notified that Serge was driving up to the ranch he cleared his desk and informed Brooklyn to put everything on hold until further notice. Serge had been a trusted employee a very long time. More importantly he had been a close friend, one of Jacobs's only true friends. There were lots of business associates, but few friends. Throughout all those years, never once did Serge demand such a meeting. He had been raised in England with a formal mannerism. Certain protocols were followed during his time at the McGinnis ranch. Appointments which were few and far between were scheduled far in advance. Maybe he had information pertaining to the fire. Whatever the case Jacob cleared his calendar.

Serge presented himself to Brooklyn, who immediately showed him into Jacobs's office.

"Serge, please, come sit," Jacob directed him to the couch near the fireplace.

"Thank you for seeing me on such short notice Jacob. I know you are busy. I do appreciate it."

"Serge, we've been together for a long time now. I assure you that you have my undivided attention whenever you require it," he told him. "What's on your mind my good friend?"

Jacob sensed Serge was off his game. He didn't seem himself. The arrogance had vanished. Whatever was on his mind was weighing heavy on him.

Serge took a deep breath, joined his hands together resting his two index fingers together then to his lips. Then he exhaled as his watery eyes met his friend's.

"Jacob, I can find no easy way to say this," he paused for a second. "I have found myself in a position that requires me to inform you that I will be resigning effective Monday."

"I don't understand Serge," Jacob was confused. "I thought we were going to be in this together until the day we die. That's the promise we made to one another."

"Jacob, I am dying."

"What do you mean you're dying?"

"I haven't been feeling well for some time now," Serge began his explanation. "This morning, actually an hour ago I received the results from my doctor. I have terminal cancer. There is no cure. He has given me three to six months. It would mean a great deal to me if I could spend that time with my family in England. I will be making arrangements to leave on Monday after the weekend races."

Jacob was blindsided. It took some time to comprehend what his head trainer and friend was telling him. Sometimes life throws you curves and they just do not seem fair. This was going to be difficult for him to accept. Jacob's general state of mind was to be in control of everything that materialized within his realm. He did not want to accept this diagnosis.

"Serge, we have access to the very best physicians in the world," Jacob began. "I will make some calls. The progress our medical professions have made with this disease is remarkable. So many people are surviving this challenge nowadays."

"Jacob, I assure you my oncologist is at the top of his field. I do appreciate your kindness but trust me, my condition is incurable."

"There must be something we can do," he said not wanting to give in.

"No, Jacob there is nothing we can do. It is what it is. I'm okay with it. I am prepared. However, I would like to spend the time I have left with my family in England. I want you and David to promote Renée to lead position. She has listened and learned—the best student I've had. Renée has established herself as a quality horse person. Her passion for our animals is something you rarely see. I actually believe she has grown to fit this role better than I do."

When passed he wanted to be assured his beloved horses were taken care of, and she was the only person he was prepared to support.

"What can I do to help, Serge?" Jacob resigned to the fact that his trainer was at peace with the meeting of his maker.

"I have everything under control. I need to resign. It is important to know that I am leaving the stables in the hands of someone I trust and that will continue our legacy," speaking to Jacob quietly. "I would ask that you not mention this to anyone until I leave for England, with the exception of Sandy, Renée, David, and Brooklyn, of course. Once Renée has accepted her new duties, a press release should be issued stating that I have embarked on a planned retirement and spending time with my family in England. It is imperative that the industry be made aware that Renée was my handpicked successor."

"Serge I would like to take care of your travel arrangements," Jacob said.

"Thank you Jacob but I have already made a reservation for Monday afternoon."

"I insist. I will have a plane waiting for you at the airport. Let Brooklyn know the time you would like to depart."

Serge didn't put up much of a fuss. He knew his boss would prevail. Actually it was a relief to be flying private and avoiding the frustrations of public transportation. He accepted.

Jacob was getting chocked up. His good friend was dying. They'd been through a great deal together. Side by side they built the most successful stable of thoroughbred horses in the country. How do you say goodbye to that. There was no proper way. Offer your love and support. That's all one could be expected to do. Respect the person's wishes. As emotional as the situation was, that's what Serge needed now.

Both men knew the conversation was nearing its end, Jacob not wanting him to leave, Serge just wanting to get on with it. They stood up, proceeded to shake hands but stopped short of that and embraced each other in a lengthy hug. Both had tears rolling down their cheeks.

"My good friend, it has been an honor to have included you in my life," Jacob expressed his gratitude of their friendship. "Anything you need and I mean anything. Doctors, money, transportation or just a conversation, you call. Brooklyn will be instructed to authorize any request from you. Please keep in touch. I will be praying for you."

"Thank you again Jacob, I've been blessed to

have known you. You're a good man."

They gave each other another hug. Serge turned and left the room. Jacob stood and watched.

Jacob went back to his desk. He was overwhelmed by his emotions. It took a few minutes to compose himself at which time he asked Brooklyn into his office. She was saddened by the news.

"Brooklyn, please arrange for a plane to fly Serge to England on Monday. He will advise you as to what time he would like to depart. Make sure the hostess is a fully qualified nurse. She must keep that to herself." He continued with his instructions, "Please enact his pension payment. Also deposit an additional ten million dollars into the account. Should he need our assistance in any way, shape or form you have my authorization. Thank you."

She said nothing, turned and left the office. Within an hour all would be taken care of.

Jacob asked her to hold all his calls for an hour or so and to close the door on her way out. He sat there and cried. This was a very sad day. He would cancel all his appointments this coming weekend and spend the two days at the track by Serge's side.

***

David completed his morning workout, called Renée and they were now eating breakfast at one of the hotel's restaurants. The nature of the discussion was all business. There was no flirtation. They compared notes gathered on the competing horses. When millions of dollars are at stake from the outcome of a race that lasted less than two minutes, you want to have all your t's crossed and i's dotted. The chat lasted an hour.

"I happened to notice Gabriela D'Angelo in the hotel this morning. Did she catch a ride this weekend?"

Renée's reply was delayed. She felt guilty, like a kid playing hooky. Not sure why. It was a large hotel. He could have noticed her anywhere. What were the chances of him knowing she made love to Gabriela four hours earlier? Even so, she was an adult and owed no explanation to anyone about how she chose to live. David picked up on the delay.

"Is there something wrong?"

"No," still hesitating, "no, she's riding Natures Gift. I'm sorry David I thought you knew. I believe I have a grasp on how she will position him. That was the basis for my race strategy. She's the one we need to beat. Again, I'm sorry, I took for granted you were aware of the jockey change when we discussed the race yesterday."

"Now I understand your wanting to position Charlotte's Choice as you do."

"Sorry, I thought you knew."

They finished eating then hailed a ride to the race track where they would spend the better part of the day. There was no mention of the past evening's activities by either of them.

***

Sandy spent the day in the Palace. After getting reacquainted with Fyad she slipped down to the

112

gym. They had promised to catch up with one another for a luncheon, at which time she would be introduced to his fiance. She opted for the gym as she didn't feel it was appropriate to take a jog outside. Although great strides were being accomplished pertaining to female rights in the country, it still was considered one of the most conservative in that regard. Fyad's mother was a strong minded person. She orchestrated a movement for women's rights within the country. Her challenges were many, being up against some hardliners, but she was making slow positive progress. Inside the Palace it was a different story. Women were seen as equals. They were now of equal entitlement once only granted to the male population.

On her way back from the gym she was approached by one of the King's special security personnel.

"Miss McGinnis," he said coming up to her from behind.

"Yes," she stopped as she replied to the man.

"If you will, the King has asked me to extend an invitation to join him in the library," he pointed down the hall towards the room.

"Absolutely," she began. "Just let me run up to the room and change into something more presentable," bringing to his attention her workout attire and that she did not want to greet the King in her present state.

"Miss McGinnis, I believe the King would like to see you now."

"Kamal," Sandy had been introduced to him at

the airport. He was one of the two men assigned as an escort to the Palace. She continued, "please inform the King that I would love to meet with him. But first I need to change into something more respectable. I will be with him in fifteen minutes."

"As you wish, I will notify the King of your plans," he conceded not relishing the thought of announcing the delay. The King planned appointments around his schedule, not that of others. He did not take kindly to being delayed.

Fifteen minutes later Sandy was ushered into the library by the two men stationed in front of its doors. It was a large room. The oak cabinet shelving provided a resting place for the volume of books shelved floor to ceiling. Given the ceiling was thirty feet high it housed over a million books. Being one who loves to read, Sandy drooled each time she entered it.

"My dear Sandy," the King held out his hand to greet her. "My security personnel were a bit distraught relaying your request to arrive late for our appointment."

"Your Highness, I would not consider myself late. We didn't have an appointment, you summoned me."

"Your Highness, my dear, you're being a tad formal."

They stood for a second than both began to laugh.

"Come here and give me a hug," the King spread his arms.

They embraced each other then retreated to one of the many lavish sofas within the room. The two spent many nights in this room discussing literature, life, and numerous other topics. They had become close friends.

"Sandy, I'm so glad you could be present for my son's wedding."

"You and Fyad are my second family. I wouldn't have missed it for the world."

"You know. I always let it be known to you that my wish would have been for you to be exchanging vows with my son tomorrow."

"Yes, Ahmed," she dropped the formality and called the King by his first name, the way she'd addressed him for a number of years now.

"Have you forgotten that I am happily married," she continued.

"I know, please forgive me. David is a fine man. However, I always foresaw you as the Princess. I will have to settle with you being the daughter I never had," a smile came over both faces.

"How is your father?" the King inquired.

"He's been in better spirits this year than he has been for some time now. His health is good, but he still works far too hard."

"He must be saddened by the tragic fire which your family experienced."

"It is troublesome, heartbreaking that two beautiful animals lost their lives."

"I understand the fire was deliberately set," he said catching her off guard by how fast the information traveled to this part of the world.

"We believe so. Your intelligence network must have more pressing issues to deal with than a stable fire in the good old state of Kentucky," while saying this she gave him an inquisitive look.

"This is the Middle East. My intelligence bureau is the single most important branch of my government. Without it there would be no country as we know it. It is my bloodline," he answered with a serious inflection in his voice.

"Exactly my point," she reinforced her earlier inquiry. "So why would you waste your resources on an incident that has no influence on your country."

"My lovely little Sandy," he said with a grin. "I apologize if I have misled you. My agency was not the source of my fact finding mission."

"Well then your Highness, where did you learn of the fire?"

He waited a moment before answering her. He was having a little fun letting her speculate as to who his source was.

"Well," she inquired again.

His grin grew wider as he was about to answer when she put her hand up and motioned for him to stop speaking.

"Wait a minute," she then said. "You've been speaking with my father, haven't you? That's where you happened upon this info."

"You've always been a perceptive one," confirming her suspicion. "Your father called me this morning to apologize for not being able to make the trip. He wanted to extend his best wishes to Fyad and his soon to be bride. Yet, I believe there was an alternative motive for the call."

"He was checking up on me," she stated.

"He did ask about you. I assured him you were

in good hands. I promised to return you as quickly as possible."

"I think you two are in cahoots with one another," both of their smiles grew larger.

"Now you mention it. We did kindle a relationship when you and Fyad were away for that year. We talked regularly, encouraging each other that our pride and joy would be safely returned to us, undamaged."

She knew they kept in touch but was surprised to learn the frequency. Her father never made reference to the friendship. When the King's name was mentioned in a conversation he referred to him as an acquaintance. Someone you might cross paths with occasionally, but certainly not someone you have spoken to often. She would have to remember to discuss it with him when she returned home.

"I had no idea you two struck up such a close relationship," she told the King.

There was a knock on the door. Strong, quick, three thumps. No one entered and the King did not acknowledge the interruption.

"That was my assistant. He strives to keep my day on a schedule. A losing cause if you ask me. But then again, I do have a country to run and a number of guests arriving who I need to welcome."

"Well, I should let you get back to your duties," she said standing up.

The King motioned for her to sit back down then said, "there are a couple of items I wish to discuss with you before we part ways."

Sandy dropped back into the chair, but didn't respond. She waited for him to continue.

"The first item I wish to discuss," he went on, "is our precious annual Dubai World Cup. Would you speak to your father about registering an entry into the race next March? I have tried for years to entice him into partaking in our race. I've even offered transportation for your entry. As you know with a purse of ten million dollars it is the richest race in the world. We wish to complement the field with the very best thoroughbreds the world has to offer. You are in possession of many of the finest."

"I will speak to him. I'm not without my persuasive tactics. I think the one we will need to convince is my husband and that, your highness, I can do. So, leave an opening on the race card."

"Thank you. It means a great deal to me. I look forward to seeing your father's face when my horse beats his," he chuckled.

"Ahmed, you said there were two things you would like to discuss with me," she inquired as he seemed to be having so much fun with the first subject she felt he had forgotten the second.

"Yes, you are correct. After dinner this evening, I am planning a good old fashion card game in this very room. I know how much you enjoy poker. I want you to attend. There will be a number of Heads of States from the Middle East. You might find it interesting," extending his invitation.

"I'm not sure some of your guests will appreciate a women sitting at their table," she said knowing full well the hardliners would not be too pleased with her participating.

"I'm sure they will come around," he said. "They might get upset when you start taking their money

118

though. But it will be fine. I insist you attend."

"Then it's a date," she accepted.

With that Sandy stood, offered her hand but the King again drew her with a hug. She went to her quarters to prepare for lunch and introductions to Fyad's future bride.

As she made her way through the Palace, she witnessed a number of guests being escorted to their rooms, most with their own entourage of security. This was going to be the who's who of the Middle East. Some of which were American friendly, some not so much.

The amount of Middle East intelligence that would be within the Palace walls for the next couple of days was irresistible. An intelligence agent would feel like a kid in a candy store.

And Sandy did. Her assignment was to tap into as much information as she could. Although the poker game was not part of the initial plan, it now gave her a perfect opportunity. It was unbeknownst to the King, but he handed her an ace in the hole before the card game even commenced.

Chapter 9

Jacob McGinnis sat alone in his office. It was now late in the evening. Brooklyn retired to her quarters. He felt alone in the world. His daughter was in Saudi Arabia. She was attending the wedding of a friend. He also knew she had an alternative agenda. Not knowing the details, but well aware any of her assignments could end with a phone call saying his daughter was being returned to him in a body bag. David was in Los Angeles. His friend Serge was dying. His wife was dead.

Whoever coined the saying it's lonely at the top certainly knew what they were talking about. Over the years he learned money could not provide someone with comfort. If used properly it could yield power. But it could not provide happiness. It wasn't able to save Sandy's mother, who had been taken far too early by breast cancer. Money provided the opportunity that saw both his daughter and son-in-law thousands of miles away. Achieving vast wealth, yet he spent most of his hours alone.

He was in need of a walk up the trail to his wife's resting place. When she passed away they built a memorial where her ashes were buried. At least once a week he'd take the five minute walk through the bush to visit her. These conversations with her nourished an inner comfort.

Standing, he grabbed his denim jacket, the one he wore when out with the horses. The thought of being alone tonight was a cold one. He was shivering before facing the chilly breeze of the evening. Jacob opened his desk to retrieve a small but powerful flashlight, one that police or military might use. It was a gift from Sandy. It cut through the darkest of night with razor accuracy.

Just as he was about to walk out of the room the telephone on the desk started to ring. It was the private line. One used for business not pleasure. A call coming through this late at night could not be ignored. So he made an about turn and walked back to his desk to answer it. He picked up the receiver.

"Hello," he said.

"Jacob," a lady's voice asked verifying she had the right party on the line.

"Yes."

"This is Madison Taylor," identifying herself.

"It is nice to hear your voice Madison. But what in prey tell is the Director of the FBI calling such an inconsequential person such as myself at this time of day or might I say night."

Madison Taylor was the first female Director in the FBI history. She was appointed to the position by the existing President shortly after he was elected. One of his campaign promises was to tap into the female population to fill top level positions in his administration. There were a great deal of women working in the White House. The problem as he saw it was few were being rewarded with the influential assignments. His predecessors had missed the boat on this. So much talent had been bypassed because of an old school mentality.

Madison Taylor did not get the position because of her gender. But she was not passed over because of it. She was by far the most qualified, graduating top of her class at Yale. Her parents were heavily rooted in the political arena. Both were lawyers. Smart, single, a rising star in every aspect of her career, tough as nails. She had an unwavering dedication to protect her country. Her duty each and every day was to assure her country was a safer place to live in. Jacob doubted she had even an inkling of a social life. That, they both had in common. So this call wasn't going to be about grabbing a coffee and chatting about old times.

"I have been asked by The President to personally oversee the investigation of the fire at your family's stables," she began.

"You get right to the point, don't you," he said.

"Jacob I have little time for idle chat."

"You know Madison, maybe we both should invest a little more of our time in this idle chat thing," he said, kind of reflecting his present state of mind. "The older you get, the quicker this life passes by."

"Maybe in the not-so-near future you and I can indulge in a tea and crumpets get-together. We can debate what life could have or should have been or is. But not tonight, I'm much too busy saving the world."

"As you wish, but tea and crumpets sounds rather delicious. I look forward to that," he answered.

"Jacob, as Agent Scott explained, the fire was purposely ignited. The technology utilized is sophisticated. The troubling factor is the manner in which this system was used. It was amateurish," she explained. "It is very expensive. Using a jerry can of gas and a match would have accomplished better results. These micro pellets as we call them can only be ignited by satellite feed. One must have coded access to a satellite which cannot be traced. Governments have them. Telecommunication companies have them, along with hundreds of other entities. The question remains, why spend so much to inflict so little damage. We believe the main objective here was one of distraction. It was meant to keep someone away or keep someone near."

"So what do you extrapolate from this?"

"They have a handsome budget but wanted to stay in the background, so an inexperienced person or persons were used for placement of the igniters. Someone in your camp was the target. It was meant to either keep them close or keep them away from the stable. Leave the details to us. We are good at what we do. But, if you could put some thought into the coming and goings of your people around that time frame, it might help in establishing who the diversion was intended for. Then we can find out the why that much sooner."

"Madison, I appreciate you're administering the investigation. I must say I'm puzzled as why this happened. What in the world could be accomplished by mounting an assault of this sort? It wasn't even a race day at the facility."

"That is what is so bothersome. I would like to solicit the aid of the CIA," she wasn't seeking his approval but rather informing him of her intentions.

"Why?"

"If we embrace this theory, which we do, it has a European connection written all over it. The CIA has agents in place that can extract the intelligence fundamental to our investigation." Continuing she asked, "Jacob I need to ask. Are you aware of any employee, friend or family that may have an association to a radical group?"

"No Madison, our screening process is quite elaborate."

"Fine, I will keep you posted," she said fulfilling her obligation to keep Mr. McGinnis in the loop.

"Will that be all Miss Director?"

"Yes, goodnight Jacob," she brought the conversation to a close for now.

"Goodnight Madison, I look forward to penciling our tea party into my schedule."

He thought he could hear her laugh on the other end of the line. They both hung up. Jacob stayed sitting to give himself a minute to digest the FBI's finding. He then got up, prepared once again for his short walk to visit with his wife. It was going to be a long conversation. He was confident the talk with Emma would provide him with some clarity.

***

Sandy met with Fyad and his bride to be for

lunch. She liked her. Very pretty, well spoken, educated. The first thought that came to Sandy's mind was how beautiful their children would be, their future little Princesses and Princes. She was as close to Fyad as she might have been to a brother, if she had one. It was important to her that he was happy with his choice of partner. He was. They seemed like the perfect match. That was good enough for her to extend her blessings.

After lunch Sandy spent the afternoon being introduced to a number of the guests who had also been extended an invitation to reside at the palace during their stay for the wedding. Some of the introductions were cordial. Some were chilly. Those who viewed the USA as an enemy would have preferred not to be put in the position of acting polite. For fear of alienating the King, they played along. After discussing Middle East concerns with a number of the guests she returned to her room to rest prior to the gala dinner, which would be a no expense spared celebration.

***

The dinner event was coming to a close. The festivity would be remembered for a long time by all guests in attendance. It was filled with live entertainment, speeches and enough food to feed a small country. The King's affection towards his son was apparent by the enthusiasm in which the occasion was staged.

The King was seated at the head of the table. Fyad and his fiance Selena were seated to the

King's immediate left. To his right was his wife. Sandy sat next to her, directly across from the soon to be princess. Her name was befitting as it meant Moon Goddess. She was unarguably enchantress this evening.

The King leaned to his right to speak with Sandy.

"Sandy, we will meet in the library regarding our conversation early in the day," reminding her of the upcoming card game.

She smiled but did not reply. She pushed her chair back, stood, and then took a few steps until she was directly behind the King.

"Are you sure you want to do this?" leaning over and whispered into his ear. "It would seem a smattering of your guests don't take that kindly to us Westerners."

"A savoring memory you will provide me with your mastery," he knew she would be on the winning side of the game.

"All right, I will see you in an hour."

"Sandy, please meet me in my office. I wish to have you by my side when we enter the library." Then added with a smile, "Sandy, please do not be fashionably late."

She nodded her head to confirm she heard him.

Sandy then began to politely extend her goodbyes to the guests before making her way to change and freshen up for the final events of the evening. Her choice of clothing was black. It had a classy look, perfect for a game of cards with a number of Kings and Princes, but functional enough for the task at hand.

True to her word, she presented herself at the office exactly at the predetermined time. The King was waiting. The second she arrived, the doors to the office swung open. Side by side they were instantly on their way down the hall. She didn't even break a stride. As they neared the library, the security detail opened the doors for them. When they stepped into the room a number of faces reflected confusion as to why a woman had been allowed access to this privileged gathering.

The King said, "Gentlemen, I believe most of you have had the pleasure of meeting Sandy. She will be joining us this evening. I've asked her to go easy on you."

"Your Highness, this is not proper. We forbid women at our table," said the leader of one of the anti-American countries.

He and two others stood in protest preparing to leave the room.

"Sit," the King said in a loud forceful voice.

He went on, "This young lady is the daughter I never had. She will be playing cards with us this evening."

"But Your Highness," another head of state began before being cut off.

"Gentlemen please sit," he proclaimed in an authoritative voice. "This is my country, my palace, my card game. We will begin. Should one of you find it necessary to leave, I assure you any financial assistance my government has allocated towards your country will cease with your exit through that door," he pointed towards the twelve foot hand carved mahogany doors which were being guarded by four security persons. Two stationed inside the room, two on the outside.

"Please sit," everyone took their chairs.

The card game commenced. Drinks were served to those wanting to indulge. Sandy declined. She required all her senses intact. They would be needed in an hour or so.

The game of choice was Texas Hold'em. As the name implies it is believed to have originated in the state of Texas. The King had to profess that the Americans should be applauded for inventing a game that had provided him with so many hours of enjoyment. When you were as wealthy as he was, it wasn't the monetary gain of the win that provided the thrill. It was the gratification of knowing you defeated your opponent.

Sandy understood this depiction of the game. She was victorious at any card table she participated in. Her exhaustive schooling in intelligence and human behavior heightened her senses to an unparalleled level. She concentrated on body movement, a twitch of the nose, a flicker in the eye, shifting of hands, or fingers, and fidgeting of the legs. Given her awareness of the minutest detail of the opponent's reflexes, she rarely lost. It also helped that she could count cards, knowing with some certainty the odds of someone was holding a better hand than hers.

Everyone settled into the game. Betting, folding, and bluffing. Sandy purposely folded or lost a few hands for the first quarter hour. Her goal was to deflect any interest she attracted by being a women in what some at the table believed was a man's world. It worked. She was no longer the center of attention. Slowly she eased herself into winning. Her opponents were wealthy. The stakes were steadily increasing. In just over an hour she displayed her uncanny skill at the discipline, to the elation of the King. She won over a hundred thousand dollars. Other than the King, the men in the room were bewildered. They had been put into their place by a woman. Mission one of the evening accomplished.

"Gentlemen," Sandy said before the next hand was dealt, "I believe it is time to retire for the evening. Tomorrow will be a wonderful day. We will witness Fyad enter into a new chapter of his life."

She collected her winnings then stood. Everyone was quiet. The King smiled. He was enjoying this. With her announcement of departure you could feel the tension in the room ease. The men could now act as men.

"My dear Sandy, we have only begun," the King wheedled.

"I appreciate your company gentlemen but you know us women need our beauty sleep," she said taking a jab at their characterization of females. She went on, "The Save the Children Foundation will appreciate your generous donation," informing them that her winnings were earmarked for the less fortunate.

Security flung open the massive wooden doors before she had reached them. She disappeared into the hallway. The card game would continue for another couple of hours if not longer which allowed her ample time to complete the next phase of her evening.

***

Eight thousand miles away Renée and David were settling in for dinner after finishing up at the track. Both saw very little of each other during the day. Renée spent the past several hours putting Charlotte's Choice through his paces and grooming the horse. David attended a number of prearranged meetings. The upcoming race day brought together a number of the important players. Breeding contracts were a very lucrative aspect of the industry. He finalized three agreements collectively worth over a million dollars.

Unlike the previous night's discussion there was no flirtation. The focus was solely on the race. Renée noticed the change in David's demeanor early in the day. She assumed it was due to the pressures of the business he was overseeing.

David was making a conscious effort not to get personal with their exchange and focus on tomorrow. Last night was still playing on his mind. The more he reran the events the more curious he was about which room Gabriela came out of. He was disappointed in himself, a grown man who loved his wife, considering crossing the line of infidelity. From this point on he intended on doing just that, controlling his emotions.

They finished eating, feeling comfortable with the plan of attack for the next day. The walk back to the hotel was a quiet one with a polite exchange of goodnight at the end of it. Then both retired to their respective suites. They would regroup early in the morning for race day.

***

Sandy swung a small athletic bag over her shoulder. It contained everything required for the task. Her objective was to gain access into a pair of the guest rooms. They were being occupied by leaders of Middle East countries who were not that cozy with the Americans. At the beginning of the day she wasn't sure who her subjects would be. After observing the visitors she decided on the targets. Her allotted time only allowed for two. The ones chosen displayed a false self-importance throughout the day. They were loose-lipped, arrogant, wanting to be noticed by the other guests, perfect candidates and also on the CIA's preferred list. With their self absorbed attitudes, chances were little thought had been put into the security of sensitive information they may have left behind in the suites. Their mindset would have been all was secure within the Palace.

She would spend a maximum of ten minutes in each of their accommodations, gathering as much intelligence as she could. A decision was made to enter each room from the hallway. Picking the locks would be a breeze. The Palace's exterior security system was as sophisticated as any USA government facility. It was so secure that there was little need for an elaborate interior system. If all went as planned, the security cameras would witness her knocking at a door and being let in by the occupant. The guards who normally patrolled the halls were gathered in the room across from the library with their counterparts. The guests not involved in the poker game would be retired by this time of night. Sandy knew she could roam freely within the complex without suspicion. What she wasn't expecting was the person sitting in front of the security monitors being Fyad.

She stepped into the hallway, walked casually to and up the staircase arriving at the floor above hers. Within a minute she was standing in front of the first suite. Knowing it was not occupied she looked to her right then to her left, then knocked with her left hand. With her back to the hall camera she swiftly used her right hand to swiftly pick the lock with a tool she earlier retrieved from the packsack. She was inside the room as quickly as anyone holding the key could have entered. Those monitoring the security cameras would believe she was visiting one of the guests. Fyad knew better.

Once inside, from her bag she took out what looked like a small pair of dark sunglasses. They were night vision goggles. The gym bag contained a number of highly technological advanced devises. The equipment was developed for the US military. Each item was then refined by the CIA, specifically designed for spying.

She immediately found the object which topped her list, a laptop. In her arsenal she possessed two pieces of equipment which when attached to a computer could extract the full contents in less than a minute. What surprised her was this particular laptop not being of military grade. It was one that a student might own. It could be bought in any of the large electronic chain stores throughout the world. She expected the leader of a country to possess a more secure system. One without USB ports, so information could only be downloaded from a main frame at headquarters. That is, unless one was equipped as she was. But hey, who was she to complain. This just made her job that much easier.

She attached a small box measuring two square inches to the USB input. Then enclosed the computer in what looked to be a clear freezer bag. Once the laptop was secured, it prevented transmissions from entering or leaving the bag. The computer was turned on and the small black box began to run millions of sequences until it broke the password. It would proceed to copy all its files. It would then, and more importantly, embed a program that would allow the agency access to all future activities of the computer. By blocking any internet waves, monitoring of the unit from its government would not pick up the intrusion. It was highly unlikely they would ever realize the security breach. Sandy touched a button. The rest would take care of itself.

She allowed herself the next five minutes for an expeditious examination of the room. The bathroom would be the first area. Her interest was in medication the subjects were prescribed. In some cases not prescribed. Knowledge of addictions or ailments of an enemy could become a beneficial weapon. She gave herself two minutes to complete the search. Next was to extract finger prints from drinking glasses, one sitting on the bedside table and two on the coffee table. Taking out what was not your everyday camera from her bag, she focused it at the glass. It then produced a picture of the finger prints that could instantly be inputted into a database search such as Interpol, but that procedure she would leave to Langley. It worked similar to an x-ray. There was no need for messy powders. Police departments would be in awe of the arsenal she had stored in the bag. The information would be stored in the CIA computers. Should whoever the prints belong to surface in any allied countries systems, the agency would be alerted. Also, thanks to the advancement of today's technology she was able to swab the glass lifting the DNA of those who held it. She then inserted it into a tiny cylinder which immediately analyzed and stored the genetic material. The swab could then be discarded. It would also find its way to the Agency's database.

Time was up. She turned the PC off then returned it to its original position. Sandy stood at the door for half a minute, listening acutely until she was certain the hallway was unoccupied. After cracking the door open an inch to confirm this, she left and walked down the hall to the other accommodation on the list.

Sandy repeated the same entry procedures. Again the computer was in plain sight, but this model was what she would expect a leader of a third world country. There were no USB ports. The only input on it was the A/C plug in the back. She was prepared for this and equipped to remove the stored data. It would take longer than the previous download. She would not have the same time frame to comb the room. This computer belonged to the leader of a country that was suspected of harboring terrorists, although it had repeatedly denied those allegations. The data collected outweighed any other information she might discover in the room.

She sealed the computer in the same sack as she did in the previous room. The only difference in this procedure was the connection. The Agency developed a sophisticated method of extraction from such a highly secured system. Since there was no USB port, the hard drive could be accessed by plugging the black box into the power input. Her unit would worm its way in performing the same functions as it does by way of the proper inputs. The only difference was the handler would have to monitor the progress as the unit would have to be prompted a few times during the process.

The download would soon be complete so she quickly scanned the restroom but found no medicine. There would be no time to take prints. One minute remained until she would disconnect from the computer, pack up, and leave. She gave the room a once over. Placed in the closet sat an attaché case. She knelt, put one hand on it and was surprised it wasn't locked so she opened it and browsed through the files. Retrieving another tiny camera from her packsack she prepared to snap pictures of the documents deemed important. There would not be time to take a photo of all of its contents. The papers seemed immaculately organized. They were properly labeled and placed in the briefcase alphabetically except for two. Those had no identification and had been recklessly tossed into it. One explanation was that they had been handed off to the owner of the case at some point during the day. Her suspicions were confirmed as soon as she opened the files. What they contained was information passed on from one leader to another. The reference to the United States was enough to peak her interest.

Although the documents only contained one sheet of paper each, she did not take the extra time to read them. She snapped a picture and returned the case. It was time to dismantle her electronic apparatus. Sandy slung the packsack over her shoulders and once again put her ear up against the door to confirm the hallway was void of any activity. This time she heard, or more like felt movement on the other side of the door. It was highly unlikely that it was the Head of State entering. He would still be fully engaged in the poker game. Chances were it was one of his assistants retrieving something for him.

One of the drills required of the participants in that yearlong exercise, had them blindfolded for a period of each discipline they partook in. If a month was dedicated to the wilderness jungle survival you would be blinded for one week of it. They parachuted blind. They swam blind. They climbed mountains unsighted. It is a well known fact a blinded person's senses were intensified to compensate for their lack of vision. When Sandy closed her eyes, she recalled this heightening awareness. What she perceived now, was someone nearing the door. At the moment she couldn't hear, but could feel the pressure of a person closing in on her.

She crouched low and tight against the opposite side of the wall of where the door would swing. Contrary to what people see in the movies, hiding on the side the door opens leaves you trapped behind it. Also, the vision of a person entering has a tendency to follow the door's movement to the right. It gives the person bent low on the left wall that split-second to exit without being noticed. Failing that, it provides the fraction of time an intruder required to have the advantage of surprise. Sandy's instincts kicked in. She was aware there were very few people in the world that she could not dominate in hand to hand combat. Within seconds she ran numerous scenarios through her head, how to proceed whether or not she was noticed. If she could not escape unscathed, she would have to incapacitate the intruder, most likely meaning the end of the person's life. It wouldn't be the first, but she preferred a clean escape, leaving no collateral damage. If force was necessary, she would debilitate him with a blow to the precordial region of the chest. If executed properly it would cause a Commotio cordis (agitation of the heart). His heart would fail. Any death in the Palace would be automatically examined by the King's doctor. Should an autopsy be performed, which was unlikely, the conclusion would be death by heart attack. She would have Fyad arrange to make sure the certificate read as such.

Her attention was focused on the door knob. She

slowed her breathing. Her hands were in an attack position ready for whoever entered the room. The door handle slowly began to move. She was braced, prepared for the inevitable. Then voices were heard of what seemed to be a conversation. The person entering was not alone. There was no doubt in her mind that she would prevail if multiple persons entered. A bit messier, but she would succeed. Suddenly the door handle stopped turning. The volume of the exchange in the hallway intensified. As if an argument was taking place. Then the door knob completed its turn. It swung open.

***

In the hallway, a personal guard to one of the visiting country's leaders, whose room was presently being infiltrated by Sandy, was running an errand for his boss. The protector was instructed to fetch cash from the safe. The poker game was getting the best of his boss. He required a restocking of chips.

As he was about to enter, he was interrupted by Fyad. Over the years the Prince developed an inclination to casually walk the halls of the Palace before he retired for the evening. He would not sleep sound unless he had seen to it firsthand that the Palace was secure of any oddities. Tonight after watching Sandy on the security cameras he concentrated on the floor she was rummaging through. He stayed out of sight. She hadn't seen him. When he saw what unit she entered he knew exactly what the agenda was. Feeling compelled to

138

oversee Sandy's safety, he would monitor her movements until she was safely tucked away for the evening in her suite. Their steadfast relationship was one whereby her motives would never be in question. A bond very few people experience.

Fyad approached the guard. He greeted him with some small talk, inviting the guard to join him for a night cap. Telling him how pleased he was they bumped into each other, as he was planning on reviewing the security details of tomorrow's wedding with the visiting dignitaries teams. The guard was having nothing of it. In fear of being reprimanded he needed to immediately return with cash. His employer expected orders to be carried out in a meticulous manner. Anything short of it was not acceptable.

When the guard proceeded to open the door Fayd moved to his left. Fyad continued the conversation with him. He put his right arm on the guard's right shoulder. His actions were similar to buddies parting ways, wishing the other good luck. He acted as if he conceded to the guard's rejection to join him. Fyad would take a step or two into the room with his arm on the shoulder of the man, making a point to continue the conversation speaking louder than what might be considered normal, to alert Sandy of his presence.

Fyad knew exactly where she would position herself. By entering the room simultaneously on the left of the bodyguard, with his arm on his shoulder, he was confident of concealing any vision of Sandy. It would allow her that split second to escape into the hallway. Once outside the room she would not attract any suspension as guests were allowed to roam freely throughout the Palace. Then he would wish his counterpart a nice evening, leave the room, and all would be well. If the man observed Sandy, Fyad would snap his neck. No witnesses. The man would be stripped and one of Fyad's details would dress in his clothing. He would be recorded walking out of the Palace, never too be seen again. His country would label him a deserter. His family would most likely be punished in some way. That was not Fyad's concern. Sandy's safety trumped all.

Sandy immediately recognized Fyad voice. Right away she knew he was purposely acting as a decoy to allow her time to exit unnoticed. The two of them were in sync. She also knew what the outcome would be if the guard did see her.

Fyad's diversion worked like a charm. Within a fraction of a second she was in the stairwell making her way back to her suite. Fyad himself only took three steps through the doorway before saying his goodbyes. After, he made his way to Sandy's room, knocked on the door. She had been expecting him

"Are you okay," he asked.

"I'm fine. You realize I could have handled it on my own."

"Sandy, it's me. I of all people am acutely aware of the damage you are capable of rendering," assuring her he hadn't forgotten about the credentials she possessed.

"Thank you," was all she said.

"Kind of like old times."

"We did have some moments, didn't we?"

"We did. Well seeing you're safe and sound, I

should be retiring. It's been a long day."

"That is a good idea. After all we have a wedding to attend tomorrow."

He was about to open the door when he turned and asked her, "You are done for the night, aren't you?"

She didn't speak, just gave him a devilish smirk.

"By the way, if you feel any of the information you've come upon this evening may be of interest to us, you know where to find me."

She winked at him. He turned and made his way to his residence. They were both feeling the exhaustion of the day. The only thing on one another's mind was sleep. They accomplished more in the past day than most would in a week.

Tired, Sandy crawled into bed. She would review her evening findings in the morning prior to partaking in the wedding festivities. But first, she couldn't resist reaching over to have a quick look at the snapshots of the two pages found in the files. At first it wasn't clear what the photos were. Once she pressed the zoom, it was apparent that what she had discovered could not wait until morning. She picked up her phone and dialed Fyad. He answered before the end of the first ring.

"Fyad, I need transport to my aircraft," she paused, listened, then said, "Yes, now."

Chapter 10

Race Day. David and Renée arrived at the track early. It was Renée's debut as head trainer. The day was worth millions to their stable if successful. The partnership had found its normality. Both absorbed in their respective race day tasks. They ate an early breakfast. Once at the track they went directly to the stables in which the horse was being housed. Renée would remain there until race time. David left after a half hour to mingle with the other owners. He would return once the race was complete.

Renée began her pre-race rituals. She had two tasks which were time sensitive. Both were equally important to her. All other duties would be scheduled around those. First, was a meeting with the jockey for a final discussion on how he was to ride the race. She would work around his or her schedule as on most race days a jockey rode in multiple races. The two discussed the blueprint for the two minute, twenty six second ride on a number of occasions. Yet track and weather conditions could alter their original strategy.

The second tradition which required her precise

timing was magical. Exactly fifteen minutes before the race parade, all her staff would back off the horse allowing Renée to talk to the animal. She would lay the side of her face on the horse's cheek. Cup her left hand around the bottom of its chin, while her right hand would brush its mane and forehead. Today's recipient of her nurturing was Charlotte's Choice. It was one of the most successful horses in the world, the favorite on today's tote board.

Renée spoke to the horse in a very low voice. Her objective was to create calmness within him. She believed the animal understood her. Anyone who witnessed this synergy would attest to the interaction being a sincerely touching moment. She would discuss the game plan for the upcoming run, or sometimes she would just talk about her life. The horse seemed to go into a Zen state. Its breathing slowed, it stood motionless. She was a true horse whisperer.

Normally after she completed her chat, she would saddle the horse then lead it through the post parade where the animal was handed off to the jockey. Today that task was given to one of their most trusted groomers. As a head trainer in a stakes race, it was expected of her to watch the race from the owner's balcony. For this she needed a few minutes to change her clothing. Out with the stable attire and into a dress that was purchased solely for the occasion.

David was already settled into the owner's box when Renée arrived. Right away he realized he had never seen her in a dress before. She chose a

Victoria Secret sleeveless, white lace tiered dress. Her shoulders covered with a new denim jacket. True to form the outfit was complimented by a pair mid-calf cowboy boots. The dress had the effect of being see-through although it wasn't. It had a loose flow to it, but yet clung to certain parts of her body. When she walked, it would slither side to side accentuating her figure. It was sexy. David took notice. The first thought that came to his mind was free. Here she stood, free of any pretentiousness. She was a breath of fresh air. Free.

Renée positioned herself beside her boss who also sported a pair of cowboy boots, jeans, and a dark blue shirt opened at the collar, covered by a grey sports jacket. There were introductions to the other owners and their families, few of which she knew prior to the day. Also present were a handful of her adversary who had been in the business for much longer. Most were skeptical on her ability to handle such a prestigious horse. The general thought was Serge would have overseen every aspect of the training, allowing Sandy to replace him as a figure head.

The sound of the bugle call echoed throughout the grounds. All eyes now turned to the track as the announcer introduced the horses and jockeys parading past the stands. Everyone in the seating area had a connection to one of the horses on today's race card. There was an eerie silence among them when the horses prepared to enter the starting gate. Renée was an even-keeled person with one exception, race time. Her adrenalin kicked into high gear.

"They're at post, they're off," the beginning of the race call was heard over the PA system.

"It looks like we have a clean break from the gate. They're running four wide with Natures Gift at the front of the pack setting the pace. The favorite Charlotte's Choice is stationed fifth along the rail. They've made the quarter in a blistering twenty three and one fifth seconds. Can Natures Gift go wire to wire at this pace?"

Everyone was fixated on the race. Renée's excitement got the better of her and she unintentionally grabbed David's arm. He didn't resist. No one else noticed Renée's tugging of his jacket. Truth be told, Renée hadn't realized what she was doing as she was so intently focused on their horse. David would be lucky if he didn't inherit finger nail marks in his arm by the end of the race.

The call continued, "as they pass the half mile pole Gabriela D'Angelo has Natures Gift a length and a half ahead of the field. Sky is running in second, followed by Remember When, and Redneck Willie now running two wide. The favorite Charlotte's Choice is taking the ground saving ride by hugging the rail, but will Mario Rossi be able to break out of the pack. Summertime and Just Call Me Great have him blocked in with Scare Me Silly trailing the tightly packed field."

"Come on, come on, come on," Renée whispered in a low voice as she began rocking, subconsciously trying to assist her jockey ride the horse. "Make your move now, you got to get him out now. Come on, come on, come on."

David was silent. His body movements weren't. He was hitting the side of his leg with the program. Mimicking the motions used by a jockey with their riding crops otherwise known as their whip. So into the race he didn't notice the arm of his jacket being pulled from his shoulders.

"They're rounding the back turn. No one wants to challenge Natures Gift. They seem content. Natures Gift may have himself a wire to wire. As they round the last turn and make their way for the home stretch the favorite is boxed in along the rail by the remainder of the group. It looks like no one is going to catch D'Angelo's ride. She's got Natures Gift two lengths ahead of her closest rival. Positions have remained the same. No one wants to race her today. Wait a second. It looks like Charlotte's Choice has found an opening along the inside of the field. How did Rossi do that? He's found himself out of the pack but can he catch Natures Gift? Charlotte's Choice is gaining ground but may run out of race track. Here they come. It's Natures Gift, Charlotte's Choice, Natures Gift, Charlotte's Choice. They're making their way to the wire. It's Natures Gift, its Charlotte's Choice. They're neck and neck, it's, it's, it's, oh this is too close to call. We're going to have to wait for the results of the photo finish. How in the world did Rossi find a line out of that crowd? What a great race. Here are the results folks. Charlotte's Choice remains undefeated."

It took a second for it to sink in before David and Renée caught on to the fact that the photo finish results confirmed their win. His jacket sleeve was pulled down over his hand exposing the blue shirt covering his shoulder.

"Oops," a wide eyed Renée said after realizing she pulled his coat half off as she tried to fix it.

He laughed it off. Then caught up in the excitement, he gave her a congratulatory hug, lifting her right off the ground while spinning her around. The white dress flowed in the air almost exposing her Victoria Secret panties.

They began making their way to the winning circle. Everyone around them was offering handshakes, acknowledging their win. Once on the main floor, security cleared the way to the gate which opened onto the track. They walked across the turf to the infield. There they were congratulated by the racing officials.

Soon Mario Rossi steered Charlotte's Choice into the winner circle. He was sporting a grin which was as wide as his face. Renée held the horse's reins. Once again she laid the side of her face on the animal similar to her pre-race ritual. She thanked him and promised him a well deserved rest. David watched. If he didn't know better he'd swear the horse answered. Her ability to converse with these thoroughbreds was transcending. In all his years, he had never witnessed anything like it.

The presentations began. The track announcer joined them with a microphone. The sound system echoed the introduction of all within the circle. The chairperson of the stakes race presented the trophy to David and Renée. Renée was also presented with a bouquet of flowers. At the end of the ceremony a groomer walked the horse back to the stables. The jockey followed an official for the winners weigh in. David and Renée crossed the track once again. They did not return to the grandstand, but instead elected to check in with their staff at the stables. Along the way Renée would be interviewed by three different networks covering the race. David stood by her side and tried to say little.

Both were drained from the rush the race had induced. They took time to visit with Charlotte's Choice, who was gently being walked around the paddock to slow his heart rate. The horse would be washed down and allowed to rest the remainder of the day before being transported home early the next morning.

"Well, our work is done here," David said to Renée. "I believe we earned the right to celebrate with dinner and drinks. Care to join me?"

"I would love to," she answered.

"Perfect. Let's go find ourselves the most expensive restaurant in town. Jacob McGinnis will be footing the bill tonight."

David reached for his phone, "I'll arrange for a ride. Can you wrap things up here? I need to give Sandy a call to fill her in on the race. Then it's dinner and a bottle of their finest."

"I've got it covered. Say hi to Sandy for me. We'll meet back here. Thirty minutes work for you?" She said then disappeared into the stables after he nodded his approval.

David dialed Sandy's number. It went straight to voice mail. Not sure what time of day it was in the Middle East, nor did he care, he pressed the redial key. He was pumped and exhausted at the same time. Again there was no answer. He wasn't going to leave a message. This was special, not something you leave on an electronic answering service. A vital part of a successful marriage is being able to share these occasions. He waited five minutes, tried once more, but it proved to be of no avail.

Back at the stable, Renée finished instructing the staff on transportation of Charlotte's Choice. The next time she would see him would be at the ranch. She thought about changing back into her everyday clothing but decided against it. It felt nice to be dressed up. Something she should do more often. She wanted to feel good tonight.

As she left the paddock area, David was approaching her.

"Our ride is here," he said. "Are we good to go?"

"Oui, everything seems to be running smoothly," Renée replied.

"Good."

Walking to the parking lot she asked, "was Sandy excited about our win?"

"I don't know. She didn't answer."

Hearing the frustration in his voice, she dropped the subject and left well enough alone. David was disappointed. It is important to share high points of your life with someone you care for. This wasn't the first time he was left feeling the emptiness.

"It's just you and me tonight kid. Let's go drink a few too many."

On the way towards the VIP parking area where a car awaited them, she could sense his disappointment. It wasn't fair, a joyful event such as this carried sadness with it.

149

David left it up to Renée to choose the restaurant. He called ahead to reserve a table for two. Directions were given to the driver. The eatery was again close to their hotel. Convenient should the alcohol consumption surpass their previous get-togethers. A walk back to the hotel would be in order.

***

Sandy heard her telephone ring. The screen displayed David's name. She just arrived at the aircraft which was parked in a private hanger and would have welcomed a conversation with her husband if she did not have such a pressing matter to attend to. In a little while, once the business at hand was dealt with, she would return the call.

She was functioning on very little sleep. During the past couple of days there were only a few cat naps. She possessed the ability to adapt to sleep deprivation. Taught to function with the utmost attentiveness during situations such as the one she currently found herself in.

After searching the hanger, confirming she was the sole occupant, she stepped into the aircraft. Although her plane was the only aircraft parked in the private facility owned by the King, Sandy would not rest until she was certain she was alone. The two employees of Fyad who chauffeured her to the airport positioned themselves outside, guarding the perimeter as was their instructions. Next, she pressed the close button next to the door. The ladder slowly disappeared into an opening below the hatch.

The door swung on its hinges and locked. Caution was imperative to safeguard the intelligence gathered during her outing.

She then made her way to the cockpit. When Sandy was recruited by the CIA, her father authorized the agency's installation of additional gadgetry within the cockpit panel. This extension to the plane's instrumentation would never be exposed during an aircraft inspection by a customs officer. An airplane's mechanism would not be questioned during this sort of examination. Secure outlets for general telephone conversations and information of a less level of security were also placed in the passenger area.

Jacob's only condition was the Agency provide two of the Air Force's finest pilots to command the jet during all of Sandy's flights. It was comforting to him knowing she was in good hands during her travels. These men were on duty as pilots only. They were ordered to observe from a distance and not act in any other capacity unless Sandy was in a life threatening situation. The pilots were not aware of her employment within the organization. They knew of her closeness to the White House and that she at times would transmit sensitive information. To whom they did not know, nor did they care. There were no questions. They followed their superior's directions. Sandy had never been officially informed the pilots her father employed were Air Force. Yet she was well aware of their appointments.

She plugged the cord from the equipment which contained the computer information into a port in the cockpit panel. Then she pressed a button that initiated the transmission of her findings to a secluded room at the CIA's headquarters in Langley, Virginia. It would be read instantly. The data which this room was the recipient of came from a select few. For the most part it contained intelligence critical to USA's arrestment of terrorism.

She proceeded to connect her cellular telephone to another open port in the panel, then pressed number one on the phone. It was a secure, direct line to Christopher Young, the Director of the CIA. He picked up on the first ring.

"Sandy, I was expecting your call," he answered, then continued. "I just hung up with the communication office. Your information is being decrypted as we speak."

"Only at Langley," she was referring to the expeditiousness of the agency.

"You were so kind as to put your life in harm's way, it's the least we can do."

"It is appreciated," was her reply.

"Christopher, I have something else of interest which I haven't transmitted," she began to explain the contents of the files she had found. "I felt it would be in our best interest if I sent copies of these two documents to you personally. I believe one of them divulges the location of an existing American hostage. The troublesome fact is, if this information is correct, it is a staunch ally of ours knowing or unknowingly allowing housing of the hostage."

"Sandy you need to include it with the other transmission," he wasn't suggesting that she do this.

He was ordering, "I have agents in place that specialize in addressing this form of intelligence."

"I understand what you are saying Christopher, but," acknowledging his instructions, then taking a deep breath before dropping the bomb, "it's Emily Wilson."

There was an uncharacteristic silence from the chief of the CIA. You don't become the head of an organization like the Agency by being tongue-tied. His position required an unwavering instant decisiveness. At the moment that attribute was absent.

"Christopher, are you still there?"

Emily Wilson was a respected journalist, photographer, spending the majority of her career reporting from the Middle East. She was considered an expert on the political atmosphere of the area. One year earlier she disappeared. There was no demand for ransom. No radical organization proclaimed responsibility.

It was first thought she was abducted. As time went on, most involved in the investigation were resigned to the fact that she had been murdered.

"Sandy you're right," he said. "For the moment this information will remain between the two of us."

Emily was a CIA special agent. She worked undercover posing as a journalist. Only a handful of people knew of her true identity. Sandy had her suspicions, but her boss never had any reason to enlighten her. At the time she went missing, Sandy was asked to keep her ear to the wall during her travels. She never did garner any intelligence on the kidnapping.

Emily earned the trust of a number of the radical brotherhoods. She was one of the selected few allowed access to the inner circle. When the group felt the need to release their propaganda to the world, Emily was the chosen one who they trusted to report their words verbatim. Such trust if found fraudulent would yield dire consequences, hence the determination that she had been executed.

"You said you discovered two items you wish to discuss," he questioned her.

"Yes the other document I believe is making reference to the location of groups we may be interested in," she explained.

There was a moment of silence both waiting for the other to continue the conversation.

"OK, there, I just sent it to you," informing him of the transmission.

"Sandy I need to get my head around this. I will call you back in an hour. Make sure you're available," he directed her.

"I'll be right here."

She wanted to take the call in the aircraft for obvious reasons. Fatigue was beginning to set in. Needing some air she left the plane to speak to the two guards waiting outside the hanger.

When she stepped out from the hanger door, she summoned both of them and explained there would be a delay in her return to the Palace. She suggested they return and that she would contact them when ready to leave. They didn't utter a word, just nodded confirming their understanding of her suggestion.

Sandy then returned to the jet. She again locked

herself in. An hour of rest would be most productive at this point, so she reclined in a seat, closed her eyes. Within seconds she was asleep. The guards continued their watch of the building. Fyad had issued a directive that they were to protect Sandy. Unless alternate orders were received from their boss or Sandy was ready to return to the Palace, they were staying put.

***

Renée and David enjoyed a wonderful dinner. Now back at the hotel they rode the elevator to their floor. The evening's conversation flowed with ease as did the alcohol. Both were still riding the high of winning one of the most prestige's races in the world. It was quite an accomplishment for Renée. Many seasoned handlers in her field will never attain this achievement. Only one trainer per year earns the distinction of being presented that particular trophy.

They arrived at her door as was the case the past two evenings. Déjà vu David was thinking.

"Renée, I'm not going be able to sleep," he began. "I'm just too pumped."

They locked eyes. She didn't reply. Being uncertain of what was on his mind, she felt it was best to remain silent so he could continue without her swaying the exchange. An invitation to extend the evening was her wish.

"Would it be inappropriate of me to invite you to my room for a nightcap?"

David knew this was so wrong on so many

levels. He was a married man. Renée was his employee. They had just polished off a bottle of wine at dinner. The alcohol might have been influencing him or allowing him to shed his inhibitions. Either way he wanted to be with her. Whatever the consequences, a few more hours with Renée was all he could think about.

"Probably," she answered.

"Probably what?" he said giving her a questionable look.

"It is probably inappropriate," then she went silent for about five seconds before accepting the invitation. "Oui David, je ne veux pas terminer ce soir," telling him in French that she wasn't ready for the evening to end.

They continued down the hallway to his suite. He unlocked and then held the door open for her, following her in. Renée took a second to take in the surroundings before making her way to the floor to ceiling windows with a breathtaking view of the L.A. skyline. She dropped into a tan leather sofa facing the mesmerizing scenery.

David stood at the bar, held up a bottle of wine in one hand and a glass in the other, offering Renée a drink. She waved him off. The spirits consumed with supper had surpassed her comfortable limit. Sitting there she wondered if the alcohol was a factor in her decision to accept his invitation.

"David, do you think you could drum up some coffee," she replied to his silent inquiry. "I believe I've had enough to drink for one day."

"Let me call room service. I'm pretty sure you wouldn't want to drink my brew."

David put the wine bottle back then opened the refrigerator. He grabbed himself a bottle of beer, opened it then dialed the hotel's room service. Along with the coffee, he ordered a few hors d'oeuvres in case they came down with the munchies.

"Renée, are you sure your okay with this?" Feeling he needed reassurance that she was comfortable with joining him. "I don't want you to feel pressured into being here just because I'm your boss. I'm still flying high by your win today. It's nice to have someone to share it with."

"David, there is nowhere I'd rather be. I'm also excited about our success. It's going to take a day or two to settle in. Until then sleep is not in the cards," she wanted him to feel at ease with her presence.

David sat on the couch beside her. He put his feet up on the coffee table, took a sip of his beer. Nothing was said for a few minutes. They gazed out the window at the brilliant light show the city was providing. A view that left them spellbound.

"Your coffee should be here shortly," David said to break the silence.

Renée smiled but didn't reply.

Maybe it was because he hadn't been able to get in touch with Sandy, or maybe it was the fact that lately she was spending more time in Europe than a home. It might be the booze or as he had referred to previously the excitement of the day. But whatever the reason, he was beginning to miss a companionship that only a female could provide. His wife's travels fed the ever expanding void in his life. Each year her travel time expanded, as did his loneliness. It came as no surprise to him and he would never complain about it. After all, this was what he signed up for. But emotions are sometimes difficult to manage.

Renée must have been reading his mind as she looked at him and asked, "David, do you think Sandy would be upset knowing we are alone in your room at this time of the night?"

"I don't think she would mind. I hope she would have an understanding with my wanting to share a special occasion like this with someone. Besides, she is rarely home these days," he immediately regretted adding that last sentence. He was verbalizing his thoughts. Something he would be mindful to refrain from for the remainder of the night.

"I hope you're right," Renée added.

There was a knock at the door. Room service was quite expeditious this time in the evening or rather morning. David gave the attendant a generous tip then rolled the cart to the side of the sofa. The day had been good to him. He felt like sharing the wealth.

"Le café est servi," announcing the arrival of her requested beverage in French.

"Merci," she thanked him.

He picked up the tray then set it on the table. Renée reached over to pour her coffee. They both nibbled on the snacks. Little was being discussed. For two people who spent so much time together it was unusual for both to be lost for words. Speaking to one another at work or sitting across a dinner table came naturally to them. Sitting a foot away from each other, alone in a hotel suite, rendered them slightly uncommunicative.

Facing David, Renée lifted, then curled her legs up onto the couch. With this she had inched a touch closer to him.

"Renée, I'm very proud of your accomplishment today. I was very fortunate to find you," he said paying credit where credit was due.

"Thank you," she responded. "But David I'm only a small part of this team. You and Serge deserve the accolades here."

"That's not true. You prepared Charlotte's Choice and he responded. There are few people who can converse with a horse as well as you," he told her. "I'll take credit for hiring you, but that's it. Today was all you."

"Thank you."

With that they were back to the silence and gazing out the window. It wasn't long before the exhaustion of the last few days settled in. David looked over at Renée. With her head resting on the back of the couch she had fallen asleep. She looked so peaceful, an alluring petite young lady. David smiled then closed his eyes. It wasn't long before he also dozed off.

An hour or so after falling asleep both seemed to wake simultaneously. Renée's head had fallen during her nap and was resting on David's shoulder. His arm which had been placed on the back top of the sofa prior to him nodding off had dropped around her side. They looked at each other, neither attempting to readjust their position, welcoming the new placement of their bodies. Whether it was the blissful state of sleep paralysis or both had succumbed to the realization that it was inevitable this was going to happen, they leaned towards each other and began to kiss.

The embrace continued for quite some time. They restricted their caressing to the face, hair and shoulders. No words were spoken. Each of them was accepting the engagement, each becoming more and more aroused.

Renée broke from his grasp. She moved her hands down to his pants then unzipped them. She lowered her head easing him into her mouth. He did not resist. David laid his head on the back of the couch and closed his eyes. Gently using a combination of her mouth, tongue and teeth she pleasured him. It soon became apparent to David that Renée was well versed in the art of oral stimulation.

A half hour passed since they awoke and still no words were exchanged. The sexual gratification was all both deemed necessary at the moment. Until Renée paused from her stimulus and looked up at him. Her dark hair partly covered her face. Her lips wet. She simpered coyly at him. He had never seen her look so sultry. David found himself fixating on her face, which was reaffirming his thought that in the last few minutes they had progressed past the point of no return.

"David, you have a nice cock," was all she said.

David didn't know how to reply. He was loss for words. Over the years he had been complimented on his lovemaking. For most part he figured his partners were caught up in the act and it was the right thing to say. But no one had said this to him. All he could come up with was, "thank you."

Short of complimenting her on her private parts, which he hadn't had the pleasure of experiencing yet, that was all he had. Just thank you.

Renée lowered her head once again and continued to please him.

After a couple of more minutes David put his hands gently onto her head to ease her off. He needed her to stop or the evening would quickly be coming to an end or at least a pause. She raised her head. He bent his. They kissed.

"We should take this to the bedroom," he softly suggested.

She nodded in agreement as he lifted all of her hundred pounds into the air and carried her to the bed. He gently laid her down. David stripped off his clothes until he was naked. Renée did the same leaving her bra and panties on. Now they were together lying on the bed. Their hands were exploring every inch of each other's bodies.

Renée maneuvered herself on top of David who was on his back. Once she had him locked inside her, she began to ride. She started with slow, precise back and forth thrusting movements. It wasn't long before she increased the tempo.

David was awestruck by the aggression of her lovemaking. He wasn't expecting her to be so ferocious. Still in her twenties and accustomed to their typical interactions, he would have thought of her being more on the reserved side. At the moment she was riding him as if aboard a thoroughbred challenging for the lead in the Kentucky Derby. The lovemaking did not last too long mostly due to its intensity and the anticipation both had built up over the past couple of years. When they completely satisfied each other they lay on the bed totally spent.

"We really crossed some line tonight, didn't we?" David was the first to talk.

"That we did," she answered, then leaned in to kiss him.

"David, that was special. I will never regret what happened here," she began. "You have my word that once we leave this room I will never discuss or make reference to it again. I promise."

"I think that would be in our best interest," agreeing.

"I'm not a delusional person. I understand this could cause both of us a great deal of anguish if we were found out. I have no intentions of dividing you and Sandy. I'm an adult. If this is a one time encounter, I'm okay with it. I'll remember tonight for the rest of my life. If it is meant to happen again, then so be it. But, if it would be easier for us, I'm willing to hand in my resignation once we get home."

"Enough," David interrupted her. "Nobody's resigning," assuring her that her employment would not be affected. "We both made a conscious decision here. It was great. I think we both knew it was bound to happen sooner or later."

"Now come here, our plane doesn't leave for a few hours," he pulled her nearer.

"David, don't you think we've done enough damage already," she said wondering if they should just clean up, leave, and put it behind them.

"We said we will not discuss this again once we leave the room. We're still in the room, at least for another hour or so. We should make the most of it."

Chapter 11

Sandy's secured telephone began to buzz. She abruptly awakened from her nap, made her way to the cockpit and answered by the third ring.

"Sandy, this information is for your ears only," the Director began.

There was no hello or any other formalities. He was a busy person. He expected his subordinates to be as diligent. No idle chat.

"Yes sir," she answered.

"Emily Wilson was," he hesitated, "or is, one of ours."

"Yes sir."

Christopher Young hadn't achieved his position being haphazard with his divulging sensitive information to anyone, unless he felt it was secure and he or his organization would benefit from it. He knew what he was about to discuss with Sandy would never be mentioned to a soul. After all, he had personally recruited her. Since that time, there were only six people who knew of her placement with the CIA. There was himself, the President of the United States and Chief of Staff. Then there was the last sitting President and his right hand man. Finally there was her father.

Jacob accepted her enlistment, but was never comfortable with it. As promised he supported her decision, not necessarily in agreement with it. She was playing with the big boys, a dangerous undertaking. Although proud, her safety was first and foremost on his mind.

"I have spoken to the President. He is of two opinions. First, leave it status quo. The agent has been missing for over a year now, presumed dead. Any active recovery has been suspended for quite some time. For godsakes, they had a funeral for her. Second, we initiate an extraction. Before the final decision is made he would like your opinion on how accurate the intel is. We need to be absolutely positive. Is there any possibility you have been set up," he explained and asked.

"There's no way. I was in and out. No one could have predicted my movements," she said trying to reassure him. "Besides, unless you are aware of someone on this side of the world knowing who I actually am, I'm convinced there is nothing else in play here."

"We have to be unfaltering with the data we are supplying to the President. He can't involve his security team because no one knows of your identity and they will surely want the face providing the intelligence. His loses are zero if he doesn't take any action. She's already presumed dead. Hasn't been on anyone's radar for six months" he explained. Then went on, "Some things are best left alone Sandy."

"You can't mean that. She risked her life for our country. We need to do whatever it takes to go in and get her," Sandy answered.

"You're going to get all patriotic on me? Might I remind you that I spend twenty-four hours a day and sometimes I wish the days were longer, trying to protect this country? I lost my wife and children for this career. This is my life. I wouldn't have let that happen if it weren't for my great love of our country," he lectured her. "So keep your emotions in check."

"Don't you chastise me," she came back at him. "My commitment to you has always been unwavering. We have all suffered personal loss due to our chosen vocation. At least you have children."

"Sandy, please let me finish without interruption," he proceeded. "The President cannot be part of this. If I convince him to authorize a covert retrieval, we have to be one hundred percent positive this is the location she is being held before he gives us his blessing. We will be on our own. Should anything go wrong he will deny any knowledge of the incident. The operation is solely CIA."

The Director paused for a short time. Sandy didn't say a word. She would give him time to collect his thoughts.

"Ok. Here's what we are going to do. I will order drone and satellite monitoring of the area. We will infra the building. If I am satisfied, I will encourage the President to secretly authorize an elite Special Forces extraction team. We will notify their government that our air activity is part of a training maneuver off one of our aircraft carriers on the Mediterranean," he was more thinking out loud rather than speaking to her.

"It won't work."

"Sandy, might I remind you again that I am the Director of the most powerful intelligence agencies in the world. When I do something, it works," he fired back.

"I know who you are. How could I forget? But that doesn't change the fact that your plan won't be successful."

"Explain yourself," not wasting words but he did want to visit her side of the story.

"You will succeed in recovering Emily. I have no doubt about that element of the retrieval. What concerns me and it should concern you is the noise we make going in. That will be on the President. Our boys will be heard. There's no way around it," she began to voice her opinion. Her boss listened. "Neighbors will be curious. Once their government gets wind of it, they will be looking for explanations. Excuse me sir, if I might, they will be pissed. The White House will spend the next month denying any involvement. Eventually it will fade away into obscurity. But a great deal of unnecessary time will be allotted to it."

"We can't call them up and say by the way your country is harboring one of our agents, who you know as a journalist. Would you mind dropping by and picking her up for us," was his response. "We have two options here. Leave her or send in a team."

"There is an alternative. One that is much

cleaner."

"I'm listening," he said.

"Me."

"You what?"

"Inform their embassy we will have aircraft flying in the area as part of an exercise. Drop me in. I go in and grab her. No one sees me. No gun fire. We rendezvous with a helicopter which your team is on board as backup. She's free and nobody is the wiser. Your PR guys put out a press release how after a year in captivity our journalist single-handily escapes her captives. After all she had a year to plan for it."

"Sandy, you gather intelligence. You're not a field OP. Hell, technically you're not even an agent. That's not what I signed you up for," he informed her.

"I must have missed that part when I read my job description."

"Sandy, you can't be serious. Let's for one minute say I was to entertain this ludicrous idea of yours, if found out, how in the world would I explain the existence of the two of you. The daughter of a wealthy American happens to parachute into a foreign country to save a reporter who has been missing for over a year," he said making his point knowing she was serious about the proposal. "Oh and by the way they both just happen to belong to the CIA."

"I won't be made. I'm in and out. You send in a team, I guarantee weapons will be discharged. There is a high probability someone will take notice. The end of the world for you, no, you can spin it, but do you have time to be justifying why we are meddling in an ally's backyard."

"Our Special Forces spend every waking moment preparing for missions such as this," he explained to her. "They are the best of the best in covert OPs. We issue orders to refrain from utilizing weapons unless there is no alternative to protect themselves or the subject."

"I am well versed in their lethal proficiencies sir. As you might recall I'm the one who trained their trainers."

"How can I forget? I knew I would someday regret authorizing your security clearance for that year."

"Listen," she interjected, "we know we can't afford to ruffle any feathers with this regime. I'm in and out within an hour. The team stations themselves on the helicopter. At the first sign of the situation going astray I initiate them into action."

"You're really serious about this, aren't you Sandy?"

"I'm already in the area. In good conscience you have to agree there are only a handful of people as skilled as I am in hand to hand combat. I will execute a controlled penetration of their refuge without so much as disturbing the flies on the wall," she said convincingly.

As absurd as it looked on the surface, the more he listened to her rationalization, the more it made sense. He wasn't at the point of acknowledging this train of thought to her just yet. A decision of this magnitude required a few minutes of thought.

"Sandy, stay where you are, I will contact you in

fifteen minutes," he ordered.

"Yes sir. You do remember I have a wedding to attend in a couple of hours."

"Fifteen minutes," he barked.

"Yes sir."

She was about to disconnect from the conversation when she heard her boss say.

"Sandy."

"Yes sir."

"The Director of the FBI contacted me this morning asking for our assistance with the investigation of the fire at your father's stables. There is reason to believe the material used may have originated in Europe. It's an odd request as I would have thought the local authorities could have brought the matter to a resolution. I would assume it may be your father applying pressure. Are you okay with it if I enlist a couple of our people to make some low key inquiries? I may need her on my side one day."

"If purposely set, I believe it is a domestic attack. I'm not the target. As much as I hate to think about it, it may have been a competitor. It's clear to me it was meant as a distraction rather than someone trying to inflict damage. Something went wrong. My theory, very amateurish," she said summing up her take on the fire. "I don't have a problem with our looking into it. I was planning to make a few discreet inquiries myself after the wedding."

"I agree with you, but it would be best if you kept your hands clean on this one. You don't want to attract any undue attention to yourself. Fifteen minutes." He hung up.

This time she stayed in the pilot's seat. With one hand holding the aircraft's yoke, the other on the control lever she began to mimic a pilot's movement. Horsing around like a kid.

Attempting a man's deep voice she said "Ladies and Gentlemen please fasten your seat belts. We have been cleared for takeoff. We are expecting a smooth flight today and will be on our way very shortly, as soon as I figure out what all these buttons are for."

She began to laugh. Overtired she spoke out loud, "I really need some sleep."

Ten minutes after she had ended the conversation with her boss, the phone indicated there was an incoming call. It wasn't the Director's number. She regrouped, snapping out of her childlike antics and answered it.

"Hello."

"Please hold for the President of the United States," said the voice on the other end.

She said nothing.

"Sandy, how are you," it was the President's voice.

"I'm fine, Mr. President," she replied, then went on. "You've caught me a bit off guard. I was expecting a call for someone else."

"Oh yes, I presume that would be Christopher," he told her. "I just happened to end a conversation with him and he was kind enough to allow me to speak with you before he made further contact."

"Yes sir, Mr. President."

"Sandy, there's no need for you to address me by my official title, please call me Andrew."

"Yes sir, Mr. President."

"I'm not going to win here, am I," the President conceded to Sandy's insistence with the formality. They had been through this a number of times and would most likely visit it again at some point.

"No sir."

"I'm expected in a meeting so I will make this brief. Christopher outlined your proposition for recovery. I'm hesitant to authorize your involvement," he informed her.

She was aware the Director and the President would visit every the scenario available to them. Both would be extremely reluctant to allow her to perform a solo extraction. It didn't change her mind set. It was the best option in this particular case and she would not easily let the idea be shut down.

"Sir, may I explain."

"The Director has briefed me Sandy."

"Sir, should you opt for a Special Forces recovery, we chance being found out. This will undoubtedly cause our country embarrassment. You will be questioned as to why we did not inform them and allow their forces to retrieve Emily for us. I believe that would be the proper protocol for the recapture of a journalist."

She paused for a second to catch her breath hoping the President would not end the conversation just yet. He was silent. Having an understanding for Sandy's devotion to her country he would extend the courtesy of allowing her to complete her plea. She did just that.

"Sir, I'm in and out. No one sees me. If I determine I can safely bring out our subject I will. If anything turns sour I retreat. You can then give the go ahead to the Special Force team," she was trying to sell this.

"Sandy, I must cut you off now. I am late for a very important meeting. My assistant just peeked into the Oval giving me the evil eye," he interrupted her.

"But sir," she felt the need to continue her plead.

"Sandy, I must go."

"Sir," she said knowing she had lost this battle.

"Sandy."

"Thank you for hearing me out, sir," saying her goodbyes. "Please give my best to the First Lady."

"I will," he said then paused for a few seconds.

"By the way," he began. "When speaking with the Director I authorized your mission. I wanted to be certain that it was your idea, not his. There will be safeguards in place. I agree with your logic. I just wish it was someone other than you executing the operation. Take care, Sandy. We will chat at the conclusion of this."

"Thank you, Andrew."

The President chuckled.

"That's all I've had to do all these years is just let you have your way," referring to being addressed by his first name.

"Goodnight, Sandy," he ended the call.

She dropped back into the pilot's chair confident that both men had been on board with her from the onset. The phone rang again.

"That was an uncharacteristically long conversation," the Director said without saying hello.

"It was a refreshing chat. I haven't spoken with the President in far too long."

"I need two to three days to orchestrate this mission," staying in form he got right to the business at hand. "You will need to remain on that side of the world until it is complete."

"I will be ready the minute you give the go ahead."

"Sandy, understand we do believe in your plan. But we would prefer to substitute another agent in your place. Knowing that will not transpire, you must understand there are going to be parameters in place that we expect you to operate within. If you alter them at all, the assignment will be aborted," he said warning her that she would be on a short string.

"Yes sir."

"I will be in contact once the logistics have been dealt with."

"Yes sir."

"Sandy," he continued.

"Yes sir."

"Get some rest," then he ended the call.

Sandy smiled as she exited the aircraft. She informed the security detail that she was now ready to return to the Palace. Elated these two powerful men agreed to the plan, the stimulus of what was to come began to set in. During her tenure with the Agency, the majority of her efforts were restricted to gathering intelligence. There were a few secretive field missions that she participated in. All were successful and saw her encounter some form of physical altercations. It was during those times that she was at her best. It was the ultimate high. The sensation was exactly what frightened her. Could she give it up?

Once back at the Palace, she tucked herself into the luscious bed. Now relaxed, it was time to return her husband's calls. She dialed his number.

It rang about five times before David answered. He and Renée had just boarded the plane for the return trip home. Once settled into his seat he answered.

"Sandy."

"What no 'hi babe' or 'honey'," trying to lighten up the mood she suspected he would be in since the call was long overdue.

"Sandy, I've been trying to get a hold of you since yesterday."

"I apologize David. I've been so busy here. Everything seems to be happening at warp speed. Each time I went to call I would be interrupted," explaining her delay on getting back to him.

"That's okay. We've been keeping a good pace going here also. If you haven't heard, we won."

"Congratulations. You've worked hard for it."

"Actually I can't take credit here. Renée stepped up to the plate and was awarded with her first stakes win."

He was proud of Renée's handling of the horse and wasn't afraid to acknowledge it publicly.

"Extend my congratulations to her."

"You can tell her yourself. She's sitting right beside me. We just boarded our flight home," he said while handing the phone to Renée.

Renée tried to wave him off, not wanting to talk to the wife of the man she had inside her a couple of hours before. Although she felt quite capable of acting like nothing happened between them, she feared Sandy might suspect something. David insisted, so she placed the cell phone to her ear.

"Sandy," she said trying to keep the tone of her voice as normal as possible. Then she added, "Hi."

"Congratulations, Renée. We always knew you had what it takes. I've been a supporter of yours from the beginning. You must be very proud," complimenting her.

"Thank you. I appreciate it. How has your trip been? It must be exciting attending the wedding of a Prince and Princess."

"It will be breathtaking Renée," she replied. "Again congratulations on your win. Could you pass me back to my husband? Take care."

It sounded like Sandy was being standoffish towards her. But then again, speaking to the wife of a man that you were just in bed with would make any woman border on paranoia. She passed the phone back to David.

"Hi," is all he said.

"I didn't realize you two were also traveling home together."

"Well in all fairness I haven't been able to fill you in on much. You've been too busy to take my calls," he had an agitated manner to his voice when replying.

"David I'm not upset. It just caught me a little off guard."

"Ok. We can talk more about this when you come home. When might that be anyhow?" Realizing he had no idea when to expect the return of his wife.

"I'm not sure, David. A couple of things have come up that might extend my stay. I won't be certain until tomorrow. I promise I will call you as soon as I know. I promise."

"Ok. I need to go we're about to take off."

"I love you, David. I really do," she found herself emphasizing her love for him.

"You too," he answered not saying he loved her rather just alluding to it.

He regretted not saying it out loud. There's no way that Sandy wouldn't pick up on it. She did. Both knew it was because Renée was sitting next to him. Renée also took note of the exchange.

David hung up, turned to Renée, smiled and said, "well you played that cool. Your voice only went up about two octaves."

With a smirk on her face, she shrugged her shoulders and lightly jabbed her elbow into his ribs.

All kidding aside, Sandy was envious of the time Renée spent with her husband. It was work. She understood that. However, Renée was a beautiful woman. She had a European look to her. Dark hair, dark complexion, brown eyes combined with her French accent although becoming less noticeable over time, a captivating young lady. Sandy was well aware that she was in no position to object to this working relationship. Besides she was the one spending less and less time at home. Hopefully someday soon that would change. But not right now. She fell asleep, a well deserved rest.

David and Renée's flight was uneventful. Both were tired from the past night's activities. They chatted a little but mostly found themselves catnapping. They landed safely, which was always a good thing. He drove her home. No kiss goodbye. Their working relationship was quickly restored. Goodbyes were exchanged with plans to meet tomorrow at the track. Then David made his way back to the ranch. Renée knew chances they would share the same bed again were slim. She was a last minute replacement for Serge. He would most certainly be resuming his position for any upcoming weekend overnighters.

***

Sandy slept for what few hours she could sneak in before having to prepare for the wedding. True to form she was one of the last to arrive at the Palace's Court where the ceremony was to take place. It was a spectacular event. Flowers, gold, gorgeous dresses wherever the eyes could see. All the bells and whistles one might expect for a Royal wedding of a Prince to his Princess. No expense was spared for the reception dinner. In the original seating plan the King had placed Sandy at the head table. Uncomfortable with the seating arrangement, she had the King alter it. Not an easy task as he didn't take kindly to being second guessed. In the end Sandy won. She was seated with a number of well-to-do American business people.

The wedding went off without a hitch. The memories of the lavish event would remain in the guest's mind for quite some time. Sandy would stay on for a day or so at the King's request. Then a decision needed to be made as where she would locate until word was received from Langley.

Chapter 12

Serge arrived at Heathrow airport Monday evening via the private jet Jacob arranged for him. The plan was to spend a day or two in London to get his bearings. He had yet to inform his relatives of the state of his health. An officer met the aircraft and quickly cleared him through customs. To his surprise, there was a gentleman standing beside an automobile on the tarmac near the aircraft. The man had a cultivated demeanor, well dressed, balding with a grayish goatee.

"Good day Mr. Thompson," he welcomed him as he opened the vehicle's door. Then he continued, "Mr. McGinnis asked if I would be available to meet you and make sure you arrive at your destination safely."

"Thank you," Serge said as he offered his hand.

"Oliver White," the man shook his hand. "Please to meet you."

"Well Mr. Thompson, where can I take you?" He asked.

"I'm not sure," Serge answered. "My thought was that I would spend a day or two here in

London. To be honest I wasn't convinced of my plans until we were landing. I guess I will call around to see what accommodations might be available."

"If you don't mind me meddling, I could make a call and reserve a room at a lovely Inn that I am familiar with," Oliver offered.

"That is very kind of you, thank you."

At that Mr. White dialed the number. Arrangements were confirmed for a suite, a quaint, but luxurious little Inn close to London's main amenities. He had recommended these lodgings to a number of people. All had been pleased with his choice.

They began to drive. Nothing much was being said. Serge wasn't upset with Jacob's intrusiveness. As independent as he was, there was something soothing about knowing you had a guardian angel looking out for you.

"Mr. White, how long have you known Jacob," Serge asked breaking the silence.

"Quite some time now," he answered. "I met Mr. McGinnis and his wife Hanna a few years before her passing."

"Oh, so you knew Hanna?"

"Yes I did. She was an extraordinarily brave woman," he replied.

"That she was. I really don't believe Jacob has ever fully recovered from his loss."

"One never recovers. Life goes on, yes. But we must reserve inner space, for those memories are never lost. We owe it to our love ones who have moved on," Mr. White told him.

Serge nodded but didn't respond to what he had heard. Speaking about death, his mind became preoccupied by his own situation. There was one other thing on his mind. He was trying to recall why he had a faint recollection of the name belonging to the man steering the car. He was positive the name was familiar but knew he hadn't met him before. Serge would have remembered his face. No, it was the name. Best way to find out is to pose the question, he thought.

"Oliver, your name seems to ring a bell. Have we met before?"

"I don't believe we have," he responded.

"Yes, I don't recall meeting you either. It's your name," he told him.

"Well, Mr. Thompson, I'm not one to follow horse racing and I haven't been in contact with Jacob very often since Hanna moved on. It may be possible you overheard him mention my name," he explained.

"You're probably right," he agreed.

The remainder of the ride was mostly a quiet one. They made some small talk about London, the weather. During the drive the name recognition continued to gnaw at Serge.

***

When David arrived home there was post-it note stuck to the door of his suite. It was a scribble from Jacob saying only I need to see you now. David was entertained by this. This powerful businessman could have called, texted or have his assistant contact him. But no, he had walked all the way upstairs to stick a note on the door.

David tossed his bag through the door then went downstairs in search of his father-in-law. He first checked the office which he found to be empty. Next would be the kitchen. Success, there he was standing at the refrigerator chugalugging a tall glass of cold milk.

"Never too old for a cold glass of moo," he said sporting a white mustache as he placed the empty glass in the sink.

He then walked by David waving him on, "come, we need to talk."

They made their way to the office. Jacob took a seat at his desk. David sat in one of the two chairs facing him, remaining silent. It was out of the ordinary to be asked to meet outside their predetermined times. Most subjects could wait until then. This must be of some importance so David did not feel the need for idle talk. He would leave the floor open to Jacob. On a normal evening the man would have been fast asleep by now.

"Son, I have some disturbing news," he started.

David's heart skipped a beat or two. He could not recall being addressed by this man as son. This wasn't going to be good.

"David," he paused, "while you were in California this weekend Serge paid me a visit. He has tendered his resignation. I have accepted it."

"I don't understand. You can't," David was confused but was immediately waved off by his boss.

"Yes I can and I did. David it's difficult to

discuss, but Serge recently learned he has terminal cancer. He left this morning for England. He would like to spend the remainder of his days with his family." Jacob took a deep breath than said, "David, he's not coming back."

With that the room stayed silent. David noticed his father-in-law's eyes had glossed over. He was having a rough time with this.

"Listen, as tough as this is, we must move on. Serge's last order of business was to make me promise to promote Renée as head trainer," he informed his son-in-law.

David remained silent trying to decipher what he was hearing.

"He feels she has prepared herself for this day. She proved that to all of us this past weekend. I tend to agree with him. Do you?"

"Well, this is a tough decision. I would appreciate a day or so to weigh our options," he was hesitating on giving the request his blessing.

His head was fogged by the events that took place the past two days and it wasn't the racing. This would mean an even closer working relationship with Renée. Promoting her would mean the two traveling together quite often. They would repeatedly find themselves sharing the same hotel floor. She had worked hard, earned her day in the spotlight. Could they, no, could he be professional enough not to hold her back because of his inability to refrain from his urges. Of course she should be advanced. He always said the job would be hers. She was an asset to his team.

"David, do you agree," Jacob broke his line of

thought. "Am I not seeing the whole picture? Is there something I need to know here?"

However heavyhearted the news of Serge was, he expected David to jump at the chance of handing the reigns over to Renée. He always spoke so highly of her. The hesitation left him a bit bewildered.

"No, no," replied David. "It's a lot to take in. I didn't see any of this coming. And yes, Renée is the only one that can fill his boots."

"Good I'm glad we see eye to eye on it," answering, but silently implying the decision wasn't up for debate.

"Now to change the subject, have you heard from my daughter? I'm sure she communicates with you a great deal more than she does with me."

"Yes, I did talk to her earlier today. She mentioned something has come up that may delay her return. I expect to learn more tomorrow when she calls. I will fill you in as soon as I know," he relayed the conversation he had with his wife.

"Why does that not surprise me? David I hope you keep us in the winning circle. I am going to need to purchase a new aircraft sooner than expected. She is going to wear out my current one."

"Will do," he stood. "I'll meet with Renée in the morning to inform her of the promotion."

They bid each other goodnight and retired for the evening.

David's life just became more complicated than it was this time last week.

***

Serge arrived at the Inn. They parked the car and made their way into the lobby. There was no desk. Patrons were ushered into a small office to complete their registration in private. It reminded him of a small library. One full wall was covered with books. The Inn did not provide televisions in the room but one could be entertained for a quite some time if they enjoyed reading. Serge's registration consisted of an older well dressed lady welcoming him with a handshake then handing him the room keys. He soon learned the lack of paper work was due to Mr. McGinnis taking care of the cost in advance.

As they were being escorted to the room, both carrying one of his two traveling bags it dawned on him. The library jogged his memory. He waited until they were alone in the room.

"Mr. Thompson, please give me a call if there is anything I can do for you. Feel free to contact me day or night," he said bidding a goodnight.

"Oliver, I now recall why I had recognized your name," stopping him on his way out. "You're a doctor. Not just a doctor. You're a renowned cancer specialist. I remember standing in front of my physician's bookcase reading the titles of his vast collection of books relating to cancer. If my memory serves me correctly, you were the author of a number of those publications."

"Well, I've been found out."

"You must be the oncologist that took care of Hanna. I recall Jacob bringing her to England for treatments," he continued.

"Yes, you are correct," Oliver began to explain. "I did treat Hanna. Unfortunately I wasn't able to save her. If I had the technology available to me today back then, I believe she might still be with us."

"Did Jacob inform you about my condition?"

"Jacob and I developed a relationship when I was taking care of his wife. When he asked if I could meet you, I agreed. He did mention your condition, but I would have agreed even if you weren't dealing with this illness," he told Serge.

"Thank you. My condition is terminal so I have come home to spend my last days with my family who I have put on the back burner for the most part of my life. There is no cure for me. I just have to accept it and make peace with myself."

"That may be true, but you will need someone to oversee your medication. I would be more than willing to offer my services. If you wouldn't mind, I could have your files transferred to my office tomorrow. I would like to have a look at them," he inquired.

"With all due respect doctor, I don't believe anymore can be done. I just need to bide my time."

"We have made tremendous inroads with the disease. We can extend people's lives much longer now. You need a doctor from this country. What would it hurt to utilize my services? It's on the house," he said trying to convince him to okay the file transfer.

"Ok, I will agree to it. Doctor I have been preparing myself for the end so I do not wish to be given any false hope. I'm not looking to extend my life for a few months if I have to spend them in bed or a hospital."

"I understand. I can only recommend as I do to all my patients. Our research is progressing at such a rapid pace that the longer one can hold on the better the chance they will be around for the cure," he explained.

With that the doctor pulled out a consent form from his inside pocket. He handed it along with a pen for Serge to sign. Serge smiled knowing full well Jacob had set this whole occurrence in gear. He signed and returned the paper to the doctor.

"You came quite prepared," he said.

"Preparation is tomorrow's success."

They made arrangements to meet at the doctor's office the day after next. This would provide time to review the files. Although Serge was prepared for his maker, human nature sways us to hold onto any glimmer of hope.

***

The next morning David went about his daily routine. Not comfortable with the authority's progress with regards to the fire, in addition to his regular duties, he began making some informal inquiries. Knowing a small number of people working in the fire fighting field, he had enough contacts to begin his own quiet, under the table, investigation.

Subconsciously he was finding everything and anything to do that morning, delaying the discussion he needed to have with Renée. As far as the staff was concerned Serge was away on business. His phone rang.

"David, last night we did not discuss reimbursement for Renée's new position. I'm not sure what you have told her but I want her to receive the equivalent of Serge's income," it was Jacob tying up loose ends before handing the details over to Brooklyn.

"Jacob, I think that's generous. That would make her an instant millionaire. I'm not sure I agree," he explained startled by the fact the salary hadn't even crossed his mind. "I believe we should ease her into a pay scale of that level."

"Is she not going to have the same responsibilities as he did? Over the past few years you have spoken so highly of her. I was of the opinion that she was ready for the job at hand."

"She is," was all he had.

"Then pay her," Jacob wasn't going to argue the fact. "By the way, how did she take the news?"

"I haven't had the chance to talk to her yet. I was planning on speaking to her this afternoon."

"Odd, I would have thought that would have topped your list of priorities," he said with what David thought was a suspicious mannerism to the comment.

"I'm busy Jacob. I will get together with her later. Was there anything else?"

"Drop me a text when you hear from Sandy." he hung up.

David leaned back in the old office chair in the office, lunchroom or storage room whatever one might call it. Deciding he had procrastinated long enough for one day, he took a deep breath then dialed Renée's number.

"Oui, David," she answered on the first ring.

"Can you come down to the lunchroom? There is something we need to discuss."

"Now?" she questioned him.

"I would appreciate it."

"I just saddled up for a training session," letting him know she was about to give one of their horses a run on the track.

"Give the ride to someone else, this is important."

"Okay, I'll be right there," she gave in.

Renée's heart rate rose to a higher tempo. Seldom did her boss display urgency for a meeting. She made arrangements for one of the junior trainers to put the horse through its paces. While making her way to the office she was stopped a few times by staff members. With Serge not there her work load increased substantially. Eventually she arrived to find David sitting behind the scrubby desk looking rather agitated, heart rate up a few more notches.

"Please shut the door Renée," he said.

"Okay," she shrugged.

She did as he asked. He was acting out of character. The only thing going through her mind was, please don't let this get personal.

"Please sit down Renée," he directed her.

"Is there something wrong?"

"Yes," he stopped not knowing how to initiate the conversation

"Renée I'm not sure how to begin here, so let me just jump right into it." He forged ahead, "after discussions with my father-in-law last night we have made a decision to promote you to lead trainer."

She didn't reply. She sat there in shock. Before saying anything she needed to make sure of what he was saying.

"Your want me to take Serge's job?"

"Yes that is what I'm saying," he answered her.

She had heard correctly. All of a sudden her face reddened. Her blood pressure began to boil. She was furious, ready to storm out of the room and never return.

"How dare you," she began. "I really thought we could deal with this past weekend like two adults. When will I learn? Every time I let my guard down, bang, someone slaps me in the head."

Renée stood up preparing to leave presuming the offer was related to their indiscretions. She didn't want or expect a payoff for sharing his bed.

"You don't waste any time do you. I cannot be bought David. You need to start making your decisions using your head, not with what's below your belt. I never would have taken you for being a person like that, serves me right."

"Renée," he tried to continue the explanation, "you don't understand, it's not what you think."

"I'm good at what I do. But I will not sleep my way to the top. I'm so disgusted with you right now."

"Renée, please here me out," he tried once more.

She turned towards the door. That was it she was leaving. He got up and made a quick move to block her. He stood between her and the exit.

"Get out of my way," she demanded.

"No, you need to hear me out."

"I've heard enough," she tried to push her way by him. "You will have my resignation on your desk in the morning. I can't do this. I'm going home."

David stood his ground. She became physical and began to shove him. She worked herself into a frenzy. He didn't budge. She bent her arms in front of him and started to bang the side of her fists on his chest. He let her work out her frustrations. Slowly David put his arms around her and held her tight. Before long, her resistance subsided until she was near motionless. Overwhelmed by the assumption of being rewarded for the past couple of days, she laid her head on his chest and began to cry. It was so out of character for the tough little French girl. He continued to console her until she was calm.

David anticipated an emotional reaction from her, but he hadn't touched on the topic expected to bring it on. It hadn't occurred to him the promotion would be construed as recompense. He knew it was his fault and that he should have gone about the explanation differently. As it turns out the news about Serge should have been the first item discussed. The difficulty was he again was delaying having to tell her. It was going to break her heart. These situations were not his forte. He waited a couple of minutes then removed one of his arms from her. Next he locked the door. It would be best for all if no one entered the room at the moment.

"Renée, this isn't what you think. I need you to sit down and hear me out. Please," he told her.

She was no longer resisting him. She was spent.

David helped her to the chair.

"Renée, I apologize I've gone about this the wrong way. Please bear with me for a couple of minutes. We would like to promote you to head trainer because while we were away Serge met with Jacob to hand in his resignation. He is no longer with us. Actually he has returned to England."

"That doesn't make any sense David," she said.

"I know it's hard to accept but it is what has happened."

"I need to talk to him. I'm sure he'll come back. Whatever the problem, I'm sure we can convince him to return." She didn't want to believe what she was hearing.

"Renée, he is not coming back," he paused. She wasn't going to take this easily. "This is not easy Renée," he took a deep breath, "Serge has cancer, it's terminal."

"Cancer?" she repeated.

"Yes the doctors have given him only a few months," he continued to explain. "He flew home this morning, choosing to spend the remainder of his days with his family."

Renée didn't utter a word. Tears began to roll down her cheeks. She covered her face with her hands. No longer weeping or producing tears of anger, she was full out crying. The actuality of passing on the news got the better of him as his eyes began to water. No words were spoken. They sat there in silence each trying to contain their emotions. The sensitivity of knowing they would soon lose a good friend, combined with the realization of the complications they had introduced into their lives, got the best of them. Their feelings were being torn apart in multiple directions. The silence of the room gave way to the weeping for the next few minutes.

***

Sandy had made her decision. She would remain in Europe until the mission was completed. It was estimated Langley would require two days of surveillance in preparation. One or two days for her to rendezvous with a Special Force back-up team. The actual rescue would only require a few hours. So her estimate was another week before she returned home. She would then be adamant about staying a month or two at home void of distractions. Her husband was owed as much. Absence makes the heart grow fonder, true enough she thought. However, extended periods of separation may lead one into the temptations of his or her surroundings, if it already hasn't.

Until the call came, she would remain at the Palace. The days would consist of her fine tuning her physical conditioning. It also allowed her time to make a few inquiries pertaining to the fire. If there was a European connection, one of her sources may have an insight to it. First things first, she had to contact David and break the news of the extension of her stay. Then she would notify her pilots of the plan.

She dialed her husband's number. It rang a number of times until she heard the robotic voice prompting her to please leave a message. She didn't. She dialed the pilots who answered on the first ring and advised them of the delay. Once again, she tried David with the same result. This time she sent a text asking him to give her a call. It was unlike him not to answer. Over the years there had been numerous calls such as this. She could count on one hand how many times he didn't pick up.

David forced himself to regain his composure. He heard the cell ring but wasn't in the right frame of mind to talk to his wife. The presumption was her calling to advise him that the trip was going to take longer than originally thought. Most of her recent calls were of the same manner.

"Renée, are you okay?" he asked. "We need to talk about this. Find a way to move on. As callous as that may seem we have a large organization to operate."

"I'll be fine," she replied as she wiped her face with a tissue David handed her.

"David, I believe the proper move here is for you to find a trainer with more experience than I have. There are some good people out there who have been in this game much longer than I have."

"Renée, Jacob and I have already made our decision. It is you we want to lead us into the future."

"But David," she began.

David cut her off, "Renée, do you trust Serge's judgment?" he asked her.

"Unconditionally, he is the best there is. I admire the man. I would have jumped off a cliff if he asked," making her point.

"His last request of Jacob was that the stable be

led by you. He insisted. We believe he wouldn't have left until we agreed," he informed her. "But he didn't have to delay his departure as Jacob and I wholeheartedly agree with him. You're who we want. You're the one Serge insisted we hand the reins to. Please accept this position."

She sat still needing a minute or so to get a grip on the proposal. She was confident that she would succeed. After all she was nurtured by the best in the business. Scared yes, but hesitating because of lack of skill, no, she would do it.

"I will do it. You won't hide on me," she asked. "I need you around, promise."

"I'll be right at your side," he said trying to support her.

"We can do this," she asked, "can't we?"

"Yes we can."

"We need to get back to work soon. I would like to call a staff meeting when we are done here to inform every one of the changes we have put in place. We also need to advise them about Serge's condition," he said trying to get back to business.

"Oh my god," Renée raised her voice as she realized her initial reaction was way off base. "David I'm so sorry. I thought, well you know. I'm so sorry for doubting you. You deserve better. Can you forgive me? I promise it will never happen again."

"Nothing to forgive, your response was quite normal. I should be the one apologizing for not explaining properly from the beginning. Now let's get to the work at hand. Are you going to be okay?"

"Oui, I'll be fine. We should talk to the staff now

before they get the news second-hand," she had composed herself.

"We will but first we need to discuss your salary which comes along with the job. Now keep in mind you are now in charge of the most recognized thoroughbred stable in the country," he was trying to justify the pay and ease the shock factor it brought with it. "So, Jacob feels you should be the highest paid trainer in the country. I agree. He insists you be paid the equivalent of what Serge made."

"David my current pay is sufficient," she was content with her current sixty thousand dollar a year. It was more than other assistant trainers she was acquainted with made.

"It's not up for debate. Your annual salary is now," he paused, "one million dollars."

Chapter 13

The call came in two days. She spent a good portion of the past forty-eight hours feeling out contacts in Europe and the Middle East. Her hope was to establish a lead or two with regards to the fire before embarking on the assignment. Some trees were rattled and the feeling was some pertinent information was close at hand. That would have to wait.

Fyad had not planned a honeymoon until later in the year. During their recent conversations he took an interest in the method used in the fire. He'd seen it before. Anyone taking aim at Sandy or her family would also have to answer to him. He accumulated a vast network of acquaintances being that he was in charge of his country's security and intelligence. At his insistence Sandy shared her thoughts so he could continue investigating while she was absent.

Fyad arranged for a military helicopter to transport Sandy to a USA aircraft carrier situated in the Mediterranean. She would rendezvous with a Special Forces team who would act as her backup. The Director insisted she be transported to the ship by an American aircraft. It was paramount to the success of the operation that her identity was not to be revealed to anyone, including the elite team. So she argued the fact that the less time she was observable by American personnel the less chance of being found out. Fyad knew she was involved in covert operations but never once asked about them, or who she reported to.

They flew in a MI-24 Hind helicopter. A Russian made machine which was Fyad's preference. It was nicknamed the fling tank, an attack aircraft that could inflict grave damage but also carry up to eight passengers. Being an accomplished pilot he took control of the flight, assisted by one of his most trusted colleagues. Sandy was the only other person aboard. It was a quiet ride.

On the ship which was preparing for the landing, tensions were mounting. This was sacred ground. Authorization being given to land an aircraft operated by a foreign country on the carrier was uncharted waters for the Captain and crew. It was a top secret mission and no questions would be asked out loud. The orders were clear. Transfer the subject from one aircraft to one of their own, where the person would accompany the Elite Team on a mission. Follow orders. Ask no questions.

ETA was one hour. In a small room Commander Miller stood in front of his Special Forces team. The squad consisted of five men including him. Each of the members specialized in a certain aspect of the group. All were smaller men. Not your weight lifting type. But that shouldn't fool anyone who had the unfortunate pleasure of challenging them in combat. These guys were deadly skilled machines. They could take down men twice their size within seconds with little effort. The five men were the best of the best, which made it all that more curious to the Commander as to why they hadn't been instructed to carry out the operation on their own rather than being designated as back up. He learned earlier in his career that an order was an order. They must be followed exactly as given. Any variation in them would most certainly jeopardize lives. Instructions filtered down on a need to know basis.

"Gentleman, in one hour we will escort our cargo to the location on your GPS. At which point we will drop him into hostile territory for a solo recovery of an American hostage. We will then retreat until we receive one of two orders," he began going over the orders.

The men sat heads down in silence intently listening. These guys thrived on action. They would jump into a volcano if ordered to.

"This is a recovery operation. Our cargo will extract a hostage being held one mile from the drop point. Once notified, we will return to rendezvous with them. If the retrieval fails our second order is to penetrate the location and retrieve our cargo. The attack will be aggressive utilizing whatever force deemed necessary," he took a short pause then continued. "If required to do so, our solo task here gentlemen is to rescue only our cargo at all costs. That is our one and only responsibility. If our cargo is returned with so much as a scratch on him we have failed our duty. We have been ordered not to speak to our cargo. He will not respond to us."

The assumption was it would be a male they were about to transport and provide back up. There were no Special Forces females.

"I do not have the answer to the obvious question. Why not just send us in. We are the Corps d'elite. We are not privy to the reasons. The directive for this op has come from as high as it gets. It's extremely secretive," he informed them. "Gentlemen, pray for the best and prepare for the worst. We board in one half hour."

Similar to a sports team they gathered in a circle extended their fists to connect in the middle. They gave each other a quick jab then went about their groundwork. Each had his own pre-ritual preparation.

Fyad was ten minutes out when he radioed the ship. He had been given a clearance code for landing. This was an awkward moment for him and the Americans. His country was not at odds with the United States. The two counties tolerated each other. He was not a fan. Distrust towards them festered inside him. There was an arrogance portrayed by them towards the Middle East. At least that is what he felt. But, this was for Sandy. That was his first and foremost concern.

On the other side of the coin, the Captain of the aircraft carrier was ordered to allow the landing, once confirming the clearance code. He knew it was from a foreign country, but not which one. He had put the ship on General Quarters alert. All on board were readied for battle.

Fyad received his authorization to land. As they approached he was being signaled as to where to set down. A spiteful thought crossed his mind. With one click of my thumb I could sink the carrier. He continued with the approach as instructed.

The mere sight of this helicopter was intimidating enough. Add to the equation that it was being flown by pilots from an unknown Middle East country. All on board were on edge.

The landing was accomplished as planned. Fyad sat the aircraft down just long enough for Sandy to disembark. As she walked away from the helicopter with her head down she stopped and turned to see Fyad peering at her through the side window. His expression was one of unease and distaste from sitting on the carrier. She gave the slightest of nods indicating she was fine. He lifted off into the darkest of the night. The landing on the deck of the carrier took less than two minutes. Once the aircraft was out of sight the tensions were eased, but the ship remained on full alert.

Sandy made her way to the waiting helicopter. The rotor blades were already in motion spinning faster with each turn. The team was positioned inside. The instant she climbed aboard, the chopper was in the air. Nothing was said. She was dressed in camouflage battle fatigues, sporting a full balaclava over her face completely shielding her from recognition. Her eyes were covered by a pair of goggles. Sandy looked similar to the team in size so it was unlikely that she would be identified as being a woman. If absolutely necessary she would reveal herself. These men held an extremely high security clearance and would keep her identity under wraps to their death. Since her face was so recognizable, it was best to keep it isolated from them.

She immediately knew the commander as Blake. He was one of the eleven who achieved the distinction of making it through that vicious year of training, as did Sandy and Fyad. There were originally thirty. Sandy had instructed him in the martial arts. She realized right there and then that her boss had provided her with a team lead by one of the best in the world. A reassuring feeling going into a not so friendly foreign country, where almost certainly one or more of their citizens would lose their life.

They lifted off. During the flight the men checked and rechecked their gear. They fine tuned their arsenal in preparation of being directed into battle. Sandy rested her head against the vibrating wall. She closed her eyes, tuned out noise of the flight and began to visualize her actions once on the ground. No words were or would be spoken. All aboard knew their duties, so there was no need for any verbal instructions.

They arrived at their destination within an hour. It was a remote, unpopulated piece of land, centered between two small hills where they anticipated not being seen or heard. The pilot positioned the helicopter stationary approximately fifty feet above the ground. Two of the men heaved a rope out the opened door. The commander gave Sandy a tap on the shoulder to indicate all was a go. She moved to the door giving the men a thumbs up. Turning to Blake she clenched her fists, touching them together with both pinkies pointing upward. The no conversation order now made sense to him. She had given him the sign of the final eleven. Only those knew the meaning. Eleven, together, always. Six of those were not Americans. He knew the whereabouts of two others and heard another had passed away. So that left Sandy. This made being designated as backup tolerable.

She rappelled to the ground. The rope was quickly retrieved and the aircraft disappeared into the darkness. It was early morning. Her attack on the compound would take place at 4 am. It was a well known fact that at this time of day human senses were in their most fatigued state.

Her destination was one mile to the north. She calculated the journey would take a half hour. The rugged landscape allowed for a brisk but cautionary walk. The moon shone brightly allowing her to navigate the unfamiliar terrain without the use of night vision goggles.

The selected route would keep her far away from any road or path utilized for vehicles. The further she kept herself from them, the less chance there was of being noticed. However, this increased the chance of an encounter with a dangerous animal. The land was home to a variety of venomous snakes and spiders. It was habitat to leopards, cheetahs and a number of other treacherous species that could quickly ruin one's day.

The trek was uneventful. Everything seemed to be sleeping at this time of morning. Sandy eased herself onto a small ridge overlooking the smallish sized building believed to be housing the hostage. She put on her night vision goggles allowing for a clearer view of the property. It was a rundown square, white building. The fencing around it provided little in the way of security. It had been dismantled in a number of spots. The structure was nonthreatening. It was similar to many of the dwellings in the area, so it fit right in. Nothing about it would invoke any undue attention. She knew that was exactly the point of selecting a location such as this. They traded off security for being inconspicuous. Smart move she thought. One would not require gates and fences to protect them if no one ever knew they existed.

Sandy's position was well concealed. A person would have to be within a few feet before they even remotely had a chance of discovering her unless they had the technology she carried with her. The small unit she took out of her packsack was a computer tablet. Not your ordinary tablet. This unit had a direct link to a CIA satellite launched in recent years, identified as a state of the art weather monitor. That was the official word from NASA.

At this minute, one of the satellite's cameras was locked onto the subject building. What it was revealing to Sandy via the tablet was a look inside the structure. By way of infrared sensors, the satellite was able to locate any living creature within its view. Its advanced technology allowed it to not only sense heat patches, but read blood pressure, heart rates, then analyze the size of the subject. Sandy was staring at the result of this information. Her screen showed five men of relatively average size and one woman. The figures generated on her screen were close to accurate. The facial features would not be exact but their stature should be similar. The characters on the screen resembled those in a video game.

The unsettling aspect of the surveillance was confirming her initial suspicions. All the occupants within the compound seemed to be moving freely. There were no guards posted on the exterior. Her best deduction from what she was viewing was that three of the inhabitants stationary, most likely asleep. The female and other two were moving from room to room. It was uncommon for a hostage to have such freedom.

It was time. No more analyzing. In a crouching position, she made her way over then down the small ridge. Every inch of her body was on high alert as she methodically approached the outer portion of the fence line, following it to the opening closest to the structure's side entrance doorway. Once at the downed section she stopped.

Still in a tuck position, Sandy stayed stationary for five minutes, listening attentively. She was able to slow her heart rate below forty beats per minute. Her goal was to achieve a meditative state of mind prior to her attack. Her awareness was at its utmost state at this point. Battles cannot be won by brawn alone.

There was no one outside. She moved stealthily to the door designated for entry. It was unlocked. The room behind it was darkened but she could still see well enough to maneuver her way to the hallway. She stopped and listened. Not a sound.

Sandy quickly and ever so quietly made her way to the room occupied by the three men who she believed to be resting. Strategically, the correct maneuver was to take out the three suspected of sleeping, easy prey. That would only leave two plus the hostage. She slowly turned the door handle. In a near to the ground position, she entered. There lay three averaged size men, fully clothed. All were out for the count. Each one was snoring. The advantage of surprise remained in her favor. One was on a single bed, the other two slept in the lower and upper of a bunk bed.

She would neutralize the man in the single bed first. If the person on the top bunk was awakened and made any attempt to descend on her, he would be dead before his feet hit the floor. The one on the bottom bed would be met with a kick that would render him unconscious, should he make a move at her.

Sandy approached to the head of the bed. With a forearm and her opposite hand she locked onto his head. In a split second he lay there with a broken neck. He was dead. No fuss, no sound.

Next, her focus shifted to the bottom bunk. The other two remained fast asleep. There was no movement whatsoever. She leaned to her right grabbing a knife from her boot. One so sharp it would put those seen on the shopping channel to shame. Again she approached from the head of the bed. With one swift move she pushed his head into the pillow exposing his neck which she sliced wide open from one end to the other. He twitched a couple of times before she stabbed him directly in the heart. Two done, one left.

Her undertakings roused the man in the top bunk. He became restless. Sandy squatted on top of the dead man in the bottom bunk. She saw a hand rest on the first step of the beds ladder. The man was beginning to comb the room in search of the rustling which awakened him. The body in the single bed looked fast asleep. Sandy knew it was a matter of seconds before she would be noticed. She grabbed her HK45CT, the handgun of choice. It was fitted with a suppressor. Holding the gun tight to the mattress above her she rapidly fired two bullets. Leaping off the bed holding her weapon with two hands one more bullet was discharged hitting the subject directly between the eyes. The first two shots had seriously injured him, the third ended his life.

All the intelligence gathered within the past couple of days and her satellite images supported the certainty of three persons remaining in the building. At least one was thought to be the hostage. Again, her concern was the free movement being afforded to all six occupants. Something was not adding up, but she felt prepared no matter how it played out.

After gently opening the door she heard a faint sound of a conversation taking place at the far end of the house. She eased her way down the hallway towards the voices. It sounded like a male and a female having a heated argument. The woman seemed to have the predominate voice. It appeared as if she was instructing the man who was disagreeing.

Sandy hid in an open doorway listening carefully to ascertain that all was clear before she proceeded any further. The only light and sound was coming from the room housing the two having the conversation. A third person could not be heard. His whereabouts was not known. This did not sit well with her. Knowledge of your opponent's whereabouts and vulnerabilities were paramount to the successful outcome of a battle.

Slowly, she eased herself forward not making a sound. Each movement was deliberate. At the end of each step she positioned herself for an attack from front or rear. This became significant as she felt the gun barrel pressed against the back of her head.

"Don't even blink," a voice precisely instructed her.

"Good, now raise your arms above your head," he continued.

Sandy followed the instructions to a tee. When a person has a semiautomatic rifle puncturing your skull, the best reaction is no reaction. At least for the initial contact until the circumstances can be analyzed.

"Now slowly walk forward. One false move, you lose a head. I would prefer to behead you right now, but I'm sure my superior will want to have a chat with you before I kill you," he uttered.

She began to move forward towards the lit room. She was confident the people inside the room were not aware of what was happening in the hallway or they would have been assisting with her capture. She decided to take out the man holding the gun to her head at the next open doorway, planning to force him into an empty space so any noise would be muffled from the remaining two.

It was three steps ahead. From the placement of the barrel of the gun she estimated her assailant's height was equal to hers. If taller the barrel would have been placed higher and if shorter if would have been lower. The projection of his voice supported her assessment. He spoke English with very little accent. His voice had a restrained quality to it. Not panicked or forced. He was applying a moderate pressure of the gun to her head. In summary, she was confident he was a well trained militant of a Middle East country with a medium height and weight. She hadn't uttered a word yet, so there was no way he knew she was a woman. He would be a capable opponent. His drawback would be his placidity of the situation. This told her he felt superior, a fatal mistake on his part. One should never take their opponent for granted. Your life depended on it. Unfortunately for him, he would never have the chance to practice the lesson he was about to learn.

When they were adjacent to the doorway, she was relieved it was open. With lightning speed she simultaneously crouched, instantaneously making herself two feet shorter while backing into the assailant before he could think of reacting. She threw her arms up grabbing and pushing the rifle upwards. There was little resistance as her actions were so swift. Knowing he would hold onto the gun for dear life, she pulled the gun forward flipping him over her. She gained control of the weapon but not before a shot was discharged into the ceiling. With the butt of the gun's handle, she hit him squarely in the face twice. He was down and out but not dead. She tossed the rifle into the empty room and then quickly dragged him into it. With her side weapon she put two bullets in his body, one in the head and one in the chest. One shot would have sufficed, but he pissed her off. Now he was dead.

Sandy immediately heard commotion down the hallway. A man ran right by the room not even stopping to look in. He must have thought the attack was at the other end of the house. Sandy rolled into the passage and put three shots into his back. He staggered for about two feet then dropped face first onto the concrete floor. That left the hostage. The building was now absolutely silent.

Sandy's alertness was peaking. The suspected hostage's free rein of the facility was disturbing. Sandy quickly made her way back into the open doorway. Something was wrong. If someone was being held against their will, now would be the time for them to be screaming at the top of their lungs. But there was nothing.

After reloading her weapon with a fresh clip, she exited the room, this time easing herself towards the light reflecting out at the end of the hall. There was still no activity. With preciseness to every movement she came to the opening. Once again she crouched with her back flat against the wall, her gun to her side. The plan was to enter the room in a squat position firing off a couple of rounds into the ceiling. If the hostage was alone in the room this would force her to take cover. A gun being fired into a room has a tendency to make one want to hide. If it was not a friendly on the other side, the discharge of the weapon would buy her a split second to evaluate the space. An enemy would aim a shot at the head or heart so being crouched bettered the chance of the bullets missing high.

She made her move. She leaped in, rolled twice while getting off two quick shots into the ceiling then to cover behind a chair. There was no return fire. Calmly sitting behind a desk was Emily Wilson, the missing CIA agent.

Sandy's suspicions were justified. She could not believe what she was witnessing. The agent was not bound in any way. Perched behind three laptop computers with her hands in the air in a surrendering position, she was unconcerned with her intruder. The gunfire did not faze her. Actually Emily had a smile on her face.

"Wow, it only took you a year to find me. I must have been a high priority on someone's recovery list," she said sarcastically. "You know I really wanted to believe that we were the greatest organization in the world."

Sandy said nothing, just kept her cover and listened with her gun zeroed in at Emily's head. She needed to hear more to decipher the kidnapped agent's state of mind. Also it was best not to expose that she was a female at this point. Was she saving someone here or listening to an enemy.

"The whole world hates the great USA. Not me, I risked my life every single day for the good of the country. I mastered the art of deception for the country. I killed for the country. Now a year after I've been to hell and back, you come in here all guns a blazing to save me," she ranted. "Let me see your face. I want to know who my savior is, who I

212

owe my life to. Who was foolish enough to risk their own life to save reporter Emily Wilson after just one year of her going missing. This must be a record for the mighty CIA to recover an asset."

Now it was time to speak. Maybe if she knew it was another woman with the gun trained on her it might help defuse the situation.

"Emily I'm here now. That's all that should count. Stop feeling sorry for yourself. You were trained for this. A year, ten years, we would have continued to search for you, no matter how long it took. Let's get you home," she asserted, without altering her aim at Emily's forehead.

"How things change in a year," Emily stated. "They send a female to save me. They've finally seen the light."

"We need to move now. This was noisier than planned. We have an extraction team waiting."

"I want to see your face," Emily demanded.

"That's not going to happen. Not now, not ever, let's move."

"I'm not going anywhere," she answered.

"Yes you are. You're leaving here with me, now."

"The United States is no longer my home. This is where I belong. The people here need me. We are the way of the future. Your country thinks they can force their arrogant style of life onto all others. Well I've learned the truth. I will remain," she explained. "Please leave. Tell them I am no longer part of their world."

"Emily, I am not leaving here without you. You have gone through a difficult year. We can work all

213

this out at home."

Listening to her talk solidified Sandy's suspicions. They had gotten to her. She had been turned. By way of torture, they brainwashed her to believe in their god, their mission. She had been taught to deal with such rhetoric, but she was now broken.

"No I'm staying. I will not kill you if you leave peacefully. My choices have been made," she responded.

"If you haven't noticed, I'm the one pointing the gun. You're in no position to be negotiating," Sandy pointed out.

Emily's hands were visible but one was moving ever so slightly downwards towards the back edge of the desk. Sandy knew exactly what she was attempting to do. Under the desk there would be an alarm button, similar to the ones a bank teller would have to alert the police in case of a robbery. The difference was this particular one was a detonation button. It would be protected by a small dome casing to avoid pressing it in error. The building was rigged with explosives. This was a common practice by an extremist group. They were willing to die for their cause. If captured, everything within the compound would be destroyed by the explosion. The remains left to rot in the ashes. Sandy couldn't let it happen. Emily may have a death wish, but she didn't.

"Don't move your hands another inch," she demanded while her finger tensed the trigger.

Emily's arm froze in mid air after dropping halfway towards the desk. All that the disgruntled

CIA agent required was another second or two and the place would be destroyed. Emily stared at Sandy. It was a blank stare. There was nothing behind it. Sandy had seen it before. The agent, journalist, had come to terms with her own death. Believing it was for the greater cause. She was lost. There was no bringing her back, at least at the present time. If Sandy could maneuver her out of the building and bring her to safety, there was a chance the Agency's people may be able to save her. Although Sandy didn't really believe it, she was too far gone.

"We will die together then. You will join me on my next journey. We will be welcomed by our lord," Emily rambled.

Her hand made a quick move for the button. Sandy pulled the trigger. One shot, one bullet to the chest forcing her backwards away from the detonator. Emily was dead. Sandy was the last person standing. She had failed the rescue. Her subject was beyond the point of no return. The death was a necessity.

As soon as the trigger was squeezed the mission's purpose switched from the extraction of a hostage, to intelligence gathering. Sandy stood silent for a minute until confident there were no others that needed to be dealt with. After all, this exercise generated a noise level in excess of what the initial plan of attack called for.

Once sure she was the sole breathing individual in the building, she gathered up the three laptops that lay on the small desk. The blood on each would remain only to be removed once DNA testing was completed. With the computers in her knapsack she scanned the remainder of the office. After retrieving a few files it was decision time. Should she carry the former CIA agent's body or leave her sitting in the chair where, by choice, her life came to an abrupt end. The verdict, she would remain as is. There seem to be no benefit to lugging her to the rendezvous area. The order would be to bury her at sea without anyone being advised of her identity. Sandy decided the complex must be destroyed to erase all intelligence that may be hidden within its walls. The country she was in dealt with bombs being detonated on a daily basis. The assumption would be the aggression was one terrorist group's attack on another. Within hours multiple radical groups would be seeking credit for the act. No investigation would be initiated. The Government was ill equipped for inquiries every time this happened. Technically the country was always at war.

She retrieved explosive devises out of her bag which Fyad provided her with. Each had a tiny microchip implanted into it. A sticky substance on the bottom allowed it to be placed on any surface in a timely manner. The first two were placed under and on the back of Emily's chair. She would not be recognizable. Also from her bag she took out a set of vials to take blood samples from all her victims. Emily was first. She would repeat this as she came across each of the other victims.

Sandy continued her exit positioning each one of the explosives on what she believed to be supporting walls. The combination of her devices along with the internal ones was sufficient to destroy any evidence which remained. It would most certainly be a noticeable explosion, but it was the only alternative. Nothing could remain intact.

Leaving the building she entered into the remaining hour of the night's darkness. Retracing her route step by step through the treeless rolling terrain in the direction of the rendezvous point she found herself that much further away from the sparse civilization.

Counting her strides she did not have to estimate when the ideal distance was achieved. At that point she took out what looked to be a GPS unit. It required a fingerprint, then a voice recognition prompt. The signal was bounced off a NASA controlled satellite. It could not be traced. She held her thumb to the screen, raised it to her face and briefly spoke into it. Still casually walking like someone out for a Sunday stroll without a care in the world, she pressed one more button on the phone. The sky behind her lit up like a New Year's Eve celebration. She continued her casual walk without breaking a stride or looking back. There would be little if anything but ashes to sift through. The other dwellings in the area were far enough away not to sustain any major damage.

"Holy shit," the commander yelled, "go, go, go, go, go!"

The team remained aboard the helicopter on higher ground ten miles from the target ready to deploy within seconds. They were expecting contact authorizing recovery of their cargo. Radio communication was the preferred method. Well I guess this works, the Commander thought.

The caterwaul of the propellers increased at a rapid speed. In no time flat they were airborne. They flew low and fast. Their destination was the drop off point. This time they did not hover above. They landed. The team disembarked one covering the front and one covering the rear of the chopper. The other three began their way towards the fireball in a V shape formation. They only gained a few yards when over the ridge Sandy appeared. She held her arms high until they were satisfied with her identity. Not wanting to speak she gave a thumbs up as the team whisked her into the aircraft. The only words spoken came from the Commander inquiring if she was all right after pointing out the blood on her face covering. She hadn't noticed an injury. It was most likely a splatter of blood from one of her victims. She shrugged it off nodding her assurance of being okay.

The team was to escort her to the airport in Saudi Arabia where her jet was still stationed. Her pilots had been instructed to have the plane prepped and ready for takeoff at an instant. The flight was uneventful. The commander reported the successful recovery of the unknown agent. Nothing else was or would be asked of him as Sandy would be briefing the Director in private once she landed.

They touched down close to the hanger in which her plane was parked. One of her pilots could be seen in the brightly lit building standing at the base of the aircraft's stairs. Sandy stepped out as did all members of the team. Once she was safely on the ground they were to return to the aircraft carrier.

She acknowledged them with a nod. With a quick jerk of her head she beckoned the Commander to follow her. He motioned to his men, directing them to stay with the helicopter.

Soon he was walking alongside of her. Once inside the hanger out of sight from the remainder of the team, she abruptly stopped, lifted the balaclava to her forehead so only he could see her face.

"Blake," she said exposing her identity to him.

"Breaker, I had a feeling."

She knew he would shield her involvement. Together they had been to hell and back. All who participated in that year long exercise were unwavering in their commitment to the sensitivity of each other's assignments.

"Breaker," he repeated calling her again by the nickname she acquired from snapping too many bones of her comrades during training. "I wasn't aware of your active duty."

The statement did not require a reply. She answered with a shrug of her shoulders. The success of the subterranean assignments this A-list group was engaged in demanded unparalleled secrecy. Their lives depended on it.

"What happened back there?" He asked.

"She wasn't who we thought she was."

"Okay." He accepted her decisions without questions.

"How have you been Blake?"

"I'm fine," not being accustomed to small talk his answer was brief.

"Have you married, have family?"

"No."

"Why?"

"I think you know the answer to that Sandy."

"We're not normal, are we Blake?"

"Depends on whose eyes you're looking through," he replied softening his voice knowing only a select few would understand the complexities of her choices.

"You've seem to have found a balance in your life," he hinted. "You appear to be handling your public life gracefully. Your newsworthiness is hard to miss."

"Yea, well, I think we both know better."

"Sandy we knew what we were signing up for."

"Oh don't get me wrong. I understand that. It's just that I was naïve enough to think I could live a somewhat ordinary life on the other side."

"I hope you do succeed," he encouraged her. "Can I ask you a question?"

"Of course," she let her guard.

"Why don't you get out? Go home. Be with your family. You don't need this anymore. You have nothing to prove. There are enough of us to take care of this end. Life's too short Breaker. Go live it."

"I'd love to, but I don't think I can," she answered then went on. "There is something wrong with us Blake. We're not right. I just killed six people and I've never felt more alive. I could go kill another six without feeling anything. We changed the day we went into training, didn't we."

"You're right. But you didn't kill six people, you killed six enemies. It takes a few of us off centered warhorses to safeguard our country so our citizens continue to live what most describe as a normal life."

"You still believe in what we do?" she asked but knew the answer.

"I do, do you?"

"You know I do."

With that she unzipped her fatigues. Under it she wore a black workout outfit like one would wear to a yoga class. She handed it along with all her weapons to Blake, keeping only the packsack.

"Thank you Blake. It was comforting knowing you had my back. Take care."

"It was good to see you. Think about what I said. Your man is lucky to have you. Don't lose him. Go home. Stay home," he was sincere with his advice.

They gave each other a hug. He turned to make his way back to the men and helicopter. Before he exited the hanger she called out.

"Blake," she paused until he looked back, "I don't think I can do that."

Chapter 14

"Hello," David answered his phone.

"David, sorry it took so long to get back to you. My buddy is not known for his quick responses."

"Not a problem. I appreciate your getting back to me. Can he shed any light on the fire?"

"He's encountered the method of burning before and just happens to be on leave for the next couple of weeks, so I suggested we get together for a beer. He'll be in town tomorrow. Are you free?"

David was talking to his friend Richard, another retired hockey player who now lived in the same area. They always played on opposite teams but became friends during the off season's golf tournaments and fundraisers. Once retired from professional sports Richard went on to become a fireman. David was reaching out to him as part of his own investigation. As it turns out, Richard did the same and asked one of his military buddy's who was an explosive specialist.

"I'm there," jumping at the chance to pick the expert's brain.

"Where's good for you?" asked Richard.

David wasn't a connoisseur of drinking establishments but he was comfortable with the favorite pit stop of the local racing community.

"Do you know The Dead Heat Bar and Grill, how about around seven?"

"We will see you then," Richard agreed.

Across the pond Dr. Oliver White sat at his desk. Serge repeated the routine of sitting opposite a physician anticipating the chilliness one felt when receiving news that your body is retiring.

"Serge, how have you been feeling?"

"Tired," was all he could think of to explain his present state.

"That's understandable. Serge I've run a number of tests and scenarios. I'll cut to the chase. Your doctors in the States were exact in their diagnosis. The thing is, we are in the early experimental stages of a new treatment. It is not a cure. What we hope for is an extension of life for those at your point. All I'm asking of you is that you give this some thought. We never know what's in store for us on the horizon."

"I'm in. What do you need me to do," a brief visit with long lost family members had changed his mind. He made the decision to fight this with every ounce of energy his body would provide.

"I'm happy to hear that. I need you here seven to ten days each month. During your stay you will be administered a combination of treatments. It will not be a cake walk. This is not going be easy. More rough times than not. But I will do everything in my power to turn your months into years. All expenses have been covered by Mr. McGinnis. We will arrange for all your transportation."

"When do we start," was the only reply he could phantom.

"How about right now," the doctor brought the conversation to an end.

Jacob McGinnis sat at his desk with the telephone held to his ear listening to FBI Director Taylor summarize their findings on the fire.

"We know what was used. We know who manufactured the material. We have determined the intent of the fire was to distract someone within your organization. It was not meant to inflict mass destruction. The persons who we believe are the distributors of the devise are tight lipped. Their clients demand discreetness. It is not illegal to sell these items so we can't ask our counterparts to utilize the strong arm of the law to apply pressure," she took a second to catch her breath.

Jacob didn't say a word. It was not his time to speak. His inquiries would come once Madison had finished her explanation.

"We have all the answers except for the final part of the puzzle, who. Every time we close in on the answers it feels like a brick wall appears. The CIA doesn't appear to be very helpful. Jacob, are you still there."

"Go on," he urged her while acknowledging his presence at the other end of the receiver.

"I will keep the file active but I need you to do some searching within your organization. Somehow, someone within it is involved," she paused. "However, there is one characteristic of this probe that doesn't sit well with me."

"What would that be, Miss Director," he inquired.

"The number of inquiries our resources have received. Others have been probing around the same areas we have. Actually it's not just the number of inquires. One in particular is bothersome, from an American. Funny thing is Jacob," she paused, "the questioning happened a month prior to the fire."

Renée dismounted from a horse she was putting through its paces when she felt a tap on the shoulder.

"Hey stranger," she heard while turning to be greeted by a smiling Gabriela.

"Bonjour, comment allez-vous?" Renée asked in French.

"Je suis bien," her answer also came in Renée's mother tongue.

"I'm so sorry that I didn't get a chance to congratulate you on kicking my butt at the finish line. You guys ran a great race," referring to coming second to Renée's horse at the recent California race. "I had another race to ride, then one thing led to another."

"Thank you. You rode a spectacular race yourself. We got lucky."

"If the rumors are true, it would seem more congratulations are in order for the new head trainer of the McGinnis Stables."

"Thanks again. This whole thing came all of a sudden. It took me by surprise. I've been pinching myself every few minutes."

"Oh you're awake. You deserve this Renée. The impact you have on these animals is special. You deserve all the accolades coming your way. I would be proud to ride any of your horses," she praised her.

"Well, thank you. David will be happy to hear that. We will work on it."

"After we're done for the day we should meet up for a drink to celebrate."

"That sounds great, but I'm too busy Gabriela."

"That's too bad," she said sounding disappointed.

"What about tomorrow night," Renée proposed.

"Perfect."

"Say seven, seven-thirtyish then," she said. "The Dead Heat work for you?"

"It's a date, seven-thirty at the Dead Heat."

Sandy was nestled into one of the aircraft's luxurious tan colored leather chairs after washing up and changing into her daily clothing. The instructions to the pilots were to prepare their pre-flight checks but not request take off authorization until she gave them the okay. Two uninterrupted telephone conversations needed to take place before blasting down the runway. The first call would be to David, the second to Langley.

She dialed her husband. He picked up.

"My long lost wife has surfaced," he answered in a slightly taunting mannerism.

"I'm doing fine thank you, and you," was her come back.

"Sandy, I'm joking. When are you coming home?"

"I'll be there in a couple of days. Clear your calendar. I'm so looking forward to the two of us

226

kicking back and doing nothing."

"That sounds good but I need to travel to Florida this weekend. We're purchasing a couple of horses. It's our only race free weekend in the near future. I'm all yours when we get back. That is if you don't fly off again,"

"Who's we?" she asked.

"What do you mean?"

"You said when we get back."

"Renée and I," confirming what she already knew or what he thought she would take for granted.

"Oh."

"You seemed surprised. I don't make a purchase without my trainer."

"Isn't that what we pay Serge for?"

"Oh boy, you don't know. We haven't talked since I got back. I thought you might have had a conversation with your father."

"What should I know David," she asked.

"So much has been going on here. When I arrived home your father informed me Serge resigned. Sandy, he's dying. He has been diagnosed with terminal cancer. He left at the beginning of the week to spend his last days with his family in Britain."

"Why didn't you tell me this earlier?"

"Are you serious? I have been trying to call you back for two days now. So don't put this on me," he answered sounding agitated.

"I'm sorry. This is so sad."

"You haven't answered my calls or text and I have been up to my ears trying to get everything in order here. He left some big shoes to fill."

"David, I will be home as soon as I can. I can help out until you find someone to replace him. I'm certain the majority of trainers out there will be jumping at the opportunity."

"Sandy, we have already filled the position."

"With whom?" she asked.

"Renée."

"Renée," she repeated.

"Yes Renée."

"Are you sure my father is on board with this. She seems an unlikely choice. She's so young. So little experience compared to others we know of. I would have thought Daddy preferred someone he could showcase as the best in the world."

"Sandy, she is the best. Young yes, but I've never seen anyone who can interact with the kids as well as her," referring to the horses.

"I'm not sure I agree," she was hesitant to give her stamp of approval.

David wasn't sure if she disfavored this appointment based on skill or concern related to the personal side of it. The guilt manifesting itself within him bred paranoia.

"The decision has been finalized. Actually this was your father's idea. He instructed me to promote her. It was Serge's last request of your father. He wanted to leave what he built in the hands of someone he had complete trust in. Renée was the only candidate. Serge felt there was no one else as capable," he explained.

"We can talk more when we both end up being under the same roof at the same time."

228

"I will be home in two days. Try to make your Florida trip as short as possible."

David's voice shifted into a low almost whispery tone, "Sandy I don't understand how your work can keep you away for so long. How can so many last minute things pop up?"

"I promise I will keep my travels to a minimum from now on. We will make this work," she tried to reassure him that their relationship was in good shape. "David, I love you so much."

They said their goodbyes.

Sandy dialed the Director. It didn't get through the first ring before it was answered. There would be no greeting, no niceties. He was upset. The explosion put him in a position of an explanation to the president without having the pleasure of first being briefed of the events.

"Let me get this straight. The reason I was led to believe you wouldn't even disturb the flies on the wall was because you planned to obliterate the whole damn compound and everything in it," he rumbled. "I knew this was bad idea. If we had sent in a convoy of tanks it would have been quieter. I've been back and forth on the phone with the President for the past hour trying to soothe him. You should have contacted me earlier. God, young lady you make me angry."

"Just feel free to let me know when you want me to explain what transpired," she said sounding a tad smug.

"How about five hours ago. We have been appeasing their ambassador for hours peddling the story that it was a coincident that our helicopter was on a training mission in the same area."

"Did he buy in," she inquired.

"So far, but that doesn't excuse your choices."

There was a lull in the conversation. Sandy went silent waiting for permission to defend her actions. Christopher Young had unloaded his frustration that had been building up for the past few hours. Deep within him, he knew Sandy would have a perfectly just explanation. She was as smart as they got. He knew once he heard her out that he would be in agreement and that her decisions would be validated. That didn't ease his state of exasperation brought on by the situation.

"Please, be my guest, enlighten me," he broke the silence.

"She turned. Not only crossing sides. She was leading this particular cell."

"So why not bring her in. There is a possibility she went under without authorization. There may have been a chance she was still with us," offering an alternative rationalization about his former agent.

"Christopher you know she would be sitting right next to me if there was even the slightest chance of that being the case."

"Fine then, but why blow the hell out of the place?"

"It was rigged. She was prepared to give her life for the cause. I was a fraction of a second away from joining her. She forced my hand. I felt my decision was the cleanest out."

"When can I expect you?"

"As soon as we are cleared for takeoff, I'll be on my way."

"Change your flight plan. You're to go directly to Washington. The President wants to sit in on the debriefing. Secret service will clear any landing delays. They will deliver you to the White House."

"I'll see you tomorrow then," was her reply. "By the way I have a present for you."

"Sandy this wasn't supposed to be a holiday where you suck up to your boss with a souvenir."

"Oh it wasn't, although the temperature was on the warm side. I commandeered their three laptops. I'm sure it will make for good reading."

The Director's mouth began to salivate at the thought of what secrets were hidden within them. He hadn't revealed to Sandy the significance of the data recovered from her success at the Palace. A number of attacks directed at the USA had been quashed, saving a lot of lives. Her importance to the Agency was unparalleled.

"Boss," she said. "No plans for the near future. I need to stay home for a while."

They disconnected. She authorized the crew to take off.

David's next call was to Renée. He asked her to meet with him.

"We need to travel to Florida this upcoming weekend."

"Okay," she lengthened the letter k coxing David to expand his news.

"We have an opportunity to buy two horses that have been in our sights for some time now."

"When do we leave?" was her response.

She was taking her new position seriously. If this was required of her then she was in. It was a pleasant surprise. Another trip with David so soon was unexpected.

"We should fly out Friday evening. Can you arrange it?"

"I'm all yours," immediately regretting her words.

Chapter 15

Fyad being good to his word found himself in Germany following up on a lead with regards to the fire. He, along with one of his men made a visit to this quaint little artisan's boutique. It was the home of master craftsman Albrecht Friedman. Many of the world's affluent were in possession of his pieces. The crafters forte was clock making. Few knew he was also the brainchild of a number of devices utilized in unethical ways.

Fyad was recognized before the door behind him closed. His assistant remained outside to inform anyone trying to enter the store that it was temporarily closed.

"Your Highness," Albrecht greeted his visitor.

Fyad's father's Palace showcased a vast array of this man's work. The dollar value was astronomical. So when the Prince paid a visit, all else became secondary.

"Albrecht, how nice it is to see you, my friend. With all the money we have spent in your wonderful little shop it's no wonder you have not retired yet. You should be sitting on some yacht rocking on the waves of the Mediterranean."

"I get more pleasure serving my faithful customers such as you."

"Why thank you."

"Fyad this is an unexpected visit. What is it I can do for you," he inquired.

"Right to the point, I appreciate that," Fayd had little time for small talk.

"Albrecht, today I will not be making an acquisition. I am trying to resolve a family matter and I understand you may be able to guide me in the right direction," he began his explanation of the visit.

"I doubt my knowledge can assist someone of your resources. But yes, Fyad, anything you ask of me I would be honored to help."

"Excellent. Recently, someone who I consider to be family unfortunately experienced a fire which was purposely set. It is my understanding the method with which it was set is one known as the Alley Marble Burn."

"I'm not sure how I can be of assistance with this," he uttered anxiously.

Fyad took notice, "Albrecht were you aware of the history of the beloved toy we all cherished as kids called Marbles."

There was no answer.

"Are you familiar with the excavation of Mohenjo-daro?" he didn't wait for a response. "During this work back in the eighteen hundreds marbles were discovered. They have been referenced to in Roman and Egypt writings. But, the interesting fact is marbles, the toy as we know them and you know Albrecht and I so enjoyed playing with them as a child, were developed in Germany."

Albrecht was a smart man. He knew exactly where the conversation was heading. Holding his reply until the story was complete was the wise thing to do. He was being enlightened by a powerful and dangerous man about a subject he knew well.

"Yes that's correct. A German glassblower invented something called Marble Scissors in 1846. This device is used to blow marbles. I would have thought you would know this as in addition to your mastery in clock making, you have graced us with some of the finest glass artwork."

"Fyad I am versed in this craftsmanship. What I don't understand is how this all relates to me," he asked.

"Please my dear friend let me continue. With today's technology one only has to tap a few keys. Overseeing my country's resources empowers my ability to acquire enormous amounts of intelligence. You know what the amusing part of this story is Albrecht?" Again he didn't allow time for a reply.

"I entered your name into a public website by the name of Ancestry.com. What I learned made complete sense. It did not surprise me in the least. Your great, great, great grandfather was that Master Glass Blower."

"You're correct. This skill was handed down four generations."

"I want to know the identity of the ones responsible for the fire," he ended the story.

"Fyad, how would I know that?"

"Utilizing a more sophisticated method of

gathering information I am quite certain you are the inventor of the Alley Marble Burn," he cut to the chase. "Now before you respond to my request, please grasp the importance of this tragic attack which was directed at someone I care dearly about. You would also be as upset as I if anyone harmed someone within your family. Albrecht, I believe you have knowledge of the persons responsible for this fire?"

"Fyad I had nothing to do with your friend's misfortune or do I know who bears the blame."

"I think you do know. You may not realize it yet, but I trust I can jog your memory," his words were meant to frighten the man.

"Yes, in the past I have fabricated these components, but it has been years. I am certainly not connected to what you speak about."

"Albrecht, I trust what you are telling me is true. On the other hand I believe there is information you possess that will be of assistance to me. I want the names of all the tradesmen who can produce this system," he demanded. Then he asked, "Within the past year has anyone made a similar inquiry?"

"Fyad my clientele rely on my discreetness. If it were found out that I provided their identities to others I would be ruined."

"You have no choice my friend. I wish there was another way but you are either going to provide me with what I have asked for or you will speak with my friend," he nodded to the man guarding the storefront.

"Please Fyad don't do this, please."

"I have little time to spare," he motioned again to

the door.

Albrecht knew that if he hoped to live until day's end it would be necessary to supply the Prince with some information, maybe not all, nonetheless some.

Fyad turned for the door.

"Wait. About a month or so ago, a man and young lady paid me a visit. I was quizzed on this very subject. They knew of my prior involvement in making the device and were looking at making a purchase. Their names were never mentioned and I did not reveal or acknowledge anything to them."

"What do you remember of them?"

"The man was an American average size and the women French, petite. She stood outside exactly where your companion is standing. They spoke to each other in French as he entered. He was the only one to speak to me but I did get a look at her when the door was opened. What I found odd was she wore a scarf wrapped around her face. It was a cooler day so I presumed she was keeping herself warm. On the other hand it seems more likely she was concealing her identity. However it is not for me to judge my customers."

"As you will recall my resources are far reaching. I am aware your computer contains pictures of every person who has entered your establishment. There are hidden cameras within the shop snapping pictures from every conceivable angle. They are automatically downloaded. We need to go look at them and you will identify these people to me."

There was no sense in resisting. They made their way to a small office. The craftsman sat then tapped a few keys on his computer. He narrowed his search to the week, then the day, then the hour which the visit had taken place. Within seconds the two faces appeared on the screen.

"Fyad please tell no one of what you have learned here," he pleaded.

"You are a good man. I wish no harm to you and your family. Please print this for me. Provide me with the identity of those making the device and our visit will be concluded. We will never speak of this again. Your secret will be safe with me."

Fyad left the store in possession of what he had come for. With his head he nodded instructions for his companion to re-enter the store while he proceeded to their automobile. His colleague was already in the shop.

"Sir, I gave your Highness all he asked for," terrified in the presence of the soldier.

"And we wish to thank you. What I would like to make clear is that no one will hear of our visit here today."

With that he took three photographs out of the inside pocket of his suit jacket. One was of Albrecht's wife, the other two of his children. He held them close enough that the craftsman could view them.

"Please, please do not harm my family. I have told Fyad the truth. I gave him everything he asked for."

"We have faith in you. We believe you to be trustworthy. But if we learn you have misinformed us or alerted anyone to our visit, you will wish you hadn't," while saying this he made reference to the pictures.

"I vow the truth has been told today. It will not be alluded to ever again."

"Good, you have a wonderful day Mr. Friedman."

He returned to the car. Getting into the driver's seat he waited for instructions from his superior.

"Let's return to the airport. For now I wish to return home. We will run face recognition on this man," he held out the picture. "You will find his location. Then you are to follow him. I want to know everything about him. Where he lives, where he works, when he sleeps, what he eats, wife, girlfriend, I want to know him like I know my family. If he was responsible for this, he will pay dearly. Run the girl. With her face being covered I doubt we will get a hit. Her eyes were clear. We may get lucky."

Jacob McGinnis with his head bowed, knelt at his wife's monument. He spent a great deal of time there yet recently the visits were more frequent. When he finished he would feel calmed, as if she had resolved his troubles.

He began to speak to her in a hushed voice. "Hanna, I pray your journey has been a peaceful one. I truly wish you were still here with me. The void in my heart grows larger each day I do not have you by my side. Isn't it ironic that our family, with all its wealth and power was unable to alter the outcome of your passing? Now one of our best friends is facing the same destiny."

He went silent for a few minutes to gather his thoughts. Jacob was tired. There had been too many nights spent alone. He felt like lying down beside her tombstone, falling asleep and maybe, just maybe he would wake up to find her by his side.

"It's not fair. I'm the one who should have met his fate. Being the ruthless one of the family, crushing others to advance my interests, which are meaningless without the ones you love by your side. Sandy is what I live for now. So much of her life is spent in harm's way. I pray each night that she will return safely. If I should lose her I could not find the will to go on. Please Hanna, speak with her while she sleeps. Tell her it is time for her to surrender to a life without being encompassed by the endangerments of the world."

Again he gathered his thoughts. Whether or not he was connecting with the afterlife of his wife was irrelevant. The console of these moments served as his antidote.

"People spend a whole lifetime searching for the reason of their being when it is staring them in the face all along. When you wake every morning beside the one you love, that is what life is all about. Money, power, poverty doesn't change that. The sad thing is too many lose the love of their life before they realize it."

He stood, "Hanna, please forgive me for my wrongs. I love you. You will always be my true love."

Jacob kissed the inside of his fingers then touched the marble monument. He made his way down the path. When the opening of the trail was reached, he turned the opposite direction of the ranch house heading towards the stables. The only occupants of the barn this time of night were the horses. As he made his way through, he patted the animals as they curiously stuck their neck out of the stalls. After spending time with the animals he exited at the other end, again not in the direction of his home. A log chalet style dwelling was the only building in his sight. It was nestled among the Kentucky trees blurred by an evening mist. Not a huge structure but beautifully designed. It featured a wraparound porch housing carved wooden chairs along with a small swinging bench. Its vaulted ceiling showcased the dominating windows on its face.

Three or four times he stopped, hesitated, turned back towards his own residence but then continued approaching the wooden structure. When he reached the stairs he once again paused.

Jacob was frequently in the company of the most powerful men in the world without so much as a hint of being the slightest bit uncomfortable. Still here he stood, second guessing himself, feeling uncommonly awkward. He took a deep breath, stepped up the porch and took one more breath before knocking on the door. There was no noticeable reaction from within. He knocked again, still nothing. Second guessing his intentions he turned towards the stairs. As he placed his foot on the second stair the door opened.

A hand on the railing provided balance, enabling him to look back at the entrance. What he saw was his assistant Brooklyn centered in the opening, outlined by the bright yellowish light escaping from the interior. With her two arms crossed at her breast holding a white terrycloth housecoat together she glowed like an angel. The professional office persona had vanished. Her long dark hair fell onto her shoulders. The glasses and touch of makeup she wore by the day were gone. Almost speaking out loud he said to himself my god she is gorgeous.

"Jacob, is there something wrong," she asked with a concerning look.

"No, no, I was just, just out for a walk and saw that your light was on. I thought I would drop by and say hello. I should go. I'm sorry if I have disturbed you. Forgive me."

Brooklyn had not experienced this clumsiness in her boss. He was in control of every aspect of his business, never faltering. She had never heard him double taking on words. And yet, here he stood rambling like a teenager caught putting a baseball through the neighbor's window. Something was wrong.

"Jacob, would like to come in for a coffee?"

"Oh, no Brooklyn, I shouldn't have bothered you. This was a mistake. I should get back to the house," the jitteriness continued.

"The Jacob McGinnis I know does not knock on someone's door unless there is a well defined reason," she said with a pleasant smile.

"Please, I insist, come in," she stepped inside with her back leaning on the opened door. "Please, I would venture to say you may require something a tad stronger than coffee," they both chuckled.

As they made their way into the living area, Jacob looked around the place. It was an impressive structure. Brooklyn did wonders with the interior decoration. The home was immaculately clean.

"I haven't set foot in here since you took up residency. The place looks wonderful. I had forgotten how beautiful the building is."

Motioning to the couch she said, "Jacob please, what can I get you to drink?"

"Coffee would be perfect. Thank you."

The chalet was open concept. The entire main floor was visible from all angles. He watched her stand in the kitchen area preparing a coffee. On occasion she mixed his brew at their office so there was no need to ask how he liked it. The majority of time he took care of his own food and beverage needs. She was paid to take care of business.

Brooklyn handed her boss his drink then sat across from him on an identical couch.

"Jacob is there something bothering you. Would you like me to dress and head back to the office with you?"

"No, Brooklyn. There is no business on the agenda this evening. I was just hoping to find someone to chat with. I think I have a touch of cabin fever."

"Absolutely, what's on your mind? I'm all ears. Actually your visit is a pleasant surprise."

"I spent some time at Hanna's memorial this evening. For years now I discuss my feelings with her and come away from our conversations with the belief she in some way talked some sense into me, solve my problems," there was a pause.

He gave her a look that said sorry for laying this on you. "Jacob, go on," acknowledging that she was open to this dialogue.

"Lately I come away from these visits empty. It's like her spirit is no longer there, like she's gone, for good. I sense she has set me free. I've developed guilt with regards to this."

"Jacob may I," asking if he would care to hear her opinion. He nodded yes.

"Hanna left us a long time ago. Your love for her is undeniable. I believe the emotion you are experiencing is closure. The length of time it takes to arrive at that point differs for everyone. A part of your heart will always be engraved with her memory, as it should be. But, there comes a time, as insensitive as it may seem, one must move on. I believe the time has come for you to step out a bit more. Attend one of the many events you are invited to. You need something other than work. You need to begin socializing."

"I'm not sure I could do that," giving her an honest answer.

"It would do you a world of good."

"You're probably right. How can a person have everything that money can possibly purchase and end up feeling so alone? I always thought my life was so complete until recently. Sandy and David are rarely around. My visits to Hanna's memorial leave me empty."

"Jacob some of us spend our whole lives chasing success. As you might have noticed my social life is, well, nonexistent, so I have given the subject a great deal of thought. I believe what happens to those of us who are so career driven is we fall in love with being lonely. We mistakenly accept the fulfillment arrived from our achievements in lieu of what's really important. Having someone to share those special moments life provides. I refer to it as, love lonely."

He was listening and shook his head in agreement when he deciphered what she said.

Their conversation continued for another half hour. They discussed solemn topics along with exchanges that provided laughter. When Jacob announced it was time for him to leave, both thanked one another for an enjoyable time. Jacob was happy with his decision to knock on her door. On his walk home the realization of Brooklyn's social life was as nonexistent as his struck a chord with him. He liked her. Maybe the two should attempt their escape from a life of solitude together.

***

David arrived at the Dead Heat at six, an hour before the meeting. He was hungry, so he took a seat at the bar. The early arrival was planned soon after setting up the appointment. It had been far too long since he had the pleasure of biting into one of the establishment's famous juicy burgers. Also missed was the conversation with Sebastian and Leven, the retired jockeys who owned the bar. They were in the riding business a long time, so if you enjoyed horse racing, their stories were entertaining to say the least.

"Leven," Sebastian called out. "David here says if you're interested in winning another Kentucky Derby he will hook you up with a ride."

Leven approached the two men, "Thanks David,

I appreciate the offer. To tell you the truth I don't think I could even climb onto a horse nowadays, let alone make it out of the starting gate without falling off. When you get to be my age, getting out of bed is an achievement. It sucks to get old David."

"I think you're selling yourself short Leven. I'm sure you've got another Derby in you. Just give me a call. The ride is yours."

David's food arrived. The two entrepreneurs went about their duties. He savored each bite, washing it down with a frosted foamy draft. The hour flew by. Grabbing his beer he moved to an unoccupied table that would provide some privacy. As he sat, his guests came through the door. He waved them over.

"David, this is my buddy Hunter."

"Pleased to meet you," they shook hands.

"Richard thanks for taking the time to meet with me. Hunter I appreciate your joining us. I'm sure you have better things to do while on leave."

Hunter smiled and Richard responded, "Anything for you my friend."

They ordered drinks while making small talk mostly about hockey. The two ex players could go on forever about the game. David inquired about Hunter's background with the military. He was a Special Forces Explosive Ordnance Disposal (EOD) Specialist. It was a dangerous line of work which saved many lives. David had an immense amount of respect for all military personnel. These women and men were prepared to give the greatest sacrifice for the safety of their country.

"Hunter. Thank you for making our world a

better place to live in. I really do appreciate it."

David's admiration for soldiers was instilled in him from an early age. His father educated him on the importance of those who serve for us. Anytime his father had the occasion to meet someone who served, he would offer his hand and thank them. David continued the tradition with heartfelt sincerity.

Just as they were embarking on the discussion with regards to the stable fire, they were distracted by the giggling of two women entering the bar. There must have been quite the humorous joke exchanged prior to their entrance. A number of patrons joined the infectious chuckling of the newcomers. The ladies hadn't realized their entrance was so grand. When they did, they gave each other a small nudge while covering their mouths, leaving only their wide eyes of embarrassment visible.

"Oops, sorry," they said to a few people sitting close to the doorway.

It took a second or two for it to register with David that the two women were Renée and Gabriela. He felt a little offish by their surprise appearance. Uncertain why, yet it was uncomfortable. Common sense told him her presence should not be of any concern. She had as much right to be there as he did.

Hunter made a comment once he turned back from witnessing the commotion,

"They seem to be having fun. Not sure they look old enough to be in here though."

"Actually they are. One of them is my lead

trainer, Renée. The other is Gabriela D'Angelo, one of the country's premiere jockeys."

The men's focus shifted back to the reason for the get together.

The women took a table on the other side of the room. Renée sat with her back to the men. They were visible from Gabriela's vantage point although she hadn't taken notice.

Sebastian approached the girl's table sporting an ear to ear smile.

"You two know how to make an impressive entrance."

"Sorry Sebastian. We promise to behave," Gabriela pledged.

"No need to apologize. Laughter can be a wonderful remedy to our rigorist lifestyle. Please feel free to laugh the night away."

"Thank you," Renée said. "Can we get a pitcher?"

Off he went to fill their order.

"Well that was a bit embarrassing," Gabriela joked.

"No more stories tonight about your wardrobe malfunction. In particular the one's broadcast on television," Renée warned.

"As I said, if I thought my Jodhpur's were going to split open," referring to her riding breeches, "I would have worn underwear."

"Stop it," Renée whispered trying to avoid another outburst of laughter.

The conversation toned down by the time their draft arrived. They talked mostly about the activities at the race track. A few minutes into their stay

Gabriela glanced around the room looking for someone mentioned in the exchange hoping to clarify something. That is when she took notice of David sitting in the back of the room.

"Renée, don't turn around, it would look too obvious. Your boss is here. He's seated along the back wall with two other men."

"David," she asked.

"Yes, of course David. How many bosses do you have?"

"Shit."

"What's wrong?"

"I didn't know he was going to be here tonight," Renée explained.

"Renée you're allowed a life outside work. He doesn't control you twenty-four-seven."

"I know. It's a little awkward, that's all. You're right, let's order some food I'm starving."

David, Hunter and Richard settled into the subject matter which was the reason for the meeting.

"Have you come across this method of arson before Hunter?" David questioned.

"No, I haven't. I've studied it. It was briefly touched on during our training. The technique is rarely used. It is extremely expensive for the minimal success it produces."

"Is there anything you could add to what we already know?"

"When Richard asked me to look into it, I made a couple of calls to some people outside the military who are well versed in this area. What I know is that the fire was started by a method referred to as a

Marble Burn. It was invented by a man in Germany. We don't believe he is still active in the manufacturing of it. There are however others with the skill who have continued the practice. A small computer chip is implanted into a tiny blown ball of glass, an alley or marble. When activated the chip heats up to a temperature which will ignite certain materials. In your case that was hay. It works similar to your stove top burners. Leave a dry cloth on it long enough it will go up in flames."

Sebastian interrupted the explanation by offering refills. All three nodded yes.

"Renée, we haven't seen much of each other since our trip to California. Seeing David reminds me of something I've been meaning to tell you. I don't think it's a big deal. But I thought you would like to know."

"What's that?"

"When I left your hotel room Saturday morning I noticed a man at the end of the hallway. I caught a glimpse of him before he disappeared into the stairwell. I've had a gut feeling it may have been David. I doubt that he saw me, but then again I hadn't looked up until I was almost at the elevator."

"You said he took the stairs instead of the elevator."

"Yes that's what it looked like."

"Shit."

"Is that your word of the day?"

"Sorry. Why didn't you tell me this before," Renée asked.

"As I said we really haven't talked much since then. Does he know about us?"

"No."

"Renée, I understand your expectations of our relationship. I'm okay with sex, drugs and rock 'n' roll. Well minus the drugs and rock 'n' roll. So I guess just sex. No emotional ties. Our time together is precious. But,"

"Gabriela, I don't want to do this right now. Let's enjoy the evening. No relation talk," Renée cut her off.

"That's not where I was going with this. I've accepted the way it is between us. What I was going to say is, be careful. David is your boss. He's married into a powerful family. You have everything going for you. A dream job, one you've worked so hard to achieve. Don't throw it away. He's married Renée. It's not worth it. Sandy and her father will crush you."

"Why in the world would you think I'm interested in David?"

"It's written all over your face. If I can see it, you can bet your bottom dollar Sandy will pick up on it."

"I'm not having an affair with my boss. I'll be fine. Thanks."

"Please be careful," Gabriela closed out the conversation.

Renée nodded yes.

Hunter continued explaining to the other two at the table about his findings. Most of what was being offered had already been brought to David's attention. There were aspects of the history and technical side of the procedure that he was finding interesting.

Summarizing his uncovering Hunter went on, "So let's say you wanted to rob a bank on the east side of a city. You strategically place these marbles on the west side. Preparation could be done weeks in advance. If one was found it would most likely end up in the trash. An hour or so before you require the diversion, you dial a number or input a code into a computer device, and there you go. Small fires start popping up all over the opposite side of town. A number of fire trucks are dispersed. A police unit for each fire to direct traffic and ambulances in case a first responder requires medical treatment. The depleted resources cause a delay in responding to your crime. Enough time for you to most likely get a clean get away. Or at least that's the theory," he paused allowing time for questions. There were none.

"The person that financed the fire had a great deal of disposable money. The placement of the marbles was amateurish. The loss of lives wasn't part of the plan. An educated guess says it was meant as a distraction. They wanted to either lure someone to the area of the fire, or keep someone from leaving. I would start reviewing the travel arrangements for those directly involved with the stable's operations. Concentrate on those whose plans needed to be altered. This might set you in the right direction. If damage was the sole reason for this, a gas can and match would have worked much better."

"Thank you Hunter," David appreciated the insight.

The explanation played in line with what the FBI

had concluded. He was starting to think this wasn't about the stable but something much bigger. It was also looking like the ones responsible may never be caught.

The chat reverted back to sports when David's phone rang. It was Sandy.

"Excuse me guys, it's Sandy," staying seated he leaned back and answered.

The other two remained leaning forward with their arms resting on the table. Richard took notice of a strange reaction made by his army buddy. When David excused himself, Hunter's body twitched, as one would do if they suddenly got a chill.

"What was that?" Richard questioned.

"What?"

"That shiver almost knocked you off your chair. You okay?"

"I'm fine. It just something David said."

Sandy was calling from an altitude of thirty five thousand feet. She wanted to inform her husband that she had one stop to make in the USA for a short presentation before arriving home. A repeat of her commitment to give this stay longevity was again interjected into the call.

"That's good news," he offered. "I'm leaving for Florida tomorrow afternoon. I'll be back on Sunday. Hope your home by then. Listen I've got go. I'm at the Dead Heat having a beer with the guys. We'll catch up in a couple of days."

He ended the call but before putting the phone back onto the table he sent Renée a text. It read, flight's at four, pick you up at one. He watched her look down to at her iPhone then his chimed with her reply, kk. The notification sounded again. This time it was Sandy, I love you. He answered with a smiley face, no words.

"Sorry again, my wife is on her way home from Europe. Did I say something to upset you?"

Hunter smiled, "I'm fine. I haven't heard the name Sandy in a long time. When I do I get a chill up my spin. Sorry David, it has nothing to do with your wife. It is part of a legend or rumor within the Special Forces community. No one even knows if it's actually true. I'm sure you guys have hockey stories that spread without really knowing if there is any accuracy to them."

"I'd like to hear more. Any story that could jolt a reaction like yours is worth a listen." David invited him to continue. "I don't get out with the guys much anymore. I'd like to hear it. What about you Richard?" who nodded yes.

"This isn't classified information, is it? You never know, it could be about my wife."

"It's not about your wife. If that were the case, you might want to sleep with your eyes open," Hunter added.

"A number of years ago it was said to be a joint, top secret training mission. It is common knowledge that members of any Elite Special Forces go through some of the most brutal training. This one however took it to a new level, one that seems too far-fetched to be true. It is rumored the United States along with a few of their allies selected a handful of their very best. I'm talking about the ones that train the trainers that train the trainers that train the trainers, the best of the best. We've heard that thirty to forty were invited into the program. Few within the military or government knew about the operation.

"Am I boring you yet," he enjoyed sharing tales like this even if there was a good possibility it was a myth. It excited him to think that this small society existed.

Both men urged him to continue.

"Okay, here's where it becomes a bit unbelievable. I'm not sure you're aware women are not permitted to be a member of a Special Forces unit. Recently they have been authorized to begin training for entry a few years down the road. But for now it is only males. Although it is said that one woman took part in this exercise. Her name or nick name or code name was alleged to be Sandy. Chances are it was not a female. It was more likely to be the name of one of the men.

"The covert program was said to be one year long. Apparently only eleven survived the duration of it. The remainder surrendered at various times. It is told the brutality of the mission was inhuman. The legendary participant called Sandy was one who endured the full term. He or she was the most feared.

"The level of clearance required to participate, was only issued to those entrusted in keeping the assignment within the group. We wouldn't be having this chat if it wasn't for one of the men who bailed early. He talks in his sleep. The men in his unit would wait for him to go to sleep then they would try to extract information from him. During

255

his many nightmares he would scream, no Sandy no, please Sandy no. In the morning the others would quiz him and he would categorically deny it."

Hunter took a breather. It felt to him like he was rambling. His listeners continued to be hanging on with interest so he would proceed. First a refill was in order. After a few good gulps, he carried on.

"It is believed the viciousness endured in their training was so extreme that no official documentation exists. The exercises were based on experiencing situations that might be encountered, such as water boarding. Each member was made to undergo this torture to acquire a firsthand understanding of its effects, should it be used if captured. It is a known fact that some carry the post traumatic stress associated with the procedure to their grave. They became experts in counter terrorism, explosives and every facet of warfare.

"Another exercise related to water was drowning. These soldiers could swim underwater longer than any record time found in a Guinness Book of World Records. The thought was if one knew the feeling of actually drowning they could learn to extend their time submerged until the last second. They were held submerged until loss of consciousness. Two divers would rush the body to the surface where CPR was performed in hopes of revival. If you wanted an insight on what you experience by death, this group would be the right ones to ask. When on a mission you would wonder if one of these guys was part of your platoon. The guy who talked in his sleep was quickly reassigned to a location where he sleeps alone."

It was time for a sip of beer. Hunter figured the guys would have had enough by now, but that wasn't the case.

"What would possess a person to endanger themselves this way," David stated.

"The goal was to make them superhuman. They couldn't be broken. Pain, torture, any form of physical or mental abuse wouldn't faze them. A couple of bullets to the head would be the only way to stop one. If in fact there is any truth to the whole story, these are the guys who are dispatched into solo covert operations."

"That's crazy."

"It is crazy David. Keep in mind they were already considered the finest in their respected fields. The eleven survivors became machines."

"And I thought our training was tough," David looked at Richard who nodded his agreement.

"Not as tough as what these guys underwent. The unit was stripped naked then left to survive in a rainforest. No food, no clothing, the only supply was an emergency beacon to be used in a life or death situation. If that call was made, the one responsible would be extracted from the group and sent packing.

"For fear of boring you I just want to wrap it up. We got on this topic because of the name Sandy. The one carrying this name Sandy, even if she was a woman, was the most feared. It is said that she was a master of Martial Arts. Her duties, besides participating alongside the others were to teach hand to hand combat. Now when I say that, we're not talking about your neighborhood Karate lesson. Apparently she could kill a man three times her size with one blow. At the end of the year the other remaining ten could do the same. Our sleep talker's nightmares were mostly related to this Sandy. The men did everything in their power not to be paired with her during the demonstrations. It was common for her partner to sustain broken bones, which would be reset the moment the sparing match was over. As legend has it, she was the scariest of the bunch.

"Now remember the only reason I can talk to you guys about this operation is because we don't actually know if it happened. The story has been floating around for years now and I'm sure it has been embellished. The sleep talker could have been referring to a bad relationship. We will most likely never know.

"One theory is the powers-to-be made the whole thing up so elite units felt more secure knowing one of these guys might be the guy in front of you. I do know each time I'm on a mission it is a comforting thought to think our commander may be one of the eleven. Although there was no way to identify one as they don't wear patches or anything to distinguish themselves from other officers. It's been hinted they got inked identically upon completion. No one but the eleven knows what the tat is.

"Well that's my bar tale of the evening. If you repeat what you've heard I'll have to kill you," breaking out into a good laugh he joked with the other two.

The three men sat for an hour or so making small

talk. It turned out to be an enjoyable evening for all. David missed the camaraderie of teammates which were part of his world since the age of five.

"I'm sorry I couldn't have been more helpful David," Hunter said as he stood with Richard preparing to leave.

"Don't be sorry. Your information will be very helpful. Thanks for taking the time to meet with me," they shook hands.

The two men exited the bar and hailed a cab. David remained at the table considering his transportation options. He hadn't planned on consuming as much beer as he did so driving was out of the question. His choice was to call a ranch hand to pick him up or take a taxi. Both options gave him the excuse to finish the pitcher on the table with one more mug of beer in it.

Once the glass was full with the final drink of the night, he looked over to the girls table. Gabriela sat alone. She caught his stare acknowledging him by raising her glass and smiling. He returned the offering with a nod.

His mind was preoccupied thinking about Hunters story. Could the Sandy be his Sandy? That was nuts. It couldn't have been. Her martial art training was a discipline not a profession. Although her recent display in New York made him the slightest bit curious. It had to be coincidence. He was so consumed by his speculation he hadn't noticed that someone was standing behind him.

"Bonjour cowboy, I was surprised to see you tonight," Renée joked.

Taking a detour on her return from the ladies

room, she came up behind him placing a hand on his shoulder.

Taken by surprise he looked up at her, "as I was to see you, with Gabriela."

"A girl's got to eat."

"How true," he agreed. "I was just about ready to call it a night," he stood.

"David, did you drive here?"

"Yes, but I think I will take a cab home. I'll send a couple of the guys to pick up my truck in the morning."

"Wait, I have an idea," she put one finger out asking him to sit tight for a minute.

Renée walked back to her table. Gabriela provided the ride tonight. They had nursed only one drink each during dinner so both were in a safe condition to drive.

"I was hoping the night wouldn't end so soon," Gabriela sounded disappointed.

"We will get together again. It's probably for the best as I have to get an early start in the morning."

They said their goodbyes. Renée then walked up to the bar to pay the tab with her credit card. Then she returned to her boss's table.

"Toss me your keys. I'll drive you home."

"It's okay Renée. I can call for a taxi."

"Keys," she insisted holding out her hand.

He complied. They found their way to the parking lot. It wasn't until they were outside did he realize the effects of the beer.

"How about I drive you to the ranch, keep the truck and pick you up tomorrow. Then we can head right to the airport."

"How about I just come home with you, we will find something to entertain us until I'm sober enough to drive."

"Bad idea boss, you're going home."

"Ok then, to the ranch we go."

There wasn't much of a conversation during the ride but they did make it. Renée dropped him off then drove the truck home with plans of picking him up in the morning.

Sandy's jet touched down at Washington Dulles International Airport. The aircraft had been given priority landing. Without delay they taxied to a private area where to Sandy's surprise sat a White House limousine with the Presidential official seal accompanied by two Secret Service Agents.

It wasn't long before they were passing through a private entrance at the White House. She was met by a Secret Service Agent who whisked her off to the Oval Office. He escorted her into the room then closed the door behind her. The President was seated at his desk while the Director paced the room.

The President looked up at her and began, "Young lady, your father is going to withdraw his generous support if I continue to authorize these outings of yours."

"Oh, I think you would survive without Daddy."

"You're probably right, but I like the old guy."

They both laughed. The Director wasn't in the mood to enjoy the chitchat. He wanted to get down to business.

"You look good Sandy. Sometime in the not so distant future we should find time for you to develop an exercise regimen for me. I'm not sure if I will commit to the diet thing, but a good workout routine I can do."

"Anytime Mr. President, you have my number."

"You're back to the formality of addressing me as Mr. President. What in the world am I to do with you?"

"I'm not sure, Mr. President."

"Well then, when we train together I expect us to be on a first name basis, deal?"

"Yes sir."

The Director had yet to crack a smile or say anything. He was only interested in jump starting the debriefing session as quickly as possible. The President was mindful of this but the process would begin when the President decided it would begin. This was his office, country, world, determining the order of business was solely his decision. Besides, he relished any opportunity for a little reminder to one of his senior staff members as to who was in charge.

"I suppose we should dispense with our little chat. We will discuss our plans in the near future. The Director seems to be quite anxious to hear about your assignment."

Her boss looked up at the two of them for the first time since she had entered the room and engaged in a conversation with the President. He'd been waiting for her to explain how a covert mission which was to stay highly secretive ended up with an explosion visible for miles.

"Sandy I want you to begin," he started but was interrupted by the President.

"Excuse me Christopher I would like to ask Sandy one question, if that is okay with you."

"Absolutely, Mr. President," annoyed by the interruption he handed the floor back to the Chief Commanding Officer.

"Sandy, do you believe your actions served in the best interest of the people of the United States of America."

"Yes."

"Well then Christopher that's good enough for me."

"Sir," the director responded seeking clarification as to whether the grilling had ended before starting.

Both Sandy and her boss were caught off guard expecting to occupy the Oval Office for a lengthy period of time deciphering her every move. That wasn't to be. The President had heard all he wanted to hear.

It was suggested the two of them relocate to the privacy of the White House War Room to remain in close proximity of the President should he be needed. Concealing his exasperation the Director of the CIA retreated to the designated chambers along with Sandy after the niceties of their goodbyes. He was thinking I could have done this in my own damn office. This isn't the only world issue on my plate. What the hell does that man think he is the only busy person in the nation? His facial expression might have hinted to his frustrations but verbalizing it was not an option.

Once secured in the bunker, the interrogation instantly commenced. They were alone. No recording or video being utilized. Two armed Marines stood guard outside the door. It would only be Sandy and the Director privy to the exchange.

"What the hell were you thinking, blowing the place to smithereens? This was supposed to be a simple in and out," the Director lectured.

"It was our only play."

"I should have sent in a unit."

"If you had, right now you would be sitting in your office calling their next of kin passing on condolences."

"Sandy, there are others quite as capable as you. They would have followed my orders."

"They would be dead. The structure was rigged with explosives. The cell was prepared to die for whatever godforsaken cause encompassed them. She knew I was alone which is why I'm here. Emily wanted to talk, rationalize the life she embraced and advocate her revolt," she paused. "I took her down a fraction of a second before she initiated an explosion. Hers would have left evidence of their existence, mine didn't."

"Do we have absolute proof of her identification?"

Sandy stood, unzipped the packsack and took out six vials of blood. Each with an attached sheet of paper containing descriptions of the person associated with it. The three laptops which were confiscated also appeared on the table.

Looking up at her superior she offered, "DNA doesn't lie."

For the first time since she arrived Christopher smiled.

"I never once doubted you," was his reply.

She gave him a look that said, I'm supposed to believe that.

The session went on through the evening. A couple of times the President dropped in to make sure the two of them hadn't attacked each other. Christopher analyzed her every move with a fine-toothed comb. Step by step each detail was discussed over and over again. The blood samples and laptop were handed off to one of the Director's assistant who had been stationed in a separate room, then rushed to the CIA headquarters. It was going to be a day or two before Sandy's recall of the mission was complete and she would be deemed off duty. When everything was wrapped up, her plan was not to step foot into an aircraft for a couple of months. The time would be spent reacquainting herself to her family, basking in the splendor of the ranch.

Chapter 16

David and Renée landed in Florida. He booked a hotel on the beach. Growing up in Canada and surviving the harsh winters, the ocean's serenity became special to him. Since there were no meetings until the next day, he planned to take advantage of the remainder of the day by frolicking in the sand and water. He hoped Renée would join him.

After check-in was completed they replayed the awkwardness of making their way to separate rooms. This time the suites were directly across the hall from one another. They chuckled realizing the irony of the circumstances.

"We are not being very fiscally responsible occupying separate suites. We could save your father-in-law some money."

"Good point. I'll take it up with Jacob next week."

She smiled then swiped the key to enter her suite.

"Did you bring a bathing suit?" he inquired.

"Oui."

"Good, get changed. Let's go play in the waves."

"I'll be ready in five," she disappeared into the room.

Within hours, Fyad's assistant verified the identity of the man in the picture. He was an American living abroad, at least at the moment. His movements would be monitored. All activities would be documented and reported to Fyad's control room on a daily basis. If it was established this person's fingerprints were anywhere near the fire, the unearthing would be disclosed to Sandy and only Sandy. What she did with it was entirely at her discretion. Although Fyad would be angered and prefer to settle it in his own way, he would not. This was her ball court and she would control the play.

Sporting bathing suits, tee shirts and towels wrapped around their necks, the two embraced the suntanned beaches of Florida. David wanted to extract every ounce of sunlight remaining in the day. Walking along the edge of the water their tête-à-tête was peaceful. They were drawn in by the hypnotic side effect the sound of the waves produced.

"Thank you for this David. How soon we forget the awesome memories nature will provide us, if we take a moment to visit."

"It's nice isn't it? I'm happy to share it with you."

At that he picked her up in both arms and tossed her into the ocean. She was caught off guard. Her body disappeared in the water for a second. A startled face gasping for air emerged, with both hands she wiped her eyes dry. Leaning her head back, she shook her hair then caressed it behind her neck. To his eyes, an angel had emerged from the ocean floor.

"Is that any way to treat an employee," she laughed.

"You looked like you needed to cool down."

Renée stepped onto the dry sand and positioned herself on the land side of David. Without even a hint of retaliation, with lightning speed using as much force a hundred pound person could garnish, she wrapped both arms around his midsection and pushed him into the water. They both tripped and fell, Renée on top, with the waves rocking them back and forth. Laughing hysterically their horseplay would have onlookers assuming the two were on a honeymoon. The remainder of the beach experience continued with playfulness.

***

The day was soon finding its way to an end when the President once again made an appearance in the war room.

"Christopher, are you close to bringing this to an end. Sandy must be beyond the point of exhaustion."

"Yes, Mr. President. We are entering the final stage and should conclude within the hour."

President Andrew Tucker directed a comment to Sandy, "I have arranged for you to spend the remainder of the evening here at the White House. The agents at the door will escort you." Then looking back at the Director he continued, "When you finish, which I trust will be soon."

"Christopher I can arrange for you to stay if you prefer to travel in the morning."

"Thank you sir, but I will be leaving for Langley soon."

"Sandy, the First Lady and I wish to extend an invite to join us for breakfast. Say seven. When I mentioned to Emma you were here, she insisted. I've been instructed not to take no for an answer. You won't disappoint me will you?"

"It would be my honor sir. Please pass on to Emma that I will be there at seven," rather relieved at the invite as she was exhausted.

"Well then goodnight," he glanced at his watch, "Christopher, soon."

The day after Jacob's surprise visit to his assistant's residence all was back to normal. Consumed by work nothing had been mentioned about their talk, albeit, reflections of last night swirled in the back of their heads.

Brooklyn's day had come to an end. Her last function each day was to verify her services were no longer required.

"Jacob is there anything further you require before I leave?"

"No, thank you. I will see you in the morning."

Draping a sweater over her shoulders for the walk, she turned off the office lights. She was surprised to find Jacob standing at the entrance of his office when turning to leave.

"Jacob is there something I can get you?" she asked.

"Actually, how about dinner?" he asked after taking a deep breath.

"Jacob?"

"Dinner. Would you join me for dinner? I can have the car brought around, your choice of eateries."

"I'd like that Jacob. Can I have an hour or so to freshen up?"

"Of course, take as much time as you'd like."

They went in separate directions to prepare for what could be considered the first time either had been on a date in years, if that's what this was.

***

David and Renée found their way back to their rooms. The plan was to order a room service dinner to be eaten in David's suite. Their intentions were to review the material pertaining to tomorrow's meetings while they ate. They washed off the oceans salt in their respective suites.

Renée dried herself then dressed in a black tracksuit. The formalities of the trip had been washed away at the beach. She envisioned a lengthy informal dinner leaning more toward socialization than business.

Spending the day with David put her in a state of tranquility. She felt refreshed, never more alive. She was aroused. They were going to have sex tonight. There was no doubt about it.

Renée wasn't looking for a relationship. That was the last state of affairs she wanted to be dealing with. Sex was a different matter. She acquired a healthy sex drive at an early age. Growing up in a rural area of France there was the occasional barn romp, roll in the hay. Self-confidence allowed her to explore this portion of her life without inhibition. She was raised to be her own self. Never be afraid to go after what she wanted. Tonight she wanted David. When experiencing a craving, Renée seldom let it go unattended. She was inventive with her solo satisfaction but partnering with someone was preferred. Man or women it didn't really matter. As long as she liked them and they were a nice person. She had a variety of partners throughout her life. Not an enormous amount but enough to have acquired a taste for its pleasures.

David was about to jump into the shower when his phone began to ring. The caller ID indicated it was Sandy.

"Hi," he answered.

"Hey babe, I just wanted to check in with you to see how you're doing. I miss you so much. It is going to feel so great to finally get home."

"It will be nice."

"I know, sorry. I'll make it up to you."

"I'm going to hold you to that promise."

"What hotel are you staying at?"

"We're at Hilton Bentley."

"Nice, Renée must be enjoying the luxuries of her new position."

"I don't believe she's the type that gets hung up on where she stays. I'm sure she would be fine with any hotel."

"She is a good kid," emphasizing her youth. "We are lucky to have her as an employee."

The call lasted a few more minutes. Sandy asked about the two horses being purchased. There was some small talk before goodbyes were said. Both affirmed their anticipation of reuniting.

Sandy had called Renée a kid. Was that a reminder of the difference in age between himself and his head trainer? He began to wonder if he was reading too much into her conversation, it almost sounded as a warning. Did she have suspicions? There was no way she knew about them sleeping together during the California trip. She was on the other side of the planet. He shook his head and wrote it off as being paranoid then made his way to the shower.

Renée grabbed her room key card, locked up, then knocked on David's door. There was no answer. She knocked a few more times. Turning off the shower he heard the last bang. He jumped out clumsily balancing with one hand on the wall then popping his head out of the bathroom yelling I'll be right there. She had just turned to retreat to her room when she heard him.

David quickly dried the water dripping off him. Still partially wet he wrapped the embroidered white towel around his waist. Making his way to the door, leaving wet footprints behind him, he opened it to find Renée on the other side looking as good as ever.

"I thought you had forgotten about me," she teased.

"Sorry. Sandy called. It delayed my shower."

"I can see that. I can come back later," she offered.

"No don't be silly," he stepped aside. "Come in."

She did. He closed the door. Seeing his partially covered wet body escalated her hunger for him beyond the point of no return. Hell she thought, throwing caution to the wind, I need him.

Renée locked the door, pushed him up against the wall and ripped the towel from his hips. To her surprise he was already aroused. Their lips met. The whole day was foreplay so there was little need for it now.

She pulled away turning her back to him. With both hands she eased her loose fitting track pants down to her knees. There were no panties being worn. Her right arm reached back to take a hold of his swollen member. She eased it into herself until it disappeared. When he was completely buried inside her she slowly moved forward then backwards. With every backward movement she pinned up against the wall.

Engulfed in the euphoric feelings of the day's activities, neither was prepared to consider the consequences of their actions. At this moment satisfying their new found appetite was all that mattered in the world.

Renée continued to thrust back and forth until David pulled out of her. He turned her to face him, they kissed. Taking a hold of her tiny waist he effortlessly lifted her off the ground. She straddled him with her legs locked behind his back. With her right hand she once again guided him into her.

The thrusting intensified. Staying deep within Renée, David sauntered his way towards the bedroom. With her legs fastened behind and arms locked around his neck she focused on gently bucking him during the ride.

Falling on the bed with him on top, the lovemaking became more passionate with every movement. Soon he was on the bottom with Renée riding him, controlling the rhythm. She rode him like she was bucking a wild horse at the rodeo. The night was a lovemaking marathon. An hour's break for dinner which was eaten in bed then back to the sex.

***

The next morning Sandy sat with the President and the first lady enjoying a breakfast cooked by the White House chef. The two women were quickly immersed in discussing fund raising ideas. Sitting at the head of the table the President read a daily paper not paying much attention to the ladies.

The President excused himself after thirty minutes or so but not before having Sandy promise to stop by the Oval Office prior to her departure. The next hour was absorbed with the girls going over plans to champion certain world causes. With the blueprints in place, a promise to meet in a couple of months was agreed on. Sandy put Emma on hold for a month or two expounding on her need to stay home for a while. Arrangements to keep in touch and goodbyes were exchanges as the First Lady escorted Sandy to the West Wing.

"Eva, the President is expecting Miss McGinnis," introducing her by her maiden name.

Legally documents read McGinnis-Watson but

in most cases she was still referred to by her father's name. For business purposes it worked best.

Eva placed her telephone on the receiver, "The President will see you now."

"Thank you," she said, then parted ways with the first lady.

"Thank you for extending your stay. Emma has a million ideas for world welfare and social reform. She relishes the opportunity to have a conversation with someone who excels in the field of philanthropy."

"You wife has been instrumental in bringing some significant issues to the forefront. I'm the one who can learn from her."

"How have you been? This last operation worried me. You're so important to the country I'm uncomfortable when you place yourself in harm's way."

"I appreciate your concern sir, but I was fine."

"I know, I know, but to make things worse your father delicately hints that if something happens to you he is going to browbeat me with a satchel of his money."

She laughed, "His bark is louder than his bite. I think you should remain relatively unscathed."

The room went silent for a moment while the President gathered his thoughts.

"Sandy I'll keep this brief as I realize you would like to get home to see David."

"First thank you for everything you have put yourself through. Secondly, all joking aside, I believe you should consider reducing your schedule to live life. Those who care about you should become your primary focus. It's important. You will realize it later in life. Don't let this time slip away. Just a bit of advice from an old guy who doesn't follow what he preaches. If Christopher becomes heavy-handed with the easing of your involvement I can deal with him."

"I have already advised him that I'm staying put for the next few months. He seems fine with it, for now. You are correct, as always. I've been entertaining the idea for a while now."

"Good."

The President stood then walked behind his desk, opened a drawer seizing a file from within it. He walked back and sat opposite Sandy, sliding the file across the coffee table so she could read it. It was titled Burn.

"What's this," she asked.

"It's the FBI report on the fire at your father's stables."

She opened it, leaning back to rest her back on the couch. The President did not utter a word. He also sat back sipping on an early day glass of scotch allowing her time to decipher the report. The report concluded what had been suspected that it was intended as a diversion. The woman who placed the actual marbles had been secretly detained. She never met or knew the persons that rendered her services. Her job was working for a feed company which supplied a number of stables. This explained why the positioning of the tiny fire bombs was amateurish as the preliminary reports suggested. The woman was paid handsomely for her participation. She was led to believe the marbles were a new product which controlled odor. The contact told her they had permission from the owners to test the experimental product. However, it was to be kept a secret from the staff. No other explanation was forthcoming. That pretty well summed it up. She put down the file.

"Do we buy the story?"

"Yes. The agents assigned are competent."

"Okay. Are we any closer to the ones who ordered the fire?"

"Sandy, would you like to interrogate her?"

"No. Cut her loose. There is no sense in creating a media circus over this. Besides the girl had no idea what she was getting into. She was just trying to make a quick buck, which she probably needs. Ruining her life won't assist in finding the one responsible. Explain to her she is catching a break but we may need to talk to her at later date. Make sure she remains accessible. Keep her under surveillance. They will know we've made her. Chances are they will want to have a chat with her."

"Done."

The room again was silent as the file was returned to the desk. The President seemed uncharacteristically fidgety with his arms crossed supporting himself by leaning his backside on the desk.

"Madison Taylor has concerns about the lack of information the CIA is providing her. On the surface Christopher is going out of his way to co-operate. There has been little substance to what he has passed on. She has reason to believe his is in possession of more."

"Sir, Christopher always knows more. That's why you allow him to run our intelligence agency."

"You have a point," he agreed. "Sandy, I have a gut feeling this fire was about you. I haven't been able to piece it together yet, but I will. Until then, watch your back. Someone other than us may know you exist. Or, and I don't want this to be true, someone within our organization that knows of your identity is behind it. If that were the case, it puts you in a dangerous position. Be careful."

"I will. Thank you, Mr. President. You have better things to do than worry about me. I will be watchful. Let's keep this close. I would prefer my father not being advised until we have everyone responsible. He would want this girl locked up forever. Would you advise Madison and Christopher?"

"Absolutely. Let me accompany you to the South Lawn. Marine One is waiting for us. I am flying past the airport. You might as well catch a ride."

"You spoil me."

They walked the hall of the White House making their way to the helicopter. As always the media would require an explanation as to this lady's royal treatment. The official word would be she had taken time out of her busy schedule to meet with the First Lady with regards to some charitable issues.

When they arrived at the lawn, the Secret Service was prepared to escort them out to the aircraft.

She leaned to whisper something to the President.

"The day is young. I believe I will adhere to your advice. I've decided to fly to Miami for a surprise

278

rendezvous with my husband."

"He's one lucky man."

***

The night was void of sleep. On the other hand it was plentiful of sex. Renée returned to her room to prepare for the days business. David did the same in his.

In a rented vehicle they drove to the farm housing their purchase. The meeting went well. Renée was immediately consumed with the two foals. The frolicking of the ponies had her grinning ear to ear. David was left on his own to handle the business aspect of the purchase. One look at Renée's interaction with them cemented the deal. She had given her approval without uttering a word. The transaction was completed and they were on their way back to the hotel by early afternoon. Renée instantly fell in love. That's all she could talk about during the ride. She was like a kid opening presents at Christmas. These two horses would be her first acquisitions as head trainer. The responsibility of nurturing them through the steps of producing two world class thoroughbreds now lay solely on her shoulders. She couldn't have been more excited.

Walking from the parking lot to the hotel entrance was the first opportunity for David to discuss anything other than the foals.

"Renée I know you're probably hungry but I have to opt out for some sleep. I think it would be best if we both retired to our rooms for a few hours.

If I invite you over, we will never get any rest."

"Should I take that as a compliment?"

"It's an acknowledgment of your prowess in the bedroom."

"Flattery will get you everything monsieur Watson."

He smiled. Nothing more was said until they reached their floor.

"Let's grab a few hours sleep then hook up for dinner."

"Sure, that sounds great."

"Renée, the gentlemen that we bought the horses off today happens to be part owners of the BB&T Centre in Sunrise Florida and he's invited us to join him in his private box tonight to see Florida Georgia Line. Are you interested?"

"Oh David, I don't think I like hockey games."

He burst into a deep laugh.

"It's not a hockey game. It's a group."

"What do you mean a group David?"

"Un groupe Renée, the hottest country band on the music charts."

"I'm not sure I enjoy that type of music. Maybe you would have more fun without me."

"No, I insist. Give it a chance. You might be swayed into becoming a country music fan by the end of the night."

"Well then okay, you're the boss. I will keep an open mind."

"Perfect. We have back stage passes. Maybe you'll get to meet the guys."

Marine One sat down in close proximity to her aircraft. She thanked the President and his staff then made her way across the tarmac to her own transportation. It seemed a bit curious to her that there was a black helicopter sitting close to her plane which seemed to be preparing for takeoff. As she approached the stairs of her father's jet, one of her pilots stepped out to meet her.

"Have you filed our flight plans to Florida?" she inquired.

"We did but they were declined."

"By who," she demanded.

"FAA," he shrugged.

Just as she was about to storm up the stairs and contact the airport authorities to demand an explanation, from behind she heard her name called. She was being addressed by two well dressed men who appeared from within the black chopper. As they approached, she walked to meet them halfway. One of the men handed her a cell phone.

"Director Young would like to speak with you ma'am."

She moved to a safe distance so not be overheard.

"Christopher, why did you have my flight to Florida denied?"

"How was breakfast? That White House Chef makes a mean omelet."

"Are these agents aware of my identity?"

"Yes. They know who you are. Not what you are. They follow orders without question. A concept one day you may grasp."

It was a hot day. The sun was beating off the pavement. Sandy was warm, she was tired and all she wanted was to get to Florida to be with her husband. The Director was wearing thin on her. Discussing breakfast or for that sake anything was not high on her priority list.

"Sir, what is it you want from me?"

"I've asked the agents to escort you to Langley. After an initial analyzing of the computers I would like to pick your brain. I need you for one more day. You will be sun tanning with your significant other by morning."

Refusing the invite was unacceptable. This was her duty. It sucked big time. But it was the reality of her agreement. Everything in life played second fiddle to the country's security.

"What will be the official line for my visit?"

"You and the First Lady are embarking on a humanitarian mission within volatile areas. Out of the goodness of our hearts, also at the request of the President, we have agreed to brief you on the dangers you face and outline security measures we will be putting in place to protect your safety."

"We will be there shortly," she said then handed the phone back to one of her unbeknownst counterparts.

After explaining the revised plan to her pilots, she boarded the CIA helicopter en route to Langley.

***

Dinner was a delight. Brooklyn was rarely subjected to the sociable side of her boss. In all fairness, she didn't think Jacob himself was very well acquainted with that part of himself. They had dined at a small Italian restaurant he occasionally frequented with clients. It featured a one page menu. No prices. Patrons had their choice of three or four main course meals. All the food was prepared fresh at the time of order. Exquisite was the best way to describe the taste.

It was during their nightcap at Brooklyn's residence that Jacob posed a question or what might have been construed as a suggestion.

"Brooklyn, please don't take this the wrong way."

Her expression turned curious. One never really knew what to expect from Jacob. Motioning for him to continue she braced herself.

"I was considering having you clear my calendar for two or three weeks."

"I will make the necessary changes tomorrow."

"Good. I want to fly to England, make up some lame excuse about being dragged there on business so I can nonchalantly run into Serge. I miss him Brooklyn."

"So do I Jacob. You two are good friends. That is a lovely idea. I've been suggesting for years that you take time to vacation. It is long overdue. Consider it done."

He waited for a short time nodding in agreement and then told her, "I want you to join me."

She didn't see this coming. Lost for words, she sat back trying to decipher what she heard. Her mind was scrambling for an intelligent reply. It wasn't forthcoming. Her brain and mouth were not wired together at the moment.

"Brooklyn, I've enjoyed our time together immensely. We seemed to have dropped our guard down. It makes me feel alive. I mean no disrespect."

"None taken," she finally found her voice. "You've taken me by surprise Jacob. I wasn't expecting such an invitation."

"I apologize. Would you at least give it some thought?" He began to stand preparing to make his way home.

You didn't serve the President of the United States as his executive assistant by being a procrastinator. Tough decisions were made instantaneously. Her work always demanded that, her personal life, not so much.

"Jacob I have enjoyed our time together. It has been years since I've kept company. It never crossed my mind that my reinstatement into that world would be with you. Would it be proper if we entertained an idea like this?"

"Who defines proper?"

Both took a drink from their glass. Jacob sat back down while waiting on a reply. No words were being exchanged. Silent, staring into one another's eyes, he anticipating her response and she was discerning right from wrong, realism from abstract. With a mind that processed as efficient as hers did, the decision was arrived at expeditiously.

"I would love to join you Jacob."

"Wonderful. Tomorrow we will make the necessary changes to our calendars for a period of three weeks. I would like to treat you to my favorite hideaways in Paris and Rome. We should plan on leaving as soon as our scheduling permits."

Jacob got up once again, this time making his way to the door. They exchanged their good nights.

He surprised her with a kiss to the forehead. Brooklyn watched as he made his way down the path to the main house. Once back inside, she locked her door and retired to the bedroom. Awestruck but feeling more vivacious than she had in years, her preference would have been to skip right to morning rather than endure a night of staring at the ceiling. Eventually sleep would triumph fostering a clear mind to forge ahead with whatever the next few weeks had in store. Well aware the latter made sense, she closed her eyes setting the stage for the sweetest of dreams.

***

Introductions were taking place back stage at the BB&T Center. Renée was conversing in French with a member of the production crew who was from Montreal. David stood beside his business acquaintances being versed on the backstage protocol. It was similar to the dressing room of a professional sports team, a sanctuary which only a select few were granted access.

David was familiar with the facility. The NHL's Florida Panthers use the arena as their home. He played against them on many occasions. Being backstage was a whole new ball game. Technicians were everywhere, fixing this, fixing that. They were tuning the many guitars, adjusting lights, kind of an organized madhouse. Taking it all in, David hadn't noticed that one member of the duo was standing to his right.

"Mr. Watson, I'm a big horse race fan. It's a

pleasure to meet you," he said offering his hand.

"Thank you. I would venture to say I'm a bigger fan of yours. You guys are awesome."

The musician held an iPad. Besides being a fan of the track he also followed the hockey world and knew of David's achievements in the game. He had been in the dressing room reading the news keeping abreast of current affairs, when he was informed of David being backstage. It was too much of a coincidence not to show his guest the article he had just read.

"You're not the only famed person in the family," smiling as he showed his guest the article headlining the political page of a news site.

The caption read, 'Prominent world philanthropist receives royal treatment from President.'

There on the South Lawn of the White House stood his wife and the President of the United States posing for the media. They were shaking hands in one of the photos and in the other stepping aboard Marine One. The article went on to describe his wife's meeting with the First Lady. It briefly outlined the plan to provide assistance to the youth of the world.

"She is a busy lady," was David's comment.

"I've read about her work. She has achieved a lot of good. Tell her if she ever needs our assistance we would be more than happy to do what we can. We can give her organizations a shout out. Better yet, a benefit concert," he offered. "We could arrange that, right Bob," directing the question to their manager who stood beside him.

"Absolutely," he agreed, handing David his business card.

"Have her call me anytime."

At that point, the other half of the duo joined his partner as did Renée with David. Show time was nearing. Technicians adjusted equipment placed on the band. The group of businessmen were about to make their way to the private suite to take in the show when one of the stars turned to Renée.

"Do you work with David?" he asked.

"I do, I train our horses."

"I'm Tyler, this is the other half, Brian," introducing himself and his partner.

"Please to meet you, I'm Renée."

"So are you a country music fan?"

David held his breath anticipating her answer.

"My boss here has assured me by the end of your performance tonight I will be," she paused, "how did he put it, oh yes, a die-hard fan."

"Your boss is a smart man. You should listen to him. Il est correct," he ended in French after overhearing her speaking with his guitar tech who had been teaching him the language.

"Maybe I could borrow you sometime. I have some horses on my ranch that have absolutely no interest in listening to me. They prance around like they own the place."

"I'm sure something could be arranged," she offered with a touch of flirtatiousness to her words.

In the background someone yelled out show time in five.

The group dispersed. The area became silent for a second until the music began to blast from the towers of speakers. David and Renée followed the entourage that extended the invite to the elevator, delivering them to the suite. While waiting for it Renée whispered to David.

"ll fait chaud David. You might be right."

Once they settled in, waiting for the concert to begin, David took out his cell phone and text his wife.

"Really S, the W H, Marine 1."

He put the phone back into his pocket. The arena went dark. The drummer began pounding out a cool beat. The crowd burst with anticipation. Screaming, singing, cell phone lights flickering everywhere, the show was going to live up to its hype. The event was sold out. Yet every seat in the building was empty, but only because every person in the building were on their feet. The duo stepped on stage and what one would think couldn't get louder, did.

The stage went black. No sound. Then the thunderous sound of a jet panned from right to left vibrating all in its path. The booming subsided, replaced by the twang of a banjo being plucked taking the band into one of its number one hits.

The ambiance of the concert was contagious inclusive of those watching from the private suite. David was impressed by the ease in which Renée was embraced by anybody she encountered. They had barely said a word to each other since entering the room yet she had not stopped chatting with everyone else. You would have thought they were all her best friends.

It was about a half hour into the performance

when Tyler spoke into the microphone.

"I would like to dedicate this next song to my new best friend. Backstage she told me if I played my cards right she would," he paused for a second then continued slowly drawing each word out, "train my horses."

The crowd erupted sending the decimal readings off the charts.

"This one's for you Renée," he announced while pointing up to the suite in which she was standing forefront with a few of the other ladies.

The decimal reader surely broke.

Renée sported an ear to ear smile. She let out a high pitched 'eeee' sound that couldn't be labeled a word. The women lauded her. David received a couple of elbow jabs from the men expressing their approval.

The girls stood with their hands in the air rocking their body's back and forth grooving as the band went on singing the song "Tell Me How You Like It"to their guest.

The ladies, except Renée, sang along knowing every word to the tune.

Tyler glanced up to the suite that housed Renée and her newly found friends.

During the remainder of the song he nodded and pointed to her several more times.

This was flirtation at its finest. Anyone within sight of her noticed the wooing. Some from the crowd below the box seats yelled "you go girl" while giving her the thumbs up.

By this point in the concert, Renée had completely embraced country music. If a guy wanted to make a girl's heart miss a few beats, this had to be near the top of the list. Being serenaded in front of twenty-one thousand devoted followers set the bar close to unreachable for any other to compete with. A new fan was born. She would find time to train his horses.

The concert was a huge success. All in attendance would remember it for a long time. No one from the private suite made it back stage at the end. David and Renée uttered their farewells promising to keep in touch. Their car was delivered to them at a special exit at the rear. They tipped the valet generously and began the drive back to the hotel.

After a few minutes of a silent ride David asked, "So, did I convert you?"

"No David I'm sorry you weren't successful."

"Ah, that's too bad. It looked like you were having such a good time."

"Oh I was. I can't remember the last time I had so much fun. They were great."

"You just said," he went on before being cut off by Renée.

"I said you were not successful in turning me into a fan. And you weren't. But, Tyler completely sold me. He has transformed me into country music's number one admirer."

"I got to give it to him. He sure knows how to sweet-talk a girl. It makes it challenging for us common folk."

"I don't think you have anything to worry about. You have your way with the ladies. I can attest to that. I'm not sure you can sing as well as him though."

"Easy now," he cautioned as he smiled at her.

"Besides you're the one who gets to sleep with me tonight, if you're interested."

"I'm there."

Once the drive was completed, they found themselves going directly to David's room. Getting undressed, jumping into the shower was the first priority. Soon both warm naked bodies were snuggled under the blankets. Opposite of the previous night, this evening's lovemaking was tenderly slow, a sensual waltz.

Morning arrived too soon. Not wanting to come up for air from the comfort of the covers, room service and breakfast in bed seemed the likely choice. They sat leaning on the backboards savoring the flavorful feast.

"Renée, I really care for you. I can't get the thought of you out of my mind," he admitted out of the blue taking her by surprise.

Wanting to understand more of what he was getting at she remained silent.

"For the first time in my marriage, I'm beginning to question my life with Sandy. I love her, yes. Raising a family with her is another question. She's so caught up in her jet setting lifestyle, being part of a family is the furthest thing from her mind."

Renée remained mute.

"When I'm with you I feel alive. You make me realize how much I've accepted being lonely. Do you suppose a person can be in love with two people at the same time?"

A clear picture was emerging. It was time to

interject. Slow things down.

"David, I'm not prepared for this. We are enjoying each other tremendously. It's complicated, wrong, immoral, but most definitely enjoyable," she began.

"Although, I believe we both had thoughts that this might happen, we did just fall into it that first night. But David, I am not ready for a relationship. That's the furthest thing from my mind. My career is flourishing thanks to you. That needs to be my focus. I care for you a great deal or I wouldn't be sleeping with you. But I'm not ready for more," she paused.

He sat silent. It was his time to listen, knowing exactly what was to be said. Realizing it was a mistake to touch on the subject, a weak moment allowing a truth from within to surface.

"I'm not in this to break up your marriage. Sandy is a beautiful person. You are a lucky guy. Don't throw it away."

Renée looked away from him towards the window as she collected her thoughts. He watched her, mindful of the fact that she wasn't finished. The bedroom remained hushed for a few minutes. He wanted to hear her out.

"David I don't feel guilty for making love to another women's husband. I don't know why. I should. What type of person am I? Maybe there is some dark reason from my childhood buried somewhere within me. The fact remains, I feel no remorse."

She adjusted the blankets. Turning towards him she placed her arm on his chest. With her bent leg positioned on top of his she snuggled up against his naked body. David's arm made its way around the back of her shoulder. They hugged.

"Whether or not we have this again, it can't be more. You have to accept that. If you can't David, this has to be our final get-together."

"Okay."

There was no doubt that both wanted to continue the relationship, albeit both viewing it differently. Two distinctive needs, same solution.

Sandy wrapped her visit to headquarters. She satisfied the agencies queries. Now that her jet was touching down at Miami International Airport, the activities of the past few weeks would be stored in the back of her mind. At the forefront was reconnecting with her husband. It was late morning, leaving plenty of time for a full day of beach. She knew how much David enjoyed the ocean.

Arrangements were made to have a car waiting for her upon arrival. It was parked beside a hanger that serviced private planes visiting the airport.

"Guys I'm not sure how long our stay will be. I do know we are here at least until tomorrow, so why don't the two of you have some fun. Get in a game of golf. Go relax on the beach. I'm going to meet up with my husband and do the same. We have earned a break. I will give you plenty of heads up time before our departure."

The officers nodded their approval. Their duty wouldn't allow for that. They would remain out of sight but always close by. Being the protectors of Sandy left little time for relaxation.

With breakfast complete, the end of the

discussion reached, David flung his feet out from under the covers finding the floor. He bent over and gave her a kiss on the forehead before making his way to the shower. Renée pulled the covers up to her neck electing to prolong her stay in the warmth of the bed.

Around the same time as David finished his shower Sandy was parking her vehicle in the hotel parking area.

"You plan on spending the rest of the day in bed? We do have reservation for a flight home later this afternoon."

"I know. Just give me a few more minutes. It's so warm. Why don't you come back to bed," she extended an invitation while patting her hand on the covers.

David smiled, "I'm going to take a walk and find us some fresh coffee. You enjoy."

He dressed, grabbed his card key then made his way to the door.

Sandy entered the lobby going directly to the registration desk. Since she wasn't expecting to visit her husband, she hadn't asked for his room number. An establishment such as this hotel prided itself on discretion so a request for his suite number would fall on deaf ears. She could use her financial or celebrity clout to demand the information but what was the sense.

"Good morning, may I help you," the grey haired gentleman behind the counter asked her.

"Yes, I believe you can," giving him a pleasant smile.

"Could you please ring David Watson's suite to

inform him that a package has arrived," she asked, then went on, "Please don't mention to my husband that I am here. I want to surprise him."

Pointing at the grouping of plush couches occupying the lobby she said, "When he arrives please tell him his package is sitting over there."

She slipped the man a nice tip then found a seat in the sitting area.

As David put his hand on the door knob the hotel telephone rang. He turned, but before he reached for the phone in the living room, Renée answered the one on the night table beside the bed.

As he entered the bedroom he heard her say, "Thank you, we will pick it up shortly."

Hanging up she looked up to see David standing there with a curious look on his face.

Before he could ask, she offered, "A package has been left for you at the desk."

"Ok, I'll pick it up. It's time to rise and shine young lady."

"This is your last offer boss. Once I'm up and around I'm not coming back to bed."

"I'll be back shortly."

He turned making his way to the stairwell on a mission to seek out a couple of freshly brewed coffees, take a peek outside to test the weather and then retrieve the package. After descending down the stairs he zoned into the hotel's café. As he passed the desk, the gentleman behind the counter spoke his name.

"Mr. Watson, your package."

"Yes, thank you, I'll be back in a minute."

"Sir," the man was being slightly overanxious

about the delivery.

"I'm just going to grab a couple of coffees then I'll be right with you.

Being persistent, the employee once again said, "Sir," with more urgency.

All the while Sandy was entertaining herself watching the interaction.

This time David approached the man wondering what could be so important that it couldn't wait until he had his and Renée's coffee in hand.

"Sir, I apologize for being so insistent. I believe you would want to be informed forthwith prior to your purchase for you and your associate that the package we speak of is sitting directly behind you."

He turned to see Sandy sunk into one of the lobbies over sized chairs smiling at him. His legs didn't seem to want to move, they were frozen to the floor. Startled, it took him a few seconds to react. Trying his utmost to act cool, calm and collected on the outside, his brain was racing. He was in search of a solution to avoid her walking into the room being greeted by Renée lying naked in his bed.

The discreet and well seasoned resort representative knew what predicament his guest was facing and was prepared to offer a solution.

"Sir," he once again drew David's attention.

"Yes," David turned his head back to the man.

Then whispering he asked, "Sir, if you would like, I could inform your associate to prepare the room for the arrival of your guest."

"Thank you, that would be wonderful," David breathed a sigh of relief then handed the man a hefty token of his appreciation.

He walked over to his wife, head still spinning. He wasn't out the woods yet, but the forest just got a touch brighter.

"This is a surprise. I thought you were heading home."

"Disappointed?"

"Are you kidding me, come here," he held out his arms to give her a hug.

She wrapped hers around him while offering an overdue kiss.

"That seemed like a secretive conversation. Are you and the clerk hiding something from me?"

"You have a suspicious mind. He was asking if we would like a complimentary bottle of champagne sent up to the room."

"You said yes I hope."

"I said no. It's morning. Coffee is what we need to be drinking. Our flight home leaves in a few hours"

"Oh yea, I forgot Renée is with you. She can catch the flight. You and I are going to spend the day on the beach. No phones, only sun, sand, and the ocean. We can head home tomorrow or the next or the next."

Meanwhile the man behind the counter had disappeared into his office, closing the door behind him. He dialed the suite's number.

Renée had arisen from the dead and was making her way to the shower. As she turned on the water tap she heard something. Turning the water off she realized the phone was ringing once again. Presuming it was David she walked naked to answer it.

"Yes."

"Ma'am this is the front desk. I wanted to advise you that Mr. Watson will be momentarily returning to his room. Ma'am the package in his possession is a woman by the name of Sandy. I believe it is his wife."

"Shit."

"Pardon me," the man replied.

"Sorry."

"I assumed prior notification of their arrival would allow time for preparations you may require. If you would like, I could have housekeeping immediately dispatched to toss the bed and tend to the room."

"That would be awesome. Thank you. I owe you one."

"All in a day's work ma'am," he hung up.

Focus was the only thought that crossed her mind. Anything that would indicate her presence in the bedroom or bathroom had to be dealt with first and foremost. Although her being in the living area was easy to brush off as a business meeting, the less implication of her company was for the best.

She rushed from room to room first tucking in the bed covers in on one side depicting a single occupancy. Picking up her panties along with her jeans and shirt was second on the list of attempting to stay incognito. Three items of clothing were all that needed to be gathered. She seldom wore bras, didn't like them. Living in the sixties, seventies, the hippie days she thought might have been a better fit for her than today's electronic society. Also, she was barefoot, so the only remaining item was her shoes. Satisfied she took a moment to scan the suite then entered the hallway.

David convinced his wife that the wait in line for the coffee was well worth it as the hotel café had perfected a fine roast.

"Three house brew please," he ordered.

"You're thirsty?"

"Sorry didn't you want one."

"Sure who's the third for?"

"Renée. I told her I would grab her one. We planned to finalize the transportation documents for our two additions this morning."

He was banking on the clerk's success in warning Renée of his wife's arrival using as many delay tactics without overdoing it. As they re-entered the lobby he caught a glance of the man behind the counter who gave him an unsuspecting nod of reassurance.

Automatically heading for the stairwell, he was surprised when Sandy tugged him towards the elevator.

"What are you doing," he asked.

"Let's take the elevator. I want you in your room as quickly as possible. Today's the day I start making up for lost time. Your meeting can wait. I can't."

"Come on let's take the stairs."

At that the bell dinged and the elevator door opened. He was pulled in. The door closed. Less than a minute until they reach their floor. If praying or touching wood or crossing his fingers weren't so noticeable he would be on his knees tapping the wooden hand railing with his knuckles.

Renée left the room then closed the door, turned towards her own suite directly across the hall. She gathered the breakfast in bed plates and placed them in front of the next door guest's room. She felt confident her tracks were covered. Turning to her door she went to open it only to realize her keycard had been left on David's coffee table.

"Shit, shit, shit," her swear word of choice rapidly blurted out of her mouth.

Stranded in the hallway expecting her lover and his wife to appear any second from the stairwell was to say the least an awkward state of affairs. What to do? Quickly weighing her options she decided to dash for the elevator, go down to the desk and request an extra key. If Sandy noticed the key in her husband's room it could easily be explained that it was left when they were going over business last evening.

She stopped after taking a few steps by the appearance of the chamber maid pushing a cart towards her from the opposite end of the hall, turned to meet her. As they met in front of David's room, she heard the guest elevator bell chime and familiar voices before they physically appeared. It was Sandy and David. They had taken the elevator. Not what she was expecting. What to do?

As they came into view, she acted like she hadn't noticed them and spoke to the maid.

"I don't believe my boss is in but let me check."

She knocked on the door obviously to no avail. After a short tap she turned to the maid.

"He's not here, so please go in. My boss is a bit

of a clean freak so can you make sure everything is wiped extremely well. Please change the bedding."

"I will," she answered.

"Thank you."

Simultaneously the maid pushed her cart through the door as she turned and began to make a fuss over the surprise arrival of Sandy.

As they met she offered, "What a surprise."

"Good to see you again Renée. Has this guy been behaving," she asked giving her husband a light punch in the shoulder.

"He's no fun. He's all business," was all Renée could think of.

"David I hope you don't mind me allowing the maid to tidy your room. I was checking to see if you were in and she asked permission to clean."

"Not at all, coffee?" offering her the cup.

"Would you guys like to sit in my room for a few minutes while yours is being attended to?"

David looked at his wife, shrugged his shoulders then said, "Sure."

Renée stood between the open door of her boss's room waiting for an opportunity to dash in to pluck her key off the table then David provided it.

"This is good. We can go over the transport documents while we wait. Then Sandy and I will be free of business for the rest of the day. Let me get them they're on the coffee table."

"I'll grab them."

She disappeared before anyone could object. In and out like a lightning bolt, she came out papers in hand with her key nestled into her jean's back pocket. Disaster averted. Despite the fact that her heart rate was racing and she could feel small beads of sweat lining her forehead, they had come out of this relatively unscathed.

"Renée, are you feeling okay? You seem a little pale," Sandy inquired.

"Oui I'm fine. I might be coming down with a touch of a flu or cold. I've been a little queasy this morning. But no, I'm good."

She swiped her card, the light flashed and they entered. The room was untouched. The bed not slept in. Towels still neatly placed on the racks. It dawned on Renée that she hadn't taken this into consideration.

"Renée you do keep a clean room," Sandy commented.

The suite looked uninhibited. All three of them took notice. Two knew why. The other had her suspicions. Then as quickly as the answer came to Renée she shared her explanation.

"I wish I could take credit for that but the truth is the housekeeper made mine up before yours," she looked at David. "You should have seen it before. I'm a bit messy."

Sandy accepted her explanation. All seemed cordial between the three of them from that point on. Their tracks had been covered up. A chat between Renée and David would take place in the near future to discuss the situation.

An hour passed before they had finished the business at hand. Renée would courier the documents necessary to fly the horse's home. She would then return to Kentucky alone. Looking at the bright side she had two first class seats to stretch out on. Sandy and David planned to frolic in the sunny south for a day or two. A rekindling of their marriage was Sandy's new mission. She was losing him.

Chapter 17

Renée made it home safe and sound. The horses were flown in without incident to join their new extended family. Sandy and her renewed center of attention extended their stay for two days, eventually finding their way back to the ranch. They split the time equally between the bedroom and the beach, occasionally taking a break to refuel with the resort's superb menu.

Life seemed to be returning to normal for the three of them. Renée immersed herself in her duties at the stable, lending too much of her time falling in love with the two new acquisitions. David resumed his daily responsibilities.

Little had been said between Renée and David with regards to their stay in Florida. David praised her quick thinking, telling her Sandy had given him no reason to believe she had suspected anything. Renée's response was suggesting they put the affair on hold for the time being. Maybe it would be best to end it right there and then. Lay low were her words. She urged David not to embrace the notion that his wife did not know of their liaison or at least have her suspicions. A woman's intuition was one of mystical powers. He agreed to the interlude, in part to protect Renée and in part because of the guilt brewing inside him.

The proper thing to do he thought was to come clean with his wife. Explaining that with their ever-increasing separation, he allowed himself to seek companionship. But that wasn't an option. He was not prepared to throw Renée to the wolves. The McGinnis's would destroy her. For now it was best the affaire de coeur remained secreted.

Jacob invited his daughter and her husband to join him for dinner. The fast paced world this family lived in did not allow for these gatherings often. Sandy jumped at the chance to dine with her favorite two men. Her only stipulation was no business was to be discussed during the supper.

When the two arrived, they were surprised to see Brooklyn seated at the table. Both had never thought of her in this capacity. She was the woman who protected her boss with an iron fist. No one got to him without being vetted by her. Neither could recall seeing her smile. Yet here she was, laughing at something Jacob said. It seemed so unusual, so out of place, although a refreshing sight.

"Oh good you're here. Please sit," he got up to assist in the seating of his daughter. "I hope you don't mind, but I invited Brooklyn to join us."

"This is wonderful daddy," putting her stamp of approval on the evening then Sandy turned to Brooklyn. "Don't take this the wrong way Brooklyn, but I thought my father expected you to work twenty-four-seven. I didn't realize he allowed you time to eat."

They all had a little chuckle knowing exactly what was meant.

"He's softening as time goes on," she smiled at Jacob.

"It's quite the opposite of what you may think," he pointed out as he looked at Brooklyn. "She's the slave driver around here. The amount of tasks she concocts for me to achieve in a day's time is inhuman. But you don't want to hear any more of that. Your request, no business is to be discussed."

Brooklyn looked stunning. Her hair was a beautiful silky black, riding halfway down her back. The glasses had disappeared. Dressed casual, yet stylish, her transformation was nothing less than astonishing. She was a striking lady. Her look was in contrast of what everyone had grown accustomed to. It reminded David of one of those movies when the nerdy girl who everyone passed over walks into her prom refashioned, stealing the awe of all her classmates.

The conversation was lighthearted. They steered away from business. Horses were considered part of the family so talking about the two adorable ponies they recently purchased was acceptable. Brooklyn opened up about her upbringing and schooling, information new to the other three at the table. David told a couple hockey stories. Sandy shared some of her touching experiences with unfortunate children from around the world that she encountered during a campaign.

It was a pleasant evening. The conversation was a reminder to the four of them how special family is. Occasions such as this provided some awesome memories. It was nice.

Jacob searched for the right moment to discuss his upcoming trip. When dessert was served, there was a pause in the exchange, no better time than the present Jacob thought.

For the short time his wife was allowed to spend with their daughter, a deep bond had been established. He was uncertain as to how Sandy would react after learning of his attraction to Brooklyn.

"Sandy, David, there's something I—" he paused, looked at Brooklyn then altered his words, "We would like to discuss with you."

The hushed dining room extended a platform for what he was to say. Searching for the proper words he was slow to continue.

"As you know I have reserved the use of our aircraft for the next month or so."

Sandy cut him off, "Daddy, no business talk."

"Yes my dear I'm aware, we agreed. However, this trip will not involve any business. We will consider this a well deserved vacation. Everyone is continually hinting that I should pull myself away from my work. So Brooklyn and I have decided to take a few weeks off to visit the sites of Europe. We have been enjoying each other's company recently and felt the time was never better than the present for an excursion such as this."

His daughter said nothing. Neither did David. He gave them time to let it sink in before he continued.

"I understand this may seem all of a sudden but we are adults and should be allowed to follow our temptations wherever they may lead us. I'm not getting any younger." He looked directly at his daughter, "Sandy, I believe your mother would approve. I have spent a great deal of time speaking to her lately. The time has come to begin the remainder of my life. My love for your mother will never waver. Brooklyn is supportive of this. The fact remains, your mother has passed and I remain. I would appreciate your blessing."

"Daddy, Brooklyn, I couldn't be more pleased," expressing her earnest acceptance.

"Thank you. Hearing that means a great deal to us."

"Jacob," David spoke as he looked at his wife, "we are happy for you. Please go, enjoy, we will keep a handle on this place."

"Thank you. Sandy I want you to stay home with this guy," pointing his finger at David. "It's time the two of you got to spend some quality time together. As I said, I'm not getting any younger. Spoiling a grandchild is high on my bucket list."

"Woo, slow down there father. I tell you what. We will give it some thought," she winked at her husband.

"Good. By the way, we plan on discreetly crossing paths with Serge. I miss him as I'm sure you do. Can I reassure him that his choice to have Renée lead us forward was the correct decision?"

David took the floor, speaking passionately, "She's the best. He knew it. There is something magical about her Jacob. Serge taught her well. Tell him she will make him proud."

"I will pass along your endorsement."

They sat around the table for a while longer until Jacob and Brooklyn excused themselves. He escorted her back to her quarters.

Sandy and David walked down the hall making their way to the grand staircase.

"Well I didn't see that coming," David pointed out.

She shrugged her shoulders not prepared to respond. As they came to the open doors of her father's office she stopped and gently led David through it.

"Let's have a nightcap."

She snagged two beer bottles from the bar fridge, set them on the coffee table located in front of the couch, which faced the picture window overlooking the pastures. David sat, grabbed one and took a swig. Sandy joined him after she turned the lights out. The darkness of the room magnified the beauty of the evening sky as seen through the window.

With the horses safely in their stalls for the night, there was little movement in the fields. With the grasslands illuminated by the cluster of activity in the sky, they sat in silence gazing at one of Mother Nature's wonders. Such a captivating view magnified one's romantic awareness.

"My mother used to sit here with me. She'd turn off the lights and we would stare into this sky for what seemed like forever," she revealed with a tenderness to her voice that he had not often experienced. Silently he listened.

"She told me that was heaven. My mother would always tell me the truth, no matter how much it might hurt. Truth is much less painful than the stinging of a lie found out. I never doubted the veracity of her words. So when she took ill as hard as it must have been for her, she sat me right here and told me her death was inevitable."

Sandy took a sip of her beer and cuddled nearer to her husband before continuing.

"Hanna McGinnis," she pointed to a particular star, "told me when the day of her passing arrived from that point on if I needed to speak with her, she would be living in heaven on that star. I named it Hanna's Capella. It was her favorite star, the sixth brightest in the sky. After she passed, I snuck in here every single night once daddy went to bed. Isn't it ironic that the person you're grieving over, the person who left a hole in your heart, is the exact same person who cured the emptiness by allowing you to believe she was hanging on to every word you spoke. When the star would flicker, I'd take it as a sign that she heard me. There wasn't one single conversation with that star that didn't make me feel better. After, I would go back to bed and sleep like a baby."

"I wish I had met her."

"She would have fallen in love with you. I know it. After all, I've been told, I am the spitting image of her."

"You stole my heart the moment I met you. If your mother was anything like you, I'm sure I would have fallen head over heels."

Sandy curled up even closer to her husband wrapping her arms threw his, then laying her head on his shoulder. It was a déjà vu moment for David. The difference was his wife was holding him not

Renée.

"David, am I losing you?" the question came out of the blue.

He wasn't expecting the sudden change of topic. Knowing his wife possessed near super powers in reading people's reactions, he strived to remain as placid as possible.

Pulling back, he looked at her, "Why would you ask me that."

"I haven't been your typical wife. My work has stolen so much of our time together. I worry. I don't want to lose you."

"Sandy I'm not going anywhere."

She pulled him tighter, "I'm going to reduce my undertakings. Stay home more. Enjoy you and this ranch."

He smiled with the slightest chuckle slipping out. "What?"

"Sandy, you slowing down is equivalent to a normal person blazing through life at warp speed."

"I can do it. Give me a chance. Don't get lost."

"Come, let's go to bed," he stood, took her hand as she rose.

Walking to their room the feeling of guilt swirled in his head. Not brought on by the actual physical affair with Renée, he had justified that by the ongoing absence of his wife. It was more associated to his growing fondness of her. It was wrong to feel this way about two women. The problem was he did.

Once nesting into bed, they made love. Unlike her natural poised demeanor, Sandy was emotional. David noticed her eyes were glossed over. He

311

thought there might even be a tear or two.

"Are you okay?" he asked.

"I've never felt better, come here."

David turned towards her, resting his head on one arm searching for the proper words to ask a question that might well determine the path his life would soon follow.

Chapter 18

Fyad completed his investigation into the fire. The findings did not shock him, although he was positive it would not sit well with Sandy. The information was best passed on person to person. The damage was done. There was little chance of a re-occurrence. The people responsible for the destruction weren't going anywhere. He was attending business meetings in the USA in the near future, at which time he would arrange a get-together with Sandy. There was no need to contact her until that date drew nearer.

Jacob and Brooklyn had the jet fueled up. The last preparations for their excursion were being finalized. The new found relationship was about to be put to the test. Both were confident it would be successful. She dedicated her entire life to a career. Since Hanna died he engrossed himself in the operations of the company. Little time was spent by either on what some say are the most important things in life. Well now was the time to explore that theory.

The first leg of the trip was enjoyed by both.

They talked the entire duration of it. It was the quickest oversees flight Jacob could remember. So engrossed in their exchange, the landing at Heathrow caught them off guard. They were whisked through customs and found themselves registering at the hotel within ten hours of leaving the ranch.

"Good day Mr. McGinnis, we are so pleased you have chosen our accommodations for your stay. As requested, we have reserved two of our finest adjacent suites" handing him the keys.

"Thank you," Jacob was about to add something when he felt Brooklyn place her hand on his.

"We will only require one room," she said to the clerk while sliding one set of keys back to him. She then looked at Jacob seeking his approval.

"Yes, sorry then, one room will be sufficient, yes, good, good. Thank you again," stumbling through his reply.

The elevator delivering them to their suite was also occupied with two other guests so they stood in silence for the ride. Once the young lady attending to the luggage escorted them to the room left with a more than generous tip, Jacob turned to Brooklyn.

"I guess that was a topic we hadn't touched on."

"If you're uncomfortable Jacob, we can make arrangements for the other suite," she smiled at him.

"No, no, absolutely not, it was, unexpected. As you might have noticed I'm out of practice at this sort of thing. To be honest I don't have a clue how to act."

"Jacob, forgive me for being so forward, but we are of the age that we have earned the right to forego the formalities we would have pursued in our youth."

"Speaking solely about me isn't it ironic at this later stage of my life I've reverting back to the clumsiness I knew as a teenager."

Brooklyn related to his way of thinking but didn't reply.

"Brooklyn we haven't so much as kissed and now we find ourselves sharing the same room. Please don't think any less of me, but the mighty Jacob McGinnis ever so feared by his adversaries, may need a little help with this."

"Jacob, come here. I promise to be gentle on you," she held out her arms.

They embraced. It was his first kiss in thirty some years, the last given to his wife after her last breath.

David arrived at the race track. He quickly wrapped up the business portion of his day before noon. His thoughts were on Renée. The hope was to happen into a give and take with her. Should that fail he would make up some excuse. Just as he was about to text her his mobile chimed.

"Hello."

"David I don't think Magical Mist will be healthy enough to run this weekend. I'm worried about his leg. The Vet is having a look at him. Can you have him scratched from the program?"

"Done," he would never second guess his trainer.

"Thank you."

Before she could hang up, he put forth an invitation, "Lunch?"

"David I'm really busy."

"Settled, noon, at the tailgate."

"Fine. Goodbye David."

Shortly thereafter, Renée made her way to the wooden fence where they met so many times. There sat her boss on the tailgate of his favorite half ton truck. It was a baby blue 1953 Chevrolet pickup. The vehicle wasn't just a means of transportation, it was a love affair. As far as he was concerned, everyone else can have all their fancy new vehicles with this option and that option. His was produced with pride not production. It was a romance that anyone who knew him was aware of.

"Hey kid, come sit."

She propped herself onto the tailgate. There they both sat, feet dangling, smiling at one another, glad to be together again. David opened the lid of a small cooler, took out a sandwich and handed it to her. He then tossed her a bottle of water. Like a guy would pitch a buddy a beer. Lunch was served. Nothing fancy, a down home meal just the way each of them liked it.

"What's on your mind boss?" she asked as she took a bite of the chow.

"I'm thinking about leaving Sandy."

Renée nearly choked on her grub. She rested her hands on her lap while shaking her lowered head, exhaling a gainsaying breath.

"David you're not leaving your wife, ne parlez pas fou. Sandy is everything any guy could ask for. You only find someone like that once in a lifetime. She's yours. Get a grip on yourself boss. We've talked about this before. I love the sex David, but I'm not looking for anything else. So make it work

316

with her. I think we need to end our," she was cut off.

"Renée this isn't about us. You've made it clearer than a sunny day on the prairies exactly what our time together is meant to be. This is about where I want my life to be ten years from now. I don't think Sandy and I are moving in the same direction. Since she's been back we've had a few heart to heart talks. She's having difficulty committing to some important aspects of how I see our journey."

"Address it again and again with her David. She will come around. You don't want to be one of those people who end up saying, if only we would have talked more about how we felt, would we both now have someone else."

"I don't know. Maybe you're right. But I want children. I don't believe she's prepared to commit to being a parent."

"David I'm probably not the ideal person to be discussing your marital troubles with."

"Sorry, I'm not thinking straight. I haven't been the same since California. You've opened my eyes to how much zeal I have for life. I want children to share it with."

"I do understand. But please give it more time. Sandy promised she will be staying home more. Once she settles in, I'm sure it will work out for you. With the amount of traveling she has been doing for the past few months, it will take her time just to rid herself of jet lag."

"Maybe your right. Sorry for bothering you with it. I'm being selfish and you're right, I shouldn't be dumping my problems on you," he admitted.

The tailgate picnic chat switched directions. They discussed the active horses stabled at the facility. Renée was exceptionally versed in each of the animal's health, progression and expectations. He had never been apprised of their conditioning in such depth. It once again solidified her promotion. Knowing their investments was in the best set of hands in the racing world allowed David time to concentrate on the business. After an hour and a half which felt like ten minutes they hopped off the truck. Renée made her way to prepare for some training laps. In the back of her mind she was hoping to run in Gabriela. The midday meeting with her boss awakened her desire for the sensual pleasures that at the moment only two people could fulfill. Under the circumstances Gabriela was the best candidate. David was heading for his office to complete his business when his cell signaled an incoming call.

"Hello," he answered, reading an unknown number on the call display.

"David, Agent Scott. I received your message. What can I do for you?"

"I'm looking for an update on the fire investigation. I understand the CIA hasn't gone out of their way in assisting your department. I've been speaking to people who know a bit about this method and have come up with a couple of theories."

"David I'd be more than happy to consider your reasoning but it would seem rather redundant at this point since the person responsible for the fire has been apprehended."

Was he hearing right? They caught the one guilty of this tragedy and neglected to inform the victims. Stopping in his tracks his blood pressure spiked. Someone was going to be held accountable for this lack of professionalism.

"What?" were all his vocal chords could generate.

"You sound surprised David. I apologize. It was my understanding that your family had been briefed."

"Well we haven't. I cannot believe that we weren't made aware of this the second you made an arrest."

"David I will make some inquiries. Although our Agency was pulled off the case and had no involvement in the apprehending of this person, it was our understanding Mr. McGinnis was briefed."

"Why was your department removed from the investigation?"

This whole conversation wasn't making any sense to him. His belief was the FBI were still actively leading the case. Something wasn't adding up. Surely if Jacob had knowledge of this, he would have passed it along.

"If you have nothing to do with this, then who the hell did."

"Don't get me wrong David. Our agency contributed a great deal in determining the identity of this perpetrator. Shortly before we were prepared to make the arrest, we were instructed to stand down."

"By who?"

"The White House. From that point on, we were issued information on a need to know basis. It is now the Secret Service who bears sole responsibility for the case."

"I don't understand. Why in the world would the White House have interest in this?"

The FBI Agent didn't have the answer to that. Normally it was his organization on the opposite side of the coin taking over cases from local police authorities. Trained to obey instructions filtered down from those above, he accepted his orders without question. In this case he presumed Mr. McGinnis's close relationship with the President was the driving factor.

"Again I apologize. I don't have any details on who within your organization was informed but I will make some calls and get back to you. David since the Secret Service is the organization now in charge, do you think it is possible that your wife was the person apprised of the situation during her recent White House visit?"

As far-fetched as the comment initially seemed, it quickly became a reasonable explanation. Recently the more he learned of his wife the less he knew.

"Thank you Agent Scott. If you do come across any additional information please give me a call."

He ended the call. With the phone still in hand he sent a text to his wife. The message was, home soon want to talk.

Back at the ranch Sandy put herself through an intense workout. Purposely she left her cell phones on her night table on silent. Her new priority in life was her husband. No longer did she want to lie to him. He could never learn of her true identity along with the purpose of her missions as it was classified information. Admitting to his suspicions was going to raise more questions but the decision was clear. What she could say is in addition to her own commitments was that she would sometimes secretly have informal discussions with political figures for the President on subjects deemed sensitive to the Nation. It was somewhat the truth. Not the whole truth but not a lie. She would tell him she advised the President during her last visit that her plan was to spend more time at home and he wholeheartedly agreed. Truth.

At the ranch's stable she saddled up her horse Beaches. There was nothing that could clear one's mind like a horseback ride through some of the most picturesque land in the State. Some of her toughest decisions were made on these trails. When her mother passed away she spent every spare minute of her time riding. It was a mending remedy.

Shortly after his text, he arrived home. The drive was a blur. One of those trips that your mind is so absorbed by something that at the end of the ride you wonder how you got there. He searched their suite for his wife but she was not there. David noticed her phones on the table which could only mean one thing. She was riding. Sandy would never interrupt the serenity of riding by the utilization of a mobile. Modern technology was wonderful but it wasn't meant to have access to certain sanctuaries.

David made his way to the stables. He immediate knew she went for a ride when he saw

Beach's stall empty. Anxious to question her of any knowledge with regards to the apprehension of the person responsible for the fire, he saddled his favorite horse. Knowing she would eventually make her way to Willow Meadows he rode off on the trail in the direction of the magnificent views the hillside oasis provided. He was sure that would be her destination. Something must be weighing on her mind. The hilltop was a favorite spot of hers to sort out worrisome concerns.

He was correct. There she sat on the cliff engrossed by the undulating landscape. So much so, his arrival went unnoticed. It wasn't until a rustling from the horses snapped her out of the spell did she realize she wasn't alone. By that point David was at her side. Sandy smiled, acknowledged his presence but said nothing as her focus shifted back to the countryside. David stretched his legs out and followed her lead. They sat silent for a good ten minutes until David broke the silence.

"We need to talk."

"We do. David I'm working on it. Now I have had some time at home, I'm beginning to get a clearer picture of what you expect of our future. But David as I asked the other night, please give me time to process. I'm struggling through a couple of issues that only I can resolve. My challenges are not visible but very real. I need to learn to deal with it by myself before I can share it with you. I don't want to lose you. We need to make choices both of us are comfortable with. Please, I'm making progress."

"As I told you I understand. Take whatever time

you need. That's not what I wanted to discuss."

There was another minute of silence as they once again gazed at the backdrop.

"What's on your mind?"

With a stern expression he turned to her and asked of her what he already knew.

"I spoke with Agent Scott today. You knew the person responsible for the fire was detained, didn't you? You knew and didn't bother to tell me. I carry the burden of losing two horses and you didn't think or want to pass that information on."

"Yes, I knew. I was briefed when at the White House, but David," he interrupted her.

"But what, you knew and didn't tell me. That's what it is. What's going on here? Why would you and your father keep this from me? Do I not merit enough respect from you two to be included."

"My father doesn't know."

"I don't get it. Is our life real or are we living in some fantasy land?"

"Can I explain myself?"

"Please, be my guest."

At that Sandy shifted towards her husband sitting upright, crossed legs with her arms resting on her knees. The contemplation was over. Her entire attentiveness was now centered on her husband. No lies.

"When I was visiting the President he informed me in private of a joint CIA and FBI arrest. The person is a young girl who works for one of the feed companies. She's innocent. Yes she did place the material in the stables. However, she was led to believe they were an odor control product that a company was experimenting with who had an odd sense of showcasing their merchandise. The kid had no clue what she was getting into. She was broke and someone paid her a great deal of money."

She continued honestly laying out all she knew about the detainee. Explaining the President decided that because of his close relationship with Jacob and the companies high profile it was best to keep it close to him until the persons who ordered the attack were brought to justice. So it was taken out of both Agencies hands and turned over to a small group of faithful Secret Service agents who the President categorically trusted. He listened believing her explanation not necessary agreeing or understanding why he had been left out of the loop.

"I want to talk to her."

"That's not possible David. She's been released."

"Who authorized that?"

"I did."

"Why."

"As I said she was blameless. The President and I felt it would be of no benefit to make a spectacle of her. The press would be damaging not just to us, but also the kid. We forced her to resign her job. They were not informed as to what happened. The President arranged new employment for her, a fresh start somewhere closer to him so he can keep a close eye on her. We believe she may be in danger. Whoever is behind it will want to clean up loose ends. I believe the President felt sorry for her."

David sat in silence trying to decipher what he learned. She was content to end the conversation hoping she had satisfied his curiosity. To his surprise, he felt a barrier had been broken or at least partially taken down. This was the first time his wife made reference to the power she wielded within the administration. He believed she was opening up with the truth.

"David we should be getting back. It is best that what we have learned stay between us. My father is not to know, for now. I promise to keep you up to date the minute I'm advised. I'm sorry I should have explained earlier."

He took a deep breath then exhaled, "Okay."

"David there is more I would like to talk about, but not here. Can we free up our schedules this evening?"

"Sure," he bent over and gave her a kiss. "I have an hour or so, let's ride."

Chapter 19

Brooklyn and Jacob sat in a rented automobile outside Serge's present residence. It was the beginning of a stay in the hospital where he would be administered an experimental drug regiment by Dr. White. Jacob had worked his magic to penetrate his friend's medical schedule. The doctor provided transportation for each series of treatments. Today the chauffeur would be Jacob, the navigator, Brooklyn.

During the past few days, the pair became tourists minus any special treatment reserved for the rich. They took in Buckingham Palace from the outside. Brooklyn once accompanied the President on a visit, but the business at hand left little time to absorb the magnificence a tourist see's while standing at its gates. Similar for Jacob who over the years attended three functions at the Royal Residence. Also checked off the list was an hour wait in line to ride the London Eye. Jacob who is not good with heights felt a little queasy by the end. In addition there were visits to St. Paul's Cathedral and the British Museum. Both were thoroughly enjoying the city as ordinary tourists.

Serge appeared from the doorway of the stoned country house. Considering his medical challenges he looked good. He'd lost a little weight but Jacob thought he could notice more color in his face.

As he approached, Jacob stepped out, walking around the back of the car and had the rear door open by the time Serge reached the car. Serge was walking with his eyesight somewhat lowered to the walkway rather than the vehicle. Obviously he was expecting a chauffeur to be attending to him so he paid little attention to Jacob. It wasn't until he was fully seated that he snapped out of his presumptuous state and recognized his boss. Quite possibly what jolted him was the presence of a woman passenger with long flowing black hair.

"Well I never, blimey."

"We were in town, thought you might need a lift."

Jacob extended his hand but Serge lifted himself out of the car and gave him a big hug. Shortly after they released each other it dawned on Serge that the passenger was Brooklyn. He stuck his head into the door opening.

"Brooklyn, how nice to see you. How in the world did you get this guy out of his office? Better yet, how did you convince him to let you out from behind your desk? God, it's so nice to see you two."

During the ride to the hospital Brooklyn and Serge did most of the talking. Jacob was struggling with driving on the opposite side of the road. Serge was feeling good about his treatment. He held no false hope of a reversal of his condition. However, the anticipation of lengthening his life expectancy was in the realm of possibilities. He thanked Jacob two or three times during the trek for the arrangements with Dr. White.

All three entered through the main doors of the hospital and stayed together until the nurse arrived to escort Serge to his room. The plan was at the end of the treatment Jacob and Brooklyn would return to drive him home.

On their way back to the hotel Brooklyn suggested they stop at a pharmacy to pick up some personal items. Next door to it was a small outdoors store that carried item such as hiking equipment and so on. Since the toiletries provided by the hotel satisfied Jacob's needs he elected to browse the little shop while she went about her purchases.

As soon as he stepped foot inside, an idea struck him like a lightning bolt. In his renewed infatuation for life, a faded teenage dream returned. He knew exactly what items he wanted to buy.

Once she returned the horse to the stables, Sandy occupied her father's office for the most part of the day taking care of business. Her first call was made on the secured phone she retrieved from her residence before settling in. It was to the Director of the CIA.

Christopher Young immediately answered, "Yes, Sandy."

"Sir, I thought we were going to keep a lid on our findings with regards to the fire."

"I have. The agents who are aware of the arrest were personally instructed by me to wipe the slate clear. Nothing will come out of this office.

Everything has been handed over to the President's crew."

"Agent Scott briefed my husband."

"Then you should have directed your call to Madison."

"No, you make the call. I know how much you two like to chat it up."

"I'll talk to her."

"Thank you."

"Is there anything else Sandy?"

"No."

"Good, have a nice day," he hung up without saying goodbye.

The remainder of the afternoon was split between her own responsibilities and discussions with a select few of her father's hierarchy. She was in possession of Power of Attorney which left her with the final word in her father's absence. But, for the most part she would adhere to the advice of those her father entrusted in.

After their ride, David planted himself in an office attached to the stables at the ranch. He called Renée for an update. They dragged out the exchange longer than need be but adhered to business matters. As he was wrapping up his cell chimed.

"Hello."

"David, Agent Scott."

"I wasn't expecting to hear from you again so soon," surprised to speak with him twice in one day.

"As I promised I dug a little deeper or tried to. David I've been shut out. I was called up on the carpet for our last conversation. The case is no longer active within our Agency. If I so much as breathe a word of it again I've been guaranteed my next assignment will be in some remote location investigating flying saucers. Sorry I wasn't able to be of more help."

"Thank you Agent Scott. I understand. For the record you were the only one I could get a straight answer from, I appreciate it. Thanks again."

"Anytime. Goodbye."

With the day's tasks complete, he took the short walk to the house. Before heading to their suite he poked his head into Jacobs's office.

"You hungry," he asked or more like motioned to his wife who held the telephone to her ear.

Sandy held up her index finger up indication she would only be a minute. He leaned against the door frame and waited. Less than a minute later she hung up.

"What did you have in mind," she inquired about dinner.

"I can throw something together. Any requests?"

"Your choice. Thanks. I need about another half hour."

"I'm on it."

With that he went directly to the kitchen, searched the cupboards, opened the refrigerator then began to fill the suite with a scrumptious aroma.

Jacob was tapping his fingers on a Smartphone when Brooklyn stepped through the door. He finished typing as he noticed her. She was surprised to see he made a purchase. She could not recall ever witnessing him go out and buy anything.

"Jacob you actually bought something."

"Yes. I found something I have been considering purchasing since my teen years."

"Well," she stood there, "let me see," making a move towards the large shopping bag.

He pulled it aside and hid it behind his back.

"No. I will show you once we get back to our room."

That is exactly what he did. As soon as they entered the suite, out of the bag came two medium sized light weight hiking rucksacks.

"What in the world," she started saying before being cut off.

"Hear me out."

Jacob took out his phone prompting something to the screen. Moving to her side he handed it to her. Still curious as to the impetus behind the suggestion, she did catch on right away after viewing the tiny screen.

"Our plan was to experience Europe. Why not do it by rail. I've wanted to do this since I was a kid. I've been so engrossed in making money it remained a dream. Let's do it now. We pack as much as we can into these and store the rest here at the hotel. If we don't come back I will make arrangements to have it flown back home."

What he showed her on his mobile was the confirmation of two Eurail passes good for a month's travel anywhere in Europe. She continued looking at him shaking her head back and forth in disbelief.

"Jacob you do realize we have a company to run."

"Oh, I haven't forgotten. That's why I hired the

best management team money can buy. Besides, it pressures Sandy to sit put for a while. She will feel obligated to help out. The two of them need together time. So, what do you think?"

"I'm all in. Truth be told, I've shared that same dream."

"Fantastic. Let's do it," he was keyed up, ready to go. "One more thing, I want to offer the use of our jet to Serge and his family for the next three weeks. I called a friend of mine who owns a beautiful island off the coast of Greece and he would be more than happy to accommodate them."

"I'm not sure Serge's health would hold. As you say, we can offer."

"Good. We will visit him tomorrow at the hospital."

She gave him a hug.

"Jacob. Where have you been hiding this element of your personality all these years?"

"I'm not sure, but it waited much too long revealing itself."

Surprisingly, Serge warmed to the idea and with the blessing of Dr. White he gathered his close family. They jetted off to the island for a two week stay. Then it was back to treatments.

Brooklyn and Jacob boarded a train, destination somewhere. Their only promise to each other was, make no plans beyond the present day. Let the journey take them whichever way the wind might blow.

Sandy and David finished dinner. After they cleaned up, she suggested they take a walk about the ranch. It was time to come clean. Her explanation would have to be modified. A promise was made not to lie. Confident her husband would understand, she would adhere to that, but there was a need to avoid topics requiring security clearance. As they walked along side of the white fence she began.

"David I know exactly how you feel about the path our marriage has taken. You are the most patient person I know. I need to be more forthcoming from now on. So if you bear with me I have some explaining to do."

"Sandy, you don't have to do this if you're uncomfortable with it."

"Actually I do. If our relationship has any chance of survival you need to know more about me. I'm a perceptive person. I know what's going on."

David's heart fluttered. He automatically referenced her comment to his indiscretions with Renée.

"Please bear with me here. Let me finish, then we can discuss anything you want."

Here it goes she thought. No lies, truth.

"One evening after I graduated college, my father was entertaining the President here at the ranch. He was spending the night in our guest house. It wasn't the first time I met him, so we were familiar with each other. When my father retired for the evening, the President mentioned to me he wasn't ready to call it a night just yet. He invited me to take a walk with him as he had something he would like to discuss. So we did, with the Secret Service in tow."

They walked a little further until Sandy propped

333

herself up on the fence. David leaned against it looking into the field lit by a full moon.

"He asked me how I felt about his administration and whether or not I had any inclination of pursuing a career in politics. It caught me off guard. I wasn't sure how to reply, telling him I hadn't put much thought into it. We chatted for a couple of hours before the weariness of the day caught up to us. As we were saying our good nights he invited me to the White House the following week wanting to continue the conversation. He mentioned he had a proposal I might be interested in."

David remained silent. This wasn't what he was expecting but it was intriguing.

"The next week I went to Washington. At the meeting, myself, the president and," she stopped for a second. "David, this cannot be repeated, ever."

He nodded his head in agreement but didn't speak.

"The other person in the room was the CIA's Director. Because of my father's contacts in addition to where my business travels would be taking me, they asked for my assistance. At times certain government concerns cannot be negotiated out in the open. That's where I come in. So when oversees, once in awhile I'm asked to meet with dignitaries to negotiate sensitive matters that need to be resolved exclusive of public knowledge. That's the reason some of my trips are extended at the last minute. But for the most part, it is our business that occupies my time. That's it. That's all. That's what I do."

"So my wife's a CIA agent."

"No David I'm not an agent. I confer with foreign officials with regards to matters that are best not made public. The world of politics has no boundaries, few rules. What you see on the news is a diminutive piece of what really goes on."

"Ok then. You're aware I always knew there was more to your trips than met the eye. However I thought it related to your father's business. So why explain yourself now?"

"There are only a handful of people who have knowledge of the delicate off the record exercises I've been involved in. I was under the impression the government would not take kindly to me sharing it with you."

"So what changed?"

"During my last visit to the White House, the President hinted I do whatever necessary to make things right with my husband."

"He's a smart man."

"That he is."

She jumped off the fence took him by the arm and gave him a kiss. They continued with a hushed walk along the fence line knowing there was more to discuss but needing a couple of minutes to let the confession settle in.

David was first to speak, "My turn?" he asked.

Her expression indicated approval.

"I appreciate you confiding in me. It goes without question that your secret is safe. Now I have concerns with your safety. Are you in danger during these undertakings?"

Not expecting that question it took a second to develop a reply as she vowed to herself there would be no lies tonight.

"David, I'm capable of handling myself. You have nothing to worry about."

"Are you sure?"

She nodded then pulled him closer. The stroll continued until David stopped, put his hands on his wife's shoulders. It was his turn to speak from the heart.

"Sandy how does this play into our future. You become evasive whenever I bring up the topic of us raising our own family."

"David you know I love children. I spend so much of my energies trying to improve their lives. I'm scared. What if I'm not home enough? What if I'm not a good mother? I can't just stop what I do. I have so many responsibilities. I know how much this means to you. David I'm afraid of not being a good parent."

Starting a family was weighing heavily on her. She started to cry. Her emotions didn't get the better of her too often but she was still human, although some thought of her as a machine. David held her tight. He would give her time, yet wanted to continue the discussion about having children.

"Sandy, listen. I don't expect you to stay at home. That's not you. I want you to continue your work. What you do is important. It's needed. We'll figure it out. I'll stay home. I can work out of the ranch. Renée is quite capable of taking on more responsibility. Sandy, your father is the busiest person I know and he raised you single-handedly. You turned out just fine."

"David I promise to reduce my traveling. I will.

I'm at that point in my life that age begins to apply its own pressure. I've been so busy it snuck up on me. There are personal issues within me that I need to come to terms with first. This is something a woman needs to do alone, at least for the time being. If I promise a decision no longer than say two months, would you be okay with it."

"Absolutely, Sandy I just want to have kids. Ok, that's a lot to absorb for one night. Let's go home."

They turned back towards the ranch house retracing their steps. Before they reached it Sandy stopped and looked her husband in the eye. There was one more issue she wanted to get off her chest.

"David there is one more issue I would like to touch on. What I'm about to say is an observation that doesn't require an answer. Actually, I don't want you to answer. I would prefer if you didn't say a word. It will alleviate the temptation to lie."

"Okay."

"You promise. Not a word."

He signaled his consent, completely at a lost as to where she was going with this, oblivious to the blind siding about to take place.

"If you are or have or are thinking about sleeping with Renée, I believe I can find it in my heart to forgive you. The extent of separation I've evoked undeniably leaves both of us vulnerable. Experiencing temptation to fill this void would be understandable."

When David began to respond she touched her index finger to his lips. He first thought his wife took notice of something in Miami exposing his extramarital relation. The enticement comment made him wonder if she was also making reference to herself having an affair.

"David no, I don't want to know. Please don't say anything, you promised."

Revealing her acceptance of what might have happened was pushing her tolerance to the max. Any expansion on the subject was sure to escalate into a seething exchange.

"Let's go to bed," she changed the subject.

"But," he started, not knowing what to say before he got the look and went silent.

If the other woman would have been someone other than Renée, someone his wife didn't know, he felt a confession would have been forthcoming before this conversation. But, to ruin Renée's life wasn't something he was prepared to do.

"David," she hesitated.

"What?" He urged her to continue.

"David, don't love her. That I can't live with."

Chapter 20

Jacob and Brooklyn extended the European vacation an additional week. They took in all the popular sightseeing destinations and some lesser known locations. Most of their nights were spent in mid priced hotels. Those where people traveling on a budget might lay their heads. A couple of nights they took refuge at a shelter normally reserved for the young. They used the excuse they were having difficulty finding a vacant hotel and that they were seeking beds to sleep only a few hours before moving on. Jacob had always wanted to experience one.

The other lodgers, mostly in their twenties, shared stories of their travels to the genuine attentiveness of Jacob and Brooklyn. The conversations were of so much interest the majority traded sleep for the narrative. Sunlight appeared before any rest could be had. Jacob was so impressed with the spirit these kids conveyed. So much so, he took a young gentleman aside before leaving, handing him his card. He encouraged the boy to complete his journey no matter how long it took. But when it was complete, a job, a well paying job, would be waiting for him at McGinnis Enterprises.

Once home it didn't take long to get back in the groove of things. Sandy was more than happy to hand back the reins to her father so she could resume her own responsibilities. The holiday had solidified what was already known, they had become a couple. They limited sleepovers to two, three times a week max, allowing this new found relationship time to flourish. Both suspected that in the not-too-distant future the log chalet would become vacant.

Sandy appreciated her brief sabbatical. Being an expert rider, she'd forgotten how enjoyable riding could be. During her visits to the track in the past couple of weeks she was encouraged by David to ride a few training laps.

Being relieved of her father's duties it was time to get back to work. Plans were in the making for some brief out of town meetings. She would make a conscious effort to restrict her travels to overnight stays, at most two nights. In one way she was surprised and in another not so much that Langley had been respective of her request to reduce her assignments. Her thought was the President had a say in it.

The first of her own commitments was arranged for the following weekend in Chicago. There she once again accepted an invitation to be the guest speaker at a fund raising event. Her hope was David would join her.

Working out of her suite, she was getting up to

refresh her tea when her cell chimed.

"Hi."

"Sandy we need to talk."

"It's good to hear from you. How's married life?"

"We will talk about that some other time. I have answers to what you asked of me," Fyad wasn't in the mood for pleasantries.

"Fyad I'm alone. The line is secure. You are aware we isolated the person responsible of placing the igniting mechanism."

"Sandy she was a pawn. I will be in Washington next week. We need to do this in person. My schedule is tight. Can you come to me?"

"Fayd are you sure we can't discuss this now."

"Sandy you're not going to like what I have for you. You may not be shocked at my findings but it will disturb you. My preference is to pass it on personally."

Sensing the seriousness in his voice, she agreed. Since she would already be speaking in Chicago during his visit, it would be a quick detour. Fyad was brilliant with regards to intelligence gathering. Actually he was the best she knew. His talents surpassed anything the CIA had to offer. The tactics used in his gatherings were not necessarily moral or legal. They did however produce exceptional results. What she was about to learn from him would undoubtedly be accurate. They wished each other well, promising to touch base once he landed State side.

Christopher Young, the Director of the world's largest, most powerful, dangerous intelligence organizations sat at his desk reviewing a file. It was presented to him by one of his agents who was uncomfortably sitting on the other side of the desk. There were no words being spoken. The boss was absorbed in the material. Before long he looked up.

"You weren't exposed."

"No sir. Our surveillance has been twenty-four seven. I assure you we have not been made."

The Director glanced back down at the paperwork.

"I see there was an appointment at the doctor's."

"Yes sir. In and out. Thirty minutes max. Some sort of record for nowadays."

"You're an expert on medical wait times?"

"No sir."

It didn't matter that the agent was a ten year veteran. Sitting in the chair he now occupied, he was reduced to feeling like a rookie applying for his first job.

"Where is the medical report?"

"Sir?"

"The doctor's report, from what you referred to as a record breaking visit. I want it on my desk within the hour."

"Yes sir."

"That will be all."

He dismissed the Agent sending him along his way with his tail between his legs, en route to the IT center to request the hacking of the physician's medical files. When the chief says an hour he means fifty minutes. The agent possessed the clout to prioritize the request and would use it. He didn't want to end up assisting the Canadians at their signals intelligence intercept facility in Alert, Nunavut on the northeastern tip of Ellesmere Island. It has the distinction of being the northernmost permanently inhabited place in the world.

David asked Renée to meet him at the fence. She arrived first and was sitting on it as he came around the corner of the stable. It had been a couple of days since they had last seen each other. He hadn't spent much time with her recently, as most of his time was spent at the ranch with Sandy. Seeing her now made his heart flutter. She looked good. As time passed he started to believe thoughts of Renée would always be present. He couldn't help it. Control of one's actions can be achieved. It's the inevitable emotions that fester within presenting themselves when caressed.

"What's up boss?" she asked as David hopped onto the top railing.

"Next weekend. New York."

"We'll be ready."

"I know."

"Are there any changes you want implemented?"

David took a moment to answer, "No."

Renée knew there was more on his mind than the race itself. She had a feeling what was to be said next.

"I meant are you ready for us to be away together again."

"David, unless one of us makes the decision to find a new job, we have to find a way to become at ease with this. Besides, now Sandy is home, won't she be traveling with you?"

He overheard one of his wife's calls making an

arrangement to be the guest of honor the same day as the race. She hadn't informed him yet, but he knew it was coming. His wife would invite him and he would decline because of his obligation at the track.

"Sandy won't be going. She has a speaking engagement."

"Okay. I have a lot to do, is there something else," trying to pry out of him what was on his mind.

"Are we going to sleep together in New York".

He felt he might as well put it out there. There was no sense spending the time leading up to the trip being preoccupied with the pleasurable thoughts of experiencing her warmth. All the cards on the table, your call.

"That's not a good idea. Your wife is back. All your energies should be focused on working things out with her. She's really trying David. That's where your mind should be. Besides, we were lucky to come out of Florida unexposed."

He didn't want to tell her he believed Sandy knew about the two of them.

"I know what you're saying is right but to be honest since California all I can think about is you."

"Can I be blunt," she felt like giving him a good back hander.

"Absolutely."

"Most men would treasure having Sandy as their partner. She's everything someone could ask for, beautiful, intelligent, and wealthy. You need to give your head a shake. Wake up from this midlife crisis you're having boss. We had sex, that's all it was.

She's the one you need to love."

"You're right again but that doesn't change the fact that I want you in bed."

David couldn't remember being this confused. He knew he loved his wife. Raising a family was at the top of his priority list or at least that is what he thought. Yet here he was fixated on Renée. The gratification from being inside her was etched into his head. He couldn't shake it off. For the first time in his life he was secretly considering scheduling an appointment with a psychologist in hopes of shedding light on his state of mind, a big step for a farm boy from Alberta. Back home people work out their frustrations by grabbing an axe and attacking the nearest log. Or they take hold of the nearest rifle and put a few rounds into some haystack or any other object not near a living creature. It worked wonders. But he was not on the farm.

"You know if we prolong ending this you will lose her and a relationship is the last thing I'm looking for."

"I know," he agreed then went on, "I'm aware of what's at stake. That's not going to take away my desire for you."

"David. I'll do you right here, right now if that's what you want. I love sex, more than that I love having sex with you. But that doesn't make it right. Cheating on your wife will ruin your future. Everything you guys have worked towards will be gone in a blink of eye."

"Why does that not bother you," he asked her.

"I'm not the one married David, you are. It's not my fault you're searching for something. Surely

Sandy realizes your needs. It's her responsibility to correct it. As for me, my downfall is sex. With you it's special, but I'll survive when it's over. And for your sake it should be."

"How can you have such a chilled attitude about what's happened between us."

"I don't have the answer to that nor am I looking for one. I believe I'm a bit of a coquette."

"No you're not Renée. You may want to pretend you don't care but you are one of the most kindhearted people I know. That tiny body of yours is chocked-full of affection."

"Listen David, we should get back to work. In New York if you knock on my door I will welcome you in my bed. As you Americans say, the ball is in your court. Just make sure you are prepared to live with the consequences before making the decision."

Renée didn't want to continue hashing about the subject. She wanted to get back to the tasks at hand. Another lesson taught by her mother was that men have a way of slipping back into their childhood. During those times, it was best to listen, but let them work it out on their own.

She hopped off the fence and gave him a look to say it was time to end the chat. He silently acknowledged it. But as she began to walk away there was one more question to ask.

"Renée, can I ask you something personal?"

The first thing that came to her mind was who asks that type of question of someone you already have been intimate with. That in itself is as personal as it gets. But obviously she would listen to where he was taking this.

"David what? I really do have to get back to work."

He posed the question which was weighing on his mind since the weekend at the stakes race. "Were you and Gabriela together in California? I swear I saw her come out of your room."

She had almost forgotten Gabriela had mentioned that David may have spotted her coming out of her room.

"Yes."

"Did you sleep with her?"

Renée stared at him for a second before an amorous smile appeared on her face. Saying nothing she turned and walked ever so slowly away from her boss knowing full well his eyes would be undressing her. Men.

David's desire for her intensified with each step she took. Picturing Renée and Gabriela in bed together drove him crazy. It was a guy thing. He wasn't sure she knew what she was doing to him. If intentional, it was succeeding.

The head of the CIA received a copy of the medical file in thirty-seven minutes flat. After dismissing the agent who delivered it, he smiled, being entertained by the uneasiness of his employees when in his company. The more fearful they were of him, the more efficient the agency operated. Their duty was to serve to the betterment of the country no matter what task was assigned.

All other files were pushed aside leaving the medical report in the center of the desk. He opened it and began to read it slowly, once, twice, then again. There was no facial expression whatsoever.

Once he grasped its contents he closed the folder and looked directly ahead with a blank stare.

After what seemed an unusually amount of time deciding how to proceed, he summoned the agent assigned as his assistant who immediately entered the room in silence awaiting instructions.

"Steven, please contact the undercover operative we have placed at the McGinnis ranch. I want a meeting in my office within twenty four hours."

"Sir, I'm not sure that would be wise. We've taken great strides to shield our identity. If brought in, it does open us up to the possibility of exposure."

"Steven, I'm not asking."

"Yes sir."

The next morning the young handler sat in the ever so feared chair waiting for the Director to explain the visit.

"I understand your infiltration has been successful. I'm told you have become a significant addition to the staffing at the ranch. You may have missed your calling when you signed up with us."

"Thank you sir, to be honest I haven't had much of an opportunity to apply what I was taught by the agency."

"Oh don't fret, your time will come. As I promised, you will be moving on in the very near future. But first I have one last task for you."

Chapter 21

Soon after their return from Europe a family dinner extended late into the evening. David and Sandy could barely sneak in a word edgewise being the recipients of a blow-by-blow account of the five week trek. Jacob and Brooklyn created the impression that one might expect from someone finding a lost treasure. There was a great deal of laughter from both couples as the stories were told.

Eventually the younger couple tired and excused themselves. Once back in their suite David made a comment to his wife about how happy her father was. Adding he felt like the older of the two men as his father-in-law could have gone on all night. Sandy wholeheartedly agreed. Actually the evening affirmed his want to have children. He visualized being the parent at the table, eventually the grandparent. Was this marriage going to fulfill his image?

"David I've committed to speaking at a fundraiser next weekend in Chicago. I know you have races in New York. I've put aside my own responsibilities to take care of dad's the past few weeks so I really should attend. They've had to postpone twice already. You okay with it? If not I will cancel and go with you."

"I heard you on the phone the other day making the arrangements. I'm good. We have three horses running so I'm not going to have a lot of extra time as it is."

"Thanks."

"Sandy, I don't want you to give up the work you do. All I ask is that you keep our discussion about starting a family at the forefront of your thoughts."

The exchange was taken place on the move. He now plopped himself on the bed. She made her way to the powder room to freshen up before retiring for the night and most likely an hour or so gratifying each other's hunger. His comment stopped her.

"To be honest with you David, for the past couple of months that's pretty much all I've been thinking about. Something inside me won't let me get my mind off it. I promised you an answer shortly and I am committed to that."

The issue was not touched on the remainder of the evening. What was talked about was her ink. When she walked naked towards the bed seeing the art on her body jogged David's recollection of the story told at the bar about the eleven phantom soldiers who survived what was believed to be the military's most aggressive training program. His wife explained the meaning behind her three understated tattoos early in their relationship. Now his curiosity resurfaced. He hadn't given much thought of the possibility his wife was the one referred to as Sandy. Actually he felt there was little chance this group even existed. Yet his interest was renewed with her recent confessions of being involved in secretive undertakings.

As she pulled down the covers he put his hand on the back of her shoulder rubbing a small tattoo. She gave him a curious look but didn't say anything.

"Sandy, how did you decide on the design of your tattoos?"

"Why do you ask?"

"I'm just curious. I think I might get one."

"I never thought the day would come when David Watson would get himself inked."

"I said I've given it some thought. I know yours are in memory of your mother, but what about this one?" he questioned her as he rubbed the back of her shoulder.

"What about it. I already explained it to you," she was becoming suspicious of his inquiry.

"I know. But why eleven stars, why not ten, eight or six, why eleven?"

"I like the way it looks with eleven," not the whole truth, not a lie.

"Your mind is on tattoos when you have a naked woman sitting beside you."

She then adjusted her position to face him sitting in a yoga position pushing the blankets aside revealing a clean shave. His interest was curious, yet she knew there was zero chance he was referring to the tattoos true meaning.

David wanted to press the issue but even if the far-fetched story was true, his wife would never admit it. Besides, the view of her naked body swiftly altered his train of thought. Her love making was more aggressive, more urgent than the norm.

The day before Sandy departed for Chicago she spent a good portion of the morning with her father. They appraised the decisions made in his absence. During the meeting he questioned her on the progress on the fire. She didn't feel comfortable going into detail with him in case he jumped the gun and began tearing people apart. Her intention was to bring closure to the investigation then review it with him. Wholeheartedly trusting his daughter, he would allow her to handle it whatever way she deemed appropriate on the promise he would eventually be briefed. The rendezvous with Fyad she anticipated would bring it all to an end.

David made his way to Renée's residence on the way to the airport. She once again sported a yoga outfit albeit different from the last but by no means less enticing. He was determined to resist the temptation of his co-worker during the weekend. As soon as she sat a foot to his right those defenses were beginning to weaken. He was entrapped by the perfume dabbed on her neck. The attire, smile, and overall unassuming allure reversed his mindset from being steadfast about sleeping alone to anticipating the pleasure of his body against the warmth of hers.

Sandy was successful in rallying the troops at her speaking engagement. A great deal of money was raised for the charity. She did cancel a meeting the day after which allowed her the opportunity to fly into Washington where Fyad was on an official business for his country. When her aircraft touched down she didn't have to wait long as he was standing on the tarmac. When she walked down the stairs of the jet he held out his hand to assist her onto the pavement.

"My dear Sandy you do look more spectacular every time I lay eyes on you. My father may have been right in wishing I married you."

"Hello Fyad. I'm sure I don't hold a candle to your beautiful Princess."

They gave each other a hug while the driver held the limousine door open. Reservations at a favorite restaurant of Fyad's awaited them. He had chosen it for both its exquisite menu and the privacy it provided. No mention of his finding was discussed during the ride. The talk centered on his new found married life. Once their orders were placed Sandy wanted to get down to business.

"Fyad what do you have for me?"

"We should eat first."

"No. Please fill me in."

He was trying to delay explaining his findings so a pleasant dinner's mood would not be dampened. However, Sandy was a professional, capable of managing her reaction.

"Ok. But I expect you to remain here and dine with me. I've been looking forward to enjoying an evening with you. We need to stay in touch with one another more frequently."

"We will. What I want now is to see if my suspicions are correct."

From the inside pocket of his jacket he pulled out a small envelope and slid it across the table. Sandy stared at him a few seconds before looking at it. She knew the fire related to her, suspecting it was orchestrated from within the small community of people in the know of her true identity, to restrict or alter her movements. What she was having problems with is the amateurish execution. Everyone in her company was an expert in their respective field. She opened the file taking a minute to review the findings before returning it. There was no verbal reaction. Her only response was a shake of her head indicating what she read was hard to believe. The food arrived.

"Let's eat," was all she said.

"Sandy do you want to discuss this. I'm concerned about you. This is a dangerous world you have aligned yourself in. I believe I can be of further assistance."

"Thank you. It is appreciated. However, I need to take care of it myself and I will. You don't have to worry. Now eat."

The next two hours were absorbed by a bottle of wine and fine food. When done they returned to the airport and said their goodbyes. After boarding the plane she dialed a number.

On the third ring she heard, "What can I do for you Sandy?"

"I'm coming in. Make the arrangements."

"When?"

"Now."

"That is not possible. I'm at the White House."

"Perfect I'm already at the airport. Please inform Secret Service of my arrival."

The Director didn't take kindly to being instructed by anyone other than the President. And there lay the problem. He knew if he didn't accommodate Sandy her next call would be the President himself and there was no doubt she would receive access to the Oval Office.

"Sandy I have little available time today. Can whatever's on your mind wait?"

"Prepare my clearance Christopher. We are going to have a chat. Maybe we should invite Andrew in on our conversation," she referred to the President by his first name to remind the Director of her influence with the administration.

"You're cleared. Please plan to be brief. My time is limited."

She hung up without extending a goodbye. Over the duration of their relationship she could not remember a single conversation ending with the formality of a goodbye being exchanged.

Brooklyn entered Jacobs's office unannounced. The sadness in her face was visible. Jacob knew as soon as he saw her something was terribly wrong. Instead of standing or sitting in the chair at the front of the desk she walked around to him and leaned on it as she laid her hand on his shoulder. The tears began to roll down her cheek.

"Jacob, its Serge. He's passed," she informed him.

"Oh no. Oh no. How can that be? He looked so happy when we left. I honestly thought he would survive for quite some time. He was responding to the treatment."

"I just got off the phone with his sister. He took a turn for the worse when they returned from the vacation. Jacob it's common for those surrounding a person entering their final days to misinterpret their acceptance of internal peace as an improvement in health."

Now tears surfaced on his face. He hated times like this. Life just wasn't fair.

"We must all arrange to attend his service."

"His family has elected not to stage a celebration of life. He's already been cremated. What they did ask is they wish to divide his ashes. They will bury half at their family plot and would like us to spread the remainder in the fields where his horses roam. I've already arranged the transportation."

He stood up and hugged her. They held each other tightly as they cried. Although the loss of Serge was inevitable it would be some time before Jacob came to grips with it.

After the pre-racing day activities, David and Renée again found themselves eating a late supper. Little alcohol was consumed as race day required both to be at the top of their game, similar to what is expected of the thoroughbreds. The evening ended with both retreating to their respective rooms without incident.

The following night was ending similar to the previous one until, when saying their good nights, Renée opened her door and David followed her in. There was no resistance. The exhilaration of winning two races and placing second in the other spilled over to the bedroom, again. The love making was powerful. This sporadic relationship was showing no signs of having an expiration date. Something drastic would have to happen for it to end.

Secret Service was waiting at the entrance gate when Sandy arrived. They whisked her through a private entrance where she found herself standing outside the Oval Office door. Expecting a private meeting with the Director she was surprised to find herself being lead in. What she had to say was suppose to be for Christopher's ears only. So when she found he was the sole occupant a sigh of relief came over her. The last thing she wanted was to involve the President.

"Sandy please come in, sit. Can we make this as concise as possible I'm expecting Andrew," calling the President by his first name to make a point that she was not the only person with a personal acquaintance to him.

"Fine by me. This won't take long."

"Good. Please have a seat."

"I'm okay right here," she voiced in an angry manner.

"What's upsetting you?"

"You. How dare you order the destruction of my family's stables. You killed two beautiful animals. Such an uncalled for, callous, bush-league operation. For what? So David wouldn't tag along to the Middle East with me. So I wouldn't be distracted in duties for this great country. Did you for one second think, maybe I should ask her to go alone. No amount of intelligence is worth the lives of two innocent horses. You're a disturbed person Mr. Director. You need help sir. I'm done."

The Director sat quietly listening to what was being thrown at him. Only when he knew she was finished and making her way to the door did he reply

"That was unfortunate. Collateral damage. I apologize for the unprofessional manner in which it was handled. I went along with an idea one of our young agents concocted and do regret it. The purpose was exactly as you have determined. We needed to be certain you would travel alone."

"I don't want to hear it. You are a troubled individual and I no longer want to be associated with you or your organization," she turned her back on him.

"Please hear me out."

"No," as she was just about to grab the door knob he got one more line in.

"Before you run away, would you like help recalling how many people you personally killed? Not animals. Human beings. You're not the little angel others are led to believe."

Sandy wanted to turn around and punch him in the head. Maybe break a bone or two. But it was best for all if she took a deep breath and leave. As she went to turn the door handle, it magically opened and there stood the President of United States.

"Sandy, what a pleasant surprise," he offered his hand.

"It's good to see you Mr. President. I was just on my way out. There were a few items Christopher and I had to clear up. I'll leave you two alone. It was good to see you again sir," she went to leave.

"Nonsense," he shut the door and directed her to the sitting area.

Both Sandy and Christopher were thinking the

same thing. Great this is all we need.

"I sense the subject you two were discussing has created a touch of friction. Is there something I should be aware of," he inquired as he sat behind the room's official desk.

"No sir, we were just tying up loose ends," Sandy offered in an attempt to ease his suspicion so she could leave.

The President glanced at them then added, "I'm a perceptive person. Please fill me in on these, loose ends."

"Sir that won't be necessary as we have brought the subject to an end," the Director was trying to assure him all had been satisfactory dealt with.

"Oh, I'm sorry Christopher. I wasn't asking about your result. I want to know the subject matter of which you were discussing."

He was making himself clear about what he wanted. The other two knew it wasn't an option to mislead him. The Director was first to put forward the substance of their chat.

"Mr. President, Sandy has her concerns with regards to our involvement in the stable fire. As a result she's informed me she will no longer accept our requests for assistance."

"I don't blame her for being disturbed by your actions. To be quite frank I'm surprised you weren't out cold when I returned," he turned his attention to Sandy then added, "On behalf of the government I sincerely apologize for the behavior of the CIA."

Sandy hesitated before entering the conversation. Surprised to learn the President had knowledge of the botched fire, she found herself becoming more upset. Not wanting to fly off the handle and make a spectacle of the circumstances in front of him she decided to remain silent for the moment until he prompted her participation.

"Sandy, I'm sorry," the Chief added.

"Sir, are we done. I would like to leave."

He got up from behind the desk, came around and sat beside her.

"You have my word this will never happen again."

"Thank you sir, but your reassurance is a little late. It won't bring back the two lives lost. To be honest I am disappointed to learn you had knowledge of this childish intrusion into my family's life," with that she got up to leave.

"Sandy, please give me a chance to explain. It was not brought to my attention until after the fact—after we spoke about the arrest of that young lady. I would never have given it my seal of approval. Christopher and I have discussed this in length. He has admitted the agencies made a grave error in judgment."

"Sir, with all due respect I can't be a part of the agencies world any longer."

"Sandy please indulge me for a minute. I would have preferred if Christopher had asked you point blank to attend the wedding alone. It was handled wrong. However none of us here can argue the outcome of your findings. Sandy the importance of the intelligence you accumulated cannot be disputed. Your sacrifice saved thousands of our citizens. We were able to prevent major attacks on our soil. You are to be commended. If your wish is to leave you may do so without our interference," he looked at the Director then asked, "that is correct, isn't it Mr. Young."

"Absolutely," he agreed thinking the President was weak when it came to what was required to keep the country safe.

"Sandy, we would prefer you take some time off without interference from our part. Then should you consider returning, we could lessen your commissions. What you accomplish on most assignments takes us years using traditional methods."

"I appreciate your confidence. My decision has been made. When I leave here today I will not be returning."

"I am disappointed to hear that," President Tucker replied.

Sandy was agitated and couldn't hold back any longer.

"Do you two listen to yourselves? You tried to destroy my stable. You killed two of my animals. All because someone didn't think to pick up the telephone and suggest I travel solo. Nothing matters to you except results. The law of the land doesn't apply. Things all three of us have done border on insanity. If the public was aware of the madness driving the leaders of the most powerful nation in the world they would be chilled. I can't be a part of it anymore. I'm going home. I'm going to see if my husband will still have me."

She stood. This time she was leaving. The Director went to speak his mind but the President put a hand on his shoulder to silence him. Sandy left without another word being spoken.

"Christopher, nothing happens to her. If I so much as suspect our not respecting her decision you will be directing traffic in Alaska. Have I made myself clear?"

"Yes sir."

The two men spent the next hour discussing a variety of security measures. Before the Director was dismissed he was scolded about the agencies decisions and warned once again not to interfere with Sandy's life. It was made clear the only way her services would be utilized again is if she rekindled the relationship. Christopher Young guaranteed her wishes would be respected.

Once secure in the rear seat of his limousine the Director picked up a secure car phone which automatically put him through to his assistant at Langley.

"Sir," was all the aide said.

"Contact our inside operative. I want this to happen now. No delays."

Chapter 22

As has been the case in the past eventually everyone found their way home, all now under the same roof. David and Sandy were informed about Serge's death. To honor his family's request, arrangements were made to set a day aside in the near future for the spreading of his ashes. The stables would be closed for the day so all employees could attend to pay their respects.

No one had any travel arrangements for a while so a goal was set to fit in as many family dinners as possible. The next one was going to provide three quarters of the guests with what hoped to be a pleasant surprise.

Jacob, Brooklyn, Sandy, and David sat around the dining table catching up on the past week's activities. The atmosphere of the evening seemed to be little more official than previous dinners. Jacob had not shed his suit and tie. The table settings leaned towards a formality reserved for the entertaining of a guest held in high regard. It was noticeable but not questioned by the others.

After their plates were cleared, dessert was in

order. Placed on a tray carried by the kitchen employee delivering the food were four plates each holding a slice of cherry cheesecake. Also on the tray was a small silver plate with a domed silver covering. The waiter placed a slice of cake in front of everyone in addition to handing the small silver tray to Jacob. It went unnoticed by the other three for the most part as it looked like a serving of butter or a condiment.

Jacob held it in his hands and stood up.

"Before we continue devouring this delicious dessert may I have a moment?"

He pushed his chair to the side, got down on one knee, looked up at Brooklyn, removed the cover and there sat the most beautiful diamond ring she had ever laid eyes on.

"Will you marry me?"

No one saw it coming including Brooklyn. She was frozen by her euphoria. Looking away from Jacob to Sandy, not being able to speak she noticed his daughter wide eyed, smiling mouthing say yes, say yes. She turned back to her future husband.

"Yes, yes, yes."

He slowly slid the ring on her finger then stood. They gave each other a hug and a kiss.

Sandy was first to speak, "Yeah, we have a wedding to plan."

Then her father was next, "Well, Brooklyn as you pointed out when we first came together, at our age we have little time for the rituals afforded to the younger generation. If you are in agreement I have invited a guest to join us."

He motioned to the entrance and in came Father

Byrne from the local church.

"You want to get married now Jacob?"

"If you would rather postpone in lieu of a more formal setting I'm okay."

Brooklyn turned to Sandy and asked, "Sandy would be so kind as to give your father away."

"Yes. It would be my honor."

They all stood, Jacob and Brooklyn facing each other with Father Byrne in the center. Sandy stood beside her father and David moved in beside Brooklyn.

"Well I guess that leaves me as the bridesmaid," he joked.

The mood was lightened as everyone laughed at David's comment. Even the priest smiled. The ceremony was touching. All four were truly moved by the union. Any hesitation on Brooklyn's part fearing she would be received as an outsider was quickly put to rest by the visible enthusiasm of Sandy.

Champagne flowed in celebration. Two hours after the ceremony David and Sandy retired. The newlyweds elected to spend the night at Brooklyn's chalet.

The next morning the office sat empty. It would be a late start to the business at hand. Sandy and David ate a light breakfast in their suite.

"Do you have a lot on your plate today," David asked.

"Nothing of any major importance. Why, did you have something in mind?"

"Not really, thought you might want to join me at the stables and ride a couple of training laps. I'm sure Renée wouldn't mind. Last time you ran the horses you came away looking so invigorated. Then maybe we could find a cozy restaurant and have an our night. After the wedding I'm feeling a bit romantic."

"Wow, how can a girl refuse an invitation like that."

"Perfect, I'm heading out in about an hour."

"I'll meet you there. I want to go for a quick run then I need to make a couple of calls. Ok?"

"Sure, just don't get side tracked."

"Oh I will be there. After all it's not every day your husband is in a romantic mood."

David made his way to the track. When he arrived he advised Renée of Sandy's intentions of jockeying. Beside herself, a couple of jockeys and two of her trusted staff no one rode these thoroughbreds. The privilege of mounting a thousand pounds of pure muscle worth millions of dollars that takes you on a forty mile an hour whirlwind ride is reserved for a select few. Renée was very protective of her horses. Although Sandy was an exceptional equestrian Renée was always nervous when she took the reins of one the animals. David was her boss so she would suppress her opposition. He was aware of her concerns but technically Sandy owned the stables and everything in it, so her capabilities would never come into question.

Shortly after lunch Sandy arrived. She first came across Renée.

"Hi Renée. Have you seen David?"

"Oh, hi Sandy. I'm not sure where he is at the

moment. He said something about having to make some calls. He mentioned you want to run a training session."

"Well between you and me it was his idea. We're really working on spending more time together and he thought it would be nice if I put in more time here. To tell you the truth I love getting on one of these guys. It's special. That is if you don't mind, after all this is your domain."

"I don't mind at all Sandy. I know you have the utmost respect for these animals."

"Renée, you're not a good liar. Girl to girl I can read you like a book. I know you would prefer if I was gallivanting around somewhere over in Europe but I'm not, I'm here. I'm really going to make an effort to reclaim my life with David."

"Really, Sandy I'm glad to see you. I don't mind at all. You are an excellent rider."

"Good. I suspect you've been doing your share of riding lately. How does it make you feel?"

"I'm not sure what you mean."

Renée didn't like the direction of the conversation. She was well aware what Sandy was referring to and feeling more uncomfortable by the second. Just as Sandy was about to stick the knife in a bit further, Renée was spared by David's arrival.

"Look at this my two favorite girls."

He regretted saying it before it even got out of his mouth but it was too late. If he made an attempt at a recovery he would just be opening the door for a comeback by his wife. Changing the subject was best.

"So what are you two chatting about," he asked.

His wife was quick to answer back, "We were just talking about how satisfied we happen to feel after a good mounting. A little thing we have in common."

"Renée who are we working out today," he asked not catching what his wife was alluding to.

"I have Ninety-Nine on the track now." A horse David named after the jersey number of hockey's Great One Wayne Gretzky.

"Royal Mist is scheduled for a few laps. I will have Mason saddle him for you Sandy."

The sooner she gets on the track the better. Renée preferred to end the one on one chat. She would follow David's instructions but put the assistant trainers in charge of preparation.

"Didn't you say Charlotte's Choice might get a lap or two in if the track conditions warranted."

"Yes David, but I was going to run him myself. I'd prefer not to alter his regimen."

Charlotte's Choice was considered the world's fastest horse in the present day. The only two people who have had the privilege of riding him were Mario Rossi his jockey and Renée. Being uncertain of how the horse would react to someone else at the reins was a gamble she did not want to take.

"I think Sandy can handle him. Go through your routine and I'm sure she will follow the instructions. Right," he prompted an agreement from his wife.

"That's okay David, Renée makes a good point. After all she is the head trainer and knows what's best."

"No, I insist," he wanted this to happen. "After all you do own the horse. Renée, explain to Sandy how you want the session to go. I have to make a few calls. Let me know when you're on the track."

David disappeared. Renée instructed Mason who was uncharacteristically hanging around as if he was listening in on the conversation. He wasn't one of the stables most motivated employees, but he was smart and efficient when asked to handle a task. Renée suspected his days were limited.

She then went on to explain exactly how every second of the session was to be handled. Her only priority was the animal's welfare. Who owned it was not her concern. The well-being of this thoroughbred was her sole responsibility. She would watch the complete workout from the rails. If Sandy altered the routine in the slightest way it would be brought to an abrupt end.

There would be five laps of the track. All four gaits would be utilized. The first half lap was to be walked. The second would be a progression from walk to a trot then a canter. The third and most important of the five was to trot Charlotte's Choice the front half of the track then in between the back turns Sandy was to run him in a gallop at three quarters speed. The forth was to be a repeat of the third. The fifth and final lap the horse would gradually be eased to a walk allowing the horse's estimated eighteen pound heart rate to return to its resting beat. At no time was he to exceed thirty miles an hour. Full out he ran over forty.

They were in agreement. The session was reviewed twice. Both were very intelligent women and respected the animal's safety. Sandy planned on following Renée's program to a tee.

Charlotte's Choice was now out of his stable, saddled and ready to run. Mason had to hold the reins tight as the animal sensed it was his time for him to shine. The three of them walked the country's number one thoroughbred to the track gate at which point Sandy would mount him.

Anytime Charlotte came on the track a crowd of horsemen would gather along the rails. It was special to watch the best of the best run if only at half speed. Today the head count increased as word spread the guest jockey at the helm happened to be the owner. There were a couple of other horses being put through their paces and would remain on the track as practice sessions were to be shared. However, they would make way allowing Sandy to work undisturbed.

The run began with the first lap ridden exactly as instructed. As the pace picked up in the second Renée watched with eagle eyes. She concentrated on the horse's temperament which seemed to be in check. On the third pass just before the increase to a gallop Renée took notice that Sandy backed her foot out of the irons leaning on them with her toes. Some expert jockeys rode like this for balance. Others say they felt the ride became lighter. Although most say the use of the toe on irons method was to avoid getting their leg stuck during a fall. Seeing the adjustment into the position added some relief as it was a sign of Sandy's exceptional skills.

Mason remained at her side but was completely disconnected from the surroundings. She noticed he had his smart phone in hand and was what looked to be texting. For the past few months his attitude towards work was diminishing. He seemed too detached. The most important requirement Renée demanded from her employees was care. This wasn't the time but soon she would speak to David asking permission to terminate his employment. It didn't matter how experienced a stable hand was, unless they possessed an undeniable affection for the horses, you didn't belong.

David was trying to cut a call short so he could take in his wife's riding. The conversation was important so he resigned to the fact that he would watch the session on video later in the day. All movements on the race track were recorded.

The third trip around went off without a hitch. Renée noticed Charlotte's Choice seems a little anxious. Sandy struggled a bit holding him back from galloping full tilt. It wasn't anything she did. The most experienced jockey would have handled it the exact way she did. This horse wanted to win. He wanted to run as fast as he could every second he was on the track. Going into the fourth back stretch Sandy let him run to what she felt was three quarters of his capability.

Halfway along the back stretch the unthinkable happened. The horse spooked. It lowered its neck, stopped, throwing Sandy forward. Everyone watching was stunned, frozen, witnessing Sandy propel through the air for what seemed to be forever. She hit the ground head first. Sandy took a number of tumbles until she came to rest at the center of the track, motionless. Renée flew over the fence running at an Olympian speed to get to her.

Sandy was savoring her short ride, such power below her. There was no feeling in the world like it. She felt the session was moving along exactly as planned. Her personal distaste for Renée would not come into play here. The trainer's requirements were at the forefront of her thinking. She didn't see or feel the unexpected bucking. As she was being thrust over the horse's head her mind clicked into frame by frame mode. Instinctively she wrapped her arms tightly around her lower chest. Her years of training took over. The goal was to relax the body and let it move freely with the momentum of the fall similar to how one might prepare for a parachute jump landing. The less resistance and less exposed limbs the less chance of fractures. She was in control of the fall until her head hit the track surface first. Then the world went black.

Within seconds an emergency horn sounded indicating a rider or horse was down. The protocol was at the sound of the horn all horsemen were to rush to the track for assistance. It took a lot of manpower to lift a thousand pounds off a jockey and seconds could make the difference in life or death. An ambulance stationed off to the side would make its way onto the race surface as soon as all other horses were safely out of harm's way.

While the other horses were cleared from the track, two remained. Charlotte's Choice was running at top speed and the only way to catch a race horse, is with a race horse. As it happened Gabriela D'Angelo was riding one of her horses and took pursuit of the unmanned runaway. Every other person within site was rushing to Sandy's side. A human perimeter was manned around the injured jockey securing her from being run over by the animal on the loose.

Renée and Mason were first on the scene. It wasn't good. She had seen a rider die in a similar accident not that long ago. Sandy was unconscious. Renée wanted Mason to relay the urgency to the first responders but he was more concerned about pursuing Charlotte's Choice. The injuries were bad. Blood was appearing from her nose and ears.

"Mason get back here I need that ambulance now," Renée ordered her assistant in a piercing yell.

He stopped his chase, looked at her, took a double look at the horse then resigned to the fact that he better obey his boss.

Gabriela drew up beside the runaway and was able to grab the reins. Bringing it to a standstill then she dismounted. She began to walk towards the gate in-between two thousand pounds of animals. A couple of the other trainers were quickly making their way to assist her. Charlotte's Choice was not cooperating which forced her to jerk his bridle hard in an attempt to bring him under control. The feel of every piece of equipment utilized in the sport was as common to her as the back of her hand. With her fingers sandwiched between the leather bridle and the horse's mane she touched something out of place. Instinct told her it didn't belong, so as soon as help arrived she handed off her own horse indicating she would remain in control of the run off. Once alone she looked under the leather.

"Son of a bitch," she said a touch too loud which

attracted attention of the two trainers walking in front of her. She waved them off as if nothing was wrong.

By the time David arrived, the first responders had his wife securely stabilized in the back of the ambulance. She had a heartbeat but was still unconscious. Her vitals were registering poor readings. The attendants were aware this was going to be a life or death situation. There was no time to delay. No time for any sort of explanation to her husband as to how it happened. He was allowed to accompany her to the hospital but told he must not interfere. David jumped into the back holding his wife's hand and praying.

Renée was visibly shaken. Tears glossed over her eyes. Once the ambulance was en route her attention turned to the jockey walking her pride and joy thoroughbred down the home stretch, suddenly realizing who it was. She ran to meet them. Gabriela stopped, deciding what her friend was about to learn was best done from a distance to all others.

"Gabriela, thank you. I'm so lucky you were out here," referring to the jockey's quick action which saved any injury to the horse.

"How is Sandy?"

She informed her, "Not good. She's unconscious and bleeding badly. Gabriela I'm not sure she's going to make it. It's bad"

"She's tough Renée. She will get through this. I promise."

"I hope to god she does. I shouldn't have given in. She shouldn't have been on that horse. This

374

whole thing is my fault."

From her pocket Gabriel took out the item found hidden under the reins.

"Renée it wasn't your fault. I found this under his bridle," she handed it to her.

"What the hell, son of a bitch, who in god's name," she suddenly realized something and stopped dead.

Looking at her pal she asked, "Can you take care of Charlotte."

"Of course."

She scanned the area looking for Mason but most had cleared the track and returned to their stables. Again running as fast as her legs would permit, she made a beeline to the barn. Once inside she yelled at the top of her lungs.

"Mason, Mason, where the hell are you. Mason. Who has seen Mason? Find him for me."

None of her staff had seen her so upset. They all just stood there.

"Now," she screamed.

Going stall to stall the shouting continued until a young apprentice who was ordered to stay behind to attend to the horses during the accident came up to her.

"Renée," she said trying to get her bosses attention.

"Not now. Have you seen Mason?"

"That's what I'm trying to tell you. He's not here."

She had Renée's attention. The kid was terrified as the lead trainer's stare cut right through her.

"What do you mean he's not here?"

"Shortly after the warning horn went off and everyone ran to the track, Mason who was already at the track came back to the stables. I thought he was heading back to the accident but he didn't. I saw him go into your office. He had an envelope in his hand when he went in. When he came out he wasn't carrying it. I kept an eye on him because I thought it was strange he wasn't lending a hand at the spill."

"Where did he go once he left the office?"

"He went right to the parking lot, got in his car and drove off."

"Is there anything else you remember?

"No. Other than he looked sad. Like someone mourning. He was confused. He scared me Renée."

"Thank you Lily, you've been very helpful. You can get back to work. Thanks again."

Renée was anxious to get to the hospital but David was there and there was little she could do. She went to the office first. After grasping a clear picture of what in god's name went on today she would join her boss. Lying on the table sat a white envelope. It was addressed to Mr. Watson. She snatched it up then tore it open.

It read, 'Dear Mr. Watson. Please accept this letter as my official resignation. An urgent family matter has unexpectedly surfaced that requires my immediately attention. I appreciate all you've done for me. In return I wish I could have been a better person. Unfortunately that was not possible. I truly pray for Sandy's full recovery. Mason.'

She didn't have the answer as to why, but she was certain it was Mason who was behind this tragic accident. Renée retrieved the small piece of electronics Gabriela found. It was a shock device that worked similar to an invisible fence used to discourage a dog from leaving its yard. She despised this method of discipline. It was cruel.

The component she was holding is activated by a hand held remote or a device such as a mobile phone. Mason shocked Charlotte's Choice purposely. Why? Why deliberately injure or kill Sandy. What was going on here? Was he insane? She had to get to the hospital to inform David. If she ever got her hands on Mason she'd drag him at forty miles an hour around the race track until the rope he was tied to wore out. She grabbed her helmet, jumped on her motorcycle and ripped out of the parking area.

***

David paced the halls of the hospital while his wife was being attended to in the operating room. There had been no update of her condition. Hell, he didn't even know if she was alive. Everything happened so fast it wasn't until after being at the hospital for two hours did he realize Jacob and Brooklyn needed to be contacted. There was no answer. He left messages on both their mobile phones in addition to the office. He then reached out to a ranch hand at the stable office and instructed him to go find his wife's father. For now he was alone, sitting there staring at the door indicating Authorized Personnel Only. Waiting for a doctor to appear with a smile on their face telling him everything went well and his wife will be fine.

Renée arrived and soon found her way to the proper floor.

"David," she called for him.

He turned to meet her. They gave each other a consoling hug.

"How is she David?"

"They haven't told me a thing. She's still in the operating room. My god Renée, what the hell happened."

"Charlotte spooked, stopped on a dime throwing Sandy into the air. She's going to make it David. She's going be okay. I know it."

"You were hesitant about her riding him. If only I had listened to you. She shouldn't have been riding him. This is entirely my fault."

"David," Renée put her hand in her pocket to retrieve the shock mechanism while saying, "it wasn't your fault. She was riding him perfectly. I couldn't have ridden any better."

"Then why did he spook?"

Just as Renée was going to explain what happened a doctor appeared.

"Mr. Watson?"

"Yes. How is she? Is she," he refrained from asking.

"She's resting at the moment. Would you like to see her?"

"Yes. Please."

"She is very heavily sedated. I need to review some results at the lab then I'll be back and I can tell you more. For the time being you should be with her."

"Will she hear me?"

"Probably not, but it's not an exact science. We like to believe a familiar hand and voice provides positive reinforcement whether they respond or not."

David looked at Renée who had backed off to provide some privacy, to see her mouth, "I'll be right here."

The doctor escorted him to the room before leaving him alone and closing the door. There his wife lay attached to a number of monitoring machines. An endotracheal tube was inserted down her throat. Her head was wrapped in white gauze with a tiny tube of what looked to be draining fluid from her brain. Both her eyes were blackened. She didn't look well, but she was alive. The graph on the screen confirmed it. That's all he could ask for now.

Back in Langley, Virginia, at the CIA headquarters, Christopher Young the Director was sitting behind his imposing desk when his assistant knocked then entered.

"Sir there's been a mishap."

"Yes."

"Sandy Watson has sustained injuries from being thrown from a horse."

"Is she alive?"

"Yes."

"Good," the Director's conversations were short and to the point.

"Sir," the assistant handed over what looked similar to an iPad.

"This her medical condition in real time. It is a

direct feed from the hospital. As the doctors learn so do we."

"Do we know the whereabouts of Brayden or Mason or whatever the hell his name is?"

"He's en route to the airport. As you requested I've arranged for one of our jets to transport him to his reassignment."

"Where did you post him," trusting his assistant's judgment.

"Our Black Site in Malaysia, sir."

"He will never step foot in the United States again?"

"No sir."

"Thank you," the agent was dismissed.

Christopher scrolled through the hospital's updates on Sandy's condition. He paused at one page.

"God dammit," he bellowed.

***

David sat at the edge of the bed. He held her hand with both of his.

"Sandy I'm so, so, sorry. Please forgive me. I shouldn't have pushed you to take the ride."

Tears rolled down his cheeks. His stomach turned. He was shaking.

"Seeing you lay in that ambulance scared me. I thought you were gone. Please don't be gone. The only thing that matters is for you to find a way to come back to us. I promise things will be different."

He wiped the tears from his face. With one hand he caressed her cheek. It was gut-wrenching to be staring down seeing his wife in this condition.

"Sandy you will get better. You will be better than ever."

"I want to apologize for my recent behavior. Seeing you like this I've realized how selfish I've been. I married you for who we are and not for what I want us to be. All I need is you. I will never pressure you to change again. A life with you is all I want. I don't know why I've been behaving like I have recently. I am so sorry. I pray you can find it in your heart to forgive me. You are the most important person in my life. I am honored to be your husband. We will see our way through this. I love you."

David bent over and gave her a kiss on the cheek. At that moment the doctor reentered, this time accompanied by Jacob and Brooklyn. David got up and gave both of them a hug. Jacob moved to the side of the bed. The doctor nodded to David to meet her in the hall.

"I'll be right back," he said to his father-in-law.

The doctor looked at the medical chart she was holding.

"Mr. Watson."

"Please, David is fine,"

"David, your wife is a very lucky woman. We've completed a full body scan and I'm happy to say she did not sustain any breaks or fractures. Which might I say is a miracle from the trauma she experienced. She is in incredible physical condition. The majority of people would have been very badly damaged. The only noticeable injury was from landing on her head. She sustained some swelling which caused a mild liquid build up. We have drained most of it. However, I would like to keep her sedated for another twenty four hours to avoid any unnecessary movement. Considering, all and all it's as good as it gets."

"Thank you doctor. You have no idea how much I appreciate hearing that."

The doctor was a bit surprised at David's overall reaction or lack of it.

"So, furthermore, the great news today is they both will make a full recovery."

"That's wonderful. I'm so," he stopped mid sentence as it sank in that he was being informed both would make a full recovery. "What do you mean by both? I wasn't aware anyone else was injured."

The doctor looked at him a bit confused until her rationalization of his comment hit home.

"Oh my god. You didn't know."

"Know what," now he was baffled.

"Your wife. She is three months into term. David, you're going to have a baby."

Chapter 23

Six months later Sandy gave birth to a beautiful healthy baby girl. They named their new family member Capella after the child's grandmother's favorite star. Life at the ranch now revolved around that little ray of brightness. David was already trying to predict what her foot size would be when she took her first steps. His plan was to contact one of the skate representatives he was aligned with to have them customize a pair for his future Olympian.

Sandy's recovery from the accident was quicker than anyone expected. The Doctors were amazed at how fast she healed. All those years of fine tuning her body paid off. Within a month of the fall she was back to her normal routine. She did however reduce her traveling quite a bit. One, maybe two overnight trips per month were all she committed to until her ninth month of pregnancy. All of her communications took place from her office at the ranch from that point on.

She explained to her husband that she had been aware of the pregnancy for the two months leading up to the accident. During their discussions on the subject, she withheld the information as she was not a hundred percent certain she was ready to become a mother. David accepted her explanation without discord. He was grateful for all he had been blessed with these past few months.

Prior to the birth of their daughter a memorial was held for Serge. The minister's sermon was heard by all existing staff, along with some past employees. He blessed a plaque that was placed on the ranch's stable which was now named The Serge Thompson Stable in memory of the trainer. They also took time to pay their respects to the two horses that perished in the fire at a small monument which was erected in their honor.

Jacob and Brooklyn fell nicely into the groove of a married lifestyle. They elected to make the log chalet their residence. Although it was only a couple of hundred yards from the main house, it provided a sanctuary away from the office.

It went without saying that the affair between Renée and David came to an end, at least for the time being. The flame still burned within both but with time it had a chance of being extinguished. To avoid falling back into the secretive rendezvous David allowed Renée to handle all the out of town races on her own. He took care of the business end from home.

Back at the hospital after David came out of the shock of learning he was going to be a father, Renée was eventually able to explain the reasoning behind Charlotte's Choice being spooked. He was fit to be tied. If Mason was in his sight he would have ripped his heart out. The information was passed on to his father-in-law whose reaction was similar, although, it didn't take either long to let calm heads prevail. At that time all their energies needed to be focused towards Sandy.

After his daughter was released and settled in at the ranch a discussion took place with regards to the shocking of the horse. Sandy immediately knew the Director ordered it and the reasoning behind it. She elected not to expose him to her family insisting that her father and husband allow her to deal with the situation. Actually she was prepared to let the whole thing slide. It only solidified her reasoning behind withdrawing her services. The more Sandy thought about it, although not in agreement with their method, she did understand why her pregnancy was an issue to the Agency. It also became obvious to her that her way of thinking was more similar to the Director than she had realized. But now was her time, not the country's.

Her father couldn't let it go. Shortly after their talk, he boarded his aircraft filing a flight plan to Washington. He had summoned a face to face with the President. Heads were going to roll. No one endangered one of his family members, especially his daughter without paying dearly. He wanted answers. Not from the various law enforcement agencies. He expected the President to have his daughter's back. Now the Chief was going to have to explain himself.

The two sat face to face on opposite couches in the center of the Oval Office. There were no niceties. Jacob was about to begin his thrashing when President Tucker waved him off.

"Jacob our government is responsible for the attacks on your family," he began.

He went on to explain it was the Director of the CIA that ordered both aggressions. The fire was to keep David near, allowing Sandy to attend the wedding by herself. The invitation list provided a once in a lifetime opportunity of intelligence gathering, making it imperative she be there alone. Without going into details, he explained to Jacob that the results of his daughter's trip ultimately saved thousands of American lives. He went on to apprise him that they were able to resolve lingering questions with regards to an operative, referring to the locating of their former agent Emily. Sandy's mission to extract her was not and would not be mentioned. Jacob was told without the sacrifice of his daughter's services over the years the face of the country would not be the same. If the necessity to shielding her involvement wasn't so imperative, she would be the recipient of every Medal of Honor the country could bestow on her.

Being a smart man Jacob sat back and listened without interruption. He was so proud hearing the President praise his daughter he couldn't help but smile. It didn't ease his being upset about the attacks, but he understood the premise behind it, not the method. He sat in silence as the President continued.

It was explained that both attacks were executed by the CIA without the knowledge or approval of the White House. No one could deny the success of the first mission. He apologized before telling Sandy's father the truth behind the shocking of the horse. The CIA accessed his daughter's medical records. When it was learned she was pregnant the Director took it upon himself to orchestrate an accident in hopes of causing her to abort the baby. Christopher Young felt he had a much better chance of retaining her services if there were no children brought into play. The Director was confident Sandy would not sustain any major injury due to her conditioning. His justification was she had been through much worse in her training. The President added that he was outraged when he learned of the attempt. It made his stomach turn to think about it.

Not expecting this explanation, Jacob was blindsided. He was fuming. His next stop would be Langley where he would personally take care of the Director. But before he exploded with anger the President put up a hand to hopefully defuse the situation by outlining his plan to resolve the debacle.

Jacob did speak up demanding the Director be removed from his position. The President went on to say that he had a heart to heart with the head of the CIA and they came to a mutual agreement that in one year's time Christopher Young would announce his retirement. That wasn't good enough for Jacob, he wanted him out now. After all he could have killed his daughter.

President Tucker laid out the plan informing his guest that it wasn't a burger joint where you could kick someone to the curb for giving his buddy a free order of fries. The Director of the largest intelligence agency in the world could not be fired on the spot. It took time to oust someone in his capacity. If he was suddenly removed from office it would mean the involvement of the House of Representatives among god knows how many more groups, his immediate staff included. This way was clean and tidy. Besides he told him, it would take that long to vet a replacement.

Sandy's father agreed on two conditions. One was the Agency refrain from ever contacting his daughter again unless she reached out to them first. The President agreed. Second was that all files relating to her existence within the organization be purged and the new Director was to know nothing of her.

"Jacob, unfortunately I can't agree to that demand. I have the perfect person in mind for his replacement but they will have knowledge of her involvement. Actually I may need your assistance in the vetting process or should I say the persuading of my candidate."

Jacob didn't understand why his participation would be required and told the Chief that it was best left to the White House to decide on these matters without public input.

"I agree that would be the norm, but in this case I am quite certain your influence of the individual I have in mind is quite substantial."

Still confused Jacob asked, "Who exactly is your candidate?"

With a widening smile on his face the President of the United States locked eyes with his long time friend and said, "Your daughter, Sandy."

To be continued...

Book 2 coming 2015

Acknowledgements

To Our Libraries...
Take a moment to visit.

About the Author

Born in Toronto and raised in Northern Ontario, Canada, I currently own a small business in the Sudbury region. My wife Diane has been by my side for 34 years, which I believe should propel her directly into sainthood. I have been blessed with an amazing and supportive family.

Creativity has always been a part of my journey. Writing seems to be a natural extension to my years in the music industry, where I had the pleasure of listening to songs I penned being played on the radio.

When not working, sleeping, biking, or writing, I am on the golf course trying to keep up with my son's Lee and Aaron.

Facebook:
www.facebook.com/williamccole

Twitter:
https://twitter.com/_WilliamCCole

Goodreads:
http://www.goodreads.com/user/show/33782347-
william-cole

Website:
http://www.williamccole.com/

Linkedin:
http://www.linkedin.com/pub/william-c-
cole/a5/76a/779/

CPSIA information can be obtained at www.ICGtesting.com
Printed in the USA
LVOW07s1700250515

439802LV00006B/630/P